THE 8TH CIRCLE

THE 8TH CIRCLE

A DANNY RYAN THRILLER

Sarah Cain

CROOKED
LANE

NEW YORK

Copyright © 2016 Sarah Cain

Published in the United States by Crooked Lane Books, an imprint of The Quick Brown Fox & Company LLC.

Crooked Lane Books and its logo are trademarks of The Quick Brown Fox & Company LLC.

Library of Congress Catalog-in-Publication data available upon request.

ISBN (hardcover): 978-1-62953-480-0
ISBN (paperback): 978-1-62953-485-5
ISBN (ePub): 978-1-62953-479-4
ISBN (Kindle): 978-1-62953-658-3
ISBN (ePDF): 978-1-62953-669-9

Cover design by Andy Ruggirello
Book design by Jennifer Canzone

Printed in the United States.

www.crookedlanebooks.com

Crooked Lane Books
2 Park Avenue, 10th Floor
New York, NY 10016

First Edition: January 2016

10 9 8 7 6 5 4 3 2 1

In Memory
of
Lily Maude
Who Knew All the Stories

1

"We're all dying, so we might as well get on with it."

Danny Ryan looked at the words scrawled across his laptop with some satisfaction and winced. He almost felt his grandmother's boney knuckle rap against the back of his head.

"Blasphemer. Do y'think He died on the cross for you to dismiss life so lightly?"

"I'm not dismissing life. I'm saying we're all headed to one end," Danny said aloud. Then he realized how ridiculous it was to argue with a dead woman.

"'I spit in the face of Time.'"

"Yeats again? Really?" But she was gone, and he was losing his mind by inches. He slammed the laptop shut.

Danny wanted to hurl the goddamn machine across the room. What happened to the words that used to flow out of his brain, through his fingers, onto the keyboard? What good was a columnist who couldn't write?

But he wasn't a columnist anymore. He was, what? His mind skittered through the possibilities: dumbass, delinquent, decayed. So many *D* words, but not the one he wanted.

Leaning back in his leather chair, he picked up the photograph of his son that sat on his desk to the left of the laptop.

Conor wore his purple soccer jersey and sported a bruise on his forehead. His huge grin showcased his missing right front tooth, and he clutched his MVP trophy in his small hands like it was the World Cup.

Danny set the photograph back on the desk and forced back the surge that threatened to drown him. He opened his drawer, pulled out an old Tokarev TT-33, and then stood and walked to the stone hearth. When he sat next to Beowulf, the dog laid his massive head across Danny's knees. He stroked Beowulf's black fur. Beowulf licked his face.

"This was my grandfather's." Danny held up the gun and drew a bead on the computer. He then turned the gun around and pointed it at his temple. "The old man gave this to me, Wolf. You know why?" He pulled the trigger. The gun clicked, and Danny set it on the hearth. "He said it was the perfect gun for a Commie asshole."

Outside, the sound of splintering wood brought Danny to his feet. Beowulf tore into the kitchen and hurled himself at the door, barking loud enough to raise the dead. Danny left the gun on the hearth and followed. He grabbed his parka, cell phone, and a flashlight and pushed Beowulf back from the door. "Wolf, stay here."

Following the beam of the light through the wind-driven sleet, he saw the hole in the fence. A car balanced precariously on the small island of ornamental shrubbery in the middle of the duck pond. Whoever sat in that car wasn't trying to get out.

Rain stung Danny's face. The wind slapped his skin, and tiny pellets of ice beat against him. He called 9-1-1 and then clambered down the slippery incline.

The flashlight lit up the back of the car, and Danny froze. Jesus. He knew that old black BMW with its "Ahh, I See the Screw-Up Fairy Has Visited Us Again" bumper sticker.

Michael Cohen. They'd fought. It seemed long ago now. The wet seeped under Danny's coat, and he shoved his phone into his pocket. He heard a crunch, and the front end of the BMW dipped into the water.

Danny sloshed into the pond. It wasn't that deep, but the freezing water sent shock waves up his legs. He stumbled in the sucking mud, and the flashlight slid from his wet hand. For a moment, it illuminated the pond in eerie green and then blinked out. He grabbed the door handle with numb fingers and wrenched it open.

In the glow of the overhead light, he could see the smashed windshield and Michael draped over the steering wheel. No airbags in this heap. Danny pushed Michael back as gently as he could, careful to avoid the shattered glass. Blood bubbled from Michael's nose and mouth and oozed down the front of his blue jacket. Michael gave a shuddering wheeze, and his eyes blinked open. His round face looked slack.

Danny could hear the faint call of sirens now. "Don't try to talk. Help's coming." The metallic stench of blood assaulted him. "It'll be all right, Michael."

Michael shuddered. "Danny." Rasping coughs shook his husky frame, and flecks of bloody foam hit Danny in the face. "I . . . I love you. Y'know? Brothers."

Danny knew Michael didn't have much time. He leaned closer. "What happened?"

"So sorry," Michael's voice came slow and thick. The light in his eyes faded with each word.

"Sorry? Sorry for what? Michael?" Police cars and an ambulance screeched around the curve. Red-and-blue lights reflected off the black water. Michael's head drooped down. When he gave a rattling wheeze, Danny grasped his shoulders. "Michael?"

Michael lifted his head enough that his lips brushed Danny's ear. "Inferno."

2

anny sat at his kitchen table and stared into his mug of coffee. The tightening behind his right eye signaled the onset of a really shitty migraine as swirls of light rippled in the dark liquid and bounced off the walls. He tried to concentrate on the copper tabletop.

"Mr. Ryan?" The younger of the two Chester County detectives moved a little closer. "I know this has been traumatic for you, but if we could just go over a few details one more time."

They were handling him. After all, he was still Danny Ryan, Boy Wonder, Pulitzer Prize winner. He'd been a national TV talk show regular. A celebrity. They hadn't figured out he was just another hustler. His stomach tightened.

"Mr. Ryan? Are you all right?"

He nodded. *All right as opposed to what?*

They had let him change out of his wet things, but despite the dry clothes and two mugs of coffee, he couldn't shake the cold that seeped into his bones. What the hell was the young cop's name? McSomething. He had a little black notebook.

"Could we go over this one more time?" McSomething said to Danny as he glanced at his partner.

The other cop stood just to Danny's left. Older. Had that ex-army posture, though his short, gray hair looked wrong. Uneven, like he cut it himself. He had a notebook too. Danny could hear his pen scratch over the page. Jesus, how many times were they going to do this routine?

McSomething said, "You were here alone when your friend crashed through the fence. Is that right?"

"I was alone." Danny pressed his fingers against his right cheekbone. *Inferno.* "I heard a crash and came outside." Lights zoomed around the room, leaving gleaming trails of white. Danny dug his fingers deeper into his cheek. He should take something to dull the growing pain.

Pain is good. It's part of the healing process. You have to let yourself feel, Danny. Wasn't that what the shrink had told him? Then he had written out a handful of prescriptions for mind-numbing pharmaceuticals.

"You understand your friend was shot, Mr. Ryan?" McSomething asked.

"Yes." Danny understood. They had tested his hands for gunpowder residue.

"You worked together on the same paper for how many years?"

"Sixteen." Michael wouldn't have had a job if his family hadn't owned the paper, but why say that now? *Inferno.* "Michael wrote *On the Scene*," Danny continued. "Half of it came right off the wire service. He had a blog, *Around Town*. His dad is Andy Cohen, the managing editor."

The older, silent cop bent closer. Danny smelled coffee and the faint tang of scotch and mint. "Anything else you can think of?" the cop asked.

"No." Danny licked his chapped lips. That smell. Scotch and mint. Just like home. Fireworks exploded behind Danny's eyes. The cop's face blurred into two, then three.

"Okay, then, Mr. Ryan, tell me again. Are you sure Michael Cohen didn't say anything to you?"

The lights in the kitchen burned his eyeballs, and cold sweat soaked into the back of his shirt. He tasted the coffee, bitter and sour, in the back of his throat as pain wormed into his right eye and tunneled down the side of his face.

"Mr. Ryan?"

Danny pulled himself to his feet, but the floor dipped beneath him. He stumbled to the sink and vomited.

*

The house creaked, and silence settled around him. In the heavy darkness, he could feel his ghosts watching, the old man sitting in the corner gloating. *God is watching you, boy.* Danny curled into a ball and pressed an ice pack against his right eye. Cold helped dull the pain while the drugs seeped into his system. His muscles began to relax.

Inferno.

What the hell was Michael doing? Buying drugs?

Beowulf jumped up beside Danny and nestled in, his paw flung across him, his wet muzzle against Danny's left ear.

Beth hadn't allowed Beowulf to sleep upstairs. She had wanted a designer dog that would look good on the cover of *Lifestyle*, not some hundred-pound Heinz 57 who thought he was a lapdog. When the magazine had come to do its cover story on them, Danny had to ask old Mrs. Norton in the house next door to watch Beowulf for the day.

Conor had loved Beowulf. He had loved dogs and soccer and the soldiers' cabins at Valley Forge Park. Danny's eyes drifted shut. He could see Conor now. Snow was falling. They'd build a snowman ten feet high when he got home with Beth from that stupid Christmas tea.

"Daddy, there's a monster under the bed."

"Conor."

Danny pushed himself up, staggered down the hall, and yanked open Conor's bedroom door. The room stood forlorn, its mementos gone. Only the double bed with its neat blue comforter, the oak dresser, and the wallpaper with the planets and stars remained.

Fuck. Fuck. Fuck.

He rammed his fist into the wall.

After the funeral and the luncheon, when the last person had left, Danny had stood in the kitchen amid the casseroles and containers of cakes and cookies he would dump the next day and stared out at the Christmas tree, still tied up on the back porch. The size and silence of the house had pressed down on him like a giant hand, and he had smashed his fists against the stone wall of the kitchen. He hadn't felt the skin ripping off or noticed the bits of rock flaking under his assault until he had seen his own blood painting the porous gray rock.

Now Beowulf bumped against him, nudging him until Danny shuffled back to his own bedroom and climbed under the covers. He pressed his head against the pillow.

Let go. I can't . . . let go.

3

When Beowulf started to bark, Danny wiped the condensation from the bathroom window. A black Crown Vic sat in the driveway, and a Crime Scene Unit waded through the pond. Headlines ran through his mind: *Death in the Duck Pond? Something Fishy in the Pond? Death Among the Duckies?*

Out of habit, Danny jerked open the door to the medicine cabinet. A whole army of bottles awaited his command—his multicolored friends, a regular rainbow coalition. He slammed the door shut. He'd taken himself off the antidepressants and tranquilizers months ago. All the medication had turned him into a zombie. Now he faced mornings clear eyed and jittery with a sense of life bleeding back into his veins. He wasn't sure he liked it.

Danny pulled on a pair of jeans and a black sweater and glanced at himself in the mirrors that surrounded him on all sides of the cavernous dressing room.

Very GQ *today, Mr. Ryan. Ready for your close-up?*

A year ago, his column had run on the front page of the Metro section, three times a week, including Sunday, and Andy had been talking syndication. After all, he had been a valuable asset in an industry dying from the competition generated by the twenty-four-hour news channels, bloggers, and online self-promoters. He still sold papers. His columns and blogs had helped staunch the hemorrhaging somewhat. Now it was a good day if he got dressed and remembered to eat. The great Danny Ryan. What was it the old man used to say about him?

You can package shite and call it butter, but it's still shite. The old man had a way with words. Maybe he should have been the writer.

Danny walked down the narrow back stairs, part of the original house built in the mid-1700s. The steps were steep and treacherous. Beth and he had debated ripping them out, but the handmade beauty of the polished oak had won out. They had settled for childproof gates Conor had quickly learned to open.

Once, Conor had wrapped the fuzzy, blue rug from his bedroom around himself, sat on his plastic, green sled, and launched himself down the back stairs. Danny had run to him, horrified.

"Look what I did, Dad," Conor had said. "Indoor sledding! Cool, huh?"

Danny had to bite his cheek to control the urge to yell, *Are you fucking insane?* Instead, he had knelt beside Conor and said, "Not cool, dude. You could have cracked your skull. Don't do it again." They had spit and shook hands.

He went into the kitchen. His great family home, minus the family.

Beowulf was still barking, but the cops hadn't approached the door. Danny opened the refrigerator. "Quiet, Wolf. Walk in a minute."

He tossed Beowulf two hot dogs. Beowulf gave one last growl, grabbed the hot dogs, and settled under the table as Danny pulled out an urn and made coffee. He opened the freezer and extracted eight enormous coffee cakes. Beth and Conor had been gone almost a year, and women still brought him food. He would stuff most of it in the freezer until there wasn't any more room and then clear everything and take it to the local homeless shelter.

But Danny knew cops loved free food and hot coffee. Why not feed them? The poor bastards were in for a miserable enough morning.

Melting frost on the sunlit windows sparkled in a dancing prism across the cherry cabinets just like any winter morning. Danny could almost believe last night was a dream.

Inferno. Michael had said that, but what the hell did it mean? Could Michael have been working on something? Danny couldn't imagine what that something could be. A play about firefighters? A hot new group? A club? It would be a first if Andy had assigned him anything serious. Andy had always treated Michael like the village idiot, even if he was his son.

He picked up his cell phone, charging on the counter. He had a missed call: Alex Burton, the paper's chief political reporter. He deleted it. Over the past two weeks, she had left messages ranging from "Yo, Ryan, could you give me a call?" to "Daniel, I really need to talk to you."

He told himself he'd call her back soon.

"Come on, Wolf." Danny pulled on a jacket, and the big dog jumped up, eager as a puppy. He attached Beowulf's leash, and they headed out to the duck pond. The two local cops from last night stood watching. Not unusual. After they'd determined Michael had been shot, the county detectives had taken over. The local cops didn't have the resources to handle a homicide investigation. Of course Michael had died here, but who knew where he'd been shot? In town, probably. That wouldn't be a surprise. Michael bought his coke in quantity, which meant he carried serious cash. Anyone could have ripped him off. It wouldn't have been a first.

When Danny drew closer, the cops turned, and he could feel them assessing him from behind their dark glasses. Wolf pulled at the leash, and Danny gave him a little extra lead. They reached the cops, and Wolf lifted his leg to pee.

"Morning," Danny said in his most ingratiating voice. Why not pretend like it was no big deal to have a CSU wading through the duck pond first thing in the morning? The press would show up soon enough, but he could handle them.

"Sorry to bother you again this morning," McSomething, the younger cop, said.

"Not at all."

"Your dog people friendly?"

Danny shrugged. "Depends on the people." He patted Beowulf's back. "It's okay, boy. Shake hands."

McSomething grinned and bent to shake the dog's paw. As soon as he did, Beowulf stood up on his hind legs and licked the young cop's face.

"Whoa. Down, boy," Danny said. "Sorry, he usually doesn't do that. He must like you."

It was one of Beowulf's best tricks. Danny supposed it was another reason Beth had banished Wolf whenever they had guests.

McSomething was good humored, though. He brushed at the shoulders of his coat and said, "We just had a few more questions."

"Sure." Danny glanced at the stone-faced older cop. No paw shaking for him. "You want coffee? I just put on some. Maybe the crew?"

McSomething shook his head. "We're fine, and they brought their own."

Danny widened his smile. "Oh, it's probably crap." He put his hands around his mouth and yelled, "Hey, guys, if you want hot coffee or food, just go on inside and help yourselves."

He could see the grateful smiles on the faces of the crew searching the pond. He turned back to the detectives. *See, I've got nothing to hide. I'm just a regular kind of guy.* The younger cop looked bemused, but Danny recognized the contempt in the older cop's eyes. This one was a hard-ass. He probably would have loved the old man.

McSomething said, "Mr. Ryan, when was the last time you saw Michael Cohen?"

"You mean before the accident?"

"Yes."

"Six months ago, give or take."

"Six months?"

"I've been taking time away from the paper. Why do you ask, Detective uh . . ."

"McFarland. Sean McFarland. And Detective John Novell."

Danny nodded to Novell. He was letting the younger guy lead, but he was in charge. Danny could sense it by the way McFarland kept looking at him for approval.

"I'd appreciate if you'd tell me what this is about, Detective."

"Do you own a gun, Mr. Ryan?" McFarland asked.

These cops didn't still think he shot Michael, did they? He glanced at Novell. His face was neutral, but Danny read curiosity, not suspicion—not yet—in his eyes. They were fishing here. "I have a Tokarev. It was my grandfather's, a souvenir from World War II."

"Anything more current?"

Danny shook his head. He had a Glock that he kept down at the firing range, but that wasn't their business. In any case, Danny doubted Michael's killer had used a Glock. He figured it must have been a small-caliber gun. Probably a .22. If it had been anything larger, the bullet would have ripped a bigger hole in Michael, and he'd have bled out much faster.

"We'd like to see it," McFarland said.

Danny stared at him for a moment. "Oh, the gun. It's in the house." Right where he'd left it on the hearth. That wouldn't look suspicious. "What does Michael's accident have to do with me owning a gun?"

Novell shifted, and Danny knew what was coming now. The big dog was about to take over. Cops were nothing if not predictable. Danny folded his arms and fought back the urge to use the old Clint Eastwood line: *Go ahead, make my day.*

Novell ran his tongue over his teeth and stepped close enough that Danny could smell his morning coffee and breath mints. He figured Novell carried a hip flask.

"Mr. Ryan," Novell said. "As far as we can determine, Michael Cohen had been missing for twenty-four hours until he showed up at your house last night. What were you doing yesterday?"

4

Detective John Novell prided himself on being a quick study. He called it his shark sense. He'd read once that sharks have a kind of sixth sense that helped them track prey. At least that was how he remembered it. In his two tours in 'Nam and twenty-five years in the FBI, it'd saved his ass more than a few times. Now it told him Danny Ryan was hiding something.

Still, he was just a witness. There was no evidence tying him to Michael Cohen's crash: The skid marks. Lack of blood splatter. Plus, the captain had warned him to go easy. Not only was Ryan just a witness, but he was also a rich, well-known VIP in these parts. Their department didn't need bad press.

Tommy Ryan's son was a liberal jerk-off with a penchant for taking swipes at tight-ass politicians and anyone else who pissed him off. He looked the part with his beard and expensive clothes. Ryan's leather jacket was probably worth a week's take-home.

Ryan seemed easygoing, but Novell sensed the tension vibrating just below the surface of his calm exterior. He had a way of talking with his head slightly tilted and his mouth curved in a half smile that projected ease. But his eyes were hard. His hands, shoved into the front pockets of his jeans, balled into fists. Still, Ryan was a cop's kid. He knew how to play along.

He wasn't much like his old man. Tommy Ryan had been a huge guy with a loud mouth and an attitude, but his kid was slim, dark, and soft voiced. The eyes were the same though: cold, deep blue. A good-looking guy. Slick. Very slick. The kind women liked.

Ryan had lost his family last year, but he also had the bucks to soften the blow. Some woman would step in and make it all better for him. That's how it went for guys like Ryan. They fell into the shit pile and came out with gold dollars.

Novell followed Ryan through the huge kitchen. No expense spared here. From the jade granite countertops to the stainless steel appliances, this palace was a showcase. The only room that seemed out of place was Ryan's office.

Tucked into a corner of the house, the room had a lived-in feeling, the brown leather furniture comfortable, not fancy. Novell noticed the journalism awards crowded together on the bookcases and the one that hung over the massive stone fireplace. Probably the only one that counted: the Pulitzer.

A huge mahogany campaign desk stacked with folders stood in front of the fireplace. On it, a photograph of a small boy in a soccer uniform sat to the left of a laptop. Except for his dark eyes, he was a tiny replica of his father, without the wariness. It was probably a safe bet that Conor Ryan had never been abused.

When he picked up the photograph, Novell heard Ryan suck in his breath, and he didn't have to wonder how Ryan handled his son's death.

Was Ryan haunted by his wife? Interesting that there were no pictures of her in the room. Still, if Ryan wasn't devastated by her death, he'd benefited from it. Beth Ryan had been born with that proverbial silver spoon, and Danny Ryan had gotten a big chunk of change when she died. Twenty-five million could buy a man a lot of comfort.

The Tokarev lay on the hearth. Ryan scooped it up and handed it to Novell, his face expressionless. More than seventy years old but in fair condition, it was a souvenir from another war. The bullet that killed Michael Cohen had come from a .22. Still, a tingle ran from Novell's fingers up his arms when he turned the gun over in his hand.

"Dangerous to leave a loaded gun lying around," Novell said.

"I was going to clean it."

Novell emptied the chamber. He grunted. "Why? Looks like your firing pin's half-rotted. Did you know that?"

"I do now." Ryan shifted slightly, and Novell saw a flicker in Ryan's eyes. He couldn't quite define it, but it bothered him.

Novell handed back the gun. "Yeah, you do."

When Novell was much younger, he'd chanced upon a book of martyrs in a used bookstore. He'd been struck by the figure on the front—a saint, pierced with arrows, who lay staring toward the heavens. Novell didn't know why he thought of that book now, nor was he sure Ryan made a convincing martyr. But the face was similar. Maybe it had something to do with those eyes.

"And you don't have any other guns in the house?" Novell said.

"No."

Novell cleared his throat. He hated Ryan's quiet voice. He hated the way Ryan looked at him, his head slightly tilted, those eyes probing. Novell despised reporters almost as much as he hated politicians.

When his career with the bureau had collapsed in ruins, Novell believed a merciful God would have taken him, but he was the man with shark sense and not much else. After he'd left the bureau, he thought he'd escaped into obscurity. He wasn't good for much, so he came to Chester County. Just a nice suburban police job to finish out his godforsaken career because a friend owed him a favor. No big deal. But he should have known that was too good to last.

Christ, he needed a drink.

*

Novell sat at his desk and paged through the preliminary lab results on Michael Cohen. They'd gotten them faster than usual because the autopsy had been done almost immediately. Respect for the family, the captain said. Andy and Linda Cohen wanted their son buried according to Jewish law. No need for bad press, Novell thought.

Gut wounds were ugly things, and despite its small caliber, a .22 could be lethal. The bullet would enter the body and career around inside doing the maximum amount of damage, but unless it perforated something like your liver and you bled out, you could survive for quite a while.

Novell set down his file. The ME couldn't be exact, but he estimated that Michael Cohen had driven around for approximately two to three hours with a hole in his gut. If he'd driven himself to the hospital after he was shot, he might have survived. So why hadn't he?

Why did he have to talk to Danny Ryan? Hell, he had a cell phone on him. If Michael Cohen drove all the way to Valley Forge, he must have wanted to give Ryan something.

Sean McFarland came into the room, his face perplexed. "Car's clean, except for some traces of cocaine. No coke in the vic's system though."

"So he just decided to drive out there for a chat?"

"Nobody just drives out for a chat when they know they're bleeding out."

Novell shook his head. "He didn't give Ryan anything."

"Information, maybe?"

"Maybe. Though he'd have had to speak fast." Novell pinched the bridge of his nose. "In any case, this isn't about Danny Ryan."

"You sure about that?" Sean stared down at the photographs from the scene. "In less than a year, this guy loses his wife and kid in an automobile accident, then his friend crashes into his goddamn duck pond with a bullet in his gut. I'd call that a pretty weird coincidence."

"Yeah, I guess."

"I checked Ryan's cars. Both engines were stone-cold. He hadn't been out."

Novell dropped the report. "Well, for now, we start looking at whatever Michael Cohen was working on."

"The father said he was writing restaurant reviews."

"Maybe he pissed off a chef," Novell said. Ryan wasn't lying when he said Michael Cohen wasn't an investigative reporter. "Well, we start there. Maybe he saw something."

"I'm still going to pull the accident report from Ryan's wife and kid from the staties."

Novell shook his head. "Stubborn."

"Yeah." Sean grinned. "My dad always says I'm a real bull-head. He's still waiting for me to give up this cop shit and get a law degree so I can join my brother and him and become respectable."

"So why don't you?"

Sean looked away. "I guess I wanted to do some good. Help people. I know it sounds dumb. I just couldn't see myself in law school. This felt right."

An idealist. Just what he needed. Novell forced a smile.

5

Danny stood in the Cohens' circular driveway and stared up at the massive stone turrets of their Gothic mansion. It dwarfed Michael's carriage house apartment, which crouched almost out of sight in the back.

The first time Conor had seen this place, he'd looked around in wonder and asked, "Is this Disney World?"

The Cohens' home had been a magic kingdom for Conor. He'd always loved that indoor pool with its turquoise-and-coral tiles, and Linda Cohen had treated him like a favorite grandson. She'd loved slipping him whatever candy she could—the more tooth rotting, the better.

Danny wasn't sure whether it was because Linda longed for that elusive grandchild or because that first time, Conor had looked her up and down and said, "Hiya, cutie!"

Beth had been horrified, but Linda had seemed charmed.

Michael had been there that night too. He had swilled tequila nonstop and watched his mother shepherd Conor around like he was the guest of honor.

Now Michael was just another ghost.

Danny walked through the front door and wandered among the people who'd come to sit Shiva and suck up to their hosts under the guise of paying their last respects to Michael. He saw

Alex Burton, the city's political reporter, across the room and waved. Her eyes widened, a look of surprise and anxiety tightening her face as she held up her cell phone.

"Daniel! Thank you for coming." Linda Cohen came up to him. From a distance, she looked fortyish, her face perfectly made up, her blonde hair styled in a sleek bob, and her black suit straight from some designer's runway. Up close, soft lines had begun to form. Linda called them her battle trophies. She'd earned them.

Linda was elegant, compassionate, and sharply intelligent, but she didn't possess mile-long legs, silicone-enlarged boobs, and the IQ of a toaster. Andy wanted to come home to Linda, but he liked screwing younger women and had the cash to ensure that those women would be appropriately beautiful.

"I'm so sorry." Danny held out his hands to Linda, and she grasped them.

"Michael always thought the world of you." Her eyes filled. "This is such a shock. No parent should bury a child." She squeezed his hands. "My God. I'm saying that to you. It's awful."

He pulled her against him, and she clung to his neck, seeming so fragile for one who had been his rock in the gray days following Beth and Conor's accident.

"It feels like a party, doesn't it?" Her voice shook. "No one even misses him. If he were here, he'd put a damper on things, wouldn't he?"

"Don't do this to yourself." He hugged her closer. Had people laughed and talked at Conor and Beth's funeral? Danny couldn't remember anything but the two white coffins sitting side by side and the endless receiving line. He'd mouthed words of gratitude while his father-in-law had taken center stage as the chief greeter.

Linda took a breath, and Danny knew she would pull herself together. That's what you did: teetered toward the edge and pulled back. When she looked up at him, she gave him a weak smile.

"Did Michael speak to you?"

Danny shook his head. "What was he working on?"

19

"Just writing about restaurants. What harm was in that?"

"I don't know."

What was he going to tell her? Michael's last words? The only *Inferno* he knew was Dante's. *Hey, traveler! Welcome to hell. Abandon all hope and join the party.* He didn't think Linda wanted to hear that.

"I've been a terrible mother. Michael called me Medea." She held up her hand when he started to protest. "No, don't. My poor Michael. He tried his best. Unfortunately, his best was never good enough, was it?"

Words had always been Danny's refuge. They seemed so inadequate now. Nothing he could say would relieve her grief. He touched her cheek.

"Michael always said you were his only real friend."

Danny didn't answer. He pitied Michael. He couldn't say he loved him. Danny added it to his list of sins.

Linda tucked her arm through his. "Andy wants to know when you're coming back to the paper." She tightened her grip when he started to pull away. "It's time. You have to go on with your life. You're still young."

He knew there was no point arguing. Linda had become his mother in many ways. She always said she felt compelled to protect the needy because she was a doctor, and Danny believed she took on people as projects to relieve the boredom of her marriage. It probably relieved the loneliness as well.

She led him down the hall and opened a door.

Andy's office had the hushed feel of a chapel, possibly because of the arched, stained-glass casement windows that opened onto the courtyard. They cast odd patterns of deep crimson, emerald, and gold light into the room.

Andy sat behind a massive ebony desk and stared out into the courtyard, but he swung around when they entered. He matched the decor with his lion's mane of unruly white hair and his severe black suit. Drinkers were supposed to have florid faces webbed with broken blood vessels and purple veins, faces like the great Tommy Ryan. But Andy was sallow with dark eyes sunk in shadow.

The door clicked shut. Linda had left them alone.

"No words of condolence." Andy held up his hand. "I don't think I can stand any more, especially from you." He waved to the black leather chair in front of the desk. "Sit down. Do you want a drink? I've got scotch and scotch."

Danny shook his head.

"For a Mick, you never were much of a drinker."

"And for a Jew, you were."

Andy pulled a bottle of Glenfiddich from his desk drawer and poured two fingers into a tumbler. "Do you think the sins of the fathers are visited on the sons, Daniel?"

"I don't know."

Andy downed the scotch and poured another. "It's a shitty thing to be disappointed in your son and have him know it."

Danny stared down at his lap. He could hear Michael's voice in his ear. *My father hates me.* "Michael did his best."

"He was strictly second string." Andy swallowed his drink. Lines of scarlet-and-gold light slashed across his face, and he pointed his glass at the cell phone on his desk. "That's all we have now. Goddamn Internet. We don't even have a police reporter anymore. We have citizens with cell phones. Papers are dying. We should be saying Kaddish for journalists." Andy poured himself another drink. "I want you to come back, Daniel. I miss you. I can see it now. Just like before. Your face on the side of a bus. 'Get your Dan Ryan fix only at the *Philadelphia Sentinel.*'"

Danny didn't want to hear it today. "That's a pretty lame slogan."

"You're pretty lame right now. You've worn black for a year. Life goes on."

"When did you move Michael off the celebrity news?"

"Who says I did?"

"Linda said he was writing about Philly restaurants."

"He wanted to expand his repertoire. Do restaurant reviews. I figured what the hell. We lost our food critic."

"Did he mention the Inferno?"

"Is it a restaurant?"

"I doubt it. It is a book."

"Touché. I'm a bit rusty on my Dante. A little too steeped in Christian ethos for my taste, I'm afraid. Why do you ask?"

"It's something Michael said. Right before he died."

Andy considered his empty glass. "Oh?"

"It has to mean something. Michael was dying. He knew it. Why would he say that?"

Andy set down the glass and looked at him. "Maybe he had a vision. Maybe he'd just read Dante, though Michael never was big on reading. How's that for irony?"

"It doesn't make sense."

"Doesn't it? Then maybe you aren't worth hiring back."

Danny's stomach twisted into a cold knot. "Jesus Christ. Maybe he found a story."

Andy shrugged. "Ah, there is life in there. Peculiar as it seems, Michael may have stumbled upon something, so stop feeling sorry for yourself and do your job. That suits you."

"Does it suit you?" Just once Danny wanted Andy to say that he was sorry about Michael, to act like a goddamn father. Christ, he was gripping the arms of his chair. He forced his fingers to relax.

Andy bared his teeth in something between a smirk and a grimace. He poured himself more scotch. "My son is dead. You should respect that."

"Why do you think he came to see me?"

"You don't have to do three columns a week. Just Sunday. Maybe Wednesday."

Danny leaned forward. "Why wouldn't he go to the hospital?"

"And a blog, of course."

"I guess I could finish Michael's article."

For a moment, Andy's face seemed to turn to stone, and then he downed his scotch. "You want to hit the clubs and pick up girls? Fine. Go find someone to suck your dick. You could use it."

"I thought Michael was doing restaurant reviews."

Andy waved his hand. "I want you to come back to work. Just like the old days. Period."

"Just like the old days." Danny didn't feel it wise to mention his case of writer's block. The words would come. Eventually.

Andy poured another and turned back to the window. Danny recognized he had been dismissed.

*

Danny slipped down the twisting path to the carriage house Michael had called home. He'd made this trip many times when Michael's pleas for company had stung his conscience. It had bothered him that Michael felt compelled to shop for food for those visits—caviar and crackers, smoked salmon, imported wine and beer—that he would leave rotting around the apartment until the cleaning service disposed of it.

"Michael," Danny had said more than once. "Why don't we go out? I'll pay." Michael had always refused. He'd hoarded those visits, maybe because he was so starved for friendship he needed to savor them in private.

Danny fitted the key Michael had given him into the lock, pushed open the door, and flicked on the lights. The place reeked of orange furniture polish, bleach, and fresh paint.

Michael's furniture had been a hodgepodge of remnants from his college days, spotted and soiled with black substances that made Danny's skin itch. It had been Michael's feeble rebellion against his father's wealth, like his battered BMW, his badge of honor, the way he'd proved he was just a regular guy, albeit with a thirty-million-dollar trust fund.

Now only a black leather couch and matching lounge chair took up the living room. Some small jade sculptures and a few decorative plates Michael had never owned lined the built-in shelves. A red carpet with bold geometric shapes covered the floor.

It looked as if a house tour was scheduled to go through the place.

It took the Cohens less than two days to clear Michael's apartment, and he wondered where Michael's memories were. Could you take thirty-eight years, shove them in a box, and pretend they weren't there? Or maybe, like Andy, you drowned them in bottles of Glenfiddich.

What the hell was the rush?

Danny went upstairs. One bedroom and bath, both cleared, save for a double bed, a chest of drawers, and a bookcase. He went to the bookcase and perused the titles. He doubted Michael had read Dickens or Twain, but *Elements of Game Theory* and *Elements of Calculus* had a well-worn look.

Michael's computer manuals sat in a neat pile. Christ, Michael had loved his computers. Online he had the personality he had lacked in person, and he had spent hours roaming the Internet looking for other lonely beings. Danny found two homemade DVDs with carefully produced labels stuck into the plastic sleeves of one of the manuals. They'd be easy to overlook among the stack of operating discs. He slipped them into his pocket. No computers. He supposed the police had confiscated them.

He went to the closet, crouched down on the floor, and groped for the loose floorboard he knew was there. It was where Michael had kept his stash.

"You should get high, Danny," Michael used to say. "This is great shit."

But Danny had watched his sister Theresa slide down that black hole. In any case, Michael had plenty of friends when he had dope.

Danny pulled the board free and groped underneath until his fingers closed over a small tin box. Inside sat a baggie about one-third filled with white powder and a plastic card. Black and white with a red teardrop in the center, it looked like a credit card but had no writing to identify it.

Danny shoved the box into his jacket pocket and was pushing the board back in place when he heard footsteps on the stairs. He spun around to face a woman who scowled at him from the doorway. Her auburn hair was pulled back in a braid, though wisps had escaped to curl around her pale face, and her deep-green eyes reminded him of a forest pool.

She leaned against the doorjamb. "What are you doing here?"

He flashed her a smile and realized he was way out of practice. "Are you a cop?"

"I can call a cop. Who are you?"

"A friend of Michael's."

"Funny. I'm a friend of Michael's, and I never met you."

He took a step toward her and held out his hand. "Danny Ryan. Michael and I worked together."

Her eyes widened. "You're Danny Ryan?"

Normally, he would have had some kind of snappy comeback, but his repertoire was limited these days. He dropped his hand.

"Sorry, I didn't mean that quite the way it came out. Kate Reid. You just look so different from the paper."

"I've lost some weight." He forced a laugh and thought he sounded a little insane. *Why yes, I've had a fucking mental collapse.* He tried to picture her with Michael but couldn't. "You dated Michael?"

She gave him a tentative smile. "No. We were friends."

"Are you a writer?"

"I'm a legislative aide. In fact, I believe you know my boss."

"Oh?"

"Yes. Senator Robert Harlan. He's here today. You should come say hello."

Jesus, she just got better and better. Danny didn't know how much of his loathing showed. He was good at keeping a poker face under normal circumstances, but his former father-in-law stretched his limits.

Big Bob Harlan. He'd gotten miles of column inches out of the senator. A mutual hate society.

When they'd first married, Beth had taken great delight in the fact that someone finally stood up to her father. By the end, she would read Danny's column, hurl the Sunday paper at him, and say, "Danny, please. Give it a rest just once, would you? He's my father, for God's sake. I have to deal with him."

He told himself he had too often given it a rest when he and Beth had married and he'd caught a glimpse of that other world, the one rumored to exist behind the doors of gated estates and clubs shrouded in exclusive secrecy. When he'd attacked her father in print, Danny had never used anything he'd learned in those rooms. Beth had looked at it differently. She'd believed he betrayed her. It would always haunt him.

"Excuse me?" Kate looked at him a little oddly. "Are you all right?"

"No. I mean, yes. I'm sorry." He'd lost track of the conversation.

Kate gestured toward the closet. "What were you looking for?"

"I don't know. Michael was coming to see me the night he was killed. I guess I feel responsible."

Her eyes narrowed like she was trying to decide whether or not he was hustling her. At last she fumbled in her pocket and pulled out a business card. "I don't know everything Michael was into, but if I can help, give me a call."

"That's very nice of you." He knew he sounded snarky. "Why did you come here anyway? Did the senator send you?"

"I told you. Michael and I were friends."

"So you did."

"As far as I know, he was doing a piece on Philly nightlife. Clubs, restaurants."

Danny touched the box in his pocket. Michael was working on something more than restaurant reviews, something that most definitely could have gotten him killed. "He didn't say anything to you? If you were friends, that's hard to believe."

"If you were friends with Michael, you know how secretive he could be." She was annoyed now. The color rose on her cheeks. "Michael also said you could be a real prick."

"No, he didn't. You did." Danny shrugged. "You're right too. Look, I need to get back."

Kate blew out a breath. "I'm sorry if I offended you."

"You didn't."

He started past her, then paused. Something about her face seemed slightly askew, as if the skin were pulled a little too tight or she'd undergone extensive cosmetic surgery—much more than a nose job. Weird. She couldn't have been older than twenty-six or so.

"Is something wrong?"

Christ, he felt like an asshole. "It was nice meeting you."

She tucked her card into his breast pocket, and the faint aroma of lavender and vanilla reached out to him and drew him a step closer. For a moment, she stood with her hand resting on his lapel, and he wanted to lay his hand on top of hers but could only stand frozen, lost inside her gaze. The ghosts in her eyes. The secrets and sorrows. Whoever she was now, Kate Reid had led a different life once. He could almost see the outline of another woman just under her skin. It was her business if she wanted to run away from her old life, not his, but it made him curious.

Her mouth curved into a tiny smile. "Give me a call. I'm not so bad once you get to know me, and I might be useful. You never know."

6

Dark all around. Cold concrete beneath his knees. Justin's hands were chained above his head. This wasn't the dungeon, was it? Not the dungeon.

The door opened. Light snapped on, blinding him for a second. Then the thin, blond man appeared. He was nightmare in a green leather tunic, tights, and weird booties; sparkling green covered his shallow eyelids, and black rimmed his eyes.

"Poor Justin," the blond man said. "Do you know who I am? I'm Mason. I've come to set you free."

He slid his hands down Justin's cheeks, his fingers long, white, and smooth like they didn't have knuckles. Justin wanted to puke. Nobody kept you chained up naked if they were going to set you free, especially not freaks like this.

"But you aren't a very nice little boy, are you? Turning tricks is such a nasty business. I'm afraid Congressman Powell is tired of you."

Who the fuck was Congressman Powell? No one used names at the club. It was just sex. Baggy old men. Sometimes a young guy with tight abs. Sometimes a woman with plastic boobs. Sometimes all three. The bodies blended together.

Who gave a shit about them? The needle made them disappear—for a while, anyway. The needle made everything disappear.

Then he remembered the guy in the red silk mask, a regular. The one with the little piggy eyes and sagging girl tits. He wore the feathered, silk G-string and liked the really kinky shit. His mask had come off the other night.

Justin bit into his tongue.

"You're young, aren't you?" Mason cooed. "How old are you, darling?"

He tried to speak, but no sound came from his dry throat.

"You remind me of someone, you know. He has blue eyes, too." Mason leaned close, pushed his fingers through Justin's hair. "Such lovely eyes. You've seen too much, my pet."

Mason snapped his fingers, and Justin heard the familiar opening guitar riff of a metal song. It was old shit, but it used to be one of his favorites because the video was so badass.

"Do you like this song, Justin?"

Justin nodded. He tasted blood in his mouth.

"Normally, I prefer Ravel, but this is a special evening. Do you like the fairies?"

Justin didn't know the answer, and his eyes stung with tears. Stuff like this didn't happen in real life. It was a video on some creepy horror channel. But it wasn't. He was in some dark place where prayers wouldn't help.

Mason spread out his arms and threw back his head. He stood for a moment with his eyes shut, then turned to the table beside him. Justin saw the flash of something metallic.

"I'm the Sandman," Mason said.

"Please." Justin managed to croak out the word.

Mason's breath caressed his neck. "Don't be afraid, Justin. Tonight, we're off to Never Never Land."

7

Two fat pigeons sat on the stone wall, their feathers ruffling in the wind. Congressman Teddy Powell had the sensation they were watching him. Stupid. He shook off the feeling and handed his ticket to the valet.

Weird to have valet parking at a wake, though you'd hardly call this a wake. Michael Cohen was already buried.

Shiva. Jews had some funny rituals. Like covering the mirrors. What was with that?

He wouldn't have come today, except he had to pay his respects. Andy Cohen would go through the guest book and note who came and who didn't, even though he'd treated that kid of his like a retard.

He'd seen that fucking Alex Burton. Goddamn bitch reporter. He'd like to wring her neck. Then to top it off, Danny Ryan showed up. If anyone deserved a run of bad luck, it was that sanctimonious prick. Teddy wasn't sure what he hated more: the phony-defender-of-the-little-guy bullshit or the watch-out-for-the-political-weasel screeds Ryan used to write. He looked like hell now. He must've lost close to twenty pounds, and it wasn't like he was a big guy to start. Maybe he'd lose so much weight, he'd just disappear.

The valet delivered his Caddy, and Teddy got in. He wondered if the asshole expected a tip. Fuck him, if he did. Who tipped at a wake?

He pulled around the circular drive toward the gates, and one of the pigeons took off. The bird flew low and swooped in right front of him. Teddy slammed his brakes.

Goddamn birds. Teddy saw the valet smirking in his rearview mirror. He hit the gas pedal and roared out into the street.

Teddy bounced over the cobblestones of Germantown Avenue, then cut back through Mt. Airy to get to Lincoln Drive. He loved the Drive, especially when there wasn't much traffic, like this evening. It was like a giant serpent twisting and turning alongside Wissahickon Creek.

Maybe he wouldn't go home just yet. He could stop in town for a drink or two. His wife didn't care. She had her career as Mrs. Congressman.

He wanted to go to the club, but they'd cut him off from the special rooms since the incident with that kid. Assholes. As if they cared about a fifteen-year-old street whore.

He was a sweet boy, though. Justin. The best he'd ever had.

Red light.

Whoa, he almost went right through the intersection. Brakes felt a little sluggish, or maybe he hadn't been paying attention. Long day.

A black Porsche pulled beside him, and Teddy was tempted to roll down his window to hear the low purr of its idling engine. Before the light changed, the driver glanced at him and grinned. He inclined his head and pointed forward, and the Porsche leaped ahead. Furious, Teddy pounded the accelerator.

The speedometer inched up close to sixty. A little too fast, but he didn't care as he flew past trees and houses. Still, the rear lights of the Porsche pushed farther ahead. Goddamn it. A warning light glowed on the control panel, but Teddy kept his eyes on the Porsche.

The traffic light was changing from yellow to red, and Teddy floored the gas. The Caddy lifted slightly from the road. Damn, he was just like Steve McQueen in *Bullitt*. Too fucking cool.

The road made a sharp curve to the right just before the Henry Avenue Bridge. Dammit, he forgot this curve. The Porsche slid through it easily, but something was wrong with his goddamn wheels. The back end spun out, and Teddy slammed the brakes. Nothing.

The rear end smashed into the guardrail. Teddy cranked the wheel, and the car careened sideways and then went airborne, rolling down toward the creek. He could hear his father talking about the Romans and how they'd built arches. He could see Justin, that pretty young face, those wide, blue eyes. The kid could have been a model. He probably hadn't even recognized Teddy; his mask had only slipped for a second and—Christ, he was going to die under the suicide bridge. Why?

The Caddy slammed into the ground, and Teddy jolted forward. The air bags exploded into him, grainy particles swirling through the air.

The car rocked back and forth on its roof.

Engulfed in the airbags, Teddy couldn't move, couldn't see, but he was alive. He smelled gasoline and heard the rush of the water close by. It was going to be all right. He just had to get out of this crumpled mess of a car.

Then he heard a soft whump, like a sack of flour being ripped apart.

Shit.

*

The driver of the Porsche continued down the Lincoln Drive and then swung onto Ridge Avenue East and back up Midvale to park on the campus of Philadelphia University. He pulled on a pair of sunglasses and walked to the Henry Avenue Bridge, where a plume of black smoke rose in the air. A small group had gathered to stare down at the valley below.

"What happened?" the driver said to a pair of young guys who looked like students.

"Oh, man. You missed it. There was a massive crash a few minutes ago," said a tall kid with bright-orange hair tipped with purple. He looked like a pumpkin on a stick.

"Really? A crash?"

"No, dude. That car flew," said the second kid. Dark haired, medium build, he might have been normal enough, except for his mass of piercings. Goddamn freaks. The driver would have happily tossed them both over the bridge, but he didn't work for free.

"A one-car crash?" He peered over the edge. All he could see were smoke, flames, and a couple of cop cars. The scream of the fire engines announced their impending arrival, but Teddy Powell was already a roasted pig. "Geez, I hope they got whoever was in there out."

"I don't think so, man," said the pumpkin head. "That car must have been going a hundred miles an hour to explode like that."

"I'll bet that was something."

"We didn't actually see it," the dark-haired kid said. "But we heard it. I think the whole world heard it."

The driver nodded. He drifted back into the crowd and sauntered back to the Porsche. Too bad his next stop was the chop shop, but details were details, and someone might have noticed his car.

Now he could report that the congressman with the big mouth was toast. That was the penalty for being a dumbass. Powell had cost them valuable merchandise. He had broken the rules. There was a price to be paid.

8

Danny almost never took Valley Forge Road through the park, but this afternoon, he did. He pulled over into a turn-off and then crossed the covered bridge by foot to the other side of the creek. The sky had turned pewter, the air raw. Soon it would probably start to pour, and he was wandering around in the woods.

He followed the path, listening to the murmuring creek as he walked. Beth had come this way. The state cops had said she'd lost control on the twisting road. The Jeep had hit a low barrier, flipped, and lost a wheel, ending up in a crumpled mess in the creek. That afternoon, it had been snowing, and Beth hated driving in it. Black ice? Could something have been wrong with the car? Something the cops missed?

"We'll take your Jeep," she'd said.

Danny sagged against a tree. Beth had been driving his Jeep. He used to get death threats all the time, but he'd never taken them seriously. If he didn't piss people off, he wasn't doing his job.

Could some nut job have damaged the car? Run her off the road? No, that was insane.

Crouching down, Danny pressed his hands against his forehead. He could smell decay and death, the cold metal odor of the morgue.

The lot of love is chosen. His mother had whispered that to him as she lay dying. Her beloved Yeats. Her lot was to marry a drunkard, bear him four kids, and die young. His was to choose Beth. He never regretted it. Never. She'd given him Conor.

Inferno.

Danny picked up a rock and threw it, then another and another. He heard them bounce off trees and splash down into the creek. The wind sighed through the trees, and Danny shivered. Branches scratched at the sky. A crow flew from the woods in a flurry of black wings, its caw piercing the raw air.

*

Novell walked behind Sean McFarland and gazed up at the redbrick facades of the row houses, now turned into apartments, on Pine Street. It was a pleasant neighborhood, filled with little boutiques and restaurants and couples out doing their Christmas shopping.

They reached the correct address, and Sean hit the buzzer. The woman's voice sounded scratchy and strained after Sean explained who they were and why they had come, but she buzzed them in. She lived on the top floor.

Kate Reid stood in the doorway with her hands on her hips, her hair pulled back from her pale face, and her eyes filled with wary curiosity. She wore black, which was fitting. Kate always seemed born to wear black.

When she stepped back to let them enter her apartment, she didn't look at him or Sean. Maybe because she knew he never appeared bearing good news. Maybe because she wanted to forget they had ever known each other. Novell didn't blame her in either case.

"Miss Reid," Sean said, "I know this must be a difficult time for you. I'm so sorry for your loss."

She nodded.

"We're looking into Michael Cohen's death, and anything you can tell us about him, anything at all, no matter how trivial it might seem, could be helpful."

Novell gave Sean points. He oozed a certain Boy Scout charm calculated to soothe. He doubted Kate was moved, but at least she wasn't cursing. She glanced at Novell for a moment and turned her attention to Sean.

"I knew Michael. I felt sorry for him. He didn't seem to have a lot of friends."

Sean tilted his head as if puzzled. "Why do you say that?"

"Michael was a bit different, I guess. He liked to hang out with me because I didn't judge him."

"But other people did?"

"I guess. I don't really know. We didn't discuss it."

"Did he mention what he was working on?"

Kate chewed on her lip. "A piece about restaurants." She stared into the space just beyond Sean's forehead and motioned to the sofa. "Please. Sit."

The sofa was expensive. Novell recognized the quality of the creamy leather that enveloped him, and the thick, blue rug with its maroon-and-cream geometric patterns looked pricey as well. In an apartment where the rest of the furniture was comprised of Goodwill specials, these pieces seemed so out of place that it was jarring. Did that matter? Novell wasn't sure.

"How did you meet Michael?" Sean asked.

"He's a reporter, and I work for a senator," she said in a tone with just enough calculated breeziness.

"But he wasn't a political reporter."

"No. If I recall correctly, I met him at the opening of a community center or something like that. I'm not sure Senator Harlan was even there."

She'd turned herself into a neatly packaged professional woman. She deserved a good life. It seemed small to begrudge her one. Novell rubbed his mouth. He'd become a sour old bastard. A scotch would taste good right now. Several, lined up like dutiful soldiers.

"So when did you last see Michael?" Sean said.

"Oh. I'm not sure. Sometime last week. He liked to drop by to watch movies. Michael liked movies. Old sci-fi, slasher flicks, gory stuff."

"Not your cup of tea."

She shrugged. "I guess I'm more of a rom-com girl."

Novell cleared his throat. That was a laugh. Kate didn't believe in love, and she'd thrown in her lot with one of the worst pieces of shit in the Senate.

"So you didn't talk to him or hear from him the day he died?" Novell said.

Kate narrowed her eyes and looked at him. "Why would I?"

Neither an affirmative nor a negative. Novell wondered if she'd learned her technique from Senator Harlan. Kate would be difficult to crack, but he'd figure out a way.

*

"Impressions?" Novell said when they were heading out of the city.

Sean hesitated for a few seconds before he answered. "I don't know. You ever meet a witness who says all the right things and seems to cooperate but something seems off?"

Novell nodded.

"Maybe it's because she just came from Michael Cohen's funeral and didn't want to talk about him. But she feels wrong. She hung out with him, but she seemed so detached."

"Maybe they weren't that close." Novell figured he might as well play devil's advocate. Not that Kate needed one.

"Maybe, but something's off. She lives in this funky apartment with a four-thousand-dollar sofa and some kind of designer rug. That's weird."

"Maybe she saved up for it."

"If you're moving up, generally you move in steps. Second-hand sofa to Ikea to a two-thousand-dollar job. You don't generally go from zero to four thousand in one leap. And that rug must have cost at least eight. I'm betting they were gifts."

"Eight hundred?"

"Eight thousand. My mom's really into that shit. Believe me, my parents' house has been redone more times than I can count."

"Maybe she has rich parents."

"If she came from money, her clothes would be better."

Novell almost laughed. Sean had his uses. He was the guy who could tell whether that antique was a genuine or phony. Maybe all kids from rich families were schooled in that. Maybe someone had paid her off. Maybe they were gifts from Michael himself. Novell wasn't sure if she knew something relevant to Michael Cohen's death or she was embarrassed by the connection.

"And didn't you think it was weird she had no personal shit anywhere? Nothing. No picture of mom and dad or boyfriend or a dog, for Chrissake. You ever walk into a place where someone had nothing personal around?"

"Not everyone is sentimental." As for the personal items, Novell understood that. Kate had nothing personal because she had almost nothing of her life to keep. "We'll deal with people he saw regularly for now."

He'd deal with Kate later. She might not know who killed Michael Cohen, but it's possible she knew why.

*

When Danny pulled into the driveway, Beowulf was waiting at the back door, so he didn't bother putting the car in the garage. He just unlocked the door and let Beowulf run free. The dog raced straight toward the pond, stopping to pee against his favorite willow tree. Danny followed. There was a lot more gray in Wolf's coat these days, and he ran much slower, but he'd always be that shivering pup with oversized paws that Danny had scooped from the trash.

Even Beth, who had been constantly exasperated by Wolf's desire to be a lapdog, would allow him to sleep on the family room sofa.

"Did you train him to put his paw up like that?" she'd said when Wolf followed her into the room one day and sat in front of her with his paw out.

"Are you kidding? He barely listens to me." It was a lie. Danny had spent weeks teaching Wolf that trick. But Beth got used to having him snuggle against her on the sofa. She never did lift the upstairs ban, but she'd give him strips of beef and buy him special bones from her organic butcher. That was the side she had kept hidden from the world, the side he loved.

"I don't know who's worse, you or that dog," she'd say as she tossed Wolf a treat from Le Gourmet de Chien, and Danny would pick her up and howl until she laughed. The good days. He didn't know how they had screwed it all up.

Beowulf came running up to him amid a flurry of honking geese. When Danny squatted down to accept his dog's affection, Beowulf knocked him over on the damp ground, and for a few moments, they wrestled just like old times. Danny could almost hear Conor giggling, and he jerked up. He took a breath, the memory a shard of glass. Beowulf pushed his head up against Danny's chest. Danny clung to him for a moment and pulled some leaves out of his thick fur. He had to get himself together.

"Race you back," Danny said and ran up the hill to the house. He was sweating by the time he reached the back door. Beowulf was there already, waiting.

"Extra hot dogs?" Danny said, and Beowulf pushed ahead of him into the house.

Later, Danny looked at the DVDs he'd gotten from Michael's place. Porn, shot in low light. From the length and quality of the picture, Danny thought it must have been shot at a sex club, a very kinky one, where the clients wore masks, cloaks, and not much else. They appeared to be mature, but the help seemed young. Too young. He tried to get a better look at a girl in a metal collar being led around the room by two dwarves. She looked no more than sixteen and seemed barely aware of her surroundings.

All stone and marble, the club was like some kind of peculiar cathedral, though it seemed to lack windows, at least in these shots. Either Michael was looking into it or he was participating. Danny knew he should show these discs to Novell, but they might not be connected to Michael's death. He owed Linda and Andy the truth before he handed these over to the police.

Novell wanted to clear a murder. Danny wanted to find out what the hell Michael was doing and where he was doing it.

His cell phone rang, and he debated answering it until he saw the name on the caller ID. Alex Burton.

"Ryan," he said.

"Yo, Daniel. We need to talk."

9

Danny stood in the crowded lobby of Seasons 52 and waited for Alex to appear. Outside a light, powdery snow drifted down. It wasn't enough to make driving treacherous, but in a few hours, the roads would freeze. A bad weather night. A chill slithered down his neck, but it was just a gust of wind from the door opening.

"Dan Ryan!" Alex said. She pushed through the crowd and made her way to his side where she gave him a hug and kiss. "You on that new starvation diet plan?"

He smiled. Alex was nothing if not direct. "How's it working? You can stop now. Ten more pounds and you'll disappear."

They followed the hostess to their table, and Danny thought of all the times he and Alex had worked together. She covered city politics but had started to widen her area of expertise to the state and national scene and had made a name for herself as the one reporter the mayor didn't want to face at a morning briefing. Pointed, pitiless, and pithy. He'd missed her company.

They were seated with drinks on the way when he said, "I gather you're upset about Michael."

"I always knew you were a smart guy."

"Has anyone talked to you about him?"

She frowned. "Not yet, but I have an appointment with two cops, Novell and McFarland, to talk about our relationship. Some relationship. Michael used to steal my pens—you know how I love my purple pens—but he did help me with my computer. He was way better than the IT guys. I always thought he should've done that, not writing." She paused when the waitress set a glass of Pinot Noir in front of her. "I heard if it was real news, you wrote his stuff."

Danny stared at his club soda. "That's not really the point."

"Isn't it?" She shook her head and softened her tone. "Hey. You were my mentor—damn, that sounds weird. But I don't think I'd have had a career in Philly if it hadn't been for you."

"You'd have been at the *Times*."

She waved her hand. "Andy offered me a column."

"And you said?"

"Hell, no. He wasn't offering me a column like yours because he said you're coming back. I would be writing about black fashion and food. Puh-lease. You know what I think?"

"I'm sure you'll tell me."

"This is serious, Daniel. I think someone was putting pressure on Andy to get me off the street."

"Come on, Alex. You've been driving the pols crazy for years. Andy loves that."

"About a month ago, I was on Teddy Powell—the late Teddy Powell. You know how there've been rumors about Teddy Powell for years—going after pages, that sort of thing—but there was never any proof?"

"That's old news, but yeah."

She leaned closer. "So I was heading out to a town hall two weeks ago, and Michael says, 'Ask Teddy Powell about Tophet.' So I'm like, 'What the fuck? Sure, whatever.' I thought, there goes Michael again. But I get there, and Teddy's doing one of his patented 'All poor people are lazy' blah, blah, and the words just popped out."

"You asked him if he ever heard of Tophet?"

She grinned. "You bet. I figured it was some kind of joke and maybe he'd just look at me like I was crazy and then go on, but that motherfucker turned even whiter than usual and says, 'No more questions.' That's it, and I didn't even know what Tophet was."

"But you do now."

"Sort of. Tophet is the name of a place in some valley near Jerusalem that was used for pagan worship. So I see Michael and I asked him why he told me to ask Teddy about some valley in Jerusalem where they had human sacrifices. Teddy Powell's an asshole, but I don't see him running around making sacrifices in a ditch."

"And he said?"

"Someone needed to do it."

"Have you told anyone?"

"Are you crazy? Michael's dead, and so is Teddy Powell. All I've got is this." She paused and glanced around before she pulled out five pages of Xeroxed notes from her purse. "Michael gave me these and said to hold on to them as backup. I started to do some research on my own."

Danny wanted to kiss her when he saw the pages and Alex's purple notations. "Why did he want backup? For what?"

"He said you didn't want them. Then he just gave me that creepy giggle and went off. So I take the list, start looking up names, ignoring the penis drawings, of course. It's a lot of weird shit, nothing that makes sense. Check it for yourself. There's Styx, by which I assume he meant the river, and Avernus, which is a lake near Naples."

Danny shook his head. "According to myth, Avernus was believed to be a doorway to the underworld. But the third one down is Tophet."

"I know, and Teddy Powell is dead. This list gives me the god-damn willies."

The last name on the list was *Inferno*. Danny's stomach twisted. He didn't need to tell her about Michael's last words. Whatever this list was, she didn't need to be involved. For her own good.

"Michael's special places," he said.

She shook her head. "Maybe. Michael was into all that 'end of days' shit, but this is weird, even by his standards. Maybe he was into devil worship and it got out of hand."

"You don't believe that."

"Look, I don't know what Michael was doing. But you take these notes, hide them good, and don't tell anyone you got them. I don't want any more accidents happening."

"What do you mean?"

She gave him a look of pure exasperation. "I go to a press conference and ask Teddy Powell one strange-ass question suggested by your buddy, and a few weeks later, both Teddy and Michael are dead. I think that's a pretty goddamn bizarre coincidence."

"Alex—"

"Listen to me. I think Michael got caught up in something funky that turned bad. Real bad. He got shot, for God's sake. Do you really think he crashed into your pond by accident? It probably took him well over an hour to get out to your place from wherever he was. I'm betting someplace downtown."

"It was shitty that night. Sleeting."

"So you need to figure out why he came out hauling ass."

"To talk?"

"Maybe, but he must have known he'd be in real bad shape by then."

"The cops didn't find anything about the Inferno or Tophet or any other hellish thing, or they would have said something, asked me about it. Believe me. I was thoroughly grilled."

"I'll bet. I just can't figure out why he gave these names to me."

"He told you," Danny said. "You were backup. He came out to my house in the summer. He said he was onto to something. I wasn't exactly receptive. Maybe he'd gotten on to this."

The waiter came to take their orders, and for a moment, Danny thought about Michael and those lost opportunities. Christ, he had been an asshole. That was the worst part.

"Don't go beating yourself up," Alex said. "Everyone knows Michael had problems. I told you, the cops want to talk to me."

"Be discreet."

"You think I want to tell the cops Michael was investigating hell?" Alex gave him her patented you-are-a-dumbass look. "He was weird, though."

Danny nodded. "He was at that, but he was also very lonely." He raised his club soda. "I've spent the day looking into underage sex trafficking."

"Oh Christ. Is that what you think this is about?"

"I don't know, but Michael had a couple of porn discs featuring kids."

"Don't you think we'd hear about missing kids?"

Danny shook his head. "What if they were runaways?" He watched the realization dawn on her.

"Throwaway kids."

"The Cyber Tipline has received more than three-point-five million reports of suspected child sexual exploitation since it started in 1998. Those are just reported tips."

She pressed her fingers against her forehead. "What do you need?"

He smiled. "I've missed you. I forgot what a good time we had working together."

"Flattery will get you everywhere," Alex said. "But be quick about it. Sam and I are leaving for vacation in a few days. It's kind of a relief. Since Michael and Teddy Powell died, I gotta tell you, I've been edgy."

"You'll be fine." He squeezed her hand. "And you've done more than enough." He glanced around. The patrons looked normal—happy couples seated in an upscale restaurant enjoying their delightful entrées. No shady men with bulky jackets lurked close by, but a niggling unease brushed over his neck like a cobweb.

"I'll follow you home after dinner," he said. "Just to be sure."

She started to protest but stopped. "He finally found something, didn't he? Poor Michael."

Danny nodded. Styx and Avernus were doorways to the underworld, but Tophet and Inferno were hell itself.

10

Sean McFarland stood at the edge of Alex Burton's cubicle and smiled. The reporter had closed her laptop at their arrival and faced them with a blank stare. Sean knew she was African American, but with her long, honey-brown hair and gold skin, she could have passed for any number of backgrounds. At present, her amber eyes assessed Novell and him. He wasn't sure her conclusions were positive.

"So, Ms. Burton. Michael Cohen was your colleague. How closely did you work together?"

"We didn't work together," Alex said. She doodled with a purple pen.

"Was he a good reporter? Competent?"

"He was adequate for the task he was assigned."

"And that was?"

"He did celebrity news, for the most part."

Sean glanced at Novell. This woman had a better cop face than most cops. "But he was working on restaurant reviews."

"Yeah. We lost our restaurant critic a few months ago. Layoffs. Most of us pull double duty these days."

"I was curious. You were at a town hall meeting a week or so ago with Congressman Powell and asked him a question about something called Tophet. May I ask what that is and why you asked?"

46

Alex shrugged. "It was a joke. Michael put me up to it. He said to ask him. I don't really know why. Seemed sort of stupid. The congressman ended the conference after that."

"He was upset?"

"I don't know. He may have had other commitments. He did seem a little upset. It was a silly question." She doodled faster. Big circles looped together across her notebook.

Sean wrote down Tophet and underlined the name.

"You didn't think it was odd for Michael to suggest a question like that?" Novell asked.

"I was running out the door to do a town hall and was late. I wasn't really thinking. When I got to the meeting, it just popped out."

Sean glanced at Novell, but Novell had no expression. Then Sean realized Novell was looking at a photograph of Alex Burton and Danny Ryan. It must have been taken at an awards dinner, and they both clutched trophies.

"Have you looked into Tophet since?" Sean said. He gave her his best Boy Scout smile. He wasn't sure she bought it.

"Sorry. Like I said, it was a joke, and I have some other stories to finish. I'm going on vacation with my husband at the end of the week. I hope that's not a problem."

"No problem at all, Ms. Burton. You've been very helpful."

*

Danny ducked into Naraka. It was one of Michael's favorite shops on South Street, filled with pentacle earrings, upside-down cross T-shirts, and other raptures for those inclined toward devil worship and the occult. He should have waited to shave until after he visited.

A girl with green hair, black lipstick, and a pentacle tattoo on her left wrist stood behind the counter. Her name tag read, "Violette," and he wondered if that was her real name. Laced into a black leather corset with a purple skirt that was high in the front and lower in the back, she looked a bit like a Goth showgirl.

The air was filled with the aroma of what he thought might be patchouli mixed with dog shit and the music of some metal band he couldn't identify. Red lights sparkled from red glitter lamps lining the walls. In the glass case stood crystal balls of all sizes and tarot cards from around the world. Something for everyone.

"Welcome," Violette said. "We have crystal balls on sale today. Twenty percent off."

"Sorry, I'm not a believer," Danny said. "I'm looking for Max."

"Max quit a few days ago. Something about his aunt dying. You don't look like a friend of Max's."

"I'm a friend of a friend. I'm from out of town, and my friend told me to look up Max."

She pursed her lips together. "I can't help you."

"I was told Max could hook me up with some clubs, you know?" he said.

"This is a legitimate business."

Danny shrugged. "I get it. I don't want any trouble. I just heard about this place called Pluto's Bowl." He didn't know why he started with that one. It was the least sinister name from the list that came into his head. "I can make it worth your while."

He opened his wallet to pull out some bills and watched her back away when she caught a glimpse of Michael's black-and-white card.

Violette shook her head. "I'm sorry. I can't help you."

He noticed her hands shaking and knew it was time to back off. "It's just a name I heard. I don't know anything about it. I'm not looking for anything too weird."

"Bullshit. You've got one of those cards. You're looking for weird."

Danny hesitated. He would have to tell her why he was here; she wasn't going to talk to someone she thought was a total pervert. "Look, Violette. I'm just trying to get information. I'm a reporter. Dan Ryan. My friend Michael Cohen was—"

"I know about Michael Cohen. I saw it on the news."

"I'm not asking you to go on the record."

She glanced up at the security camera. "I don't know where Max is. He took off in a hurry. He was scared. That's all I know."

"So he's not coming back."

"Max wasn't into clubs. Max had other business interests, y'know?" Violette sniffed. "Do you like stones? We have a ton of healing stones." She walked over to a bin divided into sections. "They're nice to touch."

"Colorful."

She smiled. "Yeah. Here." She held up a black stone. "Jet. It's really powerful. It protects you from evil and helps you heal from grief."

"What?"

"It heals. You look sad. It's your eyes. You have really nice eyes, but they're sad. You should hold onto the jet. It will help." She pointed to a bin of gray stones. "Like Apache tears. They're very good for healing grief. Not as good for protection though." She held the jet out to him.

"I don't believe in magic stones."

She closed his fingers over the piece of jet. "Maybe you should. Take it. It's on the house. Go grab some white sage, and you can pay for it and the Apache tears while I write them up. Burn the sage in your house to get rid of evil spirits. Bad karma." She selected a gray stone from the bin and walked to the counter.

"Better safe than sorry?"

"Hey," she said, "if you're smart, you'll go home and forget about clubbing. Just hold onto that stone. I think you're gonna need it."

*

Eight hours later, Danny slouched in Beth's Mercedes on a private lane in Gladwyne watching a parade of cars pull into the gated residence that sat at a discreet distance from the road. He used an infrared camera filched by Alex from the photo department to snap license plates. He'd discovered the address written in tiny letters at the bottom of his sales receipt from Violette.

It didn't seem likely to be a club, so it was probably a private party of some kind. He figured he could take a chance and pretend to be a guest. If only he'd worn his tuxedo and a black feathered mask, he would have fit in.

He pulled through the gates, swung around past the surprised valets, and left the car facing the gates. When he rang the bell, the door swung open, and he faced a tall, gaunt man with a swirl of dark hair artfully arranged on the top of his head.

"May I help you, sir?"

"I don't know. I think I'm at the right place," Danny said. The house was so quiet that except for the cars parked outside, he would have sworn no one but this ghoul was home. "I believe there's a party tonight."

The ghoul's left eye twitched. "I beg your pardon?"

"A party." Danny spoke a little louder. His voice seemed to bounce off the walls. Jesus, this place was like some kind of museum. Victorian furniture. Good paintings on the walls of Italian landscapes and naked children playing in the water. It smelled of lemon polish, bleach, and air freshener that masked another odor, something vaguely unpleasant like rotting meat. Mouse in the floorboards? Body in the walls?

"I'm sorry, sir, but this party tonight is black tie and by invitation only. You are neither invited nor properly dressed."

"How do you know?" Danny pulled out Michael's black-and-white card. "I am a member."

"I'm sorry, sir. But that card will not grant you access to this particular event. I'm afraid I must ask you to leave at once."

Danny weighed the option of trying to find the party guests and getting thrown out. Not worth it. He already had license plates. At least he could get an idea who attended this soirée. He held up his hands. "Sorry. My mistake."

"Goodnight, sir."

As he was driving home, it occurred to Danny that he should have stayed parked across the street, but it was too late now. He had no doubt the ghoul was already processing his license plate.

11

In the morning, Danny threw his research in a satchel along with the camera. He figured he could work out of the Penn Law Library for a few hours after he returned the camera. Beowulf lay by the door, his head between his paws, and watched him with his sad eyes. Had he always done that or had Conor taught it to him? The sad eyes, the silent plea for more dad time.

"I wish I knew his secret," Beth once had said.

"What secret is that?"

"How to get your attention."

"You always have my attention, Beth."

She had slumped a little. "I used to."

Danny had put his arms around her. He'd watched her try to blink away her tears before he gathered her against him. "The day you said yes to me was the happiest of my life. I've never regretted it. Maybe you have, but not me."

"I don't regret it," she'd said against his chest. "I miss us. I miss the way we were."

"We'll get it back," he'd said. And they had, to a point. Some weeks were good, especially when her workload eased, and he would see his Beth, sunlit and smiling. She'd spend hours with Conor, reading and playing with puzzles. Later they would make love like they had in the early days.

But those other weeks, when the stress had worn her down, Beth's temper would turn stormy, and Conor quickly learned to pack up his toys and head to his room when she pulled into the driveway. Danny knew she hated sitting home; he wanted her to go back to work, but Beth had begun to believe he worked against her with Conor, as if parenting was a competition to be won.

Danny looked at Beowulf and grabbed his leash. "Come on, you win. We'll go to the park, but not for long. I have work to do today."

*

Novell swallowed a cup of black coffee and refilled it. It tasted like hell, but at least it was real coffee. He eyed the young blonde sitting in the metal chair, swinging her right leg over her left. Sean entered with a soda and handed it to her with a smile, which she returned.

"So, Ashley, you worked as a nanny for the Ryans for a year?" Sean asked.

"I did. I couldn't believe it when I heard about the accident. Conor was such a sweet little guy. He was just like his dad. So adorable."

Novell filed the information away. Maybe Beth Ryan didn't like the nanny gushing over her husband and son.

Sean leaned in. "I'm sure it was a great place to work. Would you say they were a happy couple?"

"Oh my God, yes. I mean I wasn't there all the time, but they seemed happy. I think Mrs. Ryan sometimes got upset because Conor would miss his French lessons, so I started working with him. Like I'd go with him and his dad to the park and all and go over French."

"And Mrs. Ryan didn't mind?"

"No. She was fine. One time someone thought I was Conor's mom. Can you imagine? And then Conor started kindergarten not long after, and Mrs. Ryan let me go."

Novell looked at Sean. Had Ryan cheated on his wife? Did it matter?

Sean said, "Did you know Michael Cohen?"

She frowned. "The creepy fat guy? Yeah, he used to come over. Mrs. Ryan didn't like him. She told me to keep Conor away from him. Even Mr. Ryan agreed with that, and he was always so laid back."

"So she was afraid Michael Cohen would hurt Conor?"

Ashley took a sip of soda and considered. "I don't know what she thought exactly except that he was creepy. Real creepy. If a kid went missing where he lived, he'd be the first person I'd suspect."

*

Danny had gotten a later start than he planned, and it had been frustrating. He was still trying to trace the owner of the house in Gladwyne but had only a name: John Smith, whom he had traced to a holding company and then nowhere. One holding company led to another and another until his eyes were burning.

When he pulled into his driveway, Beowulf wasn't barking. Odd. He walked straight to the back door. Unlocked. The kitchen in disarray.

The drawers and cupboards gaped open, their contents strewn on the floor. Danny stepped over the mess. Every room downstairs was ransacked, but he ignored the shattered crystal and broken china, opening doors and trying to subdue his growing panic.

"Wolf?"

He didn't care about the mess. Where the hell was Beowulf? He ran back to the kitchen. Danny opened the door and stared into the growing darkness. His breath blew out in cloudy puffs, and he found himself making childish bargains with a God he knew wasn't listening. *Please let him be all right. I'll go back to church. I'll do goddamn anything. Don't take him too.*

Then he noticed the footprints. Dark against the gravel driveway, they led to the garage.

"Wolf!" Danny tried to force air into his lungs, but they wouldn't expand.

If he didn't move, everything would be all right. He knew that.

Never open that one door. It's always the thing you fear: the state cop with his kind eyes, the blue-and-red lights reflecting against the falling snow. "Mr. Daniel Ryan? There's been an accident."

He found himself walking to the garage and pulling the door open. In the dim light, he could see boxes pulled from shelves, his old college yearbooks scattered amid the tools and odd bits of Christmas decorations. Beowulf lay in the middle of the floor, still as if he were asleep, but a pool of blood encircled his shattered head.

*

Cops swarmed through his house, taking pictures of the destruction, pawing through the downstairs, upstairs, his bedroom, and Conor's room. They questioned Danny about his substantial cache of prescription drugs, each bottle untouched. They made him account for his time over and over, like maybe he'd trashed his own house and killed his own dog in some kind of psychotic break with reality.

Danny leaned against the kitchen door and gripped Beowulf's tags until the metal dug into the skin of his palm. The pain kept him focused. Kept the surge at bay.

Let go and feel, Danny. Pain is good. It's a first step.

His right hand was bleeding.

By the time the cops left, it was after eight. Only Novell remained.

Danny turned to him. "Did you forget something?"

"Thought I'd help you bury your dog," Novell said, his voice mild.

"Forget it."

"No. He's big."

"Thank you."

Danny couldn't stand to look at Novell, not with tears burning his eyes. Christ, his old man would have a good laugh if he could see him now.

The phone rang, and Danny tripped over a pile of silverware lying on the kitchen floor. He kicked at it and grabbed the receiver. "Yeah?"

"Danny Boy, you sound out of breath." The voice was little more than a whisper but full of malice.

"Who is this?"

"You got our message. That's good."

The phone slipped against his bloody palm. "What do you want?"

"This was a warning. You understand? Keep out of what don't concern you. Be smart. Give us the package and walk away."

"What the hell are you talking about?"

"The package Michael Cohen brought you."

Danny looked at the crap on the floor. Michael had a package? But he didn't. It didn't make sense. None of it made sense. "Look, asshole, I don't have any goddamn package—"

"Wrong answer."

The phone clicked.

12

Novell watched Ryan stand at the kitchen sink and run water over his hands. His shirt and the front of his suit jacket were stiff with blood, and if Novell hadn't seen it, he wouldn't have thought Ryan had it in him to heft that dog and stagger with him down to an area near the duck pond surrounded by willow trees. They buried him there, neither of them speaking. It wasn't until they got back to the house that Novell realized how ripped up Ryan's hands were.

His first thought was soft city boy, nothing like his old man. His second was maybe strength came in different packages.

"Would you like a drink, Detective?"

"Sure, I could use one." Novell wanted to forget burying that dog. He wanted to forget a lot of things.

Ryan wiped his hands on a towel and turned to face Novell. Silver lines of tears cut through the dirt on Ryan's face, and Novell thought of the book of martyrs again.

"You're a scotch man," Ryan said.

"Good guess."

"My father was a scotch man." Ryan pointed to a doorway. "I don't think they completely trashed the bar."

Novell followed him out of the kitchen into the family room and stepped over a couple of shattered crystal vases. Expensive.

Was there anything in this house that didn't cost a fortune? Books were scattered across the floor, and someone had pitched the family photographs throughout the room like Frisbees. Novell wanted to straighten the oil portrait that hung at a crazy angle from the wall. The perfect family—young, attractive, too good to be true. Novell turned away and surveyed the room.

It was three times the size of his condo—new construction made to look old with its exposed beams, high windows with leaded glass, and cathedral ceiling. The fancy furniture was all earthy greens, deep reds, and rich golds with matching pillows, now tossed helter-skelter. A mahogany bar stood in the corner. It appeared intact.

"Whoever was here left with all the beer and most of the vodka." Ryan held up a fifth of Chivas. "This okay or are you a single malt man? I've got a case of Glenfiddich."

"Chivas is fine."

"Straight okay?"

Novell nodded. "You don't drink?"

"Never was much good at it." Ryan poured a double shot of Chivas and handed it to Novell. He opened a bottle of club soda for himself. "Now I bet your partner McFarland's an imported beer man. Heineken. Guinness. Or maybe Dos Equis with a wedge of lime."

"And you know this because?"

Ryan gave him a half smile. "I grew up around cops and drunks. Haven't you done your research on me?" He laughed when Novell didn't answer. "Yeah, you have. You're too thorough a cop not to have checked me out. What were you before this? Secret Service? DEA? FBI?"

Novell swallowed his scotch and tried not to be impressed. "Door number three."

"Ah, big time. So why'd you leave?"

Ryan's quiet voice invited him to lean a little closer, assured him he was a sympathetic listener, and intimated it was safe to open up, but Novell wasn't fooled. Ryan focused on his face, like he was trying to look inside, and Novell knew he wanted to take notes. Treacherous fuck. All reporters were the same.

"I put in my twenty. It was time." Novell shifted. He didn't like the half smile that played on Ryan's lips.

"You don't strike me as a guy who puts in his twenty and quits."

Novell set down his glass on the bar, and Ryan refilled it. It was a beautiful sight, that scotch, like liquid amber. He breathed it in. "You trying to get me drunk, Ryan?"

"You drink too much, Detective?"

"Your phone call. Tell me about it."

Ryan shrugged. "Nothing to tell. I've been asking some questions about Michael, and my visitors took offense."

"That was them on the phone?"

"Sure."

"You weren't gonna tell us? Didn't it occur to you that that's the sort of thing the police are for?"

"To protect and serve? Not really." Ryan gave him that half smile, his face white, fatigue pinching the corners of his mouth. But those dark blue eyes burned with a reckless determination. Novell knew that look. It usually led to some messy ending. Guys on missions were dangerous.

Still, Novell was damned if he didn't feel an odd kinship with him. Tommy Ryan's kid was on a mission. The elder Ryan would get a grim laugh out of that.

"Was Michael carrying anything that night?" Ryan said.

"Like?"

"Like a package."

Novell frowned. "No package."

"Still, maybe there's something—"

"This is a police investigation."

"You don't seem to be making much progress."

Novell stiffened. "All right, smart guy. You said Michael wasn't an investigative reporter. Why do you think he got killed?"

Ryan's expression remained bland. "Michael was doing a story on Philly nightlife. Maybe he stumbled upon something."

Novell could tell that Ryan chose his words carefully. Did he risk pulling him in for questioning and have him lawyer up? No. Not yet. Ryan was the best lead to Michael Cohen's murder they had. If he wanted to dangle himself as bait, that was his choice. For now.

"What would he stumble upon?" Novell asked. "Drugs?"

Ryan shrugged. "As far as I know, Michael's drug use was recreational. He did clubs too. Have you looked into that?"

"We've made a list."

"Could I see it?"

Novell almost choked. "Damn it. This isn't the Hardy Boys. You don't go running off like you're some kind of storybook detective."

"Christ, if you're going to make me a detective, at least choose someone interesting." Ryan grinned, and for the first time, he looked like the man whose face lit up the sides of all those buses. Then the grin disappeared, and his face turned distant. "I knew Michael. Let me see his notes. I can help."

"You looking to win another big writing prize?" When Ryan winced, Novell looked away. Michael Cohen might have been his friend, but for all he knew, Ryan was planning his comeback on this case.

"You think winning a prize will make everything better?" Ryan's voice sank to a hoarse rasp. "I don't have anything left."

"And I can't take responsibility for you."

"I didn't ask you to."

"Losing that dog wasn't enough? If you keep this up, maybe next time they'll go after the rest of your family. I know you've got a brother. And a sister."

"Fuck you, Novell."

"No. You're the one who's fucked."

Novell watched Ryan cradle inward to absorb the impact of his words. He swallowed the second scotch and poured himself a third.

13

D anny knelt on his office floor and combed through the debris. It was after three. Maybe he couldn't face bed tonight.

Danny shuddered. He salvaged his Pulitzer from its broken frame. He'd been twenty-four years old and got it for local beat reporting. The ongoing investigation of the Sandman. His father's last case.

The Sandman killings. Over a period of ten months, the cops had found twenty-two teenage girls strangled with red ribbons in the Northern Liberties section of the city, and the strangulation had been the kindest thing done to them. Tortured over days and partially skinned, none of the girls had ever been identified.

The lost girls. Who wept for the lost?

His life had changed after that case. He'd become a star in Andy Cohen's universe, while his father had fallen into the abyss.

His father had brought down the Sandman, a derelict named Paulie Ritter, and then resigned. He had walked away after forty-two years on the job without an explanation and had gone back to their house in South Philly.

When Danny had tried to talk to him, the old man had told him to get lost.

"Give it up, you fucking vulture. I'm done. I've got nothing to say."

"Don't you want to tell your story?"

The old man's face had flushed crimson. "You don't give a shit about my story. You want to make a name for yourself. This is how you get your pound of flesh." Swaying from side to side, his father had stood in the middle of Third Street. He'd needed a shave, and his shirt was splotched with grease stains. "Stay away from me. Go suck up to that Jew and his cokehead friends you like so much. You make me sick just to look at you."

By then Danny had learned not to show weakness in front of his father. "So you're going to go crawl into a bottle and die? That's fitting."

The old man had spat in the street. "I am dead, boy. Can't you hear the banshee wailing? Don't come back."

Danny pressed his hands against his forehead. His right eye socket ached as if he'd been punched. Growing up, he'd learned how to take a punch. No choice there. He was the youngest, the runt of the litter.

He pulled out the black-and-white card. It was clearly a membership to a club of some kind. Now he needed to find the club. He turned the card over and stared at the red teardrop. On closer examination, it could have been a flame.

Under the Pulitzer was a broken frame with a picture of Conor staring out. Danny lifted it carefully and carried it back to his desk.

Often at night while working, he'd look up to find Conor standing in the doorway, his left hand stuck in the front of his pajama bottoms and his right hand clutching his blue lightsaber.

"There's a monster in my closet, Daddy," Conor would say. "I can't go to sleep."

It didn't matter how many nightlights he'd bought or how many times he'd checked the closet; Danny would end up lying on the bed that always seemed a little too narrow and holding Conor until they both drifted off to sleep. He'd wake up at three in the morning with Conor's hands twisted in his shirt and a light saber jabbing his gut, and he'd wonder why the monster couldn't take a night off.

Danny ran his fingers over the edge of Conor's picture. Now he had the king-size bed to himself and would give everything to feel the weight of his son's head against his chest again, to untangle those palms from his shirt and breathe in the light sweat and shampoo smell that was Conor.

He draped Beowulf's tags over the picture.

Before he had a wife and son, Danny had Beowulf. He'd rescued him from a dumpster, a mass of sores and cuts, and Wolf had repaid him with unquestioning love and devotion. Danny picked up a crystal paperweight Beth had given him and hurled it across the room. It smashed against the fireplace, showering chips of glass to the floor.

Who wept for the lost? Weeping wasn't enough. Someone needed to give a damn. Danny didn't care who these people were. He'd expose them. He'd lied when he told Novell he had nothing left. There was the black Irish anger he'd inherited from his father. That was enough for now.

14

Carrie Norton parked her Volvo in front of the mailbox and reached in to collect her grandmother's mail. She didn't know why Gram didn't just stop the mail when she went to Florida, but she insisted the postal service would let news of her vacation slip out, and then hordes of robbers would descend on the house.

The box was nearly full. Carrie stacked the pile of cards and catalogues on the passenger seat and then ran across the road to empty the second mailbox. It was technically for their tenant in the little white house overlooking the fields, but Gram hadn't had a real tenant in a year. She was planning to leave the land to the County Green Spaces Preserve—her way of thumbing her nose at the developers—but she hadn't gotten around to finishing the paperwork. Occasionally Carrie would find a stray piece of Gram's mail or a flyer tucked inside, but today she saw a whole package, and it was addressed to Danny Ryan.

Wasn't that peculiar? It hadn't been mailed. It was just stuck in there. Something was written very faintly in the left corner. Michael something. The last name was smudged with a brown stain.

Carrie ran her fingers over the package. She knew Reverend Gray called Danny Ryan an advocate of sin and Satan, but Carrie thought Danny was just confused because he hadn't found the healing love of Jesus. That didn't make him a bad man. He needed to come into the light.

He always was so kind to Gram, who was shameless about getting him to fix little things around her house. It was a disgrace the way Gram would ask him to change her floodlights just so she could watch him climb up the ladder.

"Good butt," Gram would say.

Carrie's face grew a little warm, and she glanced at herself in the rearview mirror. Her hair looked good. She reached into her purse for lipstick and applied a fresh coat. She knew she was indulging in vanity, but she couldn't help herself. She wished she had a tray of cookies or maybe a pamphlet from church.

Carrie pulled into Danny Ryan's driveway and parked by the back door. The stone farmhouse was beautiful, the kind of home that should be filled with children. She just loved that big, old weeping cherry tree in the front yard and the pink, red, and salmon roses that climbed against the fieldstone wall near the pool. Of course, it was dormant now, but by spring, the garden would be like paradise itself. Carrie took a deep breath, knocked at the back door, and waited.

No answer.

She could leave the package on the porch for him, but there was probably some more of his mail mixed in with Gram's. It always happened, especially at this time of year. Maybe she'd just take it with her and bring it back with cookies. The poor man was alone, and it was Christmas.

The Lord had tested Danny Ryan with a great tribulation last year. Carrie understood that finding this package was a sign that she had been chosen to help him find a way to heal. In any case, it would give her a good reason to return when she was sure he was home.

15

Danny hated church. As a kid, he would play train with his rosary on the edge of the pew until his mother would take it away from him and still his hands. After his mother died, his grandmother would drag him to daily mass and hit him on the side of the head with her boney knuckle when he'd fidget. God didn't like disrespectful little boys, she'd say. Danny would look up at the sad-eyed Jesus hanging on the big wooden cross and figure he'd probably rather play train as well.

Now Danny parked outside of Immaculate Heart of Mary Church in Roxborough and waited for services to let out.

He'd driven Beth's Mercedes today and could feel her all around him. He fingered the tiny gouge in the wood trim on the dash, the gouge made by her high heel when they'd fucked in the car.

It had started as another of those endless parties she dragged him to, the ones he hated. He'd be dressed in a designer tuxedo and still feel like he should be hanging in the kitchen with the caterers.

"You do clean up well," she'd said when they walked toward the senior partner's mansion in Gladwyne. "Please don't talk about Dad, Ken."

She'd taken to calling him "Ken" after one of their acquaintances had remarked that they were a perfect "Ken and Barbie."

"Come on, Barbie, let's go party." He'd watched the corners of her mouth twitch in an effort not to laugh.

Since the place was the size of a small museum, Danny had planned to escape to the many side parlors to avoid the inevitable political debates. He'd hold his own against them, but it always led to after-party unpleasantness.

"You can't call my father the standard bearer for toxic waste in Pennsylvania," Beth had said after one gathering.

"That's my opinion."

"I know he can be a pain in the ass, and I don't always agree with him. But I love him. I don't want to constantly have to choose between you. I don't want that for Conor."

Beth had the big money, but he had the celebrity. Danny had just published a book on the growing social divide in America that had received critical praise and decent sales. When they went to parties, her friends didn't know whether to slither up to him or treat him like a rabid socialist. It had become simpler to hide, and that's what he'd done that night.

He'd consumed his third glass of club soda and was pretending to study the painting with the bright geometric patterns of color in the music room when she'd appeared at his side, the blonde with sympathetic smoke-colored eyes. She'd nodded toward the picture.

"You like Kandinsky?"

The most he knew about Kandinsky was that he painted abstracts. "Sorry, I'm not an art expert."

"You were staring at it like it meant something to you."

He'd wanted to make up some lie but couldn't do it. "I was just faking it."

"You mean you were wishing you could escape."

"'Wishes were ever fools.'"

"'The fool doth think he is wise, but the wise man knows himself to be a fool.'" She'd shrugged when his eyes widened. "Okay. I was showing off. I was an English major before law school. Please don't hold it against me."

"Harvard?"

She'd given him a wry smile. "Yale."

They'd spent the rest of the evening talking literature and politics, and he'd felt like he'd been starving, even more so when she'd slipped him her card. For the first time in years, the night had seemed too short.

Beth had sulked in furious silence until they'd reached the driveway.

"That bitch latched on to you because you're my husband. You embarrassed me in front of our friends." Beth had kneaded her evening bag like it was bread dough.

"Nothing happened, Beth." He hadn't understood her fury. Beth had never really understood that he wasn't looking to wander; he was hers. He had always been hers.

"Do you think no one noticed?"

He'd pulled into the garage, and she'd sat still for a moment before she'd turned to him, her eyes glittering with unshed tears, and began to beat him with her fists. "You bastard! I hate you!"

He'd caught her wrists, pinned her back against the seat, and for a moment, they'd stared at each other. He'd watched the pulse pounding in her throat, her breasts straining against the deep-red silk of her dress with every breath, and Christ, he'd wanted her so much his insides bled.

In the dim light, her eyes had looked black, and then they'd changed as if a fire had begun to simmer in their depths. Her mouth had begun to sear his, her impatient hands ripped at the studs on his tuxedo. They hadn't cared about anything but that moment. It was always that way, a dangerous dance.

Danny ran his hand over the sand-colored leather. He should have driven his Jeep. He only drove the Mercedes because he knew it peeved Kevin.

Mass was over, and he watched the people pour out of Immaculate Heart of Mary and head to their cars. Danny opened the door and stepped out when he saw Kevin, Jean, and their four kids walking toward the parking lot.

Kevin looked bigger in the year since he'd seen him, though he was always the meatiest of the three Ryan boys. These days his belly jutted over the waistband of his black trousers, and his massive shoulders stretched the fabric of his checked sports jacket. He had more gray in his light hair, and his ruddy complexion had the broken veins and capillaries of an accomplished drinker.

"Kevin," Danny said, and Kevin stopped short. Danny watched his eyes shift to the Mercedes and back.

"Jesus Christ," Kevin said. When Jean gave a tiny whimper of distress, he glanced at her. "Take the kids and get in the car, honey."

"How are you, Jean?" Danny thought Kevin might backhand him.

"Oh, just fine, Danny. Great, in fact. Just terrific. Happy holidays. We have to run." Jean licked her lips and settled her small hands on the shoulders of her six-year-old son. "Come on, Tommy."

The boy stared up at Danny with wide blue eyes, but his mother dragged him away before Danny could speak. Thirteen-year-old Kelly gave her father a defiant glare and then ran over to give him a quick hug. She pulled back with a whispered, "Miss you." She grabbed her ten-year-old twin brothers and marched them to the car.

Danny had to grip the car door and grind it against his hand.

"What are you doing here, Danny? I didn't think we had anything to say to each other." Kevin stepped close until he was about a foot from Danny. He stood with his legs spread and his hands fisted at his sides. Four inches taller and at least a hundred pounds heavier, Kevin always was an expert at using his size and bulk to intimidate.

Danny held his ground. "I need to talk to you."

"About what? The last time we were together, you threw me out of your house."

"The last time we were together was at the funeral where you told me I was going to hell for burying my son in a Protestant cemetery."

"If you came for an apology, you're wasting your time."

"Apology?" Danny held up his hands in mock horror. After all this time, they weren't going to become best buds and hang at the neighborhood tappies. "God forbid. I thought I'd pop by to keep your spirits bright."

"Why can't you be normal and just celebrate Christmas like the rest of us?"

"I stopped celebrating Christmas last year."

Kevin looked him up and down another few seconds and stepped back. His hands relaxed. "What do you really want?"

"I need to talk to you about a murder investigation."

Kevin's eyes narrowed, and he shifted from one foot to the other. Cars whizzed past. Christmas music drifted on the wind. *God rest you merry, gentlemen, Let nothing you dismay.* Not in his family.

Kevin rubbed his chin. "What case?"

"Michael Cohen's."

16

"It's out of my jurisdiction," Kevin said.

They sat in a booth at the Ridge Avenue Diner. Danny sipped his coffee and stared at the gold tinsel that hung around the window. A piece had pulled away and drooped over the red plastic candle on the sill. In the background, Elvis crooned "Blue Christmas." Danny shifted on the red vinyl seat.

Kevin ordered home fries, two eggs sunny-side up, and a double order of sausage links to go with his short stack. "Don't you want something besides scrambled eggs? What's the matter with you? I'm not kidding, Danny, you look like hell. You must have lost fifteen pounds. Eat some fucking toast."

Five minutes and Kevin was already starting with the big brother act. He almost sounded convincing, but Danny knew better. When they were kids, Kevin had always been the lure with his brotherly pseudocamaraderie. He was at his best when he'd been leading Danny into whatever torment Junior and he had planned for the day.

"You know, Ma wasn't much older than you when she got the cancer."

Danny smiled. "Wishful thinking?"

"Christ. Try to talk to you like a human being." Kevin shook his head in disgust.

I'm not a human being. I'm a vulture.

Kevin drummed his fingers on the table, and Danny figured he'd finally quit smoking. Judging by the amount of weight Kevin had gained, he'd made a real effort. It hadn't improved his temper.

"You quit smoking?" Danny said.

Kevin made a face. "Eight months, and I gained thirty pounds. I'm not going on a fucking diet either." His chin jutted out defiantly. "So what's with Michael Cohen?"

"He crashed into my duck pond with a .22 in his gut."

"He probably pissed off his dealer."

"I don't think so. I think he was trying to bring me evidence."

"Evidence of what?" Kevin took a sip of coffee, then added more sugar.

"I'm not sure."

"Then why would you think that?"

"Because someone broke into my house the other night."

The waitress approached with their order. She laid Danny's platter of scrambled eggs in front of him, and he stared at them while she settled Kevin's plates on the table.

"And why is this related?"

"My house was trashed. I found Beowulf in the garage with . . ." Danny cleared his throat. It still felt raw. "They killed him, Kevin."

"Beowulf?" Kevin's face turned hard. "Someone killed Beowulf? Why didn't you call me?"

"Why would I?"

"For Chrissake. I'm your brother."

"Have you ever heard of the Inferno?"

Kevin let out a slow breath. The fine web of broken veins stood out on his nose, and Danny could see the old man in his tired features.

"Oh Jesus," Kevin said. "Not this again."

"What are you talking about?"

"Forget it." Kevin waved his hand. "Forget it."

"Jesus Christ! Tell me something."

"You're a goddamn idiot."

"Listen, Kevin—"

"No, you listen. You're just like the old man. You don't know when to give up." Kevin slammed his hand on the table. "Walk away from all this, and I mean right now."

"You're a fucking cop! How can you tell me that?"

"That last case drove the old man over the edge. I mean he lost it completely. If he hadn't quit the force, he would have been fired. As it was, they let him retire."

Danny shook his head. "But what does that have to do with Michael Cohen?"

"The goddamn Inferno. The old man talked about it. After he'd left the force. I used to meet him from time to time down at the Shamrock to check up on him because he didn't want anyone near the house. Then he'd go off on his little conspiracy trip. First the Inferno was a person or a group, then it was a place, and then it was everywhere and no one was safe, but he, old Tommy Ryan, had outfoxed them. Jesus."

Kevin dug into his short stack, and Danny considered for a moment. Something almost made sense. "Are you saying the old man knew about the Inferno?"

"I'm saying the old man lost it."

"I thought he never got over Junior." Danny shrugged at Kevin's scowl.

If Kevin was the ox of the family, Junior was the golden lion. He had the old man's strength and size, his blond hair, but his mother's fine features and bright blue eyes. Junior could run faster, jump higher, and beat the shit out of everyone in the neighborhood, but he had the lethal, aw-shucks charm that adults found irresistible. He had grown up big and bad, a beautiful bully. And Kevin, who was terrified of being called weak, signed on for most of Junior's schemes.

Junior was invincible until Paulie Ritter had managed to drive a number-two Ticonderoga pencil through Junior's right temple in the middle of writing out his confession to the Sandman murders. Paulie Ritter was a psycho and a cop killer, but he'd never been connected to sex clubs or devil worship.

The air seemed to leave Kevin's body as if he was remembering, and he slumped down on the seat. Danny's own shoulders sagged a little.

Danny knew if you wanted to survive, you took the soft parts of yourself and locked them away. When life became unbearable, you drank too much, took drugs, or drifted into a black hole, but maybe if you were lucky, someone came along and opened the door to another life, like Andy had for him. He'd escaped. No regrets.

Kevin stabbed a sausage. "Junior's dead. The old man's dead. You look dead. Let it go."

"You still haven't told me what you think about Michael Cohen. He got himself killed on his way to see me. He was trying to bring me something. I think it was tied to the Inferno."

"Bullshit."

"It's not bullshit." Danny stared at the scrambled eggs glistening on his plate, picked up his fork, and then set it down. He could still smell Beowulf's blood, feel his fur against his cheek as he carried him down to the willow that last time. "Don't tell me it's bullshit. Beowulf didn't fucking commit suicide."

Kevin set down his fork. "Then you might as well put a bullet in your brain as dig into that bag of worms."

"So you won't help me?"

"I've already lost one brother. And the old man went crazy. I'm done with it."

17

Danny drove Kevin home from the diner in uncomfortable silence.

Kevin lived in a cul de sac of redbrick twins with garages that faced the street and swing sets that filled the backyards. It helped that Jean had her teacher's certificate, though Danny wasn't sure that she dreamed of teaching history to tenth graders when she studied it at Temple long ago.

Jean wasn't a woman whom you'd pick out in a crowd, but she had an insatiable thirst for knowledge and a soft smile that left her a half-inch shy of pretty. Her eyes used to brighten with a sort of nervous energy when she'd talk about traveling or going on to get her masters and then her doctorate.

That fire was long gone, and Danny didn't know whether it was the years of marriage to Kevin that had crushed it out or just the tiny disappointments that came when life didn't work out the way she'd planned. The opportunities never quite materialized, and she watched her bright hopes fade away because she had no Andy Cohen to open just the right door.

Jean had left the Navigator in the driveway, and Danny angled in behind it. Kevin didn't get out. He sat with his arms folded and stared straight ahead. "You aren't gonna let this Inferno thing go, are you?"

"I won't bother you anymore. I can try to get a hold of Stan."

Kevin banged the dash, and for once Danny didn't flinch. He wasn't sure whether Kevin noticed or not. He no longer cared.

"Jesus Christ, you're a dumbass. Don't bother Stan. He's got problems, so stay the hell away from him."

"What kind of problems?"

"He's fuckin' dying. He don't need you pokin' around his life."

When Danny didn't answer, Kevin said, "Wait here."

He opened the door and stomped into the house. Ten minutes later the garage door rumbled open. Kevin stood framed in the doorway, a box in his arms, and he held it away from his body as if it contained dynamite. Kevin shoved it onto the seat.

"The old man's official crap," Kevin said. "I haven't looked at it since we packed up his house, so I don't know if it has anything of use or not. You know how crazy he got at the end. He cut off everyone, even his partner. At Junior's funeral he wouldn't even shake Stan's hand."

Was the old man so unusual in his grief? Was that where his darkness came from? Sins of the father?

"You want to commit suicide, go ahead," Kevin said.

Danny didn't understand Kevin. He could be such an asshole one minute and almost human the next. He'd always been that way. Maybe in a normal family, Kevin and he would have been able to work out their differences without spilling blood.

"Thanks, Kevin. I appreciate it."

Kevin leaned into the Mercedes. "Look, you wanna come in? The pregame starts in fifteen. I got friends coming over, but you're welcome."

Funny how the gulf between them never seemed so wide or so narrow as it did right now. "Thanks, but I . . . can't." He wanted to. Wanted the noise and confusion of Kevin's house, the shrieks and yells of the kids, Jean's gentle camaraderie.

"I've got to get going." Danny gripped the steering wheel. Let Kevin think he was an asshole. It was better than admitting he was a coward.

Kevin gave Danny's arm an awkward punch. "I saw Theresa the other day. She said she got out of rehab three months ago."

"She looks pretty good, doesn't she?" In truth, Danny hadn't seen their sister. He just wrote the check to the rehab facility.

"She looks straight. She said you footed the bill." Kevin frowned. "You shoulda called me. I'da helped out."

Danny shook his head. "You've got kids, Kevin. I figured. I—It doesn't matter." He didn't want to say the money meant nothing to him. Kevin would have taken it wrong.

"I meant what I said. I don't want to lose another brother." Kevin's voice wavered for an instant, and his mouth tightened.

Christ, real emotion. Danny couldn't deal with that right now. "Could you do one thing? Please?"

Kevin folded his arms. "Maybe."

"Could you run these plates?" He passed the list through the window.

"Jesus Christ. What is this?"

"I got sideswiped the other day, and we pulled these numbers off the store's security tape."

"Yeah, and I can fly." Kevin took the list. "I don't want to know."

"Thanks, Kevin. For everything." Danny couldn't believe Kevin had agreed to help him.

"And, Danny, if there is an Inferno, it's probably a club. The old man babbled about it being for elites."

"What kind of club?"

"Judging by the old man's rants, a pretty exclusive sex club where rich old coots get jacked off by high-priced hookers."

"Nothing makes sense."

"You keep digging into this, you're gonna be in deep shit fast. I sure as hell can't protect you."

"I've got to find out what happened to Michael."

Kevin shook his head. "I must be insane, but call me if you need anything."

"Thanks, Kevin. Look, could you check one other thing? There's no particular rush, but I'd like to find out some information on a local address."

"Why?"

"Just curious."

"Christ, do you a simple favor and it never ends. What's the address?"

Danny handed him the address of the house in Gladwyne.

Kevin gave an elaborate sigh. "All right. I'll see what I can do."

18

When Danny pulled into his driveway, it was just growing dark. He glanced at the garage and stopped. In the deepening twilight, the pond looked still and peaceful; the last rays of sun kissed the low hills and winked off the water as a lone duck skimmed its surface. He swallowed when he looked toward the willows. Beowulf's willows.

The fence still gaped at him. He'd have to get that hole repaired.

Danny got out and approached the hole before turning to face the road. Deep ruts still marred the surface of the grass in an almost perfect line. Michael must have come shooting down the road like a rocket. He followed the ruts in the grass to the road. What the hell was Michael doing?

The path he traced led to the top of the hill. He stood at the edge of the road and looked up. Mrs. Norton's mailbox stood in his direct line of sight, and he tried to remember if the cops talked about skid marks. There were none. It wasn't a clear shot to the duck pond, and Michael would have had one hell of a time reaching the box. He couldn't just lean over, especially not if he were bleeding, and he certainly hadn't gotten out.

Where would he put a package? If Michael was afraid, he'd hide it. In a mailbox? That seemed a bit obvious, but Michael was dying. Michael was also a gamer. He liked all that "open this door" and "look in the green box" shit.

Danny walked to the mailbox and looked inside. Just a few cards. It was not uncommon for him to get Mrs. Norton's mail and for her to get his. Danny had enjoyed her eccentricity. He had written a column about her as a break from his routine, and it had been a hit, which they'd both enjoyed. She'd feed him apple pie and give him the benefit of her tart tongue, and though he suspected she watched Beth and him with her telescope, she made a good story.

After the column, Michael had decided to start leaving her presents. Odd, inappropriate gifts: opera glasses, a black night-gown, a sex toy. Danny had managed to intercept the last gift—a large, purple, vibrating dildo. Michael was relentless. He'd started leaving gifts in the tenant's mailbox too, calling it his drop box.

If Michael had a package, it wasn't impossible that he'd put it in the tenant's box. Danny looked across the street. The tenant's mailbox stood tilted slightly back. He walked over to it and peered in. Empty. Then he saw what appeared to be a rusty stain rimming the inner edge, almost like bloody fingers had gripped the box.

Danny stared down the road. From here it was a direct line to the pond. But it made no sense, unless Michael wanted him to find the package later. Michael must have realized he was dying. Maybe he was afraid the cops would grab whatever he was carrying first, and he didn't want that. Maybe he'd left the package someplace else and had given Danny credit for being smarter than he was. He could only start here and try to think where else Michael would leave something sensitive.

Mrs. Norton was away until March, and Danny wondered who was picking up her mail. If he wasn't mistaken, she had a granddaughter or niece who wandered in and out. Danny tried to put a face on her but could only come up with a thin, younger version of Mrs. Norton. He walked up to the house, a smaller version of his own, and knocked on the door. No one home.

He'd come back.

*

In his office, Danny pulled out the notebooks his father kept from his cases over the years from the musty box Kevin had given him. The old man might have been crazy, but he was meticulous about his notes. Danny found his last notebooks near the bottom. They covered the Sandman investigation, but the last two months were missing. Surely Kevin hadn't taken them. Why the hell would he want the old man's notebooks?

At the bottom of the box lay an old newspaper with the headline "Alleged Sandman Kills Philadelphia Detective in Bizarre Interrogation Incident." Not Danny's byline. The story was about his brother, Thomas Patrick Ryan Jr., Paulie Ritter's last victim. The second cop on the scene had pumped fourteen rounds into Paulie. Stan Witkowski, his father's former partner. No wonder the old man had been so twisted at the funeral. Stan had been there when Junior died.

They'd closed the investigation after that, and the old man had lived out his days holed up in their row house in South Philly until his heart gave out almost four years later.

At Junior's funeral, the old man had stood alone. He was still a big man with powerful hands, but they'd shaken that morning. His skin had a sickly yellow cast, and he'd glared at Danny out of dead eyes with a malevolence deepened and honed by the death of his favorite child.

God is watching you, boy.

The old man didn't have to say the familiar words that day. Danny had heard them often enough. Still, he wished he'd told his father he was sorry, because only now did he understand the depths of his agony.

Danny stared down at the headlines until they blurred. They'd found evidence at Paulie's apartment. They'd found the final body there. The murders stopped after Paulie's death, so why had his father quit the force? Something must have happened. Something must have gone wrong. But it made no sense.

If something had gone down, Stan Witkowski would have left the force too. Big Stan always had the old man's back.

Still, Junior wasn't stupid, and he was strong. A god. He would never have let his guard down with Paulie Ritter. Danny knew it in a deep-down, gut-clenching way back then. He was sure now. The big question was why the old man had let it go so easily. Someday, he'd go back and look into the case again. Maybe then those lost girls would rest in peace.

Danny smoothed out the newspaper and wrapped the notebooks back in it. The old man loved to call him a vulture, so he'd probably find his current situation funny as hell. After all this time, Danny was back to the beginning, picking over dead bones.

19

The senator wouldn't approve of her being at this club, especially looking like she was open for business. The DJ played European techno tonight instead of plain old hip-hop, but it was all the same no matter what night she came. Everybody chased their loneliness with tequila shooters and exotic martinis and then crowded onto the dance floor to shake and grind and pretend it was a good time. Still, there were worse places in the city. Much worse.

"Here, Kate, you wanna run a tab?"

Kate Reid pulled out a couple of twenties. "No, it's fine, Richie. Thanks."

She didn't want to run a tab. It was too easy to get lost in a swirl of drinks, but she took a sip of her vodka martini, let her hips sway to the throbbing beat of the music, and breathed in the clouds of cigarette smoke. Kate didn't indulge her self-destructive tendencies too often, but some nights, it was the only way to forget.

Kate gulped the martini and ordered a second. When it came, she took a long swallow. She liked the cool-hot slide of the alcohol down her throat, the way it seeped into her blood, loosened her body. That was better. Now she could enjoy herself, have some fun.

She wouldn't pick anyone up. She didn't do that anymore. No matter how good a man was at night, she always woke up sore and alone in the morning.

That didn't mean she liked to drink alone, though. Sometimes she wished it weren't so easy for her to walk away in the morning. But no one came close to filling up that black hole inside her. Most of the time she felt like an empty bottle tossing about in the vast ocean. Sooner or later, she would smash to pieces, and who would care? The world was a heartless place.

Kate finished her second martini and turned to scan the club.

My oh my. There was a prospect now. She wished he'd turn around so she could see if the view from the front was as good as the back. Shit. She almost tripped over her own feet. Danny Ryan. At least she thought it was Ryan, though he looked a lot better than he had at Michael Cohen's apartment.

His hair was cut, and the homeless man beard was gone. His black jeans and leather jacket actually fit. But there was something else. He looked sharper somehow. Haggard, but that gave him an edge. Kate appreciated edges. They gave a man character.

Now she didn't know what to do. She didn't want to meet Ryan in a meat factory like this. She tugged at her skirt. It ended three inches below her ass and wasn't getting any longer.

Damn her. She'd downed those martinis too fast. Now she felt fuzzy.

Why the hell did Ryan have to show up here tonight? Michael had once told her that Ryan was straitlaced and "weirdly Irish."

"You mean like a missionary position kind of guy?" she'd said.

"I mean like a ridiculously in love with his wife kind of guy."

"What's wrong with that?" Kate had wondered what it would be like to have someone be ridiculously in love with her.

"Because Bethy is the queen of bitches. Or was." Michael's eyes had filled with tears when he talked about Danny Ryan. Kate pitied Michael, but he'd draped himself around her like a thick coat she couldn't remove.

Some days, she'd find him waiting for her when she came home from work with a two-hundred-dollar bottle of wine and

Chinese takeout. If she went to a bar, he'd follow her and buy her round after round of drinks and then make sure she got home. She'd wake to find him camped out on her couch—the new couch he'd bought her when he realized she didn't have one.

He'd follow the pattern for weeks and then disappear for a month. She should've realized something was wrong that last time he'd showed up because he'd been hysterical.

"You don't understand. I know things," he'd said, grabbing her and pinning her to the wall. "Nobody listens."

"You're hurting me!"

"Don't be mad," he'd said, tears still running down his face, snot bubbling from his nose. "I know secrets. Important secrets."

Three hours later, he'd crashed into Ryan's duck pond with a bullet in his stomach, and Kate wondered now if she'd listened, would Michael's outcome have been any different? Maybe Michael had been doomed from the day he was born. It was a bleak way to think of things, but she had a bleak Irish heart.

Well, Ryan looked like he fit in here just fine tonight, and the women who crowded around him seemed to find him interesting as all hell because they kept leaning into him to give him a better view of their cleavage. Kate wanted to gag. Could be Michael was wrong, and Ryan was a barhopping asshole. Michael didn't know everything.

She wondered if Ryan was anything like his father. When Thomas had talked about Danny, he always said, "We eat our own, Katie." He'd fall asleep in his brown corduroy armchair with a picture of his wife in his lap and his volume of Yeats opened to his favorite poem, "A Deep-Sworn Vow." When he fell ill, he gave her the book. It had belonged to his wife.

Kate slipped around the bar where she could get close to Ryan without being seen. He was talking to three women on the edge of the dance floor, and he had one terrific smile when he turned it on.

He hadn't turned it on for her.

What did she expect? The lonely, lost boy who'd bared his soul in his copybooks and left them in Thomas's house? Did she think he'd recognize her as a soul mate?

Ryan reached into his pocket to pull out what looked like a credit card, and Kate's stomach constricted enough to send the martinis rushing back into her throat. She pressed her hand against her mouth. She recognized that black-and-white card. Ryan must have gotten it from Michael.

Kate wanted to rip the card from Ryan's hands, but she couldn't move. Everything whirled around her. Her stomach gave a violent lurch, and Kate ran to the bathroom to vomit.

20

It was a long time since Danny had done the singles bar scene. It hadn't changed. The music was still too loud, the dance floors too crowded, and the people too desperate.

He'd hit eleven bars already and had no luck other than a growing collection of women's phone numbers and e-mails. When women recognized him, they snapped photos for Facebook or Twitter or WhoGivesAFuck. Nobody recognized the black-and-white card. Nobody had heard of the Inferno or any of the other names on Michael's list.

Now he stood on the doorstep of Black Velvet, a club on the edge of Northern Liberties, with his new friend Ivy, a Goth princess in a leather bustier, a skirt of shredded black lace, and a cape that seemed to be made of rat fur. Not his type, but she said she knew Michael.

"My friend Zach can help you. He knows all the clubs. If he hasn't heard of it, it doesn't exist. I can't believe you knew Michael." Ivy gave him a sleepy smile and took a step closer. The wind whipped her long, black hair into her pale face. "You have really beautiful eyes. Are you a Scorpio?"

Danny shook his head. "Sorry."

"That's okay. I'm not compatible with Scorpios."

She had a stud in her nose, six rings in her left eyebrow, and four studs below her lower lip. A snake tattoo slithered up her neck. Christ knew what other surprises she had on her body. He didn't want to find out.

A slim man in a burgundy velvet bodysuit admitted them into a dimly lit corridor that reeked of incense and a thick musk. He beckoned Ivy to come close. She handed him Michael's card, and the two of them spoke in low tones for a couple of minutes before he turned to Danny.

"Four hundred," the man said.

"Excuse me?"

"Cover charge. Four hundred. Each." The man's oily voice was threaded with steel. A black goatee rimmed his pointed chin; all he needed was a bifurcated tongue and horns and he would have made a fine devil.

"That's a steep goddamn cover charge," Danny said.

The devilman gave Danny a slow smile that didn't reach his kohl-lined eyes. "I don't know you, my friend."

Danny handed over the cash. He'd come prepared because he figured from the onset that certain kinds of clubs didn't take American Express. Michael had traveled to the land of white powder and kinky sex. Did Michael really hang out here? It wouldn't be the kind of place you'd write about in an article on Philly nightlife unless you were into the seriously twisted. Still, Danny couldn't picture Michael on the dance floor in a normal club. In this bat cave, he'd be right at home.

We've now entered the Twilight Zone.

He heard voices and music to his right, but the devilman returned the card and then led them down a corridor to the left through a door he was careful to close and lock.

Pulsating electronic music vibrated from black velvet walls. The musk odor grew stronger until they came to a square room lit by red neon lights shaped like open mouths. Squashy looking couches and tables shaped like scarlet lips surrounded an ebony bar.

It took Danny a half second to realize that bodies slithering and squirming together filled the couches. It was hard to tell where one body ended and the next began. Men with women. Women with women. Men with men. Combinations of numbers and positions.

"Isn't it beautiful?" Ivy said. "They're so natural. Just like rabbits."

Danny thought he was prepared for the sex club experience. He was wrong.

"We encourage our guests to use condoms," the devilman said and slipped back down the corridor.

Ivy took Danny by the arm. "Zach is over here." She pointed to the man behind the bar. He wore a black velvet G-string and had a tattoo of a flaming skull on his left shoulder. His light brown skin gleamed like it had been greased.

"Zach, my friend here needs something," Ivy said.

Zach smirked and held up a glass. "A little liquid fortification? It can be a bit overwhelming your first time. Say, that's a nice jacket. Is it Armani? I'd better get you a locker."

"I don't need a locker," Danny said.

"Whatever, blue eyes." Zach poured tequila into a shaker of crushed ice and followed it with a succession of clear liquors. He shook the mixture, poured it into a tall glass, and added a shot of grenadine that curled down through the alcohol like a bloody worm. "I call it a bloodsucker," Zach said. He dropped in a maraschino cherry. "It'll knock you on your sweet ass."

Danny shook his head. "Thanks. I'll pass."

"I know you. You're that reporter dude what used to be such hot shit. You wrote about Huey Newcomber—that kid got killed for stealin' a pack of dental floss? That was some righteous anger you stirred up, man. What you looking for here?"

Zach watched with curious eyes as Danny tried to dredge up the story. The memory flickered at the edges of his mind and shut off at once when Ivy leaned over his arm and he realized she had unlaced her bustier. Christ, her nipples were pierced and a chain extended from one to the other. A red crystal heart dangled in the middle.

"He's Michael C's friend, Zach. He's doing an investigation," Ivy said.

"I'm just trying to find out what happened to Michael," Danny said, and tried to judge Zach's reaction. There wasn't one.

"Michael was a strange dude. He didn't like to participate. He liked to watch. Is that your scene too? We have some private observation rooms. That's extra."

Danny felt a tiny jolt of unease, though he knew Michael always stood on the sidelines with his camera. Watching.

"Do you have a lot of watchers?" he said to Zach and looked around. His flesh felt cold and exposed.

Zach shrugged. "To each his own."

"Did Michael ever bring anyone here?"

"You mean like a date?" Zach laughed. "Michael came by himself to forget his problems. Besides, he was seriously twisted about someone."

"He ever say who?"

Zach shook his head. "No. Might not have even been human. He was always talkin' bout demons and shit. Creeped me out."

That wasn't what Danny wanted to hear. Who knew what was going on in Michael's messed-up head? *He wanted to tell you.* Danny shut off the voice in his own head.

"When was the last time you saw him?"

"A week or so back."

"Did he seem upset? Worried?"

"Nope. Just went to his observation room like always. He did leave early though. That was unusual."

Danny pulled the black-and-white card out of his pocket. "You ever see one of these before?"

Zach took a step back, and his face twisted into a scowl. "Where the fuck you get that?"

"I guess that answers my question." Danny slid the card back into his pocket. "What kind of card is it?"

"Reporter Man, that's the kind of card you want to leave home without." Zach pushed the drink toward him. "Have this instead."

"I don't want a drink. I want to know what that card is. It's got to be a membership of some kind. Ivy used it to get us in here. Is it just for here, or does it work at other places? You don't have to take me there."

"Anyone can get in here if they got the green, and I couldn't take you there if I wanted—which I don't." Zach rested his elbows on the bar and leaned close. "Listen. There's special clubs. Then there's special clubs. The Inferno ain't like this club here."

"Are you saying this is a membership to the Inferno?"

Zach looked around the room. "Low level, but yeah."

Danny's heart jolted. "The Inferno is real."

"It's real enough, but it ain't a club—not like this. It's like management. It operates clubs, and depending on your level of membership, you get access."

"Access to what?"

"Access." Zach licked his lips as if the memory gave him both pleasure and pain. "To services. The higher your membership, the more access you get."

"What kind of services?"

"Look, sweet ass." Zach straightened and put his hands on his hips. "You may be the hottest thing walked in tonight, but I'm working, and you ain't buyin'. Get my drift?"

Danny thought he got Zach's drift pretty well. He knew he wasn't interested in stripping down to frolic with the rest of the patrons. He slid a twenty to Zach. "What do you know about the Inferno?"

Zach eyed him with disdain. "Twenty? What's it really worth to you?"

Danny shrugged as if he didn't care. "I don't usually pay sources."

"I bet you got a hard-on right now for this."

"And I bet you owe at least two months' rent or you wouldn't be serving up drinks in a G-string."

Zach shrugged and shifted his weight back and forth. "Look, man, I can't talk about it now. I get off at four. There's a diner down on Spring Garden. You meet me there at four thirty. Buy me breakfast, and we'll negotiate proper. Deal?"

Danny tossed another twenty on the bar. Ivy's hand caressed his ass. "Don't worry," she said. "I'll take care of you 'til then. Don't you think he has beautiful eyes, Zach?"

21

The clatter of silverware startled him, and Danny jerked up his head. Five thirty. Where the hell was Zach?

He stared at his notes, which trailed into an indecipherable scrawl down the page. It didn't matter. If Zach was right, Kevin was wrong. The Inferno wasn't a sex club. It owned clubs.

Danny rubbed his eyes. He signaled the waitress and stared at the fat, red plastic elf that sat propped against his menu holder. It leered at him through beady eyes and held up a sign that read, "Happiness Is a Holiday Heart!"

Danny looked up when the waitress approached with a pot of coffee. Her Santa cap jingled with each step, and he wondered how any human could maintain a holiday facade at this ungodly hour. She gave him a cheerful smile.

"Y'want anything else, hon? A donut for the road?"

"No, but thanks. Hey, nice hat."

She winked and slapped his bill on the blue Formica table. "Have a great day."

*

Clammy, warm air greeted him when Danny walked out of the diner and up toward the side street where he parked. In three hours, the temperature had risen thirty degrees. Thick fingers

91

of mist curled around the lights and floated in ribbons of gray across the rain-slick street. A few cars and trucks passed up and down Spring Garden. In the murky darkness, their headlights glowed like lidless eyes.

He glanced around and wondered if Beth ever watched him from wherever she was. Sometimes he thought he could feel her with him in the darkness. A whisper he couldn't quite discern, her hand almost brushing his. Or maybe the memory of love was strongest, most bittersweet, when love itself was irretrievably lost.

He reached the Jeep and hit the keyless entry button. Nothing happened. The lights didn't blink. The car sat, silent and dark. What the fuck was this?

He took a step closer and saw the doors were unlocked. Maybe it worked after all. Christ, he was more out of it than he thought.

Danny yanked at the handle and swung open the door. The overhead light snapped on, and he stared down at his seat. It took a second for his brain to process the lump of tissue congealing in a gooey mass before Danny took a step back. The keys slipped from his fingers and clinked onto the road.

On the driver's seat, wrapped in a black G-string, sat a human heart.

22

"He's clean," the first tech said. "Not a trace of blood."

Danny looked at his hands and refrained from making a smart remark. He was too exhausted. The CSU folks had recorded the temperature of the heart and bagged it, and the cops had verified his statement with the waitress at the diner. He'd told his story four times.

"It's still warm," the second tech said of the heart. "Bet that scared the shit out of you."

Danny gave him a wan smile. He tapped out a text message to Andy and hoped he was lucid enough to read it.

"Might be arrested for murder. Will be at Center City Division soon. Please help."

*

"Where are you, you little shit?" The monster banged the wall.

Danny edged back into the winter coats. He knocked against the open boxes of mothballs, and they spilled onto the floor. Conor pulled at Danny's arm. Fear pinched his white face, but he clutched his blue lightsaber. "Hurry, Daddy."

He shoved Conor into the darkness. "Run!"

Danny tried to push through the coats, but something clamped him by the shoulder and wouldn't let go. In the flickering blue light, he could see her. The delicacy of the butterflies and drag-onflies, the twisting vines and flowers painted on her smooth, pale skull, a hideous contrast with her hollow eye sockets. Jane Doe One touched his face with her mutilated hands.

Danny tried to move, but she held him tight.

She started to shake him, and her voice grew harsh and deep. "Wake up! Wake up! Wake up! Goddamn it!"

Danny jerked backward. His head banged against some-thing with enough force that his jaw snapped together. When he opened his eyes, he lay on the floor of the interrogation room. Kevin loomed over him. Christ, he thought he might puke.

"Wake up, Sleeping Beauty," Kevin said.

Danny tried to stand, but Kevin put a casual foot on his chest and exerted enough pressure to keep him on his back. He was a bug pinned to the floor by his brother's size fourteen Florsheims.

"How about you tell me what the fuck is going on, Danny?"

"How about you let me up before I sue your ass for police brutality?" Panic made his voice crack. Why couldn't they stop this crap? Who's the biggest asshole?

Kevin smiled and pressed harder. "Assuming you get to a phone."

If he moved fast enough, he might be able to knock Kevin off balance, but his hands shook. He couldn't show weakness though. Danny began to tense, and the pressure on his chest eased. Kevin stepped back. He picked up the chair and pointed to it. "Don't get any ideas. Sit down."

Danny sat.

"Goddamn it, what in the Good Christ is going on?" Kevin's bloodshot eyes squinted at him from folds of skin that looked like wet dough. Danny bet he'd gone through at least two six-packs and half a bottle of Johnny Walker Red last night.

"I found a heart in my car. I believe you know that already."

"And you have no clue who it belongs to?"

"It didn't come with a name tag." Danny slouched back and gave Kevin a bland smile as if he were relaxed.

I found a heart. No big deal, though the G-string made it a little weird.

"So you just happened to be sitting in a diner in Philadelphia at five thirty in the morning, and you came out and found a fucking heart in your car?"

"You're very quick on the uptake."

He should've told Kevin what he was doing last night, and he would've if Kevin hadn't started off by acting like a prick. Now they stood on opposite sides of the wall. As always.

"Stop lying to me, Danny."

"Is this the part where you beat a confession out of me for a murder I didn't commit? Do you honestly think I would have called the cops if I came downtown and hacked someone's heart out of his body?"

"It's this Inferno, isn't it? You won't let it go. Goddamn it, I wish I'd never opened my mouth. I never should have given you the old man's shit."

Danny looked away. He was in dangerous territory. He was pretty sure he knew who the heart belonged to, but he also knew better than to admit it, especially since no body had turned up.

"What were you doing in that diner?"

"Having coffee."

"For two hours?" Kevin leaned close. He rested one hand on the table and the other on the back of Danny's chair. His chin jutted in Danny's face. It was almost like Kevin wanted him to make a move, so he would have an excuse to beat the crap out of him. Danny could smell the fury oozing out of Kevin's pores along with the whiskey.

"What were you doing last night?"

Danny gave Kevin his best smartass smile. "You got me. I'm a fucking vampire."

"You think this is funny? I can hold you here."

"For what? Finding a heart?"

"For suspicion of murder."

"Where's the body, Kevin? The blood? Don't you think I'd have gotten a little bloody cutting out a heart?"

Kevin slammed both hands down on the table. It used to scare the hell out of Danny when the old man would do that on the kitchen counter because it had always signaled the start of a whipping with a belt or a fist—or sometimes a nightstick. It depended on the old man's mood and whatever was handy. Danny sat very still and tried to will his heart to slow.

Kevin said nothing for five minutes, and Danny watched the hands on the clock crawl forward. Finally, Kevin stepped back. "You look like shit. Did they get you anything to eat?"

Danny blinked. "I'm okay."

"Why didn't you call me when they brought you in?"

"I figured they'd get around to it." Danny didn't mention that he'd alerted Andy. Kevin would find that out soon enough, and he'd be furious. Andy Cohen was never a favorite of the Philly PD, thanks to his paper's frequent and pointed criticism of the department.

"You must have some idea why someone would leave you this kind of calling card. What were you really doing last night?"

"I was at some bars. I told that to the other detectives. I gave them the names of people I was with." Danny hoped that the alcoholic haze engulfing most of the women would keep their sense of time fuzzy. He didn't want to tell Kevin he wrapped up his evening at a sex club with a Goth princess whom he'd last seen stripping down to plunge into a sea of naked bodies. Not yet.

"Did you run those licenses?"

Kevin blinked. "Licenses? Jesus Christ." He pulled out an envelope and slammed it on the table. "Not a lawbreaker among them. So if you hassle any of them, I'll have you brought in. And don't give me bullshit about your car."

Danny shrugged. "What about the address?"

"All right. That's weird. Technically, it belongs to a John Smith, but I can't find any information about John Smith. Still, the house was bought legally, and the taxes are paid every year. There's never been a complaint filed about the property, but I'm still checking."

Danny heard urgent voices outside. A blond detective entered and motioned to Kevin, who followed him out of the room. He didn't completely close the door, and Danny heard someone say, "You've got to turn him loose. Right now. His big-shot lawyer's here, and he's raising all kinds of hell."

23

Danny spotted Andy and then the framed caricature of him-self hanging on the wall when he entered the Palm. The restaurant sat inside the Bellevue Hotel and featured good steak and caricatures of noted local celebrities and politicians. It used to give him a rush to see himself on the wall positioned between Andy and the mayor. Now it gave him a queasy sense of his overinflated ego.

God is watching you, boy.

He ignored the curious stares and made his way to Andy's table.

Andy shook his hand. "You'll have a drink today." He looked at the waiter. "Bourbon for my friend, bring the wine list, and I'll take another."

Danny didn't argue. He could still see that heart, the dark blood oozing into the beige leather upholstery.

"I'd like to say you look better," Andy said. "You got a decent haircut at least, but you look like hell. Maybe you should try sleeping at night instead of stealing hearts."

Danny forced a smile. "Thanks for getting me out."

"You want to tell me about it?"

He wasn't sure how much he wanted to tell Andy. Yet. He took the coward's way out. "You and Linda all right?"

"How do you think?" Andy finished his scotch. "I sent her to New York for one of those women's trips. Shopping. Whatever they do. Well, she deserves it. This week's been hell enough."

"I'm sorry."

"But you're going to make my day, aren't you? I'm going to hype the shit out of you."

"Maybe no one cares about a washed-up columnist."

"By the time the PR department's done, they will. We still get your fan mail, you know. Besides, I've always had a soft spot in my heart for you. You know that, don't you, Daniel? I've always thought of you like a son."

It was true in as much as Andy looked at anyone as a son. Generally, Andy preferred the guys who tossed back the booze, did endless lines of coke, and chased long-legged blondes in short skirts. Every night was a fiesta in Andyland, and if you didn't join the conga line, he always wondered about you. But Andy was there for him when it counted.

"I've always been grateful."

Andy held up a sheaf of papers. "Good. We'll sign your contract now."

"Don't I get to read it?"

Andy held out a pen. "Have I ever fucked you? You need to come back to the living, my friend. Sign the goddamn contract."

"But I—"

"Didn't I just haul your skinny ass out of jail? At a cost of nine hundred an hour, I might add. I'm getting soft in my old age. Sign it."

Danny took the pen. He knew it was a test of loyalty. Everything with Andy was a test of some kind. He also knew Andy was a man whose word still counted for something. He signed the papers and handed them back. "You're still insane."

Andy slid the papers into his breast pocket. "Yeah? Well, only a Goy would sign a contract without having his lawyer check it out. I'll send you copies." He kissed Danny's cheek and grinned. Danny wasn't sure he liked the grin. "Welcome back. I've missed you."

The waiter brought their drinks, and Andy scanned the wine list for a second. "You can bring the Dom '98. We're celebrating. Right? That was a good year, wasn't it?"

"Yeah, it was." Danny wondered how early Andy had started drinking today. It wasn't quite noon, and he was already half in the bag.

"Here." Andy shoved an envelope into Danny's hand. "An invite to the holiday party. Didn't think I'd forget, did you?"

"I guess not." Danny stared at the silver envelope. The Cohens' holiday bash was the stuff of legend, but Michael was barely in the ground.

"Is this a celebration?"

Danny shuddered at the familiar voice. When he looked up, he found himself staring into a pair of fathomless black eyes. Beth's eyes. They always gave him a jolt staring out from Senator Robert Harlan's face.

They were in turn warm and filled with charm when he was wooing a constituent or financial backer or bleak and forbidding when confronting an undesirable human specimen. Right now they were somewhere in between.

Danny forced himself to stand and reach out to grasp his ex-father-in-law's hand. He did so only because Kate Reid stood at the senator's side. Her hair was drawn off her face, and she gave him a quick look that was almost a warning.

"Daniel, this is an unexpected pleasure." The senator's voice was warm and rich like maple syrup. No one in politics had a voice like Robert Harlan. "You've been hard to find these days."

"Have you been looking for me, Senator?"

The senator gave him a benevolent smile. "I think it's time we mended some fences."

Danny clenched his hands into fists. After the funeral, the senator had accused him of abusing Beth and had contested her will.

"We went through a terrible time a year ago, and I was hard on you. I can only say it was the grief talking. Beth was my only child. Just as Conor was yours." The senator's voice hit a dolorous note. "Grief does terrible things to a person."

"Some more than others." Danny knew he sounded harsh. Petty.

For a moment, the senator's eyes grew hard, and then he blinked and the look passed. When he spoke, his voice shook. "We all bear our grief in different ways, Daniel. We both lost a child. Indeed, I lost a daughter and grandson. Isn't our mutual loss something we can use to forge a new relationship?" He grasped Danny's hand and pumped it as if television cameras hovered nearby.

Danny couldn't answer. He fought for air.

"Daniel's coming back to the fold. He just signed a contract." Andy's face was inscrutable. "You'll have plenty of opportunity to forge a new relationship if you're keen to do so."

The senator dropped Danny's hand. "He's coming back?" His voice chilled a few degrees. "To write what?"

Andy waved his glass in the air. "I don't give a damn what he writes as long as it sells papers. Fucking newspapers have gone to hell. We need to fight the twenty-four-hour news cycle. Right, Daniel?"

Danny nodded.

"It'll be like old times." Andy settled back in his seat. "You're back on the hot seat, I'm afraid, Robert." He chuckled. "Bad joke. You heard about the congressman, I presume? Damnedest thing."

The senator's lips pulled back against his teeth in a feral smile. It made spiders of unease crawl down Danny's back.

They said it was an accident. A one-car accident. Right under the suicide bridge. Jesus, now he was getting paranoid.

"Poor Teddy," the senator said, and the warmth crept back into his voice. "Such a loss."

"Indeed." Andy patted the chair. "Sit down, Robert. We'll drink to Teddy. And Michael. And Daniel, of course. Where're your fucking manners, anyway? You didn't introduce the delicious Katie to my boy." He blew a kiss to Kate. "Come here, my darling. You can sit on my lap."

When Kate laughed, Danny could almost hear the senator's teeth grind, but he managed to sustain his genial tone. "Daniel Ryan, my assistant, Kate Reid." He turned back to Andy and sat.

"It's a pleasure," Danny said. No point in mentioning he'd already met Kate. It wouldn't matter that the meeting had been innocent. The senator wouldn't approve. Danny was the pariah who had stolen Beth and outlived her. Everything he touched turned rancid.

Kate smiled, and when he caught the faint aroma of lavender, he felt an odd sort of connection. Maybe it was the shared secret of their previous meeting, maybe something more.

Andy was already ordering more glasses and another bottle of champagne, and Danny knew it was going to be a long afternoon.

*

By four o'clock, half of the Palm had joined their table, and Danny decided to make an anonymous exit. He reached Broad Street when he heard the click of high heels behind him.

"Danny, wait!" Kate came running up to him, and it was a wonder she didn't trip in those shoes.

He stood on the street and enjoyed the view. "Where the hell did you come from?"

"The bathroom. Even servants have their limits. You're leaving?"

"All good things have to end sometime."

She took a step closer. "You didn't call."

She was still breathing fast, and her perfume curled around her like lavender smoke. It had been a long time since he'd been with a woman, or since he even thought about it. The thought was vivid right now.

Kate touched his shoulder. "If I get my coat, will you walk me home? I don't live far."

The bourbon was already careening around his system, and Danny knew he'd pay for it soon. In his present state, it didn't seem too smart to start hanging out with some protégée of Big Bob Harlan. He didn't care. "Won't the senator be annoyed that you left?"

"Probably. He won't know I left with you."

"In that case, I'd be happy to walk you home."

24

The frigid air was a relief after the heat of the Palm. Still, pinpricks of light danced in front of him, and Danny could feel that ominous pressure in his right eye. He shouldn't be here. Not with Big Bob's lackey, no matter how good she looked. Yet her sorrow tugged at him. Someone had crushed this woman. He'd seen it in her eyes that day at Michael's wake.

"How did you come to work for Senator Family Values?" he said.

"You don't believe in family values?"

"Not his."

"You married his daughter."

He watched Kate's eyes grow distressed when she realized what she'd said, and he knew he had to stop her before she apologized.

"You aren't local," he said.

Kate folded her arms around her chest like she was trying to enclose her body. "How do you know?"

"Just a guess. Where are you from?" He couldn't place Kate's flat, unaccented voice.

"Maine."

Danny was curious now. That was no Maine accent. "What part of Maine? Beth and I—"

Kate scowled. "Is this an interview?"

"It's a conversation."

"Look, I left home young, and I don't like to think about it. All right?"

"Fair enough."

The thought of home almost brought Kate to tears. He could hear it in her shaking voice.

They continued in silence toward the Academy of Music, where a group of parents and children spilled out of a Nutcracker Tea. Little girls in their best winter coats and patent leather shoes clutched cardboard teapots as if they were fragile china while the little boys took the same teapots and made pretend guns out of them.

I want to stay home with Dad.

Conor in his khakis, turtleneck, and pint-sized Brooks Brothers blazer.

"Are you all right?" Kate said.

Danny flinched when he realized he had stopped walking and stood as if he had taken root on the sidewalk. "Sorry, I—I'm more tired than I thought."

She turned away. "Look, you don't have to walk me home."

He caught her arm before she could take off. "It's not you. I . . ."

What to say? I found a heart in my car. Someone killed my dog. I lost my wife and son last year. Maybe all three.

"I'm sorry. My wife and son were going to a tea like this when they were killed." Past tense. Danny hated the way his throat tightened.

Kate slid her hand into his. "I'm so sorry."

He looked at her hand, grateful for its warmth as they started to walk again. "Don't apologize."

"You must miss your wife very much. Was it love at first sight?"

How did he explain that one when it was something he never quite understood? "I guess. I met Beth at a party. It was a strange time. I was having my fifteen minutes."

"You mean you won a Pulitzer, and you were a big deal."

"I was an asshole." He shrugged at her skeptical look. She'd taken the trouble to look him up. He'd have to return the favor.

"I was a working-class Irish Catholic kid from South Philly. A nobody. All of a sudden, my picture was on the sides of buses. I was in my twenties. I guess it all went to my head."

He told people that, and it was half-true. He was a big deal, and while he'd enjoyed the attention, he'd always had a weird sense that the clock was ticking away on the good times. Maybe he was just born with the Irish pessimism that nothing that good could possibly last, or maybe it was because his father told him he'd be sorry he made his living as a vulture.

He really had met Beth at a party, though it was more like a weekend orgy at the Cohens' home in Palm Beach. She'd come with one of those hard-drinking, fast-rising political types who deserted her once the bar was open and the lines of coke drawn up.

He could still see her walking on the beach in that white dress, her dark hair blowing in the wind. The last rays of sun had caught her face and bathed it in luminous gold. When she'd asked him why he wasn't inside getting drunk, he could only blurt he didn't need to drink when the sight of her made him dizzy. She'd told him that was an awful line but a sweet one and then sat with him on the beach until the sun went down, the shadows grew purple and then black, the tide came in, and the air became heavy with the scent of salt, orange, and her. They had danced at the edge of the shore to the strains of Sinatra drifting down from the house with her hand pressed against his heart—the heart that was irrevocably hers.

"Danny?" Kate's voice brought him back.

"It was a hell of a ride," he said. Gone. He'd let it slip away from him. He was paid to notice things, people, and he'd been blind to his own life.

"And you're getting back on the roller coaster because?"

"Because I owe Andy."

Her fingers tightened against his. "Andy?"

"Andy opened the door for me."

"Michael said you were close."

How long had Kate known Michael? He'd never mentioned her, but they must have been friends for a while.

"How did you meet Michael?"

"He hung out with the political reporters, and to tell the truth, I felt sorry for him. He was kind of like a lost puppy." Kate's voice tightened, and Danny frowned. Michael had never hung with the political reporters, with the exception of Alex, who had tolerated him. Michael had latched onto other lost souls.

"Most women didn't like Michael."

"I'm not most women."

"He had trouble relating to people," Danny said.

She nodded. "He was very smart, but nobody knew it. No social skills. I used to be terrified of him until I realized he wanted to protect me."

"Protect you?"

"Oh, yes. If you were the least bit kind to him, Michael was like a faithful guard dog. It could be unnerving. But I guess you know that." They reached an old redbrick townhouse converted to apartments, and Kate inclined her head. "This is it."

"I know what, Kate?"

"How much he wanted to protect you. He loved you."

"I didn't deserve it. I—"

Kate reached up to touch his mouth, her fingers lingering, and Danny's breath hitched before he drew her against him. Her mouth tasted of champagne and raspberry, and something stung inside his chest, almost like a pinprick, but at the same time felt unbearably tender.

Light exploded like a flashbulb, and he pulled back as gracefully as he could. In the streetlight, he could see that her cheeks were flushed. "I have to go."

"Is something wrong?"

"No, I just—I would like to see you again." He sounded jerky, unnatural. He needed to leave before something embarrassing happened—like he vomited or his head exploded.

"I'd like to see you."

"I'll call."

"Danny, there is one thing." Kate caught his arm. "It's about Michael. You can't tell anyone. You have to promise."

"I promise." Danny's right eye throbbed, and the pain tightened around his shoulder.

"I saw Michael the night he died. He was coming to see you. He wanted to give you something."

25

The migraine had kicked into high gear by the time Andy's driver let Danny off at home. He peeled off bills for a tip and stumbled into the kitchen. Tomorrow, he'd go back to Black Velvet and try to find out what happened to Zach. He'd talk to Kate, but he couldn't think straight with hammers beating inside his skull. He pulled an ice pack from the freezer.

Michael had a package. Kate confirmed that. Did the police now have it? No. He thought not. What the hell could be so important that Michael would drive out to Valley Forge rather than go to a hospital?

Michael had left something for him, and he didn't want it to be found right away. Why?

The phone wouldn't stop ringing. He finally picked it up.

"Danny Boy, how are you?"

Danny recognized the low-pitched tone. "What do you want?"

"You know what I want. I want my package, and I want you to go away."

"I don't have your package."

"I don't believe you, Danny Boy."

Danny squeezed the ice pack until his fingers went numb. "Fuck you."

"Oh, no. Fuck you. Maybe you better listen or you'll end up like your wife and kid."

"What are you talking about?"

"Not everything in life is an accident."

"What the hell does that mean?"

"You had a real nice dog. You figure it out."

Danny dropped the phone on the floor and fell to his knees, doubling over to clutch his stomach as wave after wave of agony rolled over him. Pulling himself to his feet, he slammed the phone back in its cradle and staggered to the back steps. This was a hallucination. It had to be. Everything was askew, and the floor listed so badly he fell against one of Beth's antique drum tables. Something smashed. An accident. Accidents were accidents except when they weren't.

Streams of moonlight blurred in front of him, and Danny tripped on the uneven floorboards. Damn steps. He should sell this house. It seemed to expand around him, yet every inch was crowded with memories.

Memories. Wasn't that a song?

He reached the bathroom and groped for the medicine cabinet door. Moonlight lit the room in silver, and he thought of Kate. She was like moonlight. He rested his head against the cold wall. *A moonlit maiden. What the hell is wrong with me?* His hands shook as he gobbled down painkillers, took a swallow of water, and then jabbed the Imitrex syringe into his thigh. For good measure, he grabbed a Xanax.

If I'm not careful, I'll overdose.

Oh, Jesus. It was cold. The windows in the bedroom stood open, and the sheer white curtains billowed in the breeze, filmy ghosts dancing. Danny stood transfixed, the drugs seeping into his system, the gooseflesh rising on his arms.

He hadn't left the windows open. Had he? He wasn't sure of anything right now.

Something's wrong. Someone was here. Not everything's an accident. Everything happens for a reason. Pain is good. Shut the fuck up.

Danny slammed the windows shut and pressed the ice pack against his forehead. He never should have drunk with Andy. He needed sleep. Work tomorrow.

Danny went to the bed and kicked off his shoes. He didn't bother to undress, just jerked up the comforter and slid underneath, careful not to disturb Beth. The pain began to ebb, like the tide moving out. Danny closed his eyes and took a deep breath, but his heart still skittered too fast.

"By the pricking of my thumbs, something wicked this way comes."

His grandmother liked to quote Shakespeare. She used to make him say his rosary.

His tongue stuck to the roof of his mouth. He should have gotten more water. He could still taste the bitter pills. Deep breaths.

Michael was a guard dog. The Inferno. Not everything's an accident. Happiness is a holiday heart. Why is it so goddamn cold? Someone was in my house tonight. Let go. I can't. Beth. Something about Beth.

Why did we spend so much time fighting?

"Something wicked this way comes."

I need to shut down. So tired. Too many thoughts. Like maggots. That was it. Maggots. That slightly fetid odor. Decay. Death. So very close. Beth.

Christ. Beth can't be here. Beth is dead.

Danny jerked up. He groped for the light on the nightstand and winced when it exploded against his eyeballs. When he saw the lump under the covers, he sprang out of bed, ripping the comforter and top sheet with him. He slammed against the wall and tried to focus.

"Holy God!"

The naked woman lay rigid on the bed, mouth agape, eyes bulging and coated with a milky glaze. Her chest gaped open, the skin hacked apart and her protruding ribs a shock of white against her mottled flesh. The chain that connected her pierced nipples was intact, though it stretched taut. In the middle of it hung a red crystal heart.

26

"John, wake up!"

Novell stared at Sean McFarland. He rubbed the heels of his hands against his gritty eyeballs. Dammit, he'd fallen asleep in his desk chair again. The bones of his spine ground together when he moved. "What time is it?"

"Time to go home. Shift ended two hours ago."

"Why're you still here?"

Sean's clothes still looked fresh, though his face was chalky with fatigue. "I've been trying to get a line on Michael Cohen's last day."

"You find anything out?"

"Nada. He never came home that night according to his mama, and she'd know because the Cohens have a high-tech security system. You punch in an access code to gain entry to the estate. It seems Michael never punched in."

"So we have no clue where Michael spent the last day of his life."

Sean sat on the edge of Novell's desk and pushed aside some files. "He wasn't home. He never showed up for work. Never made a phone call. Didn't go online or send an e-mail. Nothing until he crashed into Danny Ryan's duck pond."

In the beginning, Novell had thought Sean was too much of a Boy Scout with his suburban upbringing and his laid-back disposition. Too polite, too naive, and in way over his head, but he now understood this kid was thorough, the kind of cop who was obsessive about getting the details right. He just wanted to get the bad guys.

Novell shuddered. "Ryan claims Michael Cohen didn't say anything to him, and he didn't tell him what he was working on."

"Ryan's lived like a hermit since that accident last year. We know that kid was his life. That's what everyone—friends, neighbors, nanny—said. He hasn't done anything since the funeral. Until now." Sean's voice trailed off.

Novell thought of the picture of Conor Ryan, the one from the soccer game. He couldn't get it out of his head. What would it be like to lose a kid that young? It would shatter you. Given his background, Danny Ryan should have been a raving alcoholic. Novell gave him grudging points for remaining sober.

"So where does that leave our victim?" Novell rubbed his eyes as Sean shrugged. His phone went off. He fished it out of his pocket and squinted at the name and numbers, then looked up. "Guess who?"

"Michael Cohen's murderer calling to confess."

"Close. It's Danny Ryan."

27

Kevin Ryan watched his brother slump over the table in the interrogation room, his head in his arms. Detective McFarland, who had been trying to coax a statement out of him, looked up and shook his head. Kevin turned to Novell. "No phone calls."

"He's got rights."

Detective Novell spoke without inflection, and Kevin assessed him. He had that look, the FBI, uptight, in-your-face righteousness that Kevin always associated with feds. But something about the cynical droop in Novell's mouth, the faint glimmer in his gray eyes betrayed a deep-burning anger underneath. Yeah, he was the kind of guy who'd get nasty after a half-dozen scotches. Kevin was surprised Novell had been dumb enough to get caught drinking on the job.

"He's got nothin' if the DA decides to charge him with murder," Kevin said.

"It's hard to say how the DA will want to proceed. It's a difficult situation."

Novell was right. Finding a body wasn't a crime, any more than finding a heart. Other than the body itself, no physical evidence tied Danny to the murder. The body appeared to have been dead for more than twenty-four hours when Danny found it. In his bed. He certainly hadn't hauled it back from the city in Andy Cohen's hired limo. And it hadn't been in the house in the afternoon when Kevin and his partner had headed out to check, just to be sure, after getting a search warrant. Everything had been normal, except there was no Beowulf to greet him at the door.

According to the Crime Scene Unit, there was no blood spatter at the scene. In fact, the body had been exsanguinated and hosed down with great care before it was arranged in the bed. Whoever did the killing was playing some kind of mind game. Maybe the killer knew how fucked up Danny's head already was.

Goddammit, why couldn't Danny just go back to writing his stupid column? Tormenting politicians was what he did best. Kevin didn't always agree with him, but he had to admit Danny had a way of saying things that got people fired up. This poking around shit was going to get him killed.

"Your brother have a substance problem?" Novell said.

"It's the headaches." Kevin turned back to Danny, who cradled his head in his arms. He took a deep breath. "He fractured his skull when he was a kid."

"Excuse me?"

"Danny. He fell down the stairs and fractured his skull. He started getting them after that. The migraines. The doctors said it happens sometimes." Kevin tried to unclench his fists.

So much goddamn blood. It'd soaked into the floorboards in the front hall. Some nights, Kevin would dream it all over again. He'd hear the crack of Danny's skull against the radiator and wake up in a cold sweat. Those nights, there wasn't enough whiskey in the world to drown his guilt.

"Maybe you could let him sleep for an hour or two?" Kevin said.

"We can proceed however you'd like, Detective Ryan. I'd say we have a jurisdictional nightmare here. It's going to take some time to straighten it out." Novell was all business now.

"Agreed. Though the Philly PD will probably get priority. We got the heart when it was fresh. That means in all probability, the murder occurred in Philly, and the body was dumped out here. Assuming the DNA matches. The heart definitely belonged to a female."

"Which means it's unlikely your brother had anything to do with her death since his time is accounted for from at least three thirty AM yesterday on."

Kevin knew Novell was waiting for him to say something, but he continued to stare into the interrogation room. He wanted to break through the door and grab Danny by the throat. Goddamn him. Why couldn't he listen?

"But you still want us to treat him like he's the number one suspect. Mind if I ask why?"

Kevin turned back to Novell. Novell might turn out to be a rat bastard, but there was no point trying to lie. Novell was too smart a cop. Those cold eyes of his didn't miss much.

Kevin took a deep breath. "All right. It won't make much sense to you, Detective, but I'm trying to save his life."

28

Danny lay on the narrow cot and stared at the ceiling. As cells went, this one wasn't bad. It was clean and relatively quiet, and he didn't have to share quarters. He'd been able to sleep for a few hours at least.

The fuzz from the medicine had worn off, but the world around him seemed gray, like the color had bled out, and he hovered somewhere between substance and shadow. Wasn't that the first sign of mental illness? The world around you became unreal? Danny pressed the heels of his palms against his cheeks. That felt real enough.

He heard Novell's voice down the hall and then approaching footsteps. The cell door rolled back. He sat up and swung around to face Novell.

"Good morning," Novell said. He looked pretty wrecked himself. Eyes bloodshot, cheeks stubbled, face wan. He held out a container of coffee. "It's black, but I can get you cream and sugar."

Danny took the cup. "Thanks. I take back every bad thing I ever said about cops."

"How about we stop dancing around and you talk straight to me."

"Are we dancing?" Danny eyed Novell and wondered why they were going through this routine here instead of an interrogation room.

"What did Michael Cohen say to you?"

"How do you know he said anything?"

"Because whenever there's a weird murder, you're right there. And before that, near as I can determine, you qualified for zombie of the year."

Danny ignored the dig. "I think I should call my lawyer."

"You aren't being charged with anything. The DA doesn't think we have enough to proceed to a grand jury; therefore, no indictment. Yet."

He wanted to tell Novell, but something held him back. His residual distrust of cops, his natural inclination to hate authority. Who could he trust? He wasn't sure anymore. But he knew this whole situation was getting out of control.

"Michael was dying," Danny said.

Zach had said the Inferno was management. Maybe Michael found out who those managers were. *Maybe that was the information he was bringing the night he was killed.*

"Answer my question, Ryan, or you're on your own. And trust me, right now, you really don't want to be on your own."

That sounded ominous. "Because?"

"The press has gotten wind of your heartless girlfriend. We have media guys all over the place. Looks like you're a celebrity again."

Danny could almost hear the cameras and feel the heat of the klieg lights. He could hear the old man laughing. *The vultures are after you now, boy. Serves you right.*

Danny looked at Novell. "He said 'Inferno.'"

He thought Novell would laugh, but instead he sat down on the edge of the cot. "Are you sure?"

"Yeah. I'm sure. I think it's tied to sex clubs in this area."

"Michael Cohen told you that?" Novell's face turned the color of ash.

"What do you know about it? I can tell you know something."

Novell hesitated and patted his pockets as if feeling for a pack of cigarettes or a flask. "A few years ago, there was an FBI investigation into the Inferno. They turned up nothing, but two agents were killed. It was a clusterfuck from the beginning."

"You ever hear of Tophet?"

"I heard a lot of things. But nothing panned out. The investigation was shut down. Lack of evidence." He looked at Danny, his eyes tired. "I'll tell you this much. If you're poking up that particular sewer, get out. Some things were meant to be left in the dark."

"You don't believe that."

Novell sighed. "Maybe not. But you'd better."

29

Carrie Norton stood in the middle of her kitchen surrounded by the aroma of butter cookies and cinnamon candles. She swallowed the last of her chamomile tea, took a deep breath, and dialed Danny Ryan's number. The phone rang and rang until the voice mail kicked in, and she hung up. She'd already left three messages. She'd tried his e-mail. Nothing.

He'd stopped by Gran's house, and she'd missed him. Now he just wasn't around.

Could he have gone on vacation? She didn't hear his dog bark when she went to the door. Maybe he went away with someone.

Another woman? Gram told her that women were always visiting, dropping off food. Gram knew because she liked to use her telescope to watch out the window. Those women smelled money, she said. That's what always happened when a man lost his wife.

"You better get down there if you want a shot," Gram had said before she left for Florida. "Those women are worse than hyenas. Danny Ryan'll be married again, and he won't know what hit him. Mark my words. And for God's sake, wear something that doesn't look like a potato sack."

Carrie had the dress all picked out. Something modest, but everyone told her that blue brought out her eyes. She just hoped he'd notice. Poor Danny had seemed so distracted when she'd stopped by at Thanksgiving with grief counseling pamphlets and pumpkin pie. Overmedicated, Gram had said. He'd looked so gaunt. He needed someone to take care of him.

Maybe she'd wear some mascara and eyeliner with her lipstick. If only her hair were long and dark like his late wife's. She shook her head and stared at her shoulder-length hair in the mirror. It was just so mousy. Maybe she could get a few highlights. Would that be vanity? Gram would approve, but she wanted her to get a bikini wax when Carrie would never ever wear a bikini. Reverend Gray would be appalled.

Carrie flipped through the stack of mail. No bills. Mostly Christmas cards that got mixed in with Gram's and this package. She picked up the box. It was heavy for its size. There wasn't a return address, and the brown paper wrapping was spotted and dirty. It probably wasn't anything urgent, but she'd feel better handing it to him. Then she could give him the cookies and the Christmas flyer she'd just gotten from Church of Good News about the Christian singles' night.

She'd mention it casually.

In the meantime, she'd see about getting those highlights.

30

Until he ran the gauntlet for himself, Danny had hoped Novell had lied about the media. But they were waiting as promised, and he had to push through the jostling reporters and duck the cameras, microphones, and cell phones thrust into his face.

He tried to ignore their shouted questions as he walked between Novell and McFarland to Novell's Crown Vic, careful to keep his head down and his eyes on the ground. He was grateful McFarland shielded him from the cameras. The young cop's dark eyes were sympathetic, but lack of sleep left his face wan, his lips drawn tight with tension.

"You all right?" McFarland said.

Danny nodded. "Where are you taking me?"

"We can take you home to get your things, but you can't stay until the CSU is finished." McFarland exchanged a look with Novell. "Do you have a friend you'd like to stay with?"

"I'll stay in a hotel."

"You might consider buying a new bed," McFarland said.

A new bed. A new house. Maybe a new life. Just as soon as he figured out who was behind this insanity. If they thought they'd scared him off, they were wrong. All he had to do was figure out who they were. Before they cut out his heart.

Danny wondered if Zach gave up Ivy to save himself or if he was tucked away in a freezer someplace just waiting to be thawed out and dumped in pieces. Maybe he'd find Zach's liver in his shower next or his head on a platter with an apple in his mouth. The possibilities were endless, and the holidays added a whole new festive dimension.

Someone called his name, and he looked up. Stupid. Cameras whirled and clicked. McFarland gave him a gentle nudge.

Danny slid into the car and stared out the window at the crush of reporters who had followed them through the police parking lot. A thin, blond man lowered his camera and pushed against the car. He wore a black scarf that covered the lower half of his face, but he pressed against the window, his pale-blue eyes filled with a terrible longing.

A vulture. Or worse.

"Let's move," Novell said, and McFarland pulled out of the parking lot.

31

Rain pounded on the roof of the church like giant fists, and Kate suppressed a shudder. The cold sunk into her bones. *Look, Ma. I'm in an Episcopalian church, and I haven't been struck dead yet.* She summoned the thought as if bravado would fight off the persistent feeling of doom. She woke up with it, her mouth tasting of ashes.

Kate bowed her head and tried to concentrate on the priest and his sermon, but the words wouldn't register. On Judgment Day, would the Lord reunite Congressman Powell with his body? He didn't need to be cremated. He was already incinerated; now he sat on the altar in a silver urn, mixed in with parts of his Cadillac. Salon de Powell.

What an insane thought.

She wondered where Danny was. When she'd told him that Michael had been with her that last night, his face had turned the color of milk, and she'd thought he was going to be sick.

Someone close by was wearing cologne so intense, it made her eyes water, and in the raw, damp air, it smelled sweet and foul at the same time. Death sat here.

Dear God, he's come for me.

Kate glanced around. Dignified mourners filled the rows. She noticed the blonde woman on her left who clutched a handkerchief and pressed it against her face, but the woman's hands, those long, white fingers made her shiver. Kate had seen hands like that before.

Hinky dinky corny cup, how many fingers have I got up? She guessed three, but two it is.

Kate could hear the screams echoing through her head, and she wanted to press her hands against her ears. She started when the senator put his hand on her shoulder and leaned close.

"Are you all right, Kate? You're trembling."

"I think I've caught a chill." She couldn't look at him, couldn't let him see her panic.

"But why didn't you say something? Come." He linked his arm in hers and led her from the pew. She slid a glance toward the woman. All Kate could see was a sleek bob of blonde hair, the line of her cheek, streaks of dark gray shadow across her eyelids. The same, yet not.

"Senator, I'm so sorry," she said when they reached the vestibule.

"You have nothing to apologize for," his voice soothed. "You clearly weren't feeling well this morning. We'll slip out, and I'll have Albert drop you home."

"I'm sure I'll be fine."

"Nonsense." His eyes were filled with concern now. "I hadn't planned to return to the office today. It will do us both good to take an afternoon."

"You've always been very kind to me, Senator. I'm grateful." Kate knew she sounded stilted, but something about him demanded her formality and distance. Maybe it was the decorum of his office, or maybe there was something about the way he carried himself. If someone placed a crown on his head and draped him in robes of ermine and scarlet velvet, he would have looked perfectly normal.

In truth, he'd barely acknowledged her the first few years she worked for him, and she'd cringed whenever he did. But it had changed when his daughter died and she had left him that ridiculous healing stone. After she'd put it on his desk with the sympathy card, she'd wanted so much to retrieve it, but it was too late.

She'd quaked when he'd called her into his office, and the gloom of the late December afternoon had filled the room with long shadows. Among the fruit baskets and flower arrangements, her offering had seemed both foolish and insignificant, and she hadn't been able to look at him.

He'd said nothing for so long that the colors in his Oriental rug smeared into a blur.

"I've received many expressions of sympathy," he'd said at last. "But yours may be the most heartfelt. And unique."

His chair had creaked when he'd risen and walked to her. He'd placed his hand on her shoulder. "I believe I've overlooked you, Kate."

From then on, he'd seemed to take a special interest in her. Kate couldn't quite define it, but she'd understood that at least for the moment, she'd gained his favor.

Now the senator paused in the vestibule to slide into his coat. "I've always been grateful to you for your hard work and loyalty." Did he emphasize the word loyalty just slightly?

He reached into his suit pocket and produced the green stone.

"You see? I still carry this with me. I never forgot. You're very special to Mrs. Harlan and me. We feel protective of you." He paused and took a breath. "Especially since we lost our Beth."

"It was a terrible accident, sir."

"I'm not sure it was an accident." The senator's voice was filled with such sorrow that she thought her heart would break, but his eyes were black tunnels. "I was foolish. I lost what was most precious to me because of my damnable pride."

"I don't understand." The chill crawled down under the collar of her coat and spread over her like a fine web. She couldn't stop shaking.

"My daughter was headstrong. Too much like me, I'm afraid. She made a very regrettable marital choice, and we fought about it. We never fully reconciled. I've never forgiven myself. Life is so short. You never think, as a parent, well, the worst will happen."

He sounded so sincere, so melancholy, yet his eyes seemed so fathomless, so dead.

"I'm sorry, Senator."

"My poor Kate. You're trembling with cold, and I'm talking about myself. I'm afraid it goes with the territory." The senator's voice grew warm, and his eyes filled with life. Kate almost laughed. She was an idiot. Of course he looked solemn. He was talking about his daughter.

"Let's get you home right away, dear. I happen to know there's a restaurant near your apartment that makes excellent soup. Seventeen varieties. I'll order you some and have Albert stop on the way to pick it up."

The senator gave her shoulders one last squeeze. He opened the church doors and led her out into the storm.

32

Since he was officially deemed cured, Mason kept his exceptional treasures hidden in his special room, a place filled with wonderful things. An antique Aubusson covered the parquet floor, and the furniture, including the white divan, was Louis XVI. The eyes, specially preserved in acrylic cubes, glistened like rare gems in the clear medium. Most beautiful of all were the wings that hung from the arched ceiling.

It had taken a long time to perfect the art of preserving the skin of the wings. His first attempts had been so dry and brown. The trick, of course, was to maintain the fine grain of it so that once it was stretched and hung on a frame, it looked almost translucent. Irish, Scottish, and English skin had worked the best. So pretty and soft, as long as it wasn't covered with freckles, though it was hard to procure. Mostly he had been forced to settle for the Eastern Europeans, but that skin had often been sallow and needed more decoration. Still he had learned to make do. It occurred to him now that skin the color of black coffee would have made a dramatic addition to his gallery.

Once the wings had been completed, he had decorated them with ink, sequins, and jewels. All were exquisite, and the sun pouring through the skylight made them shimmer with unearthly light. They fluttered with every puff of air, tiny motes of dust drifting around them like the very breath of magic. His fairy wings. But then he was a fairy child. Hadn't Mother told him?

Everyone always said he was such an exceptional boy. He didn't understand why that had displeased Father so much. Why had an appreciation of lovely things made him so unpalatable?

Father had never understood when he built a garden in his bedroom and filled it with the butterflies and dragonflies he had collected. He'd tried to explain it was for the fairies. He hadn't understood why Father was so upset when he saw the pretty white Persian cat curled up among the rocks. He'd broken its neck cleanly and done a magnificent job of hollowing it out and stuffing it. He'd learned taxidermy by reading about it. Didn't that show his superior intelligence? "Jesus Christ. Is that Lissa's cat?" Father's eyes had turned as hard and cold as marbles. "Get that monstrosity out of here. As for you . . ." He'd never finished what he was going to say. Mother had stopped him, but from that day forward, he could feel the burn of Father's cold eyes in his back. Accusing. Always accusing. Every time an animal had gone missing, Father would search his room. He had to start hunting in other neighborhoods, an inconvenience at best.

Mason ran his fingers over the photographs that covered the wall in front of him. "You'd understand, wouldn't you? Your father treated you badly too." Mason turned away. "Such a lonely little boy. Such a sad man."

He pulled out a new black-and-white photograph from a manila folder. The man in the photo had been walking with his head down, but he looked up just before he climbed into the waiting car. Oh, that delicious face with its lovely cheekbones. Those eyes.

If the eyes were the window to the soul, this man's soul was an ocean of pain. And he had captured it. In another life, he might have been a photographer or an artist—though in a way, wasn't he already an artist? Someday, perhaps his talent would be recognized.

Mason unscrewed his jar of rubber cement and fastened the photograph to the wall. He stepped back, pleased with his handiwork. So pleased that he hugged himself. "We'll meet soon. Very, very soon."

33

Danny pulled through the gates and parked in front of the Cohens' house. Andy's red cashmere scarf flapped in the wind, a gash of color against his whites. He carried two squash racquets.

Andy slipped into the front seat. "You didn't come dressed to play. No matter. We'll pick up what you need at the pro shop."

"I didn't come to play squash."

"My partner canceled on me." Andy glanced around the Mercedes and winced. "Damn it, Daniel. You've become a real old lady. Why the hell are you driving this? Nothing says stodgy better than one of these cruise ships. Well, at least I can warm my ass. Why don't you trade it in for a convertible?"

"You have one."

Andy laughed. "I only use it for funerals. How 'bout a Jag?"

"How 'bout you tell me about Michael."

Andy fingered the racquets, as if buying time while he searched for just the right words. Funny that. Andy never took care before.

"What about him?" Andy said at last.

"Jesus Christ, Andy. Michael was looking at more than restaurants. Didn't he talk to you at all?"

Andy gave him a tight smile. "Our relationship was less than cordial. You know that."

He should've told Andy up front what Michael said that night. "It's just that I think Michael stumbled upon some kind of sex club operation."

"He said that?" Andy's voice hitched. "Did he have proof?"

Should he tell Andy about his conversation with Alex? Danny figured it could wait. "I thought he might have discovered something, so I started to—"

"You started to dig into his death." Andy pulled a slim, silver flask out of his pocket and downed the contents in one long gulp. "Turn here."

Andy led him on a series of twists and turns through the streets lined with stately old Chestnut Hill mansions into the slightly more modest neighborhoods of Mt. Airy until they came to Henry Avenue.

"Isn't this the long way?" Danny said.

"We're making a little detour. Pull over."

Danny maneuvered into a spot just off the road. Andy jumped out of the car and headed for the Henry Avenue Bridge, a massive stone-and-cement structure with graceful Roman arches that loomed about a thousand feet over Fairmont Park. Danny followed reluctantly. From where they stood, it just seemed like another stretch of road. Perspective was everything.

"Teddy Powell died down there the other day. Burned to a crisp. Who gives a shit, right?" Andy turned and grinned at Danny. "You know, they used to call this the suicide bridge. Does it bring back old memories?"

Danny looked away. He didn't need to acknowledge the question. Andy already knew the answer.

June 30, 1996. His third week at the paper as a full-timer, Danny had been driving over this bridge when he spotted the girl who clung like a spider to the streetlight that protruded from the flat stone railing. Amy Johanson. Age fifteen.

"How long did you talk to her, Daniel?"

"Four hours, twenty-two minutes."

"I remember that story. All those nice details. You always noticed those little things. The smell of the tar from the road being paved. The humid air. The heat shimmers. You had a gift for seeing the grim and the sublime. Misery and beauty. I used to let you get away with writing that shit because people seemed to like it."

"About Michael . . ."

"Amy Johanson. How did she manage to hang on so long? She must have been part monkey." Andy patted the streetlight. "I don't think I could dangle for four hours. How do you really think she felt? Do you think she was scared? Or maybe she was having the time of her life."

"It was seventeen years ago!" How could Andy bring him here to mock that of all stories? Did Andy believe for a second he'd forgotten her?

For those four hours, they had gone back and forth until he thought he had won her over, and then, just at the point when he was ready to pull her in, she had said, "Will you remember me?"

"Yes. Yes, I'll write about you. Just come in. Let me help you."

She'd smiled. "I'm free. No one can catch me now."

She'd closed her eyes and tilted her head back then loosened her left hand. She'd held it in the air, and he'd watched the fingers of her right hand release their grip. For half a second, she'd seemed to hang suspended. And then she was gone, and he'd heard the screams of the people at the bottom. He didn't know what haunted him more: the look in her eyes or the remembrance of her hand cutting through the air.

Danny had gotten drunk for the first time that night. He'd consumed ten shots of scotch from Andy's special reserve. Andy had found him vomiting into his trash can.

Now Danny leaned over the bridge to stare at the Wissahickon Creek. It stretched like a slender, brown ribbon so very far below. If he closed his eyes and listened hard enough, he could still hear those screams, see Amy Johanson's tiny body mangled on the rocks in the shallow creek. He had thought of her when he saw Jane Doe One and her mangled fingers.

Ghosts.

"Your first column, if I recall," Andy said. "I put it on the Metro Page. You were still working the police beat."

Danny felt the pressure of Andy's hand against his shoulder. It took every ounce of forbearance not to shake it off.

"Do you remember what I told you that night?"

Danny turned to him. "You told me if I was going to puke, I should have the decency to do it in my own space."

"After that." Andy narrowed his eyes against the sun, and Danny could see the deep grooves in his face, the sagging pouches of tan skin. Andy looked every one of his sixty-whatever years this morning.

"You said my job wasn't to save the world."

"That's right. Get the story. Don't become it."

"Michael came to me," Danny said.

Andy pulled him to the side of the bridge where the guardrail was crushed down and crowded into him. "Why didn't you tell me about Michael?" Andy clamped both his hands on Danny's shoulders.

When he looked in Andy's eyes, he saw sorrow and something else. It was dark and cold and made him want to pull away and run. "What was Michael into, Andy?"

"It got him killed. Isn't that enough for you?"

"No. They kill people." Danny tried to pull free, but Andy held him fast.

"They?"

"What the hell are you doing?"

Andy's fingers dug into his shoulders. "Tell me!"

"Michael said something about the Inferno. The night he died, I think he was trying to bring me evidence about a group that operates sex clubs, among other things. They leave human hearts as calling cards, for fuck's sake. I found the woman who went with the heart in my goddamn bed!"

"God almighty, listen to yourself. You sound like a fucking lunatic!" Andy shook Danny hard enough to make his jaw snap. "And even if by some fucking miracle what you're saying is

131

true—" Andy took a deep, shuddering breath. "You can't bring them back."

"Are you saying there's a connection?"

Andy dragged Danny over the crushed guardrail into the open space between the end of the bridge and the high shrubs that lined the road. He was on the wrong side of the bridge now where the ground sloped off, and the footing was treacherous. Kids cut down this way into the woods to drink, but one wrong step could send you over the precipice to the creek below. Dry leaves and twigs snapped, ominous in the early morning quiet.

Andy still gripped his shoulders. He leaned close until his face was inches from Danny's. "How do you think she felt? Amy Johanson? What would make a fifteen-year-old girl jump off a bridge?"

"She ran away from home," Danny said. "No one claimed her for almost six months."

"A throwaway kid."

The hair on the back of Danny's neck rose. When he tried to pull away, Andy released him so quickly that he stumbled. He grasped for Andy, but he only succeeded in ripping off Andy's scarf, which fluttered out of his fingers in a blur of red. Danny hung in the air like Amy Johanson before Andy grabbed his arm at the last second. Andy threw his weight backward and dragged Danny through the dead leaves to safety.

Danny's breath came in painful gasps, and he could only sprawl on the ground next to Andy. He stared at the blue sky and wondered what had just happened. At last he glanced over at Andy, who lay heaving for breath. Danny touched Andy's shoulder. His hand shook. "Andy . . ."

Andy hunched over, his face waxen. Bits of brown leaves and twigs stuck to his clothes and hair. His red scarf, caught on a tree branch twenty feet below, fluttered in the air. "It's easy to die, Daniel. Now, get me the hell out of here. I need a fucking drink."

34

He had to get out now.

Zach stuffed clothes into his duffle. All he wanted to do was get to the other side of the roof and down the fire escape to the street. Just in case anyone was waiting, like that big guy in the black watch cap who'd stood on the corner all day. He tried to blend into the crowd that gathered near the newsstand and pretend like he was just waiting for a bus. Well, he could stand there 'til his balls froze.

Zach had a back way out. He'd jump the roof to the next building in the back. No big deal, no more than ten feet, and he was in shape. He was pretty sure no one knew about that route. Then he'd cross the bridge to Camden and hop a bus to New York.

Gone. He'd be gone.

He saw them take Ivy. Man, that's what happened when you got friendly with reporters. You got dicked every time.

He probably should've just hit the road then, but he needed his cash. They'd been here before he got back, but they hadn't found his stash. He figured they thought he already blew out of town.

He opened the refrigerator and pulled out a Coke can. *Things go better with Coke, all right.* Zach took a knife and hacked it apart. Jackpot. Out popped a bunch of twenties and the occasional fifty. His lifesavings. He didn't stop to count. He jammed the cash in his pocket and headed out.

It was bitter cold on the roof, and he paused to zip up his jacket. The distance looked wider than he remembered. More like twelve, maybe even thirteen feet, but he licked his lips, took a deep breath, and went for it. His feet pounded against the asphalt. Faster and faster.

Five yards from the edge, he saw them right near the fire escape. That big fuck, Lyle, and his sidekick—Zach never could remember his name. Dark silhouettes against the setting sun, Zach knew they'd been waiting for him the whole time.

Too late to stop now, and they'd never follow. Slugs. He kicked off the edge. Arms outstretched. Airborne.

His legs scissored, as if he ran on the air itself.

Yeah, he was gonna make it. He heard two pings hit a pole to his right. One pop hit to his left, but he could see the top of the building. His head roared.

Then something burned through his back and exploded out of his chest in a spray of red. It couldn't be. He was so close. So goddamned close. He could see the asphalt rooftop. He reached out his hands, but he couldn't feel anything. Only darkness.

35

Linda Cohen fastened the gold collar around her neck. Andy called it her Cleopatra collar. He'd bought it for her years ago after they first wed. Before he found it necessary to seek out younger, fresher women. Or maybe she deluded herself. Maybe the women had always been there, and she chose not to see them.

She was dreading this holiday party. It seemed callous to throw such an enormous gala so soon after her son's death, but Michael would have said they were acting in character.

Linda's eyes filled, and she blinked back the tears. They came too often lately, and she hated self-pity.

"Damn it!" Andy stood in the doorway to her bedroom. His dress shirt gaped open and he struggled with his French cuffs. "Help me with this, Lin." He shook his arms in exasperation.

Linda couldn't help but smile. Andy was such a child. She went to him, took his hands, and finished with his cuffs. Then she attached his studs, knotted his bow tie, and smoothed down the front of his shirt. Perfect.

She stepped back, and he gave her a kiss on the top of her head.

"You're wearing the collar," he said. "It still suits you." He rapped on it and kissed her on the lips this time.

She pushed him away when the need swelled up. "It still suits me." Hurt crushed her heart, and she folded her arms against her chest.

He cleared his throat. "I'm sorry, Lin. I know this has been hell for you."

"Did you talk to Danny?"

Andy's eyes shifted away, and Linda's insides chilled. He didn't do the one thing he'd promised. She wasn't surprised. She knew how much Andy dreaded that conversation.

"Andy, you have to talk to him."

"He won't listen."

Linda wanted to punch him. "You're a coward, Andy. I love you, but you're a coward."

"He'll walk away."

She heard the tremor in his voice, and the anger drained out. It was replaced by a hollow resignation. Funny that Danny should be one person whose approval Andy craved. Maybe because Andy viewed him as his creation, the son he wanted so desperately. If only he'd loved Michael half as much.

But wasn't Andy's failure her own? Hadn't she cringed away from her own child, even while she pretended to embrace him? Michael, her wretched Caliban. God had seen her hypocrisy and punished her.

"If you don't talk to him, I will."

Andy's shoulders slumped, but he nodded. "I'll talk to him after the party. I promise."

36

"Welcome to the Four Seasons, sir." The doorman snapped to attention and smiled like he'd been waiting all night for Danny to arrive. "Enjoy your stay."

In the lobby, Danny paused to let the old feelings pour over him. Beth and he used to meet here for those romantic weekends. No one made an entrance like Beth. She didn't walk; she seemed to glide. He never tired of watching her. They'd order room service and make love until they were spent. And talk. Once he thought they would never run out of things to say.

A year ago, they were right here at the Four Seasons for the same event, the Cohens' holiday party. They had been dancing, and the orchestra was playing "I Can't Get Started." Halfway through it, Beth had begun to cry, silent tears sparkling on her cheeks, and he'd kissed her and said some inanity or another. He couldn't remember now. Couldn't remember why she'd been crying, but they'd gone home and made love for the first time in months with a new sort of gentleness. He'd thought they had reached some sort of understanding because he'd wanted to believe they'd rekindled something that night.

Now a year later, he stood in the lobby of the same hotel. Pretty weird, considering Andy had almost pushed him off the suicide bridge. But he hadn't. If Andy was crazier than usual, perhaps he had reason. Maybe Danny needed to find out that reason.

A flash exploded in his face. The light blinded him for a moment before Andy took him by the arm and led him through the crowded ballroom toward the bar. He caught glimpses of the cell phones trained on him and sighed. No escape.

"Good thing for you it's only the society reporters tonight—and the citizen bloggers, of course," Andy said. "I've managed to keep our coverage of your involvement with the heart lady to a minimum. I hope I don't live to regret it."

"I don't know how she got in my bed."

"You're going to disappoint me. I can feel it. Well, come have a drink. No pussy club soda. You gotta have vices, babe." Andy draped his arm around Danny's shoulder. "Have you got any? Vices, I mean."

"I think we all know I'm a little bit nuts."

"That's pathos, not vice." Andy leaned closer. "Come on, Daniel. Haven't you ever crossed the line? What's the worst thing you've ever done?" He backed Danny up against the bar. "You do the nasty with the heart chick? Before she was croaked?"

"Jesus, Andy."

"Did you?" Andy waved his hand to the bartender. "Scotch for me and bourbon for my friend here. Straight. We'll do shots. Why don't you like to drink? That's always bothered me. Never trust a man who doesn't drink. I wonder if he's keeping notes, and you do, don't you?"

"That's my job." Danny wondered how many shots he could manage before he began to see stars. "Don't you think it's a little early to get hammered?"

In the semidark, Andy's face reflected the twinkling gold lights on the ceiling. They gave his eyes a peculiar glow, like lit coals. He seemed so pleased with himself that Danny supposed this was one of Andy's new tests of manhood.

Andy always was big on tests of manhood for Michael and him. Crazy-ass shit like who could come up with the most depraved murder on the police beat. Michael wilted under the tests, but Danny always preferred hunting down a story—even if it was an insane one—to hanging at the clubs with Andy and his crew of merry sycophants.

The bartender set down two shot glasses, and Andy picked up both. He handed one to Danny.

"Down the hatch," he said.

Danny bolted the bourbon. It burned down his throat.

Andy held up two fingers to the bartender. He winked at Danny, looking a little like a satyr. "You didn't answer my question."

"Which question was that?"

"What's the worst thing you've ever done?"

"How is that your business?"

"It's not. You're my business. I own your ass."

"Slavery was abolished a while back."

"You think so? Maybe you're not as smart as you think."

The bartender set down two more glasses, and Danny wanted to beg him to pour more slowly.

"Drink up, pal. The night is young," Andy said.

The second shot went down easier. Danny set down his glass, and Andy held up his hand to signal for two more.

"You ever do cocaine, Daniel?"

Danny shook his head. Heavy-duty drugs were his sister Theresa's province. "I used to sell dope in high school. Does that count?"

Andy's face brightened. "Ah, yes, the famous essay. Heroin?"

"Pills. Weed." Danny felt almost embarrassed by Andy's look of contempt, like he should have been a big-time dealer. He had sold a little coke, but in his neighborhood, most of the kids couldn't afford it.

"Michael used to smoke dope. Poor bastard. He loved you. Did you know that?"

"I know. Michael was a sad guy." The bourbon was already buzzing around his system, and Danny cursed himself for not eating.

"What's the worst thing you've ever done?" Andy's eyes bore into him, not accusing. Probing. "Did you ever hit Beth?" Andy's hand clamped down on his arm. "Did you?"

The bartender set down two more drinks. Danny pushed Andy's hand aside and downed the bourbon. It was a game. He knew that, but he still wanted smash the empty glass into Andy's face. "I never hit Beth."

"But she—I thought—"

"You thought wrong."

Andy swallowed his scotch and slammed down his empty glass. He signaled for two more. "Goddamn you! Why didn't you say something? Everyone thought—well, everyone but Linda."

"Christ, Andy. What difference does it make now?"

"She had pictures, you idiot."

"What are you talking about?"

"She had pictures. She said you beat her. I saw them, Daniel. She was bruised. Her wrists. Her back."

The drinks arrived, and they swallowed them in unison.

"I never beat her. You want the truth? She was having an affair. Maybe he did it."

Danny had to grip the edge of the bar. He'd said the words he hadn't admitted to anyone. Beth was having an affair. Michael had told him six months before the accident, offered to show him photos, but Danny had been unable to bring himself to look. He hadn't wanted to acknowledge the truth. He'd known somewhere that life was falling apart, but he had always believed he could fix the cracks.

He knew where she got the bruises. That night in the Mercedes after they had fought. They both had them, but if Beth had pictures, that could only mean she planned to file for divorce and claim spousal abuse. He'd believed they could turn their marriage around because he hadn't wanted to face the truth, and she'd played him. His stomach felt like it had caught fire.

"Jesus Christ, Andy. I loved her. I always loved her." He heard his voice crack.

Andy said nothing for a moment, but he didn't signal the bartender. He drummed his fingers on the bar, then slipped his hand into his pocket. "Here." Andy slapped a sheath of cardboard containing a plastic room key into Danny's hand. "Stay here tonight. I don't want to worry about you driving."

Danny started to shake his head. "I'm okay."

"Yeah, you think, but you're a candy-ass. Can't drink worth shit. I don't want you on my conscience."

"Who else is on your conscience, Andy?"

"Find Linda and say hello. She'll be upset if you don't. Make sure you tell her how good she looks." Andy ran his hands through his hair and managed to make it stand up around his head in white spikes. "Go ahead. Pick up someone and have sex. You're still young. You don't have to be a goddamn celibate."

Danny wanted to ask if he'd passed the test or not, but Andy had already turned to the bartender and ordered another scotch.

*

"Don't you look handsome tonight." Linda Cohen kissed Danny and rested her hands on his shoulders. "I do love a man in a tuxedo."

"You look terrific yourself," he said, but he thought Linda looked more worn than she had at Michael's funeral.

"I'm so glad you're coming back to us."

"Andy's a hard man to refuse."

"He needs you. You understand that, don't you?"

"I let him down." Where did that come from? The bourbon? Danny felt fuzzy around the edges. Still trying to comprehend Beth's treachery. Still hurting.

"You never let Andy down. Damn it, he's such an idiot." Linda drew a shaking breath. "All this nonsense with the police. About that woman, I mean. Whatever you need, we'll be there for you."

He bowed his head against hers, overwhelmed.

She fumbled in her purse. "Take this." She handed him a plastic CD case. "I took it from Michael's computer before the police confiscated it."

"What is this?"

Linda took another breath, then smiled and squared her shoulders. "I want you to use the CD, no matter what."

"What do you think I'm going to find?"

"Just promise."

"I promise, but—"

"Linda, darling, you look fabulous!" Three women surrounded her, cooing and fawning, and Danny watched her compose herself.

She mouthed, "Later." Danny nodded. He slipped the disc into his pocket and then stepped away to blend into the crowd.

*

"Danny Ryan?"

Danny turned at the sound of the low voice to face a blonde in a black velvet dress that hugged her slender body and puffed out in ruffles of taffeta at her hips. Under a million layers of makeup, she had eyes the color of aquamarines and skin so flawless it could have been made of wax.

When she laid her hand on Danny's arm, he noticed her long, white fingers, so smooth they seemed not to have knuckles. They tapered almost to points made more obvious by her frosted white nails. Then her perfume hit him in a wave that smelled like death—it probably had some stupid name like Agony.

"Do we know each other?" He forced a smile.

She bared white teeth under her wet, red mouth. "We've met."

"Not to sound clichéd, but I'm sure I'd remember you."

"You're looking so well tonight. Come to steal some hearts?"

The blonde licked her lips, like she was sizing him up for dinner. Danny shuddered. "What did you say your name was?"

"I didn't."

"Maybe you'd tell me where we met?"

"Why? It's much more fun watching you try to remember."

Danny tried to force his mental Rolodex to function. Normally, he was good with faces. He wished he hadn't done those shots with Andy.

Then he saw Kate walk into the room. His shoulders relaxed, and the tension began to drain from his body. It was like the relief of a cool rain that washed away the dank humidity of a long

142

summer night. When Kate blew him a kiss, the blonde gave him a feral smile.

"Someone you've been waiting for?" she asked.

"A friend."

"I won't keep you from your friend." The blonde kissed him full on the lips. Her nails dug into the back of his neck. "Think about me, Danny, and I'll think about you." She winked and sauntered away.

Danny pulled a napkin off a tray to wipe his mouth. In the dim light, the lipstick looked like blood.

*

Danny walked up behind Kate and kissed the side of her neck. She leaned back against him. He slid his hands down her arms, and his knuckles just skimmed the sides of her breasts. Her perfume made him think of moonlit gardens. He wanted to breathe her in, lose himself in her. Christ, he was half in the bag.

"You have a bad habit of not calling, Ryan," she said, but she didn't really sound angry.

He was glad he stood behind her so she couldn't see his face tighten. "I suppose you've seen the news."

She turned in his arms and put her hand on his cheek. "You should've called anyway."

He couldn't stop staring, and he wondered what she'd say if he told her that he had a room for the night. Probably slap his face. "You look nice, Kate. I mean terrific." Danny winced. *The great Pulitzer Prize winner sounded like a moron.*

"Now there's a line to knock a girl off her feet. I hope you did better with that blonde."

"I'm pacing myself."

She picked up her glass. "Why? You think you're going to get lucky?"

He wanted to come back with something, but all the cracks that came so easily when it didn't matter fled him. He cleared his throat. "Maybe you'd like to dance?"

*

Danny knew he'd pay for the champagne on top of the four shots of bourbon, but right now, he didn't give a damn. He let his palms rest against Kate's back and let the longing soak into him. She was smaller, more fragile than Beth, her warm skin so pale against the green velvet of her dress. They gave up the pretense of dancing but instead clung to each other, as if making up for lost time. That sweet ache convulsed his chest. He couldn't put a name to it, but it was like feeling the sun break through the heavy purple clouds on a winter morning. Despite the bitter cold, there was a hope of spring.

He glanced up and saw Robert and Patricia Harlan enter the room. The senator wore his benevolent face tonight, and Mrs. Senator, her frosted-blonde helmet firmly in place, was the picture of decorum in a tasteful ice-blue gown.

Patsy Harlan liked to tell people she was from an old Southern family, but Danny knew she was raised on a Georgia pig farm. He figured there was nothing wrong with growing up on a pig farm until you began to intimate it was really Tara, with the darkies singing "Swing Low Sweet Chariot" in the cotton fields.

Still, he'd always felt sorry for Patsy. He knew she'd worked hard to mold herself into a perfect senator's wife, always smiling, always complimenting, never able to let down her guard. Maybe that was why she hated him. She knew he recognized her as a fellow outsider.

"Your boss is here," Danny said. "He has his wife with him."

Kate's eyes narrowed. "And you're suggesting?"

"I'm suggesting that being with me won't do your career any good. I wasn't their favorite son-in-law."

Kate slid her hands back around his neck. "Do I look worried?"

37

Kate staggered a little. Too much champagne. It always made her lightheaded. He'd held her like she was made of spun sugar, a confection of sweet and delicate perfection. How long had it been since a man treated her like she was something that exquisite?

God almighty. Now what was she going to do?

Kate walked down the hall to the ladies' room. She just couldn't let things get out of hand. She'd have to slip out like Cinderella, no matter how much she wanted to be with him. The problem was that she didn't know if she had the willpower.

No. Dammit. That wasn't true. She could get through anything. She saw her da and two brothers shot on the street in front of their flat. She'd been hungry enough to go begging and needy enough to sell herself. She was a survivor above all.

So what to say? *Hey, Prince Charming, now that your wife is dead, you can carry me away and we'll live happily ever after.*

Good God. She sounded as crazy as Michael.

Maybe he'd turn out to be a creep. Why should he be any different than all the others? Why ruin it with all that ugly reality when the dream was a lovely iridescent soap bubble, too fragile to touch.

Kate leaned against the wall. She didn't need Danny Ryan. She didn't need anyone.

Her isolation had never bothered her until now. Strange how wanting someone made her feel so ragged. Like she stood on the other side of a window and stared in at a sumptuous feast. Kate, the little match girl.

Or maybe she never thought she'd ever be close enough to get what she wanted. Danny and she must have walked the same paths thousands of times, entering and exiting rooms within minutes of each other, and it took Michael Cohen of all people to bring them together. Not a promising omen.

Kate opened the ladies' room door and froze when she heard a peculiar gurgling, almost like a clogged drain. She expected to find a puddle of water and instead saw the woman who slumped against a cushioned chair, her hand pressed against her throat. Blood spilled between her pale fingers. Linda Cohen.

Kate screamed.

38

Voices swirled around him like the bits of ice caught in the howling wind outside. Danny squeezed the velvet curtain and tried to force himself to breathe. In. Out. His chest ached.

In another life, he would have been interviewing the assembled multitude.

How close were you to Linda Cohen? Can you think of anyone who'd want to hurt her? How do you feel about this?

Once he had to interview a family whose twelve-year-old son had been killed in gang crossfire. Just another day at the office, but he'd researched the kid. "I'm so sorry about Darnell," he'd said to the mother who hadn't talked to any reporters. "Look, I know you must be going through hell, but I don't want to go over that night again. Won't you tell me about your boy? TV says he wanted to be a wideout for the Eagles, but I hear he wanted to study physics and could build anything out of Legos." She'd paused for a full minute, and he'd been about to hang up when she invited him to come to the house. He'd gotten an exclusive.

"You're the first one who really knowed anything about my baby," she'd said. "I look in your eyes and see somethin' real. Mebbe you'll understand."

Even he hadn't known whether he'd felt anything real or had been faking it to get a column. Now he was paying for all those days. He couldn't think about Linda without feeling his throat close.

She'd been the first person he'd called after the accident. His one act of self-preservation. Jesus, she'd looked so fragile on that gurney when they wheeled her out, and he could do nothing except pray she wouldn't die—only prayer wasn't going to help now. Grief would only hold him back. Danny couldn't afford to mourn Linda, or Beowulf, or even his family. He could only stumble forward. He fumbled for the CD in his pocket.

Don't let me fuck it up.

*

"This is a terrible tragedy. Just terrible." Danny heard the voice by his elbow and looked down to see an elderly man in a wheelchair. He recognized Bartlett Scott because he was a fixture in Philadelphia's philanthropic circles: he was building a new world-class performing arts center down on Walnut Street; he had raised the money for the Scott Cancer Research Wing at Children's Hospital; he had created the Scott Center for Academic Excellence in West Philadelphia to help bright kids from struggling families make it to college. Bartlett Scott was the closest thing Philadelphia had to a saint.

Now, felled by a stroke a little less than a year ago, his left arm curled up against his chest, but his face was still red cheeked and benevolent, his glowing white hair full and wavy. He nodded at Danny, his pale-blue eyes filled with concern. "Daniel Ryan? I thought it was you. My goodness. Terrible to see you under such circumstances." He spoke slowly but clearly.

Danny squatted down to better hear him. He took hold of Bartlett Scott's proffered right hand. "Yes, sir. It's an awful night. Would you like me to speak to the police? Perhaps they could move you to more comfortable quarters."

Bartlett Scott shook his head. "I'm a witness here like everyone else." He glanced over at a middle-aged blonde sitting near him at the table. "My daughter Melissa may feel differently, of course, but I don't mind waiting. Poor Andy. God awful thing."

He paused and looked at Danny. "Waiting is hard, isn't it? Waiting to hear? I daresay you know all about that."

Danny stood. "I've had my bad nights, yes."

"I've always admired your column. You've taken on some of our sacred cows. It's good for the city."

"Thank you, sir." Danny cleared his throat and tried to remember if he had written anything particularly unflattering about Bartlett Scott. He thought not; the old man seemed to have been a genuine force for good in the city.

"I've often thought of you. I remember the funeral for your wife and boy. So sad. Terribly sad. I thought of Blake then. 'Some are born to endless night.' Yes, I thought of that line then. It's hard to lose a child." He caught Danny's arm again. "I haven't always agreed with you, but I always thought you were a good man." He sighed. "'Endless night.' Would you agree, Mr. Ryan? I believe we share that in our own way."

Melissa Scott was on her feet. She gently pried her father's fingers off Danny's arm and then settled the old man. "Dad, please. I'm sure Mr. Ryan has enough to worry about right now." Her face looked pinched, and Danny realized that she was concerned with what he'd write about her father. He turned away but felt her touch his hand.

"Don't mind Dad," she said. "He's not himself these days. He gets confused. I hope you'll try to remember him as he was. He hasn't been the same since Mother passed away."

Who wanted to write that Bartlett Scott was losing his mind? Or maybe he wasn't. Maybe he saw something true. Danny's parade of sleepless nights hadn't started with Conor and Beth's accident. *Some are born to endless night.* Now it would be one more thing that would rattle through his mind. Danny's flesh was crawling. Christ, this party had become a circus of the macabre. He glanced back at Bartlett Scott. Something bothered him: The old man's serene expression? Or maybe it was those almost colorless blue eyes. They reminded him of something.

Melissa Scott was watching him expectantly, and he nodded. "I'm sure your father's exhausted. It's been a very upsetting evening for everyone."

She gave him a chilly smile. "Indeed. I hoped you'd understand."

*

Danny watched the cop who guarded the door to the ballroom and wondered if the police intended to interview everyone or hold every person prisoner until someone confessed out of boredom. They'd taken Andy away in the ambulance with Linda. When Danny asked the cop by the door where they had taken her, he just shook his head. It wasn't a surprise. Danny didn't expect police cooperation, not with a hostile crowd circling.

Where had they taken Kate? What hell was she going through? He tried texting her but got no reply. He needed to find her, but he was stuck in this room for now.

Senator and Mrs. Harlan sat near the door, and Danny didn't understand why the senator hadn't made a discreet phone call to get their asses out of there. Then again, why make a scene? If Bartlett Scott could wait it out, why not Robert Harlan? After all they were comfortably enjoying their coffee, dessert, and after-dinner cocktails on Andy's tab.

The senator waved to him as if they were friends. Robert Harlan smiled when Danny reached the table, but his eyes remained cold. Mrs. Harlan's lips twitched, and he thought she might spit at him. Danny leaned over and kissed her cheek just like a dutiful ex-son-in-law. Her hand clamped down over his, and her long, red nails dug into his flesh, but he ignored the quick stab of pain and said, "Awful night, isn't it? You holding up, Patsy?"

He called her that because he could get away with it, but he still got a rush when he saw the twin flashes of fury in her eyes. She made no effort to disguise her feelings. He was the usurper who had stolen her daughter. To him, she was an old fraud with infinite amusement value. If she had possessed a sense of humor, they might have gotten along. He knew she'd taken etiquette and speech classes so she could learn to fit in the Washington social scene and hired a tutor to help her polish up on history and literature. Patsy Parker, farm girl and former Miss Georgia Peach, always maintained herself with the rigid discipline of a drill sergeant. He'd heard the senator dismiss her more than once with a quick "Don't talk about things you don't understand" put-down, and he'd watched her face tighten into an obedient smile. Danny had never seen her relax or drop her facade, and he pitied her, even though he knew that if given half a chance, she would have strung him up and gutted him along with one of her father's prize sows. Some people lived with stress. Patsy was a virtual pressure cooker.

"It was most unfortunate that our poor Kate stumbled across the crime scene," the senator said.

Danny looked at him for a moment. "Maybe it saved Linda's life." Linda couldn't die. Not the Linda who brought him containers of chicken soup and thick corned beef sandwiches wrapped in waxed paper when he first started at the paper. Not his Linda. Christ, he needed to hold it together. "She's not dead."

The senator shook his head. "It's my understanding that Linda's throat was cut. Of course, Linda and Andy will be in my prayers."

"I'm sure that'll be a comfort to them." Danny knew the sarcasm sounded hollow.

"I'm glad to hear you say that." The senator smiled as if Danny had told him Christ had come down for a chat. "God will sustain Andy in his hour of need just as he sustained you through yours. That's how you came to accept that Beth and Conor moved on to a better place. It was God's will. No matter how difficult."

Danny wanted to tell the senator to go fuck himself, but the surge welled up. He forced it back. The senator's eyes turned black with pure venom. The bastard knew he'd scored a direct hit.

"I don't accept anything."

"Accidents can be very upsetting."

"This wasn't an accident." Danny said.

The senator's eyes grew darker. "No, of course. This was quite deliberate, wasn't it?"

"What the hell is taking so long?" A tall man with flowing chestnut hair swept across the room to stand with them, and Danny recognized him at once. Bruce Delhomme. Philadelphia's hottest restaurateur. Party boy. Andy's asshole buddy. He bristled with the kind of self-important impatience that made Danny hope he was the last on the interview list.

"Calm yourself," the senator said in the no-nonsense voice a parent would use on a petulant child. Delhomme pouted and folded his arms. Danny waited for him to stamp his foot.

The door opened, and John Novell appeared. He said something to the cop and then motioned to Danny. When Danny headed toward him, Delhomme also approached the door.

Novell looked at him. "May I help you, sir?"

Delhomme tossed his hair. He could've been in a shampoo commercial. "We've been held captive here for almost an hour! I demand to know what's taking so long!"

"The detectives in charge will be in soon to interview you. It won't be much longer, sir."

"Do you know who I am?"

Novell waited.

"I'm Bruce Delhomme, goddammit! I don't have to take this crap!"

"Now, Bruce." Robert Harlan stepped forward and laid a hand on Danny's shoulder. "I'm sure the police are doing everything they can. Perhaps, you'll put in a good word for us, Daniel?"

Danny would have said, "In a cold day in hell," but Novell's face stopped him. It twisted like someone yanked his muscles with a wire.

"Senator Harlan," Novell said.

"Agent Novell, isn't it?" Robert Harlan's voice oozed like syrup. "Miss Reid is a member of my staff. My wife and I would consider it a personal favor if we could speak with her."

Novell spun away. "If you'll excuse us." He jerked his head at Danny and strode out the door.

Danny followed Novell into the hall. "So what's with you and Senator Charm?"

Novell grunted.

"Come on, it'll keep me from asking you what you're doing here. Did you tail me?"

Novell turned so fast he caught Danny off guard. He backed him up against the wall and leaned into him until there were mere inches between their faces. Danny could smell the scotch under Novell's breath mints, and for a moment he thought Novell might throttle him.

"Do you give a shit about anyone? A woman had her throat cut tonight. Did that register with you?"

Danny's mouth dropped open. Did Novell have a clue? He took a breath. Fuck Novell. He could think what he wanted.

"So about you and Big Bob?"

Novell's face turned scarlet. "That bastard is the one who screamed for an investigation into the Inferno. Then he interfered from day one, and when the operation collapsed, he turned around and said it was our fault. Our agents got sloppy. The bureau fucked up. Sanctimonious prick. As far as I'm concerned—" Novell clamped his teeth together and bit off his words.

Danny stared at him. He wanted to ask Novell more about the operation, but somehow this didn't seem like the time.

"Jesus, Novell. Harlan's not my choice for man of the year either. What are you doing here anyway? The Philly PD doesn't call in outsiders on this sort of thing. Particularly not suburban cops."

Novell pointed to an alcove. "Wait there. I'm getting Kate before Harlan gets a chance to talk to her. I've persuaded the Philly PD that you're part of my investigation. But you're sick. You get migraines. So keep your mouth shut and look sick. You got someplace to stay tonight?"

Danny handed him the key card. "Yeah, here."

Novell took it, studied it for a minute, and then put it in his pocket.

"Anyone know you're planning to stay?"

"Just Andy and Linda."

"You're valet parked?"

"Yeah, it's in with the key card, but what—"

"Can it, Ryan. I'm not in the mood." Novell stalked off, leaving Danny to wonder what the hell was going on.

39

Lights exploded in Danny's skull just after five. He rolled out of bed, fumbled for his tuxedo jacket in the dark, and staggered into the bathroom, Imitrex in hand. Lights popped around him like fireworks. Orange. Red. White. They pulsed and ran together as the ominous tightening in his right eye socket began.

His hands shook when he jabbed the needle into his thigh. He slumped down on the toilet and pressed his palms against his forehead. When the light show in his head began to diminish, he filled the basin with water and plunged his face into it.

Danny could almost feel hands on his back the moment his face hit the icy water, and he jerked his head from the basin with a shudder and combed his fingers through his hair.

Once just for fun, Kevin and Junior had pissed in the toilet and held his head in it just to see how long he could stand it. The brawl had been life as usual with the Ryan boys, until they had broken his mother's Waterford rose bowl. Even Junior had been scared that night when the old man had come home stinking drunk. Already furious.

Funny the things he remembered: the darkness of the closet where he had hidden, his father's footsteps in the hall, his fear that reeked of mothballs.

Danny walked back into the bedroom where Kate still slept. Last night, after Kate asked to stay with Danny, Novell had escorted them to this suite. She'd removed her gown, wrapped herself in the complimentary terry cloth robe, and curled into a white ball beneath the covers. Danny had offered to sleep on the sofa, but she'd said, "Don't leave."

He didn't know what comfort she took from his presence twenty-some inches away in that king-size bed. In the darkness, they might as well have been twenty miles apart.

Kate slept with her hands balled into fists, as if sleep itself was a battle. Danny wanted to slip in beside her and take her in his arms, but he figured he'd get a fist in the eye. He smoothed the covers around her and kissed the top of her head.

He wandered to the outer room of the suite. A gift basket sat on the coffee table, and he fingered the cellophane. The gift card read, "From Linda and Andy, Welcome back." Danny crushed the card in his hand when the grief swept over him.

The first time he'd met Linda, she wore a black satin gown and had been searching for Andy. Danny had fallen asleep at his computer terminal after completing his last obit, his cheek resting in a small puddle of drool.

"I'm thinking of cheating on my husband tonight." At the sound of her voice so close to his ear, he'd snapped up, almost connecting with her chin. She'd surveyed him with a knowing smile and then reached into her evening bag to offer him a tissue. "I hope you finished whatever you were writing."

"Yes, ma'am." He'd scrubbed at his cheek.

"Does my husband keep you chained here at night?"

"No, ma'am. I—"

"That's good to know. And you find your employment here satisfactory?"

Danny had nodded, trying to think of something to say. He'd realized this was Andy's wife because Andy kept a picture of her on his desk and spoke of her with great affection.

"Perhaps you'd like to help me cheat on my husband. If I'm not mistaken, he's hiding out somewhere around here with

Miss Philly Cheesesteak or something like that. So here we are, you and I. Are you the kind of man who's willing to help a lady in need?"

Danny had felt like a train was bearing down on him. No matter what he'd said, he'd be flattened, but he'd croaked, "I think you'd be way out of my league, but I'd be happy to see you home."

She'd said nothing for a moment, then leaned close and touched his cheek. "Don't sell yourself short."

He hadn't helped her cheat on Andy, though she did give him a ride back to his dorm in her limo. And she'd begun checking in on him, the first time with a box of cookies from Termini's. Later she sent more substantive food: corned beef sandwiches and chicken soup. Then came the clothes: cashmere sweaters, a leather jacket because she'd thought he looked cold, a Burberry scarf. He'd try to refuse; she wouldn't hear of it.

"My son won't let me be a good mother," she'd said once. "Indulge me."

He'd always thought Michael would resent him, but Michael had been philosophic. He'd knocked back a double shot of tequila and said, "They didn't like the son they got, so they got themselves a new one. You should change your name to Jacob. What the hell, it gets them off my back. Just wait 'til Mother Wonderful is telling you how to live your life."

Linda had never told him how to live his life, though she'd stood by him through enough disasters. But something had been wrong with Linda last night. Linda and Andy. Something had been wrong since Michael died. It was like Michael's death opened the door to some alternate universe where everything looked the same but wasn't.

How could Beth and Conor's crash have been anything but an accident? Danny tried to remember the accident report. Beth had lost control of the Jeep. Black ice, the state troopers had said.

Not all accidents are accidents.

That voice came back to him, low and hoarse and evil. And along with it came the senator.

This was quite deliberate, wasn't it?

So many accidents. Beth and Conor. Michael. Teddy Powell. Too many. It didn't make sense. Maybe nothing made sense anymore.

And why did Andy have to talk to him about Beth? Why did he even care about her? Danny's head sunk toward his chest. It felt so heavy. Too heavy to hold up. If he could just sleep for an hour or two more, he'd be able to function. The hangover didn't help.

Something he needed to remember. It seemed important, but his mind was too unfocused. Where had he seen those eyes?

*

"Hey."

A hand brushed down Danny's cheek to linger on his neck. He opened his eyes. Kate leaned over him, rested her hands on his shoulders. Her hair hung in a damp tangle, and she still wore the terry cloth robe. She smelled of lavender and vanilla.

"You look like hell," she said.

"You look beautiful."

She bowed her head, but not before he saw tears fill her eyes.

"What's the matter, Kate?"

"I had a bad dream."

He drew her into his lap and tried to ignore the way the robe slipped off her shoulder, the way she fit against him. He put his face against her hair.

"Don't say anything." She inched closer until their mouths almost touched. "I want you to make the ghosts disappear for me, Danny. And I can do that for you. We can do that much, can't we?"

He wanted to tell her that ghosts never went away, that you could never close the door to them and keep it closed. Even soft spirits like Conor haunted you forever. Instead, he let his fingers slide under the fabric of her robe.

"We can try, Kate." He heard the lie in his voice and hoped she didn't. "We can try."

40

Novell felt like an old shoe—worn out and broken down. He trudged through the elegant lobby of the Four Seasons and punched the elevator button.

He'd already started the day with a fight over his lack of regard for proper police procedure. The captain didn't appreciate the shark sense that had made him tail Ryan. The Philly PD brass didn't find his impersonation of an FBI agent amusing either, though Novell knew he did a damn good job of it.

Everything was fucked up.

Linda Cohen remained in intensive care, and Novell suspected Ryan was next on the hit list.

No doubt Ryan would still want to keep digging, and Novell wanted him in protective custody today. The trick was to get Ryan to agree. The brother would help. Novell was sure of that, if he could get them together. But it was not a promising way to start Sunday morning.

His phone vibrated. The Philly PD. Again. Novell slid it back into his pocket. He'd deal with them later.

He reached the door and gave a quick knock. No answer. Fuck 'em. It was almost eleven. They need to get moving.

Novell slid the plastic key down the slot and opened Ryan's room door. A white robe and a trail of clothes led to the bedroom, but it was quiet. Thank Christ. At least he wasn't walking in on a show.

Novell opened the minibar, pulled out a bottle of water, and strolled through the sitting area to peer through the doorway. Kate would pick him, of course. He was young. Good looking. He had something to offer.

Stupid old jackass. Novell's fist tightened on the water bottle.

Kate lay with her head on Ryan's chest, the picture of innocence, but he knew better. Kate's heart had turned to stone long ago. He stalked over to the side of the bed, opened the bottle of water, and poured it on them, just like a fountain.

"Jesus fucking Christ!" Ryan leaped up when the cold water hit him. Kate shrieked. Ryan wiped his face with the back of his arm. "You goddamn prick, Novell."

"Wakey wakey." Novell noted the old scars that crisscrossed Ryan's forearms. Defensive wounds.

Ryan pushed Kate behind him. "Who the hell do you think you are?"

"I'm the man who's telling you to get up."

Novell assessed the anger burning like blue flame in Ryan's eyes. Damned if there wasn't something of his old man in him after all. Ryan's hands balled into fists, and he tensed like he was looking for his best shot. He'd be mean in a fight. Novell sensed it, and he took a step back. Could it be the wife had reason to be afraid? Or did Ryan have that temper under ironclad control? Novell watched the control assert itself. Interesting. Ryan's hands relaxed, but his face drew tight, ashen. The effort cost him.

"You aren't paying for this room, Novell." Ryan's voice was soft now but threaded with fury.

"Neither are you." Novell tried to make his tone conciliatory. "Look, it's eleven o'clock. Check out is eleven thirty. Get up and get dressed."

That half smile curved Ryan's mouth, though no humor lit his eyes. He glanced at Kate and then back at Novell. "Did you plan to stand here and watch? It doesn't matter to me, but I don't think the lady wants an audience."

Novell's face heated up. "We'll talk on the way," he said and shuffled to the door.

41

The morning seemed surreal, like maybe he'd taken too many drugs and was caught in a dream, though Danny was pretty sure he now stood in front of the Four Seasons turning into a human Popsicle.

"What's going on, Detective?"

Novell ignored him. Danny asked for his ticket for the Mercedes, but Novell shook his head. "We'll take my car," he said. "I'm just around the corner."

Kate folded her arms against her chest, and Danny put his arm around her shoulders. He could feel her shaking and wished she'd say something, but she stood rigid and unyielding. She hadn't spoken since Novell had appeared.

Novell nodded toward the Crown Vic illegally parked at the corner. "Your car isn't there. I had it towed last night."

"What do you mean you had it towed?" Danny stared at Novell. Who did this asshole think he was?

"Right after I saw someone fucked with your wheels."

*

They rode in silence. Novell kept the front window half-open and cold air blasted through the car.

Andy Williams sang "The Most Wonderful Time of the Year" on the radio, and Danny wondered whether someone really messed with his wheels or Novell was jerking his chain. He wished Kate would look at him.

"Your boss wants to know where we're hiding you," Novell said to Kate. They parked in front of her apartment. Danny tried to take her hand, but she pulled away. She stared at the floor.

"Make up a story. Tell him the police had you looking through mug books all night, do you understand? You don't tell him where you were." She didn't answer. "Kate?"

"I got it."

"Get moving then." When Danny started to get out with her, Novell caught his arm and jerked him back. "Not you."

"Fuck you, Novell."

"Christ almighty!" Novell pinned him against the seat. "What's wrong with you?"

"I'm fine. What's your problem?"

"You're a goddamn idiot. Didn't it occur to you that someone might be watching you? And if they are, the minute you get out of the car, you put Kate in danger?" Novell glared at Danny.

"Jesus." The sick realization churned through his stomach. If someone was watching—he knew damn well someone was watching. "How could you just leave her like that?"

"Kate can look after herself. It's you I'm worried about." Novell pulled away from the curb and headed up Walnut. They hung a right on Twenty-Second Street and waited at the light on Chestnut. Flakes of powdery snow drifted down from the leaden sky and blew across the windshield.

"Look, Ryan, the people who killed Michael Cohen want you dead."

Danny closed his eyes. There was nothing like stating the obvious, or maybe Novell thought he found hearts and bodies regularly. "I've gotten death threats before."

"These aren't threats, pal. If you drove home last night, you'd have ended up like your wife and kid."

"That's my problem."

"No, it's mine, so I guess there's only one thing to do."

"And that is?"

"Protective custody."

"No way."

"The way I see it, you don't have a choice."

Novell was starting to sound like Kevin with his I'm-a-cop-and-I-know-best attitude. If he didn't take it from Kevin, Danny sure as shit wasn't going to take it from Novell. As for protective custody . . .

The light turned green, and Novell inched toward the inter-section. Danny grabbed the door handle, jerked it up, and hurled himself out of the car.

42

D anny heard Novell curse, but he kept moving. When he rocketed out of the car, his palm hit the pavement, and his knee slammed against the curb. A shot of agony tore through his body, but he ducked behind a taxi and took off down Twenty-Second Street.

He cut through an alley and ran with a shuffling limp until he reached Walnut Street. Despite the icy wind, sweat ran down his back. At least there would be stores here. He ducked inside some kind of unisex shop to buy a coat, gloves, jeans, and a sweater.

Where to go? Not Kate's. Novell would look there first. Not home. He lingered in the doorway and searched the street for the black Crown Vic. Snow fell thicker and faster. It already coated the pavement. A police cruiser drove past, and Danny pulled back. His heart started to race.

He wasn't a criminal. Novell couldn't put out an APB on him, and he couldn't force him into protective custody. Could he? Danny had a feeling Novell could do whatever the hell he wanted.

Danny pushed out the door into the street. He could call Kevin, but he didn't want Kevin to give him a ration of shit. He wanted more substantial shoes but didn't see any place where he could grab a simple pair of snow boots. He settled for sneakers.

He trudged toward Broad Street, his head bowed against the wind and snow. Pausing on the corner of Fifteenth, Danny stared up at the traffic light that swayed in the wind. The answer came to him, and he prayed the Broad Street subway was still running.

43

"Jesus God, Danny! What the hell happened to you?" Theresa pulled him in the door.

Danny couldn't feel his toes. Melting snow ran in rivulets down his head and neck and seeped under his collar.

"Did you walk from Valley Forge?" He shook his head and watched his sister unbutton his coat. "Don't say nothin'. Go upstairs and take a shower right now."

The water burned his frozen skin, but the chill drained out of his bones and swirled down the drain. Danny breathed in the clouds of steam, felt his muscles relax, and wondered how long it would take Novell to figure out that he had a sister who still lived in South Philly. Maybe he was already on his way. Danny was too tired to care.

It seemed to take hours to walk the twelve blocks from the subway to her house. Once he knew the neighborhood so well he could've found his way blindfolded; now the narrow streets were alien to him. The redbrick row homes all looked alike. Maybe it was the snow; maybe it was because he found himself turning toward the old man's house more than once.

He didn't know what would make him want to go anywhere near that place. He'd closed that door on his life and triple locked it, but his father always hovered outside, his personal monster.

Danny could hear him working away at the locks, testing the knob, always pushing, waiting for his chance.

Danny would hear him those nights when Beth would chatter about her latest plan for grooming Conor into a proper gentleman, and he would smart over his own lack of culture, inferior education, and missing pedigree. The shame and anger would coat him like a thin, red haze, but he kept the door shut tight, even if it took all his strength to keep it closed, because he swore he'd never be like the old man. To what end? From the depths of hell, Danny swore his father was laughing. He turned off the water and stepped out.

Theresa left him clothing. Her husband's things. Heavy socks. An extra large, extra ugly, green velour jogging suit with an Eagles logo. Danny knew Vic wouldn't care. Dead men didn't need clean clothes.

Theresa was sitting at the table when he came into the kitchen. She stood and tried not to smirk. "Your stuff's in the dryer."

"Thanks." He slid his arms around her. The years had hollowed out Theresa. Her hair stuck out in a chaotic frizz around her head. An inch of black roots frosted with gray clung to her scalp, and it was hard to reconcile this hard-bitten woman with the popular prom queen who'd once been his sister.

She pulled back to look at him, her pale-blue eyes sharp with curiosity. "Danny, what happened to you? You look fuckin' awful."

"I need to hide out for a few days."

"You need to eat a square meal and tell me what's wrong." She nodded toward the stove. "I got lasagna. I'll make it, okay? So you sit and tell me what's wrong. Jesus Christ. You showed up half-froze on my doorstep."

"Maybe you don't want to hear this."

Theresa put her hands on her hips. "I grew up with the Iceman. I was married to Vic Ceriano for fifteen years and did two years in the slam. I been through detox six times. What're you gonna tell me I can't handle?"

"I didn't kill that girl, the one in my house. In case you were wondering."

"Never crossed my mind."

"Because you don't think I'm capable of murder?"

Theresa gave him a sly smile. It was a look he remembered well. The look she got whenever she pulled one over on the old man. "I guess if you had to do murder, you could, but you wouldn't be dumb enough to get caught."

"I got caught selling dope."

"And look how that turned out for you." She went to the oven and pulled out a pan of lasagna. It smelled decent; then again, he hadn't eaten today. She scooped out a generous portion onto a plate and set it in front of him. "The old man did you a favor when he tossed you in jail."

Theresa had a way of looking at things that was stripped of artifice. Maybe it had to do with all those years of rehab.

Danny dug into the lasagna. The noodles tasted like rubber; the cheese had the consistency of plastic, and the sauce was straight from a jar, but right now he couldn't shovel it down fast enough.

"It's okay?" She twisted her fingers together and stared at him as if his approval was important. When he smiled and nodded, she took a deep breath and relaxed.

"It's great, Theresa. Thank you." Danny started to reach out for her, but she just plopped another helping on his plate. He wanted to bury his face in it.

"Christ, it ain't that good. Vic always said I was a shitty cook."

"What did he know?" Danny wanted to tell her it was the first time in a year he felt hungry, but he didn't. He finished the lasagna, pushed back from the table, and rested his hands on his stomach.

"So what were you doing with the Goth chick anyway?"

"Research."

She sat down beside him. "On what? Findin' true love?"

"Sex clubs."

Theresa chuckled. "You at a sex club? That I'da paid to see. You're so goddamn straight."

Danny didn't know whether to be insulted or not. "I guess you have intimate experience with them."

"Don't get huffy." She lit a cigarette and blew the smoke at him. "I was married to a dope dealer. I didn't hang out at the Four Seasons with all them big shots like you, though Vic did sell 'em a lot of drugs."

"I was at a place called Black Velvet."

"Yeah, Vic dealt there. It's a real hole, but there's worse places."

"You ever hear of the Inferno?"

Danny felt her leg jerk under the table. He heard the faint crackle of the cigarette when Theresa took a long drag that must have pulled the nicotine down to her toes.

"The Inferno? That what you're into? Jesus Christ, does Kevin know? He'll smack the shit outta you."

"Kevin's an asshole."

"You're both assholes. Two hardhead Micks." She picked a piece of tobacco from her front tooth, examined it, and flicked it at him. "You tryin' to write about them? The Inferno?"

"Maybe."

"I got Vic's guns upstairs under my bed. Go pick one and blow your brains out instead. The Inferno. That ain't no club. You can't go there."

Danny let her words sink in. He didn't know why it hadn't occurred to him sooner to speak to Theresa. If anyone would know about the underside of Philly, she would.

"Come on, Theresa, talk to me."

"Just like that? Why should I?"

He saw the avaricious gleam in her eyes before she looked away, and he knew that she wasn't going to volunteer anything out of sisterly affection. Stupid of him to have forgotten the family creed: fuck everyone. "I'll pay you."

"Money's no good if I'm dead."

"You'll be dead if you don't lay off the cancer sticks."

169

"Fuck you. I gave up everything else. Not everyone's a saint like you."

Danny didn't argue. It wasn't worth the effort. "I won't use your name. I just want information."

"Vic never clued me in on his business."

He could've reminded her that she was a drug mule for Vic, but he didn't. It would've pissed her off, and she'd have shut up for good. When she didn't say anything further, Danny wondered how long she planned to stretch it out. She shifted in her chair, but he ignored her.

"Must be great to be rich, huh, Danny?" She sounded bitter, and he swallowed his anger. He hadn't been rich when she'd broken into his apartment and stolen almost everything he owned for drugs.

Kevin had wanted him to press charges, but he couldn't do it. "Junkie bitch," Kevin had called her, but Danny never could bring himself to judge her. Theresa was a survivor; she did what she had to do to get by.

"So how much money're we talkin' about?" Theresa said.

What difference did it make? She was right: he was rich. Money wasn't going to bring Conor back. "Pick a number."

She smiled. "You're nicer than Kevin at least."

Danny massaged his right eye socket. "Does the Inferno own Black Velvet? Pluto's Bowl? Tophet?"

"Where did you hear about Tophet?"

"Does it matter?"

"I guess not. Not sure what it is, but there's a club in Northern Liberties."

"And?"

"And nothin'. I don't know the name. All I know is its some extreme S and M club open to members only. Vic had a special card. Real weird gold thing with this black drop in the middle."

Danny clutched the sides of the table. It sounded similar to the card Michael had. He wished he had brought it with him, but it sat in his safe. "You still have the card?"

"How the fuck should I know?"

Danny watched her calculate what it was worth to him, but he didn't care. He wanted that card. "What else?"

She gave him a blank look born of years of practice on the old man and later on cops in general. "What do you mean, Danny?"

"Come on, Theresa, you know more than that."

"I was so strung out at that time I didn't know my ass from a hole in the ground. All I know is Vic dealt with this subhuman named Lester or Lenny or something like that. A big ape with a square head. I'll never forget him."

Theresa stared into the thin, blue ribbon of smoke that snaked up from her cigarette, and it struck him that she looked a little wistful. Maybe she'd loved Vic at that. She'd stuck it out with him despite the beatings, the constant stream of whores, the arrests.

"So how do I find him?"

"You start lookin' around for the Inferno, he'll find you."

"Did he find Vic?"

She took another drag on the cigarette. "Who the fuck knows? Vic sampled too much of his own product."

"But no one came after you."

She smiled a little. "Vic wasn't all bad. He had friends who took care of me. It's good to have friends, Danny. You might remember that."

"Did he kill Vic?"

She looked away. "I don't know. Seriously. But Vic saw somethin'. He never said what, but it was bad. Real bad. And two weeks later he OD'd. Coulda been he got careless. Wouldn't have been the first time. But . . ." She shrugged and let it hang.

What were the odds?

44

Kate sat on her window seat and stared out at the street below. In the darkness, the lights glowed pinkish yellow against the swirling snow. Only the plows traveled tonight.

She rested her head against her knees. Why had she let him get close to her? She hadn't planned on sleeping with him. She'd planned to slip out, call a taxi. But she'd seen the cartridge from his medicine in the waste can. If she'd been smart, she wouldn't have stood by the side of the chair and watched him in his uneasy sleep. But she'd claimed him as her own fallen angel, the hell with the consequences.

And there were always consequences.

She'd never let anyone see her naked in the daylight. But he wasn't appalled at the white scars on her rib cage, the pucker just below her right breast. He'd kissed it and told her she was beautiful.

"I wish I'd met you before," he'd said.

"Before what?"

He didn't answer immediately, and she watched him trying to frame his answer. He did that a lot. Danny was careful with words. He enjoyed coaxing them out of people, but he liked being careful with his own. Was it the deceiver in him or his fear of exposing himself? Maybe it was both. It allowed him to insinuate himself into people's lives, however briefly, and walk away with little nuggets he would polish into gems.

Was she real to him or just another little nugget of a story he would store away in his mind? Kate pressed her fingers against her eyes and willed herself not to cry. She wished she could be like the snow and dance away on the wind.

She heard the soft knock on her door and went to open it. Novell. She tried to slam it in his face, but he stuck his foot in the doorway.

"I don't have any booze," she said.

"It's not a social call." He pushed past her. "Where is he?"

Kate folded her arms. "Who?"

"Ryan."

She tried without success to force down the bubble of laughter that rose in her chest. "Jesus Christ, Novell. You lost him?"

Novell caught her by the shoulders. "Tell me where he is or—"

"Or what?" She grinned when Novell let go of her shoulders.

Novell leaned close. She knew he did it because she hated it, but she didn't flinch. "You just remember, Kate. I know who you are. If Ryan comes here, you call me. Linda Cohen was a warning. I can protect him."

He didn't believe that. Kate would have sympathized if her anger hadn't run so deep.

"No one can protect him, Novell. He'll have to take his chances."

"That's cold. So cold I almost don't believe you."

Damn him. She hated that he knew her so well. Once it was almost a relief having one person she didn't have to lie to, and she felt a pull toward him—even though he was a million years old. Sometimes she still felt it. Faint, almost bittersweet, even though Novell thought she was a whore.

Hell, she'd been that. She made no apologies. But her most unforgivable sin in Novell's eyes was going to work for Robert Harlan.

"Ryan's still in love with his wife," Novell said. "Funny, isn't it? She was a bitch too."

Kate gave a shrug as if she didn't care, but cold sliced into her chest. Still, she wouldn't give Novell something else to hold over her head. Novell knew her at her worst, clinging to the edge of a toilet, barely able to stand. It didn't give him the right to tell her how to live.

"You used to be kind of decent, Novell. You get religion or what?"

"I'm just warning you, Kate. Don't think he's some kind of hero because you had sex with him."

"Why is it that men think women can't get over getting laid?" Kate examined her nails. She had a chip in her manicure and glared at the offending triangle of white in the smooth burgundy of her thumbnail. "Believe me, Novell. You see one dick, you've seen 'em all. Someday, I'll get me a dog, then I'll be content." She sat back down on the window seat.

"Ryan attracts some heartless women."

She pulled up her knees and rested her head on them. Heartless. That was almost funny. "How's Linda?"

"Still unconscious. You talk to the senator?"

"I told him I was with the police."

"You need to watch yourself with him."

Kate heard this lecture before. "I'll be all right."

"I'm serious, Kate. He's a predator. He likes to isolate—"

"He's never done anything improper." She didn't understand why Novell thought Senator Harlan would do anything to her. Sure, he was strange, but he'd always been kind to her. Sort of like a mentor.

Novell shook his head. "He doesn't work that way. He'll suck you dry and then discard you. I'm warning you, for your own good."

Kate focused on the salt truck that drove down the street. Its amber light flashed like a beacon. If she concentrated on that light, the snowplow, she could shut out the terrible pain in her nonexistent heart.

"Don't you have somewhere to be, Novell?"

"If Ryan comes here, you let me know."

"He's not stupid. He got what he wanted from me. Why should he come back?" That was what Novell expected. Cynical Kate. The whore.

What else could she do? When Thomas had died, she had to survive. She didn't have anyone to look out for her. If he'd lived a little longer, things might have been different. She didn't know why Thomas had signed on to be her angel, but he'd told her once she was his penance and redemption.

All she knew was that Thomas had paid for the surgery on her face. He'd given her a place to stay, helped her find a new identity. A girl with the same first name because he said it would be easier to remember, and Katie Shay of Belfast, Ireland, became Kate Reid of Deer Island, Maine.

It would've alarmed Thomas to see her with his son, the boy he'd been at odds with forever. One of those nights near the end, when the pain was bad and he was living on morphine, Thomas had told her Danny was conceived in anger, and he couldn't look at him without feeling ashamed.

"The Lord punished me," he'd said. "He took my Mary and left me with—every time I look at him . . ." He'd buried his face in his hands, his gaunt cheeks marred with tears.

No, Thomas wouldn't be happy, but it was too late. She'd jumped in the deep end. Or maybe that happened long ago.

Novell said, "Goodnight, Kate."

She startled at the sound of his voice.

Kate turned back to the window and reached out to touch the cold glass. She wanted to cry for Thomas and Danny Ryan and Katie Shay, the girl who died in the flames. The lost one.

45

Danny slid the disc Linda had given him into Theresa's laptop. He'd bought the computer for her when she insisted she needed it because she was going back to school any day. The trouble was that every few months, she had a new idea: dental hygienist, medical assistant, interior designer. He gave her points for sticking with the receptionist job she'd managed to secure with Jimmy Manisky. He wasn't sure if it was Theresa's typing skills or the fact that Jimmy had been sweet on her all his life. Now divorced from his third wife, Jimmy was still sweet on Theresa and had a thriving dental practice, despite his penchant for cheating wives and bad toupees and his unfortunate resemblance to an overweight Chihuahua. If Theresa had given him the slightest encouragement, he would have been her slave, but even Theresa had her standards.

He opened the files that popped up. The first was a restaurant review. The Red Door. Michael rated it four stars plus.

"Look behind the Red Door for Bruce Delhomme's real specialties. . . . Any fantasy your palate desires will be fulfilled here; Red Door caters to the outrageous . . ."

Kinky, for a restaurant review. Michael's style had improved, though it was out of place here. Or maybe it wasn't. Bruce

Delhomme of the shampoo commercial hair and overindulged child manners served up exotic food and what else?

Bruce Delhomme, friend of Andy and Robert Harlan. Danny made a note to check through the senator's campaign filings to see if Delhomme was a contributor and, if so, how big. The most recent filings wouldn't be out for a few more weeks, but he could go backward. He added Bartlett Scott to the list and then called Linda's appointment secretary and cajoled her to e-mail him the guest list.

"Linda wanted me to check out some names quietly," he told her. She had agreed tearfully after informing him she'd sent the same list to the police.

He didn't expect surprises. Most of the people who appeared were bound to show up on a donor list for Robert Harlan. It was always politically wise to hedge one's bets when donating to a candidate, even in the bitter partisan political atmosphere. Robert Harlan wasn't likely to be defeated in Pennsylvania; therefore, major donors were going to line his pockets whether they liked him or not. It guaranteed an audience. Robert Harlan was a business conservative: he talked family values but never let those hardcore conservative beliefs interfere with business interests.

Danny went back to the restaurant reviews. Twenty more restaurants—some of which he knew well. Michael rated fifteen of them four stars plus. It all seemed innocuous, except for Michael's vaguely obscene prose and the fact that half of them were mediocre places at best. Danny couldn't believe someone killed Michael over smutty restaurant reviews, and he didn't see the connection between upscale eateries and the Inferno.

Still, there had to be one or Michael wouldn't be dead.

Danny opened another file: Black Velvet. Michael rated it four stars plus and called it "a delightfully decadent feast for the voyeur but not hard core." Black Velvet of the lip-shaped couches and naked bodies was a whole different kind of feast, not exactly a place you'd recommend as a top nightspot in a mainstream paper. He wondered what Michael considered hard core until he opened the next file.

Club Midnight in Northern Liberties, which was, according to Michael, a Bruce Delhomme Enterprise, though not one on the record books. "Club Midnight is not for all tastes. . . . Private rooms upstairs have the real action. . . . The dungeon is reserved for special members. . . . Luscious leather and chains are available for those who like it hard. Bring your own whips and fantasies. Pain guaranteed. Four stars plus." Just below Michael had typed "Tophet." Danny wasn't sure if it was part of Club Midnight or a new entry he hadn't filled in.

None of this made sense. How could Michael compare sex clubs to restaurants? Unless the four stars plus wasn't a rating but some kind of code. A code that signified a connection to something. What did restaurants and sex clubs have in common? What did Club Midnight and Bruce Delhomme's upscale restaurants have in common?

What was it Zach had said? "It ain't a club—not like this. It's like management. It operates clubs, and depending on your level of membership, you get access."

Access to what?

A sex club where rich old coots got jacked off or something more? The Inferno was management. Maybe they managed clubs and provided special services. Danny was sure that Midnight was the sex club Theresa described. The one that specialized in S and M. She said there were levels of membership, and after they negotiated for a while, she even remembered where she put Vic's card. It was similar to the one he found at Michael's. This one was flashier, gold divided by a red line with a black drop in the center—just the thing for a dealer on the rise.

Amazing what money could do to jog the memory.

Dumbass. Concentrate.

One file remained: an image. Danny wasn't sure what he expected, maybe a dominatrix complete with whip and full leather ensemble. He wasn't prepared to see a photograph taken more than nine years ago at his father's funeral.

It had reached one hundred and four that day, a new record for the city. He remembered that Kevin's face had burned bright red above his dress uniform, and a waterfall of sweat had run down his forehead.

Poor Jean's pregnant belly had strained against her black cotton dress, and her ankles had looked like mottled sausages. Danny had held her arm when Kevin had accepted the American flag that had draped over the old man's coffin. Jean's arm had been slippery and fragile, as if the slender bones might snap under his fingers, and she labored to catch her breath. When he'd whispered to her to come back with him to the limo to sit in the air conditioning, she'd looked up at him both stricken and surprised.

"Oh, no, Danny. I couldn't, but thank you. I'm fine. Really. Please, no, this is your father's funeral."

"He's dead. He won't care."

Her mouth had dropped open, and that was the moment caught in the picture, seconds before the ubiquitous piper began to play "Amazing Grace" and they threw handfuls of dirt on the old man's coffin. Danny thought it would've been more fitting to dump shots of Dewar's in the grave but then figured the old man might come roaring back from hell if he knew they were wasting a drop of his beloved scotch.

Why did Michael go to the trouble to look up this picture? It was a strange choice.

Danny squinted at the photo and tried to decide what Michael might have been looking for in that sea of faces. Some were familiar. Cops for the most part. His coworkers from the paper. Curiosity seekers. A girl with her back to the camera, but something about her carriage reminded him of Kate. Weird, or perhaps he had Kate on his mind.

A face in the corner caught his eye, and he leaned closer. Bartlett Scott. Now that was peculiar. Danny tried to remember if he had spoken to the great man himself and decided he hadn't. In the photograph, Bartlett Scott looked vigorous, with a full head of blondish hair and a slim build. It reminded Danny of someone, but he couldn't force the image into his head. He made a note. He needed more information. He knew Bartlett Scott had lost a son to cancer, and of course, there was the daughter, but he thought there was a second son. Why was Bartlett Scott at the old man's funeral? He hadn't come because Thomas Ryan was a kindly man. More likely, he wanted to make sure the old man was dead.

Why had Michael pulled this picture? Did he have suspicions about the great philanthropist of Philadelphia? Bartlett Scott built hospital wings and performing arts centers. The thought of him prowling around a place like Black Velvet made Danny's skin crawl. *Some are born to endless night.* Was Bartlett Scott talking about himself when he dropped that gem?

This just got weirder and weirder.

Michael must have been nosing around clubs and discovered the Inferno. That much made sense. Danny's own father had talked about the Inferno—Kevin had admitted that much—but what had he meant? What the hell did Michael find? Some kind of link? Zach had told him the Inferno was management. It provided access. The more money you paid, the more access you got. But what did that mean? He needed to get out of here and talk to Andy. He needed wheels.

He should have talked to Michael when he had the chance, but he'd been too busy popping pills and wallowing in his own misery. God, he loved those pills. He'd line them up and swallow them down until the pain faded to a tolerable ache and life lost its hard edges and bright colors. He'd drifted into a perpetual twilight, like falling into deep snow.

"Can't you see what you're doing to yourself?" Michael had said that night when he'd dropped in unannounced and unwanted. Michael had paced the family room and swallowed tequila straight from the bottle.

It was summer, and he'd worn a hideous red, orange, and purple Hawaiian shirt that had gaped open enough to reveal his massive beer gut. Danny had heard Beowulf growl beside him, and it snapped him out of his stupor enough to pay attention.

"You've got to stop this shit right now." Michael had slammed down the bottle. "I love you. Conor and Beth are dead. I'm your brother. I won't let you kill yourself." He'd headed for the stairs.

It was the only thing Michael could have done that got Danny running, but he'd tripped on the uneven back steps. The toilet had flushed before he'd reached the second floor. When he'd skidded through the bathroom door, Danny had seen the pill bottles lying empty in the sink. A few of his precious friends had scattered across the floor like jewels against the beige tile.

"Asshole!" He'd started toward Michael. "You have no right—"

Michael had pulled out a .22 from behind and aimed it at him. "I'd rather shoot you than see you like this!"

Beowulf had barreled through the door, and Danny had grabbed his collar. The dog's momentum had driven him to his knees and dragged him halfway across the bathroom, but he had known if he let go, Beowulf would go for Michael's throat, and Michael might shoot.

"Put the gun down, Michael." Danny had forced himself to speak in a rational voice. If he weren't afraid for Beowulf, he would have launched himself at Michael and hoped for once Michael wouldn't screw up.

"You don't know." Great sobs had racked Michael's body. "Listen to me. I know things. You have to come back."

"You know shit. You want me back because I've saved your sorry ass for the last sixteen years. Who's rewriting your column now that I'm not there?"

Michael had slumped as if he'd been kicked. His mouth had opened and closed. The gun had drooped in his hand. "But you have to . . . You can write—"

"I don't want to write. I want to be left alone." Danny had pulled himself to his feet and dragged Beowulf with him to the master bedroom. "If you're going to shoot me, go ahead. Otherwise, let yourself out. Don't come back."

They didn't speak again until Michael had crashed into his duck pond.

Now he knew that Michael was right. He knew things.

Not all accidents are accidents, and Beth and Conor certainly hadn't been one. Beth and Conor were dead because of him. They had been driving his car. If he hadn't fallen apart, he would've realized something was wrong about the crash. He should have known.

Beth was in awful shape. Danny hadn't recognized her at first, and he'd stood for a long time, staring until her features began to rearrange themselves into their familiar lines and angles.

But there hadn't been a mark on Conor's body. He'd just been so cold. And Danny had thought if he could only hold him, Conor would grow warm again. His heart would start to beat, and his skin would turn pink instead of that bloodless white.

Familiar pain gnawed at his stomach. He'd let them slip away. He couldn't hold on to Beth, to Conor. To anyone. The sense of his own impotence overwhelmed him like the thick silence that lay over the house. He bowed his head against the window. Cold. He was cold. He was so good at using smartass remarks or, worse, silence as a shield. Because nobody was ever going to beat him up again. Ever.

A car door slammed, and he jerked up his head.

Theresa's street hadn't been plowed, and most of the cars still stood buried under thick drifts. Only Theresa's footsteps leading away from the house disturbed the pristine white. At the end of the block, though, Danny could see a black Crown Vic parked lengthwise. It blocked the intersection.

Novell walked toward the house alone.

46

Ravel's "The Fairy Garden" played, and Mason settled back on his white brocade divan to watch his movie. Though a tad underlit, the film possessed a softer reality, and the gold lights on the ceiling twinkled like fairy lights.

Amazing what you could do with those miniature cameras. You could hide them almost anywhere.

Mason clasped his hands together. It was all so lovely, except that Danny Ryan hadn't been like he'd imagined. He pictured a meeting of minds, a joining of souls, but it wasn't that way at all.

Ryan preferred that tarty redhead. Lovely skin, but clearly a harlot. She draped herself around Ryan like a boa constrictor. Mason clicked off the movie in disgust.

The woman came between them. Kate Reid, Robert Harlan's assistant. She looked oddly familiar. He would have to find out more about her.

It didn't matter. They'd promised him. They wanted information from Ryan, but after that, Mason had a special place for him. Right here.

Mason looked up at the wings that glittered above his head; they spun slightly in the air. Pale streams of sun bled through the skylight. It reflected off the jewels and sequins and sent shimmers dancing across the room. Fairies come to call.

For a moment, his wall of photographs glowed with an unearthly golden light, and Mason felt his breath catch at the back of his throat. Those eyes. Tears slid down his cheeks.

Here was beauty wrought by the exquisite hand of suffering. That was Ryan's destiny, his true purpose. It was glorious, really, to bear such torment in life.

And Mason knew it was his purpose to help Ryan find redemption through his pain. It would be his greatest achievement. His masterpiece. The last photograph he would add to his collection. The one he would take when Danny Ryan's spirit fled his body forever.

47

Vic Ceriano was a drug dealer, a wife-beater, and a low-life son of a bitch, but he had an extensive gun collection. Danny gave him a silent blessing for that when he pulled out the gun case from under Theresa's bed and selected a Glock. It was oiled and loaded. Danny took a moment to enjoy the feel of it in his hands before he chambered a round.

He heard the front door creak open. Novell would check out the downstairs first. Danny unscrewed the hall light and crept to the stairwell. He listened to Novell's measured footsteps and heard him click the light switch. The hall remained murky.

If he was lucky, Novell was hungover.

The footsteps came closer, and Danny gripped the gun in both hands. He saw Novell's feet and then his knees. He pointed the gun at Novell's chest and said, "Detective Novell, I'd say nice to see you, but I wish you'd leave me the hell alone."

"You really don't want to point that gun at a police officer." Novell sounded calm, but Danny could see the irritation and surprise that twisted his mouth into a grim line.

Danny came down three steps. "I can use it too. My father made me learn to field-strip a gun before I was eight. Impressive, don't you think?"

If he didn't get it right, the old man would make him start from scratch. If he still couldn't do it, the old man would take his belt to him. Instruction through intimidation. Thomas Patrick Ryan wrote that book.

"You can't stay here," Novell said.

"And you can't force me into protective custody. I'm a citizen. I've got rights."

"You won't have anything if you're dead."

"I'd appreciate it if you'd lay your weapons on the floor. You can start with your SIG and finish with the .22 strapped to your ankle."

"I just want to talk."

Danny's fingers tightened on the butt until his knuckles blanched. Guns always had that power over him, as though when he picked one up, a switch went on. Maybe that's why he was able to hit those perfect clusters on the shooting range—one of his few skills that had always earned his father's approval. He was the best shot in the family.

Danny met Novell's eyes. "The guns. On the floor. Now."

Novell laid his SIG Sauer on the floor, and Danny watched him gauge the distance between them.

"Put down your backup and step away."

"This case is bigger than Michael Cohen's murder." Novell nudged the SIG toward Danny, but it stuck in the brown shag carpeting.

"No shit, Sherlock. Your backup too."

"All right. The feds have been looking into the Inferno for more than eight years, and you want to know whose name keeps popping up?"

"I thought you weren't a fed anymore."

"I'm not. That doesn't mean I don't have connections. I was part of the original investigation. I knew all about you long before Michael Cohen crashed into your duck pond."

"What are you talking about?"

"You were under FBI surveillance for a year and a half."

Danny leaned against the wall and tried not to let Novell see the impact his words had. Christ, was someone peeking through the windows of his home? He cringed when he thought about the times Beth and he made love in the pool or on the floor in the family room. When they fought. All their intimate moments.

"Why in the hell would I be under surveillance?"

"As a possible link to the Inferno."

"You pull my name out of your ass?"

Novell shrugged. "You sold drugs for your brother-in-law."

"And that's bullshit." A red haze began to cloud Danny's vision. He was tired of Novell's head games. "You know, I might be a little out of practice, but I can probably take out your knee-cap from here."

"You aren't that stupid."

"I'm that pissed off. Why investigate me?"

"You put down the gun, and I'll tell you."

"Do I look like a fool? I put down the gun, and you arrest me."

"I won't arrest you. You have my word."

"What assurance do I have?"

"None. You'll just have to trust me."

Trust me. I'm from the government; I'm here to help. One of the five great lies. Danny's finger tightened on the trigger. He could shoot the bastard and plead self-defense, but he knew he wouldn't. Some doors were meant to stay locked.

"Tell you what," Novell said. "I'll give you a name, then you can decide whether or not to shoot me."

"All right, Novell. Go ahead."

"Senator Robert Harlan."

48

Kate balanced her notebook on her knees and scribbled. Her pen jerked when the limo bounced over the cobblestones on Dock Street and then turned onto Delaware Avenue. She hoped she'd be able to read her writing when she got back to the office.

"And, Kate," Senator Harlan said, "one more thing. Albert will take you out to the house this morning. Mrs. Harlan needs you."

"Sorry?" Kate almost dropped her pen.

"For the party at the Pyramid Club. She'll go over the guest list so you can get out the press releases. She may have a few errands. You know how important this night is going to be."

"Of course." Kate swallowed. She was sure there'd be more than a few errands, and the next two weeks now promised to be pure hell. The real reason Mrs. Harlan wanted her was it was almost Christmas and she had errands to run. Stamps that would have to be stuck on letters—and not just stuck: measured and placed exactly one-sixteenth of an inch from the top and right edge of the envelopes. Thousands of them.

He leaned a little closer. She wanted to move away but forced herself to sit still.

"I've been meaning to talk to you, but it's been awkward with all the unpleasantness over the weekend."

Unpleasantness? An odd way of putting it. "You mean Linda Cohen?"

"Exactly."

His black eyes seemed cold and dead. Then he smiled, and she thought she must've imagined it. Why did Novell's warning keep echoing in her head?

He's a predator.

She knew he could be difficult. He expected his staff to perform up to exacting standards, but he had an image to uphold. When she went out into the world, she represented him. Naturally, he worried about her behavior. That was normal. Wasn't it?

"I'm concerned about you."

"Me? Why?" A niggle of unease began to bubble in her stomach. She closed her notepad and folded her hands.

He'd fired his former legislative aide because she had a smart mouth. She wore her skirts too short and too tight. She dated the wrong guy. Whatever happened to her? Kate didn't know. She moved away. Didn't leave a forwarding address.

But the senator was different with her. Kate heard the whispers in the office. She knew everyone thought they were sleeping together. Hell, even she expected him to put the moves on her. What difference would it have made? One more guy she had to fake it with. When he didn't, it confused her because he seemed weirdly paternal, kind in that formal way of his. Sometimes she caught him watching her, not the way the pigs in the bars did, like they were ready to take her right on a table, but with a strange, almost bemused look, like maybe he'd surprised himself.

The senator cleared his throat. "At the Cohens' party, Patricia and I noticed you dancing with Daniel Ryan. You seemed . . . intimate."

"Intimate?" Kate frowned. "We were dancing. He's very good at it."

Good at dancing. Good at a number of things. An unexpected rush of warmth coursed through her body. Mother of God, she was blushing.

"You know I feel . . . well, protective of you, Kate. I hate to say this, but Daniel's a very troubled young man."

"Troubled?"

"You know he was married to my daughter."

"Yes, I—"

"Unhappily, I'm afraid." The senator pressed his lips together. "Patricia and I warned Beth, but she only saw the charm. The good looks." Tears welled in his eyes, and he paused to catch his breath. "He came from an abusive background, so I suppose it wasn't entirely his fault."

"He was . . . abusive?" A cold lump in Kate's stomach replaced the nice, warm glow. She didn't expect this. Danny always seemed so gentle, but so did Thomas. Her saint. She knew he'd been a drinker. She knew he took his rages out on his sons. Even if she hadn't read Danny's notebooks, she'd seen the scars on his body.

"My father was handy with a belt," he'd said when she fingered the fine web of white lines on his back, though he didn't comment when she touched the ugly six-inch line that cut through his dark hair into his scalp. If you called abuse discipline, did that make it acceptable?

The senator put his face in his hands. "I was such a fool. I should have stepped in, but I didn't want a scandal. I was weak, Kate. I lost my daughter. My grandson." His voice shook. "I'm sorry. It sounds trite, but to lose a child . . . Beth was everything to me."

"I'm sorry. I know—I . . . I'm so sorry." Kate squeezed her pen against her damp palm. It was horrible. She didn't know what to do. In the entire time since the funeral, the senator never once betrayed any emotion like this in front of her.

Even at the funeral, he was calm. It was so terribly crowded that she never went through the receiving line, but she remembered Senator Harlan. He spoke to people like they were there for cocktails. Smiled, shook hands. Worked the crowd.

Danny was the one who looked hollowed out and alone. She didn't know how he could be surrounded by people yet appear so solitary. Maybe that was part of his appeal. He was a lost one too.

Ryan's still in love with his wife.

She tried to forget Novell's words, but they remained stuck. She hated him for saying them. Why was it never her turn? A tear spilled down her cheek before she could blink it back, and she swiped at it in horror. Thank God the senator was still looking down.

The car stopped at City Helicopter, and Kate watched the senator take another deep breath. When he looked up at her, though, his face appeared composed. That quickly, he pulled himself together.

"I'm sorry to have burdened you, my dear," he said and patted her hand. "It's just that you've been with me for some time now. I think of you as, well, family."

"I appreciate your concern, sir."

"Then you aren't seeing him?"

"We were dancing. You're kind to worry though."

He watched her for a moment longer, and Kate wondered why she felt like he was reaching inside her, touching her in some strange, intimate way, as if she sat naked in front of him. Kate clasped her notebook and pen against her like a shield. "Is there anything else, Senator? Any last-minute instructions?"

"There is one thing, Kate. You've worked for me for some time now."

Kate nodded. Almost three years, but who was counting? It was a good job, and she'd been lucky to get it. The only time trolling the clubs ever paid off for her. She picked up the senator's campaign manager. He got laid, and she got a job. A good deal all around.

"I've been thinking it's time you made the move from Philadelphia to Washington."

"Washington?" Two weeks ago she would've been elated. Today it sounded like he condemned her to Siberia.

"I know it would be a change, but you don't have family here, do you? And it would mean a raise in salary as well as many other benefits." His voice spread over her like oil, thick and suffocating.

"It's so sudden." Kate couldn't look at him. "I'm flattered."

"Of course, this move is your choice, Kate, but I'm sure you'll recognize it for the opportunity it is."

"Yes, Senator."

Kate knew that Washington wasn't a choice. She would go or else. Kate wasn't sure what the "or else" was.

He leaned forward and placed his palms on either side of her legs. His long fingers just brushed her thighs, and her skin shuddered away from his touch. She was trapped, his face inches from hers.

"You're a very bright girl, Kate, and a lovely one. You'll make the right decision."

It was a wonder she could hear him at all. Her blood pulsed so hard that it seemed to roar inside her head. The air felt thick and heavy, and she wanted to scream, but it was as if a boulder lodged in her throat. When she looked at the senator, his eyes glittered in triumph.

"We'll have a more intimate discussion after the holidays, my dear."

He sat back and knocked on the window. Albert opened the door, and Kate watched the senator walk to a waiting chopper. His navy overcoat flapped like giant wings.

49

"Jesus, Andy."

Andy huddled on a bench just inside the ICU waiting room. His unshaven face looked gray, sunken. His hands shook. Andy still wore his tuxedo, and his white hair stood in matted clumps around his head. Danny sat next to him.

Andy licked his raw lips. "You wouldn't have a pint in your pocket, babe? I keep asking, but no one will humor me here."

"How bad are you feeling?"

Andy's eyes filled, and he took wheezing breaths that sounded like he was choking. "Ran out this morning."

Danny glanced around the room. He wondered where all the party guys were—the ones who sucked down Andy's liquor and snorted Andy's coke, who vacationed at the Palm Beach house and partied at the clubs, always on Andy's dime.

"I'll get you a pint." Danny put his arm around Andy. "You need anything else? A change of clothes?"

"Goddamn woman. Drove me crazy. I cheated all the time." Andy's voice cracked. He cleared his throat. "But we're a team. I love her."

"I know you do."

Andy pulled back and ran his hands back and forth through his hair. "No, you don't. You don't have a clue. You didn't love Beth. You didn't give a damn about her."

But it wasn't true. That was the hell of it. Long after the giddy melody of their courtship faded, Danny would watch Beth in those unguarded moments when she was just drifting off to sleep or reading to Conor and see the sunlit woman he loved. She had always hidden her best self: the woman who would buy gourmet treats for Beowulf, who would build Legos with Conor, and who would ruin a four-thousand-dollar dress pulling him into the swimming pool to make love.

"Do you need anything else? Besides a pint."

Andy's hand clamped down on his shoulder, but Danny wouldn't look up. He concentrated on the white tile floor, trying to shut out the tightness in his chest. Andy leaned closer. He smelled fetid. "I want you to go to my house. I'll call ahead and have them pack me a suitcase, but I want you to go to my bedroom. There's a safe in the wall behind the Picasso. I'll give you the combination. When I die, I'm leaving it to you. The Picasso, that is."

"Don't you think a museum would be more appropriate?"

"You are a museum, with a head filled with little factoids. Someone should display you in a case."

Andy looked entirely capable of sawing off his head, like some insane mortician with his spotty tuxedo and three-day-old beard.

"What do you want me to take?"

"There's a package inside."

"What kind of package?"

"Just get it." Andy pulled Danny against him. "I'm sorry, Daniel. Sorry you got dragged into this. I thought we'd get a chance to work together again."

"Andy, I—"

"Don't waste your breath, and don't come back without a pint."

50

Danny wasn't certain what to expect when he ventured into Andy's bedroom: a trapeze hanging from a mirrored ceiling, multiple handcuffs attached to the back of the bed, boxes of foil. Nothing would have surprised him. The room, however, was disappointingly normal if ornate, filled with heavy mahogany furniture covered with purple-and-gold velvet upholstery. A selection of paintings in the style of Rembrandt decorated the walls; they clashed with the Picasso hanging over the bed. Danny didn't know about the other paintings, but he knew the Picasso was genuine, a blue nude with pendulous breasts.

He wasn't sure whether Linda had genuinely liked the painting or had been making a statement when she bought it at auction. He did know she'd paid a small fortune for it and never displayed it publicly.

"He's sleeping with multimillion dollar breasts," she'd said once. "Even they don't satisfy him."

Andy had always called it the blue-tit horror. At the hospital, he'd been somewhat more restrained.

There was nothing in the safe. At least nothing that counted as an insurance policy. Twenty thousand in cash, some monogrammed cuff links, and what appeared to be a full baggie of coke. Danny removed the coke and flushed it. Let Andy bitch and moan. The last thing he needed was cocaine sitting in his safe.

Danny went down to Andy's office and fired up the computer. Like most people, Andy kept his passwords in his desk drawer hidden in a small address book. Danny scrolled through quickly, looking for anything that looked suspicious. There wasn't much. Andy had fought the onslaught of the computer age with great vigor. Even computer porn lacked a certain entertainment value Andy craved.

He liked his sex live.

"When I'm ninety-two and can't get it up, maybe I'll like all that shit," he'd said more than once. "Some of those sites are fucking sick."

Danny checked Andy's bank accounts. Every month on the fifteenth, Andy withdrew one hundred thousand dollars from his main checking account and noted the withdrawal as "business expenses." There were smaller withdrawals from some of his other accounts always around the fifteenth, which were similarly notated. It added up to two million a year. In Andy's world, it wasn't a great deal of cash, but Danny wondered where the hell the money went. Booze? Nose candy? Women?

Something was definitely amiss in Andyland.

*

"What do you mean, empty?" Andy's face turned a deep red, and he glared at Danny as if he were lying.

"There was nothing there."

Andy slumped down on the bench and held out his hand. Danny handed him a fifth of Glenfiddich. Andy opened the bottle. He downed a quarter of it without pausing for breath.

"What was in the safe?" Danny crouched in front of Andy and peered up at him.

Andy stared straight ahead. "Insurance." He lifted the fifth and sucked down another gulp. "Life insurance. One hell of a policy." Andy let the fifth fall from his hands, and Danny caught it before it crashed onto the floor. "Well, we're all fucked now. No getting around it. Sins of the father, Daniel."

It had to be the package. "Why the hell didn't you check for it after Michael died?"

"Why would I? Michael didn't know about the safe. Or the combination, as far as I knew."

"Michael probably cracked the goddamn safe in a minute. He was bringing me whatever was in it. So what was in it?"

"Let's just say your worst nightmare."

Danny wanted to hit him with the bottle. "Could you be more specific?"

Andy took a breath, and Danny watched a tear roll down his cheek. "You know, you were fifteen when I met you. Do you remember that? You wrote that essay about your night in prison. I still have it."

"It was a long time ago, Andy." What the hell was wrong with him?

"You were a tough little bastard and so fucking talented. Where does that come from? Why you instead of Michael? We gave him everything, but we couldn't give him that."

"Jesus, it always comes back to Michael, doesn't it?"

Andy reached down, clutched Danny's free hand, and dragged him closer. "No, you idiot. It always comes back to you. I loved you, and he knew it. He was bringing you that package because he knew you'd take care of it."

"I was sitting on my ass trying to put two sentences together."

Andy shook his head. "You were stewing in your own self-pity, but that doesn't work for you. Michael knew that. It's anger that drives you. Your best stuff was ninety-nine percent fury, and every bit of it was aimed at your old man. But you can't say that, can you?"

Danny stared at the liver spots on Andy's hand. The antiseptic hospital smell overwhelmed him.

"No, you can't say it. Just like you could never admit that every time you looked at that boy of yours, you wondered how much of your old man really was inside of you. Whether one day you'd lose it just like he did." Andy's fingers closed like pincers against his bones. "And everyone always said, 'Look how wonderful Danny is with his son. Look how patient.' But I could see that deep down, you were scared. You were fucking terrified."

Danny gritted his teeth against the pain. He wanted to scream at Andy to let go, but he didn't. If he opened that door just a little and let the anger out, he might not get it back inside. Or maybe if he began to scream, he never would be able to stop.

"Why didn't you tell me the truth about Beth?" Andy said.

"What the hell are you talking about?" Danny thought Andy's fingers might go through his hand.

Tears ran down Andy's cheeks. "I thought you beat her! Goddammit!"

"Andy, she's dead! Why does it matter?" Danny began to shiver. It was like they teetered on the edge of the abyss again.

"Because I—Why couldn't you just have had vices like the rest of us? But you couldn't, could you? And I should've known. I did know. Oh fuck. It doesn't matter anymore. Just tell me that I saved you after all. Kept you from the seventh circle of hell. Give me that much, Daniel."

Maybe Andy did save him. If it hadn't been for Andy, he might still be in South Philly hustling drugs. Or worse. "You gave me my life."

Andy relaxed his grip on Danny's hand, and he smiled. "Now I will most certainly be in the eighth circle with the other hypocrites and frauds, but don't worry. I won't be alone."

Danny looked at the little mole to the left of Andy's nose and tried to ignore the stench of scotch that made his stomach pitch and roll. Then he understood. The circles of hell. The Inferno. And Andy was right up at the top of the order.

"Oh Christ, Andy, you're one of them."

"That essay you wrote will be worth money someday. You'll want it back, Daniel, but I won't give it to you. You'll have to wait 'til I've shuffled off this mortal coil."

Danny didn't care about the goddamn essay. Andy was a member of the Inferno. He was sure of it. "Christ Jesus, Michael was your son."

Andy kissed Danny's forehead, and Danny knew that Andy was somehow pulling him close and pushing him away at the same time. Maybe for the last time, and Danny wondered why he always seemed to be standing on the other side of the window. Looking out or looking in, it didn't seem to matter. He was always on the wrong side.

Tears welled in his eyes, and he blinked them back. Goddamn Andy.

"It's not so tragic, Daniel. You Irish enjoy your sorrows too much."

"It gives us an excuse to drink." The words scratched his throat.

"But you don't drink. That's always been your problem." He looked for a moment like the old Andy, full of life. Full of the devil. "You're my mitzvah. When you write the story, don't let me down." Andy fumbled in his pocket and pulled out a black card from a silver case. Both shiny and matte, it was divided on the diagonal by a red line, and in its middle, a gold teardrop outlined in red glittered in the fluorescent light. He pressed the card into Danny's hand. "This is one of four. Don't show it to anyone."

Before he could answer, Danny heard the soft squeak of padded shoes moving across the floor. The ICU nurse beckoned to Andy. "Mr. Cohen, you may go in now." She smiled at Danny. "Is this your son?"

Andy's shoulders slumped, and the years piled back on him. "My son's dead." Andy pulled himself to his feet and lurched toward the door. He paused and said, "My mitzvah." Then he was gone.

Danny couldn't move. The ground seemed to yawn beneath him, and he clung to the slenderest of threads. The Inferno. Michael had grabbed the biggest story of his godforsaken career all right. He'd stolen it from his father.

51

lbert held the car door open for Kate. "What time should I pick you up tomorrow, Miss?"

"You don't need to pick me up, Albert."

"Senator Harlan asked me to make sure you got to and from work safely, Miss. Shall I be here at eight?"

"Make it eight thirty. I'm exhausted."

He nodded. "You want me to see you to your apartment?"

"That won't be necessary. Thanks."

It seemed like it took hours for her to climb the steps to the third floor. If she could throw herself into a hot bath, maybe she'd no longer hear Patricia Harlan's voice barking out commands or feel watched by photographs of Beth Harlan. Danny's wife.

Most important, maybe Robert Harlan would no longer coat her skin. Kate unlocked the door and pushed it open, but before she could hit the light switch, someone grabbed her and pulled her close. A hand closed over her mouth.

"Don't scream," Danny said.

*

Kate pulled the heavy living room curtains closed. Bits of dust swirled in the air. She always meant to get rid of the curtains because they were old, worn things made of heavy brown material and stained and tattered with age. Now she was glad for them.

"What are you doing here?" she said. "How did you get in?"

He stepped from the shadows of the tiny foyer and gave her a half smile. "Your friend Novell. How long have you two known each other?"

Kate wasn't sure whether to feel glad or furious to see him. She decided on anger. "Novell had no right."

"I'm sorry, Kate. I was afraid someone might be watching. I don't want you to get into trouble because of me." Exhaustion replaced the cool amusement in his voice.

"I'm already in trouble because of you. Senator Harlan thinks you're a dangerous man."

He didn't answer, but a muscle in his jaw flexed. She saw the anger, controlled but smoldering in his eyes, tightening his mouth. She felt unsure of him. Or maybe intimacy made her feel vulnerable. Naked.

She wished he hadn't seen her naked.

She'd slept with men. She'd never left herself open to any of them. Until now. What wonderful timing on her part. "The senator said you were . . . abusive." The word sounded so harsh, so ugly hanging between them.

Danny winced, but the half smile remained in place. "That's rich. Sorry to disappoint, but it wasn't quite that way."

She could still feel his hands on her. The way he pulled her against him. He was capable of violence, she was sure of it, but he hadn't hurt her. Scared her, but nothing more. "Then how was it?"

"Beth and I were going through a rough patch. Her family never thought I was good enough for her."

"Why would she say you were abusing her?"

"She thought we were heading for a divorce, and she knew I'd fight her. Beth was a very smart woman. A lawyer. She was laying the groundwork."

Kate stared at him in disbelief. How could he talk so calmly about his wife? As if they'd had a minor spat?

"Why would you want to stay married?"

"Conor." The word came out so soft, she barely heard it. "We had a hard marriage. Neither of us was easy, and Beth could seem tough if you didn't know her. I was the one who took Conor to playdates, handled school, you know, Mr. Mom, all that, but she loved him. She read to him, played with him. Her schedule was just difficult."

"She thought that would hurt her chance of custody."

"Yeah. Weird, considering the money angle, but I had a shot. One of the top divorce lawyers in the city agreed to represent me—if it came to it—pro bono. I met her at a party about five months before the accident." Danny's voice started soft and grew so quiet that she had to strain to hear him. It was almost like he was talking to himself. "Beth wanted to raise him the way she'd been raised—you know, Princeton prep? He had his own squash pro, golf and piano lessons, and a tutor. She wanted him to be just like her, and he just wasn't. Too much like me, I guess. It drove her crazy. We both did. He was five years old. He liked running in the park and playing Star Wars. He could write stories, you know. Little stories. He used to tell her he wanted to be a writer like me. She felt like a bad mother, and her parents didn't help. We had some battles, but I never hit her. We always found a way to work things out."

Danny looked away, but not before Kate saw the flicker in his eyes. Something deep and raw, like a festering wound. She watched him take a breath. When he turned back to her, his face was unreadable, almost as if he had drawn a shutter closed, and Kate knew it didn't matter what Beth Ryan was or wasn't, Danny wouldn't discuss her any further. However their marriage ended, he'd once loved his wife very much. And wasn't it funny to be jealous of a dead woman?

"Look, I'm sorry. I didn't mean to scare you. I shouldn't have just shown up like this," he said. "I'll go and check out Michael's club tonight."

"What are you talking about?" Cold curled around her insides. He'd gotten in trouble already checking out Michael's clubs.

"Someplace called Midnight. Maybe he mentioned it to you."

Kate wrapped her arms around her stomach. "Does Novell know you're planning to go there?"

"I didn't mention it to him." And from the tight, cold note in his voice, she was sure he didn't plan to mention it.

"Don't you need to be a member to get in to a place like that?"

He hesitated, then reached into his back pocket and pulled out a gold-and-silver card with a black flame in the center. "Would this get me in?"

Kate leaned back against the wall. Danny hadn't gotten that card from Michael. "Where did you get that?"

"Are you all right?" He put the card back and wrapped his arms around her, pulling her against him. "What's wrong?"

What could she say? She promised not to speak.

She wanted to tell him about so many things. The truth about Michael. That card he held. Thomas. But she was afraid, so she rested her head against his shoulder, closed her eyes, and let him soothe her. As if he cared.

He didn't push her for an explanation, but Thomas always said Danny was the smart one.

"I have two sons left," Thomas said. "Kevin's slow, but he has a good heart. Danny's got a brain. No heart, though, and he'd sell out his mother, God rest her soul, for a story. Don't forget that, Kate."

But Thomas was wrong. Danny had a heart. He just kept it locked away. She had to believe that.

"Don't go." Not when everything was coming apart.

He framed her face with his hands. "Kate."

"Don't talk. I don't want to talk."

Danny lowered his mouth to hers, and it was like the night they danced at the Four Seasons, when they swayed together like branches in a summer breeze, and she felt overcome by that giddy, light-headed rush. She wanted him then. She needed him now, and though she knew better, she'd hope for a happy ending.

She slid the gold card out of his rear pocket just like a pro.

52

"There's a monster in my closet."

Conor stood at the foot of the bed with Beowulf at his side. He wore his Batman pajamas and gripped his blue lightsaber in his right hand. His hair stood up around his head in a sleep-tousled mess. "There's a monster in my closet. I can hear him, Daddy. Make him go away. He says he'll eat me."

Danny reached out but felt nothing. He shook with cold, and he moved so slowly, he didn't know what was wrong with him. Then he realized it was the mothballs. Thousands of mothballs. They lay in shining heaps on the floor. He tried to push through them, but they grasped his ankles with tiny hands and held him back.

"Daddy! Make the monster go away!"

Danny could hear Conor crying in the dark, and he tried to call to him, but his voice was paralyzed.

Panic settled over him, thick and suffocating, and he could hear his own heart thunder in his chest. Dear God, he needed to move. What the hell was matter with him?

The monster screamed, "Where are you, you little shit?"

Danny saw the closet door ahead, but when he jerked it open, Andy Cohen stood inside with a .357. He held it out to Danny and grinned. "This is for you, pal."

*

Danny knocked against Kate's orange crate bookcase. It caught his elbow and sent a shot of agony to his fingertips. At six o'clock in the morning, enough ambient streetlight washed through the window to enable him to see. He could hear the cars move down Spruce Street. Somewhere, a door slammed. A siren wailed.

He took a deep breath. There was comfort in the early morning traffic, the warmth of Kate's body, the shivers of pain that ran from his left elbow into his hand. They were real. He could focus on them. *Don't think about Conor. Don't think about Beowulf. Don't think about the monster. Don't think about Andy and his one of four cards.*

Kate shifted and moaned, and Danny eased himself up. He pulled on his jeans and went into the bathroom. He needed to act normal, but his life no longer bore any resemblance to normal.

He rested his head against the mirror. Waiting for the tightness in his chest to pass, he gripped the sides of the sink.

It was never going to end.

He had to pull himself together. Danny lifted his head and stared at himself in the mirror. People used to tell him all the time he looked young for his age, and before the accident, some smartass bartenders or liquor store clerks would card him. No one would make that mistake now. He looked as waxen as Conor when he lay in the morgue.

Danny went back to the bedroom. Kate had left the window open, and he could see his breath. He closed the window, sat on the edge of the bed, and looked at her, at the way her hair spread in a dark tangle across the pillow. He leaned closer to finger an errant curl.

Kate had awakened the desperate need in him to be close to someone again. When he was with her, he wanted to memorize her body with his hands, every curve and plane and line, every glorious imperfection. It scared the hell out of him because she was opaque; shadow and form he could feel but not understand.

They moved well together, their rhythm perfectly matched. If less frenzied than with Beth, it was also less of a battle. Loving Beth was ferocious. They devoured each other.

Kate was different. When he kissed her, he tasted both her hunger and her doubt. Her loneliness. It curled about her like a faint echo. She was like the dreams he used to have when he first left home. He would be walking down corridors opening doors, but after every door there was another door to open, another knob to turn.

She knows about the Inferno. The thought came unbidden. He wanted to push it away, but it wouldn't go—the way she reacted last night when she saw the card Theresa gave him. He wondered if she knew about Andy. Kate knew Michael, Novell. Something about her accent bothered him. That flat voice. She was no more from Maine than he was.

Danny looked around the bedroom. Who lived like this? She had no pictures. None of the little personal things, the mementos people collected over time. If his home was too filled with memories and reminders, it at least bore witness to the lives lived there. If Kate disappeared tomorrow, she would go without leaving any footprints.

He squinted at her bookcase. Jammed among the paperbacks sat a worn copy of *The Collected Poems of William Butler Yeats*. His mother had loved Yeats; he remembered reading the poems out of a similar volume to her when she lay dying. He wondered what had happened to it. Kevin never had much of a poetic streak.

He leaned closer and pulled out the book. How many afternoons had he spent reading to his mother? "Brown Penny." She loved that one. "The Wild Swans at Coole." Peculiar. This looked just like her book with the same water stain on the front. He began to flip through it when he found a photograph stuck between the pages as a marker.

Danny almost dropped the book. The photograph inside had to be at least ten years old because Kate was little more than a kid herself. Slender and small with her thick hair hanging over her shoulders, she looked like a good Catholic schoolgirl in her St. Maria Goretti uniform, and she held the hand of a man who smiled down at her as if she were his most precious treasure.

Thomas Patrick Ryan. His father.

53

"Danny?"

He heard her groggy voice and slammed the book shut, shoving it behind him. Kate pushed herself up, her face still soft with sleep, and he stared at her in a sort of panic.

She slid her hand down his arm, and her fingers left a warm trail against his flesh. Even now he could feel her begin to melt into him, seep beneath his skin. "Get under the covers. You're freezing."

He started to lean toward her when the vision popped into his head: Kate and the Iceman, Lolita in a Goretti uniform with her grinning Humbert Humbert. He jerked back as if she'd grown a viper's head.

"What's the matter?" He watched her coil up inside herself, shutting him out. Before his eyes, she was turning into someone else. A stranger.

"Who are you, Kate?"

She pulled the covers around her, her eyes flat and wary. "You know who I am. What's the matter with you?"

"How did you know my father?"

She caught her breath. "What do you mean?"

"My father. Thomas. Patrick. Ryan." He fumbled for the book.

"I don't know what you're talking about."

He pulled out the photograph and shoved it under her nose. "Does this jog your memory?"

"Oh God." She pressed her hands against her mouth as if she were going to be sick and began to rock on the bed.

"How did you know him, Kate?"

She had to know the man in the photograph was his father. She had to know. Unless . . . Danny's stomach twisted. It wasn't possible that the old man had another family stashed someplace in South Philly, was it? He caught Kate by the shoulders. "Jesus Christ, Kate. Who are you? How did you know him?"

"Danny, please—I can't—I didn't—I—"

"Don't lie to me. How did you know him?"

"You won't understand."

He wanted to understand, but nothing made sense in this alternate universe. Maybe he wasn't really here at all. Maybe he was lying in restraints in the psych ward screaming his head off because he had finally gone over the edge.

"Talk to me, Kate." He should've been moved by the look of terror on her face, but he was way past that. His fingers dug into the flesh of her arms, and he tried to relax his grip. Deep breath. Couldn't anyone tell the truth? "Goddamn, you!" His hands squeezed tighter. Christ, he'd leave bruises if he didn't stop. His fingers caught in her hair when he wrenched himself away.

His breath came in painful gasps, and he pressed his shaking hands against his face. Just like the old man. No. He wasn't. He could shove his fury back into the closet. Lock the door. Christ, he hurt, but to let go was to fall into the abyss. The surge almost doubled him over.

He felt a movement behind him and turned. Kate had started to slide toward the edge of the bed.

"Please."

He wasn't sure if he spoke aloud, but she stopped. He could see she had given in by the way she bowed her head and held up her hands, like she wanted to push the memory away but no longer had the strength. And he knew then that he didn't want to hear what she was going to tell him.

"Who weeps for the lost ones, Danny?"

A chill started in the base of his gut and began to work its way up. "What do you mean?"

"You wrote it. Don't you remember?"

"I know I wrote it."

"But you didn't weep, did you? Your father did."

"I don't understand."

"I was your father's last case."

The impact of her words hit him like a bullet. "But that was . . . the Sandman case. You would've been—"

"Fifteen. I was fifteen. He liked us young." Her body trembled, and her eyes were wide as if she stared at something only she could see. As if he were no longer there. "We were the lost ones. We lived in a cellar."

"Kate . . ."

"Once you got taken, you never came back." Her voice sounded so small, so faint. Danny could see the red imprint of his hands on her skin. Contrite, he tried to put his arms around her, but she shoved him away. "No! You wanted to know the truth. Now you can listen."

Danny tried to comprehend the horror of a child waiting in a cellar to die. He could almost see Jane Doe One stroll into the room to sit beside Kate on the bed. For a moment, they were all there, the lost girls, and the walls of the room seemed to fill with the raw stench of blood. Danny pressed his fists against his eyes.

"Pretty little girls all in a row." Kate's thin voice snapped him back. "He liked to dress up and play games. The Sandman. 'We're off to Never Never Land.'" She swayed back and forth and stared at him with unseeing eyes. "Once they were finished with us, some went away—I don't know where—but some of us were given to Mason."

"Oh, Jesus. The lost girls," Danny whispered.

"They told me I could be an au pair. Work with kids. I spoke English. A lot of the girls didn't."

"They kept you with Mason?"

"Before. They kept us in a basement before and after. I don't know. He made films. He'd show us what he did to the others. He said they'd been bad. He used razors and other things. He said if we didn't cooperate, they'd do it to us. Some tried to run away anyhow."

"You ran?"

"Only once." She began to tremble. "He strung me up. He said I had beautiful skin, but I had to be punished."

"Kate." He wanted to hold her until her pain soaked into him.

"Hinky dinky corny cup, how many fingers have I got up? She said two but three it is, and now she'll feel the razor's cut."

"Oh, Jesus."

Danny watched her clutch at the comforter and ball it into her hands. He wished she'd strike out at him rather than make those strangled whimpers of torment.

"Who had you in the cellar? Was it Paulie Ritter? Was Mason's real name Paulie Ritter?"

"No. Not him."

"Who then, Kate? Who hurt you?" He kept his voice soft, as if she were a child.

"Thomas said not to tell. Thomas said not to tell anyone or they'll find me. 'They're above the law,' he said."

"But you have to tell now, Kate."

"Not you. Thomas said if I told you, you'd get me killed."

The bitterness welled up. Why did it matter anymore what his father thought? Funny, after all this time, the old man still packed a punch, or maybe some wounds never did heal.

"Kate, he may still be out there."

"He'll put me back in the cellar."

"He won't put you in the cellar, Kate. I swear it."

Danny moved closer. When Kate didn't push him away, he slipped his arms around her, and she clung to him as if he were a spar on her storm-tossed ocean. He murmured quiet words of comfort until her breathing slowed and her trembling eased.

It struck him then that Beth had stopped seeking solace from him. Was it because she thought he had none to give? Had he become that much of a cipher to her? Or maybe the crushing weight of things left unsaid had suffocated them. Love, like any living, breathing thing, needed air and space to thrive, but their marriage had become a vacuum.

This time had to be different. He couldn't screw this up.

Danny rested his cheek on Kate's head. "I won't let him hurt you."

"Funny. You almost sound like you care." Her voice sounded too small for her to bring off the sarcasm.

He tightened his arms around her. "I do care."

Kate went rigid for a moment before she relaxed against him. He wanted to tell her he loved her. But the words wouldn't come.

In the photograph on the bed, the old man smiled, and Danny looked away.

God is watching you, boy.

Kate stirred in his arms. "Your father was a good man, Danny. I'll never forget him. He was my angel. He saved my life."

54

Kevin Ryan's jaw cracked when he yawned, and he rubbed the back of his neck. His bones ached. Jean was right. He needed to cut down on his drinking. He picked the last jelly donut out of the bag and finished it in two bites. Powdered sugar dusted the front of his coat, but he didn't brush it off.

"Why d'ya suppose they asked for us this morning?" he asked and picked up his coffee to take a sip.

His partner, Jake, maneuvered their unmarked car through the early morning traffic. He swore and jammed the brakes when a taxi cut him off.

"I should give that cocksucker a ticket." Jake lifted his arm to make his favorite Italian gesture and then shook his head. "Fuck it." They lurched to a stop at the light on Eighth Street.

"Well?"

"They wanted you. We're a package deal." Jake grinned at him, and his newly whitened teeth seemed a little too bright for morning. He drummed his fingers on the wheel. Kevin looked away.

A scrawny Salvation Army Santa rang his bell in front of the Gallery. Even decorated for Christmas, the mall seemed forlorn. "Space for Rent" signs were as prominent as wreaths, and trash whirled across the wet street into piles of dirty snow. Under swaying tinsel Christmas stars, drunks sat propped on steaming grates already sucking down rotgut from brown paper bags.

Peace on earth.

Who the hell came down here to shop anymore? Everyone went to the suburbs. Or moved there. Like Danny.

Why couldn't he stop thinking about his brother?

"He wouldn't even stop in for a beer," Kevin had said to Jean last Sunday. "Too high and mighty."

She'd just shaken her head. "What did you expect, Kevin? Didn't you even look at him? He's half a ghost."

When he'd seen Danny that day, Kevin almost hadn't recognized him. It hadn't just been that he'd lost weight. It was the emptiness in his eyes, a look Kevin had only seen in rape victims, kids who'd been abused, and a twelve-year-old gangbanger he'd been forced to strip search.

An instant flare of remorse had burned through him. Kevin had let a year pass without so much as a phone call to check on his brother. All because of a stupid fight, one he'd started. What difference did it make where Danny had buried his son?

Grains of sand. Wasn't that what Ma used to say? Life was like grains of sand that slipped through your fingers? Must've been some stupid Irish thing.

Kevin swallowed the rest of his coffee. He still felt cold inside.

Jake rolled down Market and turned right, twisting in and out of traffic to the address they'd been given. He parked next to a squad car. Once Old City was the commercial district, packed with warehouses and taverns; now it was the trendiest part of Philadelphia, a neighborhood of pricey loft apartments, upscale restaurants, and cute cobblestone streets that ripped up your tires and suspension. Danny's kind of place.

It hadn't always been. Maybe what he resented most was the way Danny had repackaged himself. Turned slick and forgot who he was. Thought he was better than the rest of them when he was nothing more than . . .

A punching bag.

213

Christ, was that what pissed him off? Kevin didn't know anymore. How was it Danny always made him feel like an asshole?

Kevin's stomach tightened when they got out of the car at the far end of the alley. Someone banged out a manic "What Child Is This?" on a piano. The notes crashed through an open third-floor window, and Kevin shuddered. Despite the cold, sweat ran down his neck under his collar. A group of uniforms and CSU people were already at work.

"The elves are busy," Jake said. "Must get the mess cleaned up so the civic association don't bitch." He pulled out a camera from the trunk.

Kevin held up his ID to a uniform who stood guard and signed them in. The uniform offered him a pair of latex gloves, and Kevin snapped them on.

"What've we got?" Kevin said.

The uniform waved toward a black tarp that lay in front of the dumpsters. "White male. Ain't pretty."

"And he was found by?"

"The trashmen."

"We still have trashmen?" Jake said and shot Kevin a grin. "Hell of a way to start their day. You start to canvass the area?"

"Nobody's seen nothin' so far." The uniform nodded at the tarp. "Uh, Detective Ryan, you really need to take a look at this."

Kevin exchanged a glance with Jake. Another shiver of unease ran down his spine. The uniform looked pale, shaky, like maybe he'd hurled. This guy was no rookie. Not a good sign. "How bad?"

"You better see for yourself." He jerked back the tarp. Overhead, the pianist pounded out the insane carol.

Kevin clenched his fists, and he heard Jake say, "Holy fuck."

The corpse was a male with a terrific head of white hair, though it was matted and stuck out around his head in greasy clumps. He appeared to be in his sixties. Naked, his ankles and wrists were bound with duct tape; his body was a mass of bruises, cuts, and burns.

Someone had hacked off the poor bastard's penis and scrotum and shoved it in his mouth. A red-and-white, candy-cane-shaped pen protruded from his right temple. A green bow tied around his neck fluttered in the breeze.

Kevin felt his breakfast rush into the back of his throat, and he forced it down. He leaned closer, unbelieving, to read the words scrawled across the victim's belly in crimson marker: "For Detective Kevin Ryan. Send this gift to your brother."

55

"You shouldn't go to work," Danny said.

He watched Kate pull her hair straight back into a ponytail. She wrapped it in a bun and jabbed bobby pins into it to hold it tight. It looked almost as painful as the rigid set of her jaw. When she brushed past him, he caught her arm.

"Don't . . . please. Just don't." Her voice rasped, and he heard the desperation in it. "I have to go. Pretend it's all normal."

"Kate. I'm sorry."

"I know." She used her free hand to wipe at her eyes, and he hated himself for bringing her to this state. He pressed his fingers against her arm and brushed his mouth against her neck. "Kate."

"Don't. Oh, please, Danny."

But he couldn't let go. How did he explain when he held her, felt her against him, breathed her, the world took on a radiance he hadn't known before. He wasn't sure she'd believe him if he told her.

She rested her head against his shoulder. "I don't know what's left inside me."

"We've got us." He pulled her closer. "It's something. A place to start."

"I did stuff, Danny. Drugs, the clubs, other things . . ." She wouldn't look at him.

Did she think he gave a damn about any of that after she'd lived through hell? "The black hole."

She nodded. "Novell helped me get straight, more or less, and I guess I thought I owed him. I used to tell him stuff I heard just being around at the clubs. But we had a falling out."

"When did you fall out with him?"

"After I went to work for the senator. Novell hates Robert Harlan—I'm not sure why. Probably when the original Inferno investigation went bad. Two agents were killed. Novell took a lot of heat."

"No wonder Novell's so twisted."

"Your father believed they were set up."

"My father? My father told you that?" Danny shook his head. This whole case kept getting weirder and weirder.

"He said it was like a poison that infected the city, at least parts of it. He said it was all about money and power."

"Did he say anything else?"

"If he hadn't died when he did, I figure we would have left the city and started somewhere new. He had money saved up. He gave it to me before he died and told me to get out."

"He took out a mortgage on the house," Danny said.

"Yeah. He didn't want anyone to know. He said the money was for me because nobody gave a damn about the girls. He was friendly with Novell, you know? Novell helped me find a place to live, looked after me."

"If you aren't working for Novell, what's holding you? We could chuck it and get out of town today," Danny said. Maybe if they left right now, they had a chance.

He could almost picture a house by the ocean. Someplace quiet. They could go anywhere. Just the two of them. He could write that novel he'd always thought about. And Kate wouldn't care about parties and being seen by the right people. The things he'd always hated. Kate. They would make love to the sound of the waves, and he'd keep her safe. And one day, the nightmares would go away for both of them and . . .

"You'd always wonder why you didn't stay to write the story. You couldn't live with that." Kate pulled back, and Danny jerked out of his reverie. He started to protest, but she laid a finger on his lips and gave him a smile that broke his heart because he knew she was right. "They won't let you get away now anyway."

"What do you mean, Kate? Who?"

"Them." She looked past him, her face hardening. "Mason. He was one of them. The Inferno. At least that's what Thomas believed. And they're above the law."

"This Mason who wasn't Paulie Ritter. He was big, small?"

"I don't want to remember." She closed her eyes as if she were a child, as if that would make the monster disappear. But monsters never really disappeared. They just hid in closets, under beds, or in dark places inside your mind.

"Kate, please try to remember. Was he big?"

She looked at him and spoke in a rush. "No. He was thin, blond. I don't know how tall, but I remember his eyes. He had horrible eyes, like chunks of blue glass."

"He was a member of the Inferno?"

"Yes. I don't know. All I know is we were illegals. No family to come looking for us. We were the lost ones."

Her eyes turned dark with pain he couldn't begin to fathom. It didn't matter that he bore witness to Jane Doe One and the others. Once in his arrogance, he believed he'd told their story with the honesty and integrity they deserved, despite the flawed ending. Now he knew better. He'd wanted to make a name for himself. No wonder the old man despised him.

"No one knew about me. That I lived, and Thomas said if I told anyone the truth about Mason, they'd find me. If he knew more, he never told me. He wanted me to have a clean start. He gave me a home, paid for my face to be fixed."

"So he took his secrets with him to his grave."

"He took me in when I had no place to go. He kept me safe. He was good to me, Danny. My angel."

Danny finally understood why his father hadn't wanted him to poke around the Sandman case. It made sense now. The old man had preferred to die in disgrace then expose Kate. Despite all those citations, maybe it was his one real act of heroism.

"I used to go looking for Mason. Dance with the devil because I was ready for him, but I never found him. And now . . ." She shrugged.

The sorrow washed up against his chest. "What are you going to do?"

She leaned close to slide her hands up his face, and he caught her in his arms. He wanted to pull her inside of him, afraid if he let her go, she would be lost to him forever.

The downstairs buzzer rang.

"I have to leave." Her voice trembled.

Danny could feel the brush of her damp eyelashes against his cheek, and he breathed in the scent of lavender that surrounded her.

Say something, you idiot. "Kate." The word tore from his dry throat like a prayer.

The buzzer sounded again. She jerked free and blinked back her tears. "Thomas loved Yeats. Did you know that? Because of your mother. He missed her terribly." She dabbed at her eyes. "Find Mason for me. Tell your brother. He's a cop."

Something was wrong. She wouldn't look at him. "And you'll be here," he said. "Tell me you'll be here, Kate."

"Promise me."

"I promise, but tell me you'll be here."

"A deep-sworn vow, Danny. I'll give you that." She leaned close to brush her mouth against his, and then she was gone.

56

Danny prowled Kate's apartment. He picked up the volume of Yeats and paged through it to the photograph. He ran his thumb over its surface, not sure why he felt so uneasy. The old man looked sick, stooped and gaunt, yet happy, his face radiating a kind of pride, like he'd found something he'd lost. Danny didn't know why the picture bothered him. Was it the shining adoration in Kate's eyes? The only person who ever looked at him that way was Conor.

He understood Kate's devotion to the old man. He'd saved her after all. Protected her. But why was it so easy for the old man to love a stranger and not his own flesh and blood?

Maybe it was because Kate asked for so little.

Danny stared at the page. He'd been lost all his life and finally found his way home. He'd found her, and they'd start over. It seemed so urgent to talk to her. Try to take away her sorrow.

A deep-sworn vow. I'll give you that.

Jesus, that poem—A floorboard creaked, and he spun around, the thought gone. Novell stood in the doorway looking like he hadn't slept for a year. The lines on his face made fissures in his gray skin, and black rings circled his eyes.

Novell emanated the tense, barely controlled anger that reminded Danny of the old man when he came home after a bad shift and too many hours at the Shamrock, and it only took one wrong look or word to ignite him.

Novell gazed around the room. "She's gone?"

"Why didn't you tell me the truth about Kate?"

"The truth is a relative thing, my friend. You should know that. Come on. We have to go." Novell tossed Danny his jacket. He looked as though he wanted to say something more, but he didn't.

"I'm sorry about you and Harlan."

Novell jerked his shoulder. "Does it matter?"

*

Danny followed Novell down the stairs to the front door. "Where are we headed?" Novell stopped so abruptly Danny collided with him. "Sorry."

"No, I'm sorry, kid. We're not going anywhere. You are."

Kevin stepped out from behind the steps. "Do what I say, Danny, so we can get this over with." Kevin used his best cop voice.

Danny started to move, but Kevin grabbed his arm and shoved him against the wall, pressing his shoulder against him. He twisted Danny's right arm behind his back and then his left so quickly that he had the cuffs on before Danny could react.

"What the hell is this? I haven't done anything."

"No more running, Danny," Kevin said.

Novell stared at the ground. "You'll keep me informed?"

"I will. Thanks." Kevin yanked Danny with him. "Let's go."

"Danny?" Novell said. "I'm sorry."

Danny glared at him. "Go to hell."

*

When they walked into the city morgue, the stench of formaldehyde assaulted Danny's nose, throat, and mouth. His arms ached and his hands were numb, but he wouldn't ask Kevin to take off the cuffs. It was Kevin's little power trip to bring him here like this. Let him enjoy it.

"I've got something for you to see," Kevin said.

Danny didn't answer.

They marched into the autopsy room where a body lay on a table. Under the fluorescent lights, the body had a curious purple-green cast, though it was hard to say if that was from death or the bruises and swelling. It bore the familiar Y-shaped incision of a recent autopsy.

It took Danny a second to register the body before he recognized the white mane of hair and the tiny mole to the left of the once prominent nose that now lay in a pulpy mass on his blackened face. A large hole gaped in his right temple. They'd put his head back together, but his face looked like a mask.

"Jesus. Oh, Jesus." Danny doubled over like someone kicked him in the balls.

"You know him?" Kevin's voice came from a million miles away.

You're my mitzvah, Daniel.

Danny staggered against a cart that held a tray of instruments. The tray spilled with a metallic clatter, and Danny heard an animal moan escape him.

"Danny! Christ almighty, let me get you uncuffed."

Kevin unlocked the cuffs, and Danny ripped his right hand free fast enough to make a fist and connect it with Kevin's temple. "You sadistic son of a bitch!" Kevin stumbled back in surprise.

Something hot exploded inside Danny's skull and burned down through his body. He wanted to smash his fists into Kevin's face until there was nothing left of it but twitching nerve endings and gore. Kevin might have size and bulk, but he was slow. He didn't have thirty years of fury stored up. Despite the pins and needles in his hands, Danny grabbed the metal tray and swung it at Kevin's head. It hit with a solid thunk and opened up a gash in his forehead that began to pour blood.

"You bastard!" Kevin made a grab for him, and Danny raised the tray again. He cracked it against Kevin's jaw before Kevin sent it flying.

Danny hurled himself at Kevin like a pit bull. They slammed against the gurney where Andy's body lay, and it careened across the room to crash into something that landed with a wet splat on the floor.

He heard footsteps, shouts, but he didn't pay attention until hands closed over him and dragged him backward. Danny didn't know how many cops had him, but he kept struggling. Fists rammed into his kidneys and ribs. They forced him facedown onto the floor, cursing and kicking, then a shot of agony reverberated through his skull.

Darkness.

57

Kevin walked into the room, and Danny looked up. A neat, white bandage cut across Kevin's forehead. Stitches? Danny hoped so. Kevin's jaw had a deep purple bruise. He carried an ice pack.

Danny tilted back in his seat. "What's next, Kev, a strip search? Or are you just gonna cuff me to the chair and beat the shit out of me?"

"What's going on, Danny?" Kevin was back in cop mode.

"Is this an official inquiry?" Danny drawled out his words and watched Kevin's jaw tighten. "If it is, I'm entitled to a lawyer."

"Do you need a lawyer?"

"Between you and Novell, apparently I do." He shifted and winced when his bones and muscles protested. Philly's finest hadn't lost their ability to deliver an ass kicking.

Kevin sat opposite Danny. Someone had scratched "Blow me" into the top of the table. Kevin set his ice pack on top of the words.

"You can ID the body."

"Like you didn't know that already." Danny slouched lower in his seat and began to draw circles on the table with his middle finger.

"No. I didn't." Kevin pulled four photographs from his pocket and slid them across the table. "That's why I wanted you brought in. You see what's written on him?"

Danny shoved the photos back at him. He couldn't stand to look at Andy laid out like a slab of beef with those vile words printed on him, but he forced down the ripping pain and concentrated on his fury. "Do you want me to thank you? Thanks, Kev. You're a terrific big brother. May I go now? Or should I kiss your fat ass first?"

Kevin turned the photos face down. He pinched the bridge of his nose and looked up, his light eyes filled with exhaustion. Danny's anger cooled. He knew he was acting like an asshole. Kevin always brought that out in him. They brought it out in each other.

"I don't want—Whatever you're into, Danny—Christ, I warned you!"

You're my mitzvah, Daniel. Danny's throat closed. He forced himself to breathe. *Oh Jesus, Andy, what the hell happened?* "It's Andy Cohen." Danny heard his voice shaking.

"From the paper?"

"None of you geniuses recognized him?"

Kevin pressed his fingers against his temples. "We don't travel in your elevated circles, Danny. God almighty, are you sure?"

"Yeah, I'm sure, and no, I didn't kill him."

"I didn't say you did."

"Then why did you bring me in like a goddamn criminal? You going to throw me in jail next?"

Kevin banged his fist on the table. "Are you stupid?"

"Am I being charged with a crime?"

"I can charge you with assaulting a police officer. How 'bout that, smartass?"

"I want to call my lawyer."

"Danny, listen. Novell's right. There are dangerous people out there, and they want to hurt you. I can get you into a safe house—"

"No."

"Jesus Christ, you're stubborn! Do you want to end up dead?"

Danny wished Kevin would just give up and let him go. What was the point when neither of them was going to give in? Theresa was right. They were both hardheaded Micks. "Still burn your ass, don't I?"

"Fuck you."

"Why did you take the old man's notebooks out of the box? What didn't you want me to find?"

"What the hell are you talking about?"

"The old man's notebooks for the last two months of the Sandman case are missing."

"If they are, I didn't take them!" Kevin's face turned scarlet.

Danny leaned back in his seat and smiled. "You can't cover up forever. I'm going to figure it out. I have a witness."

58

"You have no goddamn respect for police procedure!" The captain's voice boomed through the closed door.

"Fuck police procedure! If you'd just listen—"

"I'm tired of listening, Novell. I'm tired of dealing with your shit!"

Detective Sean McFarland tried to ignore the shouts that came from the captain's office. He didn't know if John Novell would still be working the case with him when he was done fighting with the captain, but right now, he was too busy working his way through the state police report on Beth Ryan's accident to care.

It had taken them long enough to forward it to him, and it was, at first glance, straightforward. The victim had made a right turn onto Route 252 and lost control of her car. She had run off the road, gone through a barrier, and crashed into Valley Creek. Sean examined the photographs of the Jeep. It lay on its left side, squashed in like a trampled tissue box. The right rear tire lay in the creek.

Wait. How the hell had that happened? The Jeep lay on its left side but was missing its right tire.

According to the report, the tire came off in the crash, but in the photographs, it looked undamaged.

He looked at the autopsy photos. Beth Ryan had taken a beating. She was knocked unconscious when rocks had broken through the window and had two skull fractures, though the listed cause of death was drowning. Sean barely recognized her, but the little boy, Conor, was strapped into a car seat and didn't have a scratch. It wasn't impossible that the child's neck was broken. Whiplash, maybe. But his car seat—the top brand on the market—was on the right side of the car. The car didn't jerk backward. It rolled down and landed in the water.

This report was bullshit. It didn't appear that anyone had checked to see if the brakes or wheels or anything else had been tampered with.

Something was wrong here. Sean was sure of it, and nobody gave a damn.

59

"What the hell is the matter with you?"

"Shut up and walk." Kevin dragged Danny from the interrogation room down the stairs and out to the parking garage. Their footsteps echoed in the cavernous space.

Danny had forgotten how strong Kevin was. He wasn't as tall as the old man, but Kevin had been a First Team, All-State tackle in high school, back in the days when Kevin could see his toes and dreamed of playing for Penn State. Danny didn't know if Kevin had any dreams left.

They reached Kevin's Navigator.

"What do you mean you have a witness?" Kevin pinned Danny against his car. "Stop playing games with me, or right here, I'll beat the shit out of you. You can call your goddamn lawyer later."

Danny could feel the fury rise off Kevin, like heat shimmers over hot asphalt. Sweat rolled down his forehead and his breath came in rapid puffs of white steam. He waited for Kevin to stomp the ground and snort like a bull, which would have been funny if Kevin's big hands weren't clamped around his shoulders.

"Paulie Ritter didn't kill all those girls—if he killed any of them. At least one lived, thanks to the old man."

Kevin stepped back as if Danny burned his fingers. "Holy fuck! Are you sure?"

"Yeah, I'm sure. The guy who had her called himself Mason, and from her description, he wasn't Paulie Ritter."

"Maybe it wasn't. Maybe it was a copycat."

"I don't think so. According to her, Mason was tied to the Inferno."

Kevin waved his hand in disgust. "Are you back to that again?"

"The old man talked about the Inferno."

"The old man lived inside a Dewar's bottle too." Kevin looked past Danny, and the lines around his mouth grew deeper.

"What happened to the old man's notes?"

"I don't know. I wasn't his partner. You know the way he got at the end. He holed up in that house like a rat."

Danny started to argue the point but then stopped. Why would Kevin take the old man's notes? Maybe the old man did have reason to get rid of them. Maybe he had something to hide. Where did he get the extra money? Was it just from a second mortgage?

"You think he was on the take?"

"Hell, I don't know. He took out a mortgage on the house before he died," Kevin said.

"You were the executor of his estate. Why didn't you check it out?"

Kevin gave him the cop look. "Because I didn't want to know. Jesus, you're so goddamn self-righteous."

Danny let the sting of Kevin's words sink in.

"Y'know, the old man wasn't just your tragedy. We all got to share in it. Maybe you got it the worst, but no one escaped that house without scars." Kevin's staccato voice hit him like punches.

The dingy walls of their house seemed to close around him, and Danny smelled the suffocating stench of scotch and mothballs. At least he'd made it all the way out. He thumbed his nose at the old man and walked away, but Kevin stayed tied. Brothers in blue. In the end, which of them bore the worst scars? "Kevin, I—"

Kevin waved him off. "You eat anything today?"

When they were kids, Kevin would find him after school and go through his battery of questions: "Did anyone hassle you? Did you behave in school? You got any homework?" It always ended with, "Did you eat anything?" Most of the time, Kevin would shove a half-eaten hoagie into his hands and stand there, his face contorted in a scowl, until Danny choked it down. He used to believe Kevin did it to push him around. How stupid was he?

"You look like walking shit, Danny."

He felt like walking shit. "Where did they find Andy's body?"

"Old City. Why?"

"Will you show me?"

"It's an ongoing investigation."

Danny gripped the door. "Andy gave me my life. I . . ."

The awful truth doubled him over, and the bitter dregs of his stomach emptied themselves on the asphalt. He clung to the side of the car. "I'm sorry." Danny wasn't sure for what. Everything. He didn't know if Kevin even cared anymore.

Kevin jerked his head. "Get in the goddamn car."

*

Danny stood in the alley and peered down at the row of dumpsters that lined the walls of the redbrick buildings. A piece of bright-yellow tape stuck to the edge of a trash can, but all other evidence of the morning's crime scene was gone. There was just the odor of grilled beef and the beeping of a truck backing into the alley from the opposite end.

Danny folded his arms against the ache inside his chest. A door opened, and he could see into a restaurant kitchen. The truck backed into place at the loading area. Two kitchen workers smoked on the platform. Their uniforms bore a red rectangle with the embroidered words, "The Red Door." A man with an impressive head of chestnut hair walked out and said something to the workers, who tossed their cigarettes and disappeared inside. He turned toward Danny, and for a moment, their eyes met and held.

And Danny could almost hear Michael Cohen whisper in his ear, "Look behind the Red Door for Bruce Delhomme's real specialties . . ."

60

"I can't arrest Bruce Delhomme!" Kevin watched Danny, his expression as pained as if Danny had asked him to change water into wine.

"Why not? Andy and Delhomme knew each other. What else do you need?"

Kevin sighed. "Some physical evidence would be nice."

"Like a body in a dumpster?"

"We found the body here. The ME says he was killed elsewhere."

"Yeah, like in the Red Door?" Danny didn't care what Kevin said. If Andy was found here, it wasn't a coincidence. "You know Bruce Delhomme is involved in a bunch of sex clubs that are connected to the Inferno."

"No. I don't have proof of that, and neither do you. You have some half-baked article your friend was writing. That's evidence of nothing. All I can do is ask Delhomme to answer some questions. We have nothing to tie him to Cohen's murder."

"But—"

"I haul Delhomme in, and he calls his high-priced lawyer who has him on the street an hour later. Five minutes after that, my ass is called into the commissioner's office for hassling a highly regarded citizen."

"Jesus, Kevin. I know this guy's involved." Did Kevin think he'd pulled Delhomme's name out of the air?

Kevin threw up his hands in exasperation. "I'm a good cop, Danny. It may not mean much to you, but I am."

"I know you are."

"You always looked down on Junior and me 'cause we were just cops."

It surprised Danny that Kevin gave a damn what he thought, but he sounded wounded, raw. The undercurrent of anguish in Kevin's voice was an insubstantial thing, almost like a call borne on the breeze, a whisper from across the room, but Danny realized it had always been there. He didn't know why he never recognized it before. Christ, it was a day for discoveries. First on the list: he was the world's biggest asshole.

Danny opened his mouth to apologize, but Kevin said, "You gotta let me handle Delhomme. If I take you to the impound lot to pick up your car, will you promise not to come back here and hassle him? I got it repaired."

"Will you talk to him?"

Kevin clenched his fists. "Let me handle the police work. You go write a pretty story."

"Will you talk to him today?"

"Jesus Christ, you're annoying!"

"And you'll let me know what happens?"

"I don't have to let you know jack shit." Kevin jerked open the car door, but Danny heard the resignation in his voice.

Let Kevin handle Delhomme. He had someone else to see.

61

"Mr. Delhomme, thank you for seeing us," Jake said to Bruce Delhomme. Kevin wanted Jake to lead off. Right now, Jake was sharper. Fresher. He was happy to listen and take notes.

After spending five hours with Danny, Kevin's head ached, and the crimson carpet made it worse. Photographs of ebony carousel horses covered the walls. Their red eyes seemed to watch him.

Delhomme stood behind his desk, an ugly thing made of dull, black metal, wound with a strip of scarlet. On the floor sat a huge lava lamp filled with blobs of black slime that slithered in a hypnotic rhythm through blood-colored liquid.

Delhomme frowned and tossed his hair. "We open for dinner in two hours, gentlemen. I don't have much time."

"Mr. Delhomme, you're aware we found a body in your dumpster this morning?" Jake asked.

"Yes. A vagrant, wasn't it? It's a terrible thing, but I'm not sure what it has to do with me. I own three restaurants, so I wasn't even here last night. I was at the Golden Palette. I already spoke to a detective about this."

"Then I'm sure he told you we'd be asking all the local merchants for help identifying the body." Jake's voice was smooth. "You were at the Golden Palette all evening?"

"I was there from four o'clock until sometime after three AM. Then my driver took me home. I wasn't alone, and if I must, I can provide you with her name."

Jake waved toward a stack of cards held by a black porcelain hand. "Maybe you could just write it down on one of your fancy business cards. Say, you're friendly with Andy and Linda Cohen, aren't you?"

Delhomme's eyes narrowed a little, but he nodded. "Yes, I am."

Jake glanced at Kevin. "Andy Cohen wasn't at the Golden Palette last night, was he?"

Delhomme looked confused. Kevin didn't think he was faking it. "I'm sorry, but Andy's wife was—he—I haven't seen Andy since Friday night. His wife—Dear God, haven't you people seen the news?"

"So you've had no contact at all with Andy Cohen?"

"I believe I've made that clear, Detective. Has Andy said otherwise? Is there some problem?"

"No problem, Mr. Delhomme." Jake leaned a little closer. "We're just trying to get a positive ID on the body we found this morning."

"Oh dear." Delhomme laid a manicured hand on his chest. He wore clear nail polish. Kevin almost snorted in disgust. What sort of asshole wore nail polish? "I suppose this is absolutely necessary, Detective?"

"We'd like to try to get this done as quickly as possible so we don't inconvenience you. It'll be easier if we do it here than, say, down at the morgue. And a whole lot less unpleasant." Jake reached into his pocket for the photos. "I should warn you, he's a little beat up."

Jake laid out the photos in a row across his desk. Delhomme looked down at them, and Kevin watched the color drain from his face.

Delhomme drew in a breath. "Oh my God. It's Andy Cohen."

"Andy Cohen?" Jake said. "Your good friend?"

Delhomme's head snapped up. His eyes locked on Kevin's. "You got your ID, gentlemen. Which I think you already had before you walked in. Isn't that right, Detective Ryan?"

Kevin held Delhomme's gaze. He could feel Delhomme's righteous fury. He could also smell his fear.

Kevin leaned in, resting his hands on Delhomme's desk. "Now what do you suppose Andy Cohen was doing in your dumpster?"

62

Danny turned off the Schuylkill Expressway onto Roosevelt Boulevard and headed to Northeast Philly. Coming here as a kid had always seemed like traveling to some distant land. Sure, there were row houses, but some people lived in single homes with yards and grass. People like Stan Witkowski.

They used to call Big Stan Witkowski "Bear" when he was the old man's partner because of his massive build and lumbering gate. Danny had once seen him pick up two mouthy perps by their collars and smack their heads together, just like something out of the movies. Everything about Stan had been larger than life: he didn't just laugh, he roared; he didn't shout, he bellowed.

Big Stan had always called him "kiddo" even when he was on the police beat. He had been the cop who let him see the remains of Jane Doe One, though Danny wasn't sure whether Stan had done him a favor or not.

"Play square with us, and I'll make sure you get your exclusive." He'd clamped his big hand on Danny's shoulder. "You're family, right?"

Now if it hadn't been for a drooping tattoo of a rearing black bear on his bicep, Danny wouldn't have recognized the shrunken man who stood before him. Shrunken might have been the wrong word. Tethered to an oxygen tank, Stan Witkowski seemed to be collapsing upon himself. His once florid face had turned a pale gray, his lips had tinged blue, and his dark eyes had sunken deep into the hollows of his skull.

"Stan?" Danny reached out a hand to touch him to see if the apparition was real.

Tears filled the old man's eyes. "Jesus Christ, Danny Ryan." He took a deep breath and leaned close. His hands seemed oversized now, but he squeezed Danny's shoulder with surprising strength. "Emphysema. Your dad would get a laugh out of that." He gave a wheezing snort. "Don't suppose you gotta cigarette on you?"

"I don't smoke. Sorry."

"It don't matter." He motioned Danny into the hall and closed the door. Danny recognized the heavy, sickroom smell that clogged the air. The stink of soiled linens not quite covered by antiseptic mixed with the bitter tang of medicine. He could see his mother all over again lying in her bed, whiter than her sheets, her hands like wax.

"How's Muriel?"

"You don't gotta whisper, kiddo. She's upstairs. She ain't so good these days. She got the cancer, just like your mom." Stan sucked in a gulp of air and let it out with a rattling wheeze. "She's dying. She got morphine for the pain so it ain't so bad."

"Jesus, Stan, I'm sorry. Is there anything I can do?"

Stan shook his head then let it droop forward. "We got hospice care, so it ain't so hard. What the fuck, we all gotta die, right? Better she goes first." He took another wheezing breath. "Here . . ." He motioned down the hall toward the kitchen.

Danny glanced at the pictures of Stan, Muriel, and their daughter Lily Jean that covered the walls, wisps of memory that reached out to him.

He'd spent so many Sunday afternoons here before his mother died. Stan would barbeque steaks until they turned black, downing beers with the old man while the women smiled indulgently. Lily Jean and Danny had hid from Junior and Kevin in the shrubs, and she had made him tell her stories until his throat got sore. Theresa had sat in the sun, her nose in a movie magazine, and ignored them all. Just two regular families.

After his mother had died, Danny had wanted to go back to the comfort of their ritual, but when he'd asked the old man, he'd gotten a punch in the mouth that loosened two teeth.

Danny swallowed the lump that almost choked him. Maybe what made it all the worse was that once things had been normal. Not perfect. Just normal. Maybe the old man had drunk too much, and his mom tolerated it. Maybe Junior and Kevin had ganged up on him, and Theresa had acted like they were all beneath her. But at one time, they'd been a family.

Maybe you couldn't learn to hate someone unless you once loved him.

Kevin was right. The old man wasn't just his tragedy. The Iceman's self-loathing became a poisonous cloud that choked them all.

"You comin'?" Stan stood in the doorway and beckoned him into the kitchen.

Not much had changed. It was still painted bright yellow, though an array of pill bottles lined the white Formica counter. Two huge, gray oxygen tanks sat by the door.

Stan opened the refrigerator. "Beer?"

"No thanks."

"You never was a drinker." Stan shut the door. "Sit. I gotta call the oxygen guy. He's late today. I only got half a tank left." His face had a flush that turned his skin a peculiar shade of light purple, and a muscle in his cheek twitched. Danny listened to him make a quick call, and then Stan pulled up a chair.

"What did you want to ask me?"

"It's about my father. About that last case."

"The Sandman case."

Stan sat beside him like a priest and placed his hand on Danny's arm. "I think we better start at the beginning, kiddo."

*

"It's one hell of a story." Stan's voice exuded sorrow, regret. It pulled him in, but a weird unease nagged at the base of

Danny's gut—something Kevin had said, something about Junior's funeral.

"I need to know if my father was on the take, Stan."

"It ain't so simple, Danny. At the end of that case, we were no closer to catching the Sandman. We had the FBI crawlin' up our ass, the mayor, the press—Christ, you were there. It was a three-ring circus. No one slept. I never even saw Muriel or Lily Jean."

Danny remembered those months. He knew the cops had been running on fumes by the end. The cops. The FBI. It was like the Sandman was a demon, and one who understood enough about criminology not to leave clues. Worse, because the victims couldn't be traced or identified, the police didn't know if they were runaways or local prostitutes.

Stan stared off into space. "After ten months, we got a break. Someone called in a description of a car with a partial license plate. Your father and I told no one, not even the FBI. We chased down every car that matched and came up with a possible, but it was registered to Mason Scott, son of Bartlett Scott, the big developer. The guy who gave all that money to Children's Hospital and the Avenue of the Arts."

Mason Scott. Kate's Mason? Danny thought of all the development going on around the city. *Another improvement brought to you by Scott Development.* Bartlett Scott's daughter Melissa was running Scott Industries. Did she know about her brother? She had to know.

Some are born to endless night. He supposed that was true enough.

"At first, it seemed ridiculous—that is, until we started to tail this Mason guy, found out he hung out at a warehouse in the Northern Liberties section. Then it was like—it all seemed to come together. Too fast. Both of us got a look at him and knew it. But you can't get a warrant on looks. We just didn't have enough evidence—especially considering who he was, and we knew as soon as we went before a judge we'd tip our hand."

Stan wiped his face, and his wheezing breath turned ragged. Danny heard the anguish in his voice. Even after all this time, it was still there. The old man used to talk about soul-breaking cases. He never understood until now.

"It was like the little bastard knew we was watchin' him. He'd go in and out of that goddamn warehouse every day, but we had nothin', and he didn't do nothing. And we couldn't stop him or be there all the time. Finally, your father said, 'I'm goin' in. We'll worry about gettin' a warrant after the fact.' But then we get an anonymous tip about Paulie Ritter.

"We go to check him out, and don't you know, we find Jane Doe Twenty-Two in his place still warm?"

Danny remembered too well. Stan and the old man leading Paulie Ritter out of his rat hole, Paulie still covered in Jane Doe's blood. Trouble was, Paulie hadn't seemed aware that he had a dead girl in his home.

"We knew he'd been set up," Stan said. "It didn't matter what the CSU found in his place. We knew. Paulie Ritter couldn't draw a stick man. How could he paint all them pretty flowers on those girls? Your dad got so pissed, he just threw his badge across the room and walked."

When the police spokesmen hinted that the old man had gone over the edge, Danny had been surprised, though not alarmed. He'd wanted to believe the old man's sins caught up with him, and the old man's fall from grace made a good story. After all he'd done, the time had come for the old man to enjoy the benefits of his own poison.

Stan's voice broke through his thoughts. "We went back to that warehouse. He was determined, and I couldn't let him go alone. I always had his back, you know. And he always had mine."

Danny nodded. The Iceman and the Bear. They had always been a duo. Supercops with feet of clay.

"He must have been expecting us, though I don't know how. We step in the door and the place goes up in flames. I remember hearing those girls screaming." He looked at Danny with haunted eyes. "He kept them like animals, Danny. Worse than animals. We could only get one out alive."

"But I don't understand. You had the girl as a witness. Why didn't you go after him?"

"You didn't see her, kid."

But he did see her. For the first time, he finally saw Kate. He had let her walk away. He should have run with her when he had the chance.

"You wouldn't know she was a girl, except she had long hair. Hell, I seen a lot of awful things in my time, but this girl was bad. Your father carried her out and she held onto him like he was Jesus Christ. Her face all torn to hell. She'd been broke, Danny. She'd never have held up on a witness stand. She couldn't even talk straight.

"Even so, your father went to see Bartlett Scott. Told him he had a witness that could put his son in jail, and they made a deal."

"What kind of deal?"

"I don't know. The kind that put Mason Scott in the nut house for a while and let your father walk away with compensation for the girl."

Danny wanted to puke. "I can't believe the old man would agree to put an innocent man in jail so Mason Scott could get off."

"It was the best your dad could do. Like I said, it ain't so simple."

"And he believed Bartlett Scott would keep his word?"

"He made a tape of the whole thing. Bartlett Scott had no choice, and don't forget, he was always worried about his reputation."

"What did my dad do with the tape, Stan?"

Stan shook his head. "I don't know. I figure he hid it good. It was his insurance. No one ever found it." He pushed away from the table and stood.

"And the girl. What happened to her?"

"She disappeared." Stan looked away. "That girl. Your father felt like he had to save her. I always thought it was on account of he couldn't save your mother. He never forgave himself for that, for her dyin'. And you. Jesus God, you look so much like her. It killed him. But this girl was like a second chance. I don't think he touched the bottle again after he found her, and he was in a bad way. It changed him, Danny. He never was the same again."

Stan's words soaked through Danny like bitter rain. It all sounded true, so why did it feel rehearsed? Stan had no reason to lie. Not after all these years. Christ, he needed to get out of this rotting house.

"And what did you get out of it, Stan? Why did you go along?"

"I didn't have a choice. I had a family. Muriel. Lily Jean. When you got people you can't bear to lose, you'll do anything to keep them safe. You close your heart. Do things you never thought possible."

Stan gave a shrug, and Danny saw both resignation and defiance in the gesture.

"I'm sorry. I can't say I had lasting regrets about Paulie Ritter. He was a rapist and a thief and a low-life scum who shouldn't have been on the streets. Your father knew that. He did what he had to do not just for that girl but for you and Kevin and Theresa. To keep them from going after you."

"Then what do you regret?" The words stuck in his throat, and he knew what bothered him. The old man and Stan were partners. They had each other's backs, but the old man didn't want to see Stan after he retired. At Junior's funeral, he wouldn't shake Stan's hand.

Kevin's words. And Stan never mentioned Junior.

Stan looked away. "It was a long time ago."

Why would the old man turn against his best friend?

"What do you regret? You and Dad were partners for years. Why wouldn't he shake your hand at Junior's funeral?"

Stan shuffled closer and took hold of Danny's arm. "We all have to make hard choices. It damn near killed me."

Danny understood then. "Junior. It was Junior, wasn't it?"

"We'd been partners, friends for so long. But I didn't have a choice, Danny. It was a test. If I didn't do it, they'd have killed

Lily Jean. You understand, don't you, kiddo? It wasn't personal. You had a wife, a kid. You gotta take care of your family."

Danny wanted to push Stan away. Hadn't he always questioned how Paulie Ritter managed to kill Junior with a lead pencil? Andy hadn't let him go down to the jail to write the story. "You're too close," he said. But Danny knew something was wrong. Deep down, he'd always known.

Now he understood why Kevin kept steering him away from the Sandman case. Kevin knew. Somehow he knew the truth. *Let me handle the police work. You go write a pretty story.* He wasn't condescending. He knew. Stan had killed Junior. *At Junior's funeral, the old man wouldn't shake Stan's hand.* That was Kevin's oblique way of warning him off. And now it was too late.

"Those people killed my family, Stan."

"You should have let them rest in peace." Stan squeezed his arm and glanced around. "Go. Get out now, and don't come back. Please, Danny, I—"

There was a sharp knock on the back door, and Danny saw two huge men in dark-blue windbreakers. Stan shrank closer. His fingers dug into Danny's arm when the back door swung open.

"Hey, Stan," the larger of the two said. He had a square head that sat on his shoulders like a box. "You got a pick-up today?" When he smiled, he bared a set of crooked, yellow teeth.

"Sure, Lyle." Stan's voice trembled, and he seemed to diminish in the presence of these giants. Danny stood.

The second man walked around the room until he hovered behind Danny. His mouth turned dry. *Run.* The thought jumped into Danny's head and clung on like a mosquito sucking at an open vein. But he couldn't. No matter what, he couldn't leave Stan.

"Hey, I know you." Lyle walked toward Danny. "You're that big-shot reporter that lost his marbles when his wife and kid died. A real tragedy."

Stan's fingers tightened on his arm. Tears ran down his sunken cheeks. "You shouldn't have come, Danny. I still got a daughter. I got no choice."

Danny didn't care about Stan and his choices. Something dark and evil twisted his insides. "What do you know about my wife and son?"

A pair of arms locked around him from behind, and he tried to pull free.

"What do you know about my family? Tell me, you son of a bitch!"

Lyle shoved Stan to the floor and then landed a punch on Danny's gut that doubled him over. He grabbed Danny's hair and jerked up his head. Lyle leaned into Danny's face, and his breath stunk of whisky and cigarettes. "I know you're gonna join 'em, asshole."

63

Kevin stood by Danny's back door. No lights. Danny never came home. It wasn't a surprise, but Kevin had to start somewhere.

He held his brother's life in his hands. He'd failed him before.

Kevin had gone along with Junior pissing into the toilet and holding Danny's head in it because it had always been easier to pick on Danny than to have his older brother call him a pussy. They just hadn't counted on Danny putting up such a fight or breaking that goddamn rose bowl or the old man coming in drunk and in such a rotten mood.

That night, Kevin had scrubbed up the blood from where Danny hit his head on the radiator. It had soaked into the sleeve of his shirt, and for a long time, he'd sat and watched his brother's blood turn from bright red to brown.

When Danny had gotten back from the hospital, Kevin had made him promise to come get him if the old man came in drunk.

"Why should I?" Danny had said.

"Because you could get hurt, dumbass."

When Danny's eyes had shifted past him the way they always did, Kevin had put his hand under his chin to force his head up. "Look at me, so I know you're listening."

He'd recognized it then. The animal fear in Danny's eyes. He'd remember it later on the job when he walked into the homes of other kids who'd been beaten, kids who learned to keep their heads down and their mouths shut, and every time he did, he saw his brother.

"You won't come." At the age of ten, Danny's voice had a cynical edge, hoarse and low for a kid so young.

"I'll come. I'm your brother."

Danny had just given him that half smile, and Kevin had known he part wanted to believe and part thought Kevin was full of shit. He had never come to him, and Kevin had always resented it.

Now after all that time, Danny needed him, and Kevin didn't know where the hell to begin.

He was about to try the door when a car pulled into the driveway, and he spun around to see a woman get out of a Volvo station wagon. She tugged at her pink scarf, gave him a nervous smile, and tucked a strand of blondish hair behind her ear.

"Oh, I was—you aren't . . . I'm Carrie, Mrs. Norton's granddaughter from next door."

"My brother's not home."

She seemed to crumple from disappointment. Her thin shoulders slumped, and her chin quivered as if she were about to cry.

Kevin glanced at the red gift bag and bakery tin she clutched to her chest. "Is that for Danny? Do you want me to pass it along?"

She gripped her packages tighter, as if she wasn't sure he was trustworthy, and Kevin tried to give her a reassuring smile.

"I'm a policeman. Here's my ID." He flipped it out and held up his shield. Jesus, she stared at him like he was about to rape her, and he wondered where Danny found these kooks.

She flushed. "This happens every year when Gram goes to Florida. Danny's mail gets left in her box. I only get over every few weeks or so. I made cookies, too." She swallowed a few times and held out the bag and the tin, offering them to Kevin as if they were Holy Communion.

"Thanks," he said, keeping as much space between them as possible when he took the bag and the tin. The bag was heavy. What kind of mail did Danny get? More than letters.

"Danny's feeling better then? I haven't seen him in a while."

This was all he needed: a chat with the president of Danny's fan club. "He's fine."

"If he needs anything . . . I mean, the holidays are so hard and all." She looked at Kevin like she wanted him to say something, but Kevin didn't know what to say. He wanted the earth to open up and swallow her.

"There's a Christian singles group at my church. I left a flyer in the bag. We're having a get together on Saturday. It's a big step, but it's that first step that's the hardest, right?" She bobbed her head.

Kevin smiled at the thought of Danny at a Christian singles group. "Thanks. I'm sure he'd enjoy it."

"If he doesn't want to go alone, he can call me. I left my number. Okay? Well, okay. Merry Christmas." She turned away then paused. "Oh, I didn't get your name."

"Kevin," he said. "Kevin Ryan."

"I'm Carrie. Carrie Norton. It's a pleasure to meet you, Kevin. I'm sure Danny is grateful to have a brother who cares about him," she said. "You can come too, if you'd like. It's a wonderful chance to meet new people."

"What?" Kevin's jaw flopped open.

"You can come to the singles night if you want. Well, I have to go now. Have a blessed Christmas."

"Yeah. Likewise."

She got back in her car, and Kevin watched her roll out of the driveway. Danny sure did attract some odd ducks. Kevin opened the car, got in, and dropped the bag and tin in the back of the Navigator.

A blessed Christmas. That would be a fucking miracle. Why the hell couldn't Danny have listened to him just once? He banged the steering wheel. "I won't let you die."

He started the engine and threw the car into reverse.

64

Danny's arms and shoulders burned. He hung by his wrists. Naked. He struggled to breathe.

Overhead, muffled music pounded, despite the thick foam insulation that packed the ceiling. The dank room had stone walls and a massive wooden door. A cot stood in one corner and, next to it, a sink and a small, covered table. The concrete floor had a drain in the middle of it. He hung over a fucking drain. That couldn't be good.

If only he could figure out some way to loosen the chain that held him up, but he couldn't bend his neck. A metal collar prevented him from tipping his head. His left eye was swollen shut.

The door opened, and a man entered. Small, thin, and unnaturally blond, the man wore the tightest green leather pants Danny ever saw. They were tucked into green leather booties, and over them he wore an unbuttoned green silk shirt. His eyes were lined in black; his face was pale and smooth.

"Hello, Danny," he said as if they were meeting at a business lunch. "I'd shake hands, but you don't seem to be in the position." He chuckled, a sort of high-pitched little cackle. "I'm Mason." He came closer and nodded toward someone Danny couldn't see. The chains loosened, and Danny slumped to his knees.

Though his hands were still above his head, the ripping agony in his shoulders eased.

"That's better, isn't it?" Mason ran his fingers down Danny's cheeks. A caress. "Such a nice face."

Don't fucking touch me. Danny recognized those hands. The long, white fingers all adorned with heavy gold rings. Fingers so smooth that they seemed not to have knuckles. The blonde at the Four Seasons. The photographer at the police station. Mason. Kate's Mason.

Mason pulled Andy's black card from a pocket in his shirt. "Where did you get this, Danny?"

What the hell happened to that other card? But he knew what happened. Kate had stolen it. For whatever reasons.

Mason took Andy's card and pressed the edge of it against Danny's neck and then drew it across like a knife. "Did you get it from Andy?"

Mason made a tsk-tsk sound and backhanded him with surprising strength. "When I ask you a question, I expect a reply. Did you get the card from Andy?"

Danny tasted blood in his mouth. It dripped down from his nose. "You look like the porno pixie," he said. What was it the old man used to say? *Never show fear or you're dead.*

Mason caught a drop of blood on his finger and examined it. "Oh, Danny, I do like you. You have that Irish pugnaciousness. I've always liked the Irish, but you know that, don't you?" He slid his finger into his mouth. "Yummy."

Mason walked in slow circles around him, and Danny could sense his pent-up excitement. It lay over him like a fine, glistening oil.

Blood and bile almost choked him, but Danny forced it back. "I thought you liked girls, Mason."

"I did make my reputation with girls, but I was never exclusive. No, never exclusive. I'm touched. You've been curious about me."

"Yeah. I like freak shows."

Mason slid his fingers through Danny's hair with gentle, almost loving strokes. Then he pressed the metal collar against his throat until Danny struggled for air. Mason released him, and he sagged down.

"A little respect, please. Especially when we have so much in common." Mason leaned close and pushed Danny's face against his crotch. "We both hated our fathers, for instance. Did you know my father placed me in a hospital? They called it a sanitarium. Quaint term, don't you think?"

Danny couldn't move. He was suffocating, the leather sticking to his skin, Mason's thick scent overwhelming him. He tried to pull back, but Mason clasped him tight, grinding his face against his dick.

"Really, I had your father to thank for that, Danny. Who'd have thought an ignorant Irish cop would be so clever? He was much smarter than you, but you're much prettier."

Mason shoved him away and moved behind him. "And now you're mine." He ran his hands over Danny's shoulders.

"Yes, your father was quite a man. The scars on your back. Did he use a belt? Did it bring you closer to God when he beat you? I've always believed that pain brings us closer to God. The mortification of the flesh."

Maybe all he could do was let go. Let Mason wash him down the drain. When Mason was done, he probably wouldn't want to live.

"Have you ever played Hinky Dinky Corny Cup?" Mason walked his fingers up Danny's back. "How many fingers have I got up?" He leaned close to Danny's ear, his tongue flicking out to touch the rim.

"You belong in a goddamn hamster cage, Mason." Danny's voice cracked. He couldn't get enough saliva into his mouth. *How long would it take to die? A day? A week? But I won't die. Mason won't kill me. Not yet.*

"Oh, Danny, Danny. I expected something more original from you. Maybe it's this place. So depressing. Too much concrete."

Mason walked to the table and pulled back the covering. Danny could see a row of metal instruments.

"My old man should've killed you."

Mason turned and studied him for a moment. "Silly, he tried. I had to set fire to my pretty toys to get away. Such a big fire. The flames were so roasty toasty. Can you imagine, he tried to save all those lovelies. For nothing."

Not for nothing. He saved Kate. For a moment, she felt so close, her scent curled out to Danny, and then she was gone.

"But he couldn't kill me because we have a destiny together. You need to understand that."

"We don't have anything."

"Do you know we were born on the same day? June 4th, 1974. A little after midnight at Pennsylvania Hospital. We lay together in the nursery. We share a destiny. And very soon, you will hear the voice of God. But first we need to talk about boring things. The package."

Danny knew he wouldn't be hearing anything but his own screams soon. He didn't have a clue where the package was. But that didn't matter. After a few hours with Mason, he'd say anything.

"This can be easy or difficult. Talk to me, darling. Tell me about the package," Mason said.

Danny tried to get to his feet, but as soon as he did, Mason snapped his fingers. The chain jerked tight, and pain shot up his arms when it wrenched his body off the floor.

"I don't know about any fucking package."

"Truth is beauty, Danny."

"Here's a truth. You're a maggot."

"Feisty, aren't we?" Mason picked up a filleting knife. A glitter of light danced off the thin blade as he motioned to someone. "Secure his legs."

Metal clamped around Danny's ankles. He wasn't feisty. He was lost.

Mason gave him a feral smile and gestured to the table. "So many shiny instruments. I wonder what they all do."

65

Novell lived in a puke-green wood condo that backed up to the 202 Expressway in Malvern. When he got to the door, Kevin heard the blaring television from inside and hoped Novell wasn't drunk.

The door cracked open, and Novell peered out. He didn't look too far gone, but he didn't look good either. He needed a shave, and his bloodshot eyes sunk into sagging purple flesh. He put up his hand like he was fending Kevin off and then dropped it. His head bowed as if he were resigned.

In that moment, Kevin thought of Danny cringing away from Junior and him like a whipped dog because they'd smacked him one too many times, and he felt ashamed.

"What do you want?" Novell said.

"I need your help."

"My help?" Novell gave him a bitter smile. "My help isn't good for much. I'm on suspension, Ryan."

"Danny's disappeared, Novell. I think they grabbed him today. I told him to go home and wait for me, but he wasn't at home."

"Doesn't mean he was grabbed."

"I can't raise him on his phone, and Stan Witkowski's dead."

Novell blinked and wiped his mouth. "I thought you had him."

"I did, but I sent him home. I need your help."

Novell's face was working, and Kevin knew he was fighting something inside himself.

"Novell, you know what they'll do to him." Kevin almost choked on his desperation. Every minute he stood here, he was wasting time. "You've got to have some idea where they'd take him. Please."

"You'll probably get suspended yourself, Ryan."

"He's my brother."

Novell nodded. "I know where we have to start."

66

Kate didn't say anything when she opened the door and saw Novell with the big man she recognized as Kevin Ryan. She let them in and watched Novell do a double take when he saw her hair. She had dyed it sable brown, cut it shoulder length, and blown it straight just that afternoon.

"That color is all wrong for you," the stylist said. "And why would you want to get rid of all those beautiful curls? It makes you look older. Not like yourself."

And wasn't that just the point? She wouldn't be herself. Maybe she'd call herself Beth and lose herself in a dead woman's identity. She'd pretend she was a princess and say once someone was ridiculously in love with her.

Of course Novell would show up tonight. She had forty-five minutes to get to Thirtieth Street station and then she was out of here. A new identity in a new place. It was her only hope. She'd always be damaged goods to Danny. No matter what he said, he'd never love her, not the way she wanted or needed.

She'd thought about it all day. She could go to the club—that gold card would grant her access to every room—and she could look for Mason. Or she could leave. Just disappear. This time she'd go west. She'd always wanted to see California.

Goddamn Novell.

She glanced at Kevin Ryan. He had his father's face, though it was less harsh, and he was bigger than Danny, not so much in height, but in weight and build. Kate wouldn't have pegged them for brothers except for their eyes. Not the color. Danny's were cobalt while Kevin's were almost gray, but the shape—the wide set and slight downward cast—was similar. It gave both of them the look of lost boys. What horseshit. She wanted to shake herself. "What do you want, Novell?"

"We need your help, Kate. It's important." Novell sounded tired. He hadn't come making threats, and he hadn't come alone. That was a surprise.

"Oh?"

"They got Danny. They'll probably kill him if they haven't already, so we need to move fast. Where do you think they'd take him?"

The air rushed out of her lungs. She looked at Kevin Ryan once more and waited for him to say something, but he didn't speak. His face betrayed nothing. He was a cop all right, and if he was anything like his father, probably a good one.

Dear Christ. Nothing made sense anymore.

This was her last chance, and she knew she didn't have a choice. She'd help them because she owed Thomas, because she loved Danny, even though she was ready to disappear and never see him again. Maybe that's what love did. It took you outside yourself, opened you to some bigger world, even if you knew in your heart it could never be yours.

"If they know you're coming, they'll kill him. You know that, Novell." She nodded at Kevin. "I can get him inside. Maybe. Not you."

"Where, Kate?"

She looked away.

67

Cold water hit Danny like liquid nails. He shook so hard he thought his bones would break. They loosened the chain behind him and yanked off the metal collar. He flopped onto the wet concrete floor and let his eyes drift shut.

Arms wrapped around him and dragged him across the floor to flip him onto a mattress that stank of blood, piss, and death. His head banged against the edge of something, but the pain barely registered.

Someone wrenched his arms above his head, and he heard the sound of tape ripping. The tape slapped down on his wrists and bound them to the metal frame of the bed.

"Tape don't stick too good," someone said in disgust. "He ain't got much skin left. You think Mason'd think 'bout shit like that."

"Mason don't think about nothin' but pain," the second voice said.

These were new voices. Danny didn't recognize them. How many people worked down here in this hellhole? He wanted to open his eyes, but it was too much effort.

"Think we need to tape his ankles?"

"What for? You think he's gonna go for a stroll? He don't know where the hell he is. Anyways, Bruce wants him rested up. He don't want him dyin' like that other guy."

"I'm surprised he ain't dead already. He didn't scream as much as most of 'em. That's weird, ain't it?"

"He'll scream. Mason's just getting started."

They laughed, threw a blanket over him, and then walked out of the room and closed the door. A second later, the lock turned.

Danny didn't open his eyes. He was sinking below the water. The deeper he went, the less it hurt. The relentless bass grew fainter, and he could hear the wind hiss through the sea grass and the tide crash against the shore. If he were to reach out through the rippling darkness, he would be able to touch her, to die inside her the way he always had, and she would love him again. She seemed to pull him down, smiling, her eyes glittering black.

But he shifted, winced. He was no longer sinking. He could see Kate's long auburn hair tangled against the pillow, feel her shadow and substance, and he longed to trace the scar beneath her right breast with his mouth, to smell the scent of lavender that clung to her.

"Don't leave me."

There was no answer, and the room came back into horrible focus.

I have to get out.

When Danny pulled himself closer to the edge of the bed, the tape slid a little on his arms, and he was able to catch it in his teeth, just like an animal. He didn't know how long it took him to gnaw through it to free his right arm. He used his teeth and numb fingers to pry loose his left arm.

The feeling was coming back into his hands now, and the rush of blood crackled acid hot through his veins. His hands looked like purple balloons; the fingers so stiff, he could barely bend them. He understood why the tape didn't stick: the outer layer of skin was shredded. He didn't think there was a part of his body that wasn't shredded in some way.

Don't pass out. Don't pass out.

He had lost all track of time. He might have been here a day or a week. All he knew was that fucking bass line and Mason's voice. "Talk to me, Danny. Tell me about the package." And pain. He knew a lot about pain. Mason was right. He was an artist.

But not a professional. How did he know that?

The fuzz began to clear from Danny's head. Mason got off on the pain. He didn't care about the package. Danny took a breath. He could hear his ragged, wheezing breath and feel the stabbing agony that meant something was broken. Ribs, maybe. Or his heart.

Danny Ryan died of a broken heart. Christ. Focus.

Mason. What about Mason? Mason liked pain. A professional would have known after an hour that he didn't have a clue about the package, but Mason didn't care.

The next round would be worse. He couldn't just lie here and wait.

Danny pushed himself up, and the room tilted. He shuddered with the effort, but he levered himself off the bed onto the floor. Cold seeped into him, and he tried to summon the strength to go on. Every muscle protested when he began to crawl along the floor like an insect. He had to get to Mason's table of instruments.

When it finally loomed above him, he pulled himself up on his knees to stare at the array of toys Mason had laid out. A curved knife drew his eye, and he reached for it, careful not to disturb the rest of the tools.

His jeans and shirt lay on the metal chair, and he managed to grab them. He used them to wipe his blood trail from the floor when he crawled back to the cot. It took him a long time to pull on the jeans. The fabric felt like sandpaper against his tortured skin, and blood soaked through the knees. Danny hoisted himself back onto the cot. He pulled the blanket around him and gripped the knife against his side.

Could he pry open the drain? No. It was too narrow to fit into. No strength to try to scale the walls, and even if he could, there was no place to go. Maybe pick the lock? Vic taught him how to pick locks, but he wasn't up to it now. No, he had to think.

He sat with his back against the wall, trembling with cold, even while sweat ran down his body. The salt burned and stung, but he didn't care. It proved he was still alive.

The room drifted out of focus, and he pressed his hands against his forehead. Pinwheels of light spun around the room and shattered off the walls. Orange. Yellow. Red. Shards of pain sliced into his right eye. Danny wanted to curl his body into a tight ball, but he couldn't surrender. Not now. He clenched his teeth together when tears filled his eyes.

If they killed him, they'd win. He wasn't going to let them win. Not without a fight.

68

"That's it, Novell," Kate stared out of the car window at the purple neon sign that glowed above Club Midnight.

The club stood alone on the edge of the Northern Liberties business development district in a four-story renovated factory surrounded by deserted warehouses. No neighbors to complain about the music that pulsed like a heartbeat or the nasty business that went on inside.

Even in the old days, Kate only came here when she felt especially self-destructive.

Kate knew that certain membership cards bought entry to special rooms, and in those rooms, you could get special services. All she ever found was sex in its most basic animal form, enhanced by leather and whips and pain. There was a rumor that things went on downstairs in the dungeon. They called it Tophet, though she wasn't sure why. She never went there. As far as she knew, no one who did ever talked about it.

If Danny was anywhere, he was in the dungeon.

"We'll go in the front way," Kate said. "Try to find Delhomme. He likes to come late, so he's probably here. When we find him, we'll call you, Novell."

Novell nodded. "I'll go around back. See if there's another way in."

Kate glanced at Kevin Ryan. So far he'd said nothing to her. Only grunted.

"I'm sorry if it pains you to be with me," she said to Kevin when they were walking toward the club. She tugged on her leather skirt. It felt too short, too tight.

"It doesn't." He gave her a sidelong glance, and she could feel him assess her. "You a fed?"

"I'm a friend of your brother's."

"I can see you with Danny. You look a little like . . ." He paused, and his eyes swept over her again. It made her feel naked. "He always went for classy women."

She fumbled in her purse to hide her discomfort. "I'm not so classy now, am I?" They stood near the door. She couldn't break down.

"You either are or you aren't. Don't matter what you wear."

Kate pulled out the gold card she'd stolen from Danny. She didn't know why she'd taken it. Maybe she believed if she had it, he couldn't get into too much trouble. Then she could run with a clean conscience. Or maybe she hoped he'd follow her. She made him promise to find Mason, but she didn't expect him to do it. She wished she'd lied about Thomas. She wished she'd run away with him when he asked her. Now he was going to get killed, and it was her fault. She gave Kevin a weak smile. Classy wasn't the word she'd use to describe herself.

He put his hand on her arm. "Delhomme knows me too. I questioned him, Kate."

"We'll have to move fast then."

Kate looked at his hand. It was big and solid like his father's. She swallowed. "You know, Danny's probably dead."

Kevin's fingers tightened on her arm. "You were leaving tonight. I saw your suitcases. Why were you leaving?"

"We'd better get moving."

But Kevin didn't move. "Why did you change your mind?"

Kate stared down at the asphalt.

"Kate." She heard the tremor just under the calm surface of his voice, a tiny crack in his armor. "Holy God. You're the witness."

"Danny told you about me?"

"He told me about Mason, but he wouldn't tell me who you were. Kate, you've got to get out of here. He'd never want you to be involved."

She could take some comfort in that. Danny wouldn't want her to be involved. He cared for her in his way. "You'll never get in on your own. You need me. I can do this."

"I can't ask you—"

"You didn't ask." She wanted to tell Kevin her choice wasn't a choice at all. She was bound to Danny, to all of them, the day Thomas pulled her from the flames. She had to help because maybe then Thomas would rest in peace. Maybe then she could forgive herself. But she didn't say that to Kevin. Instead, she leaned close and kissed his cheek. "I have to do it. Here. Unbutton your shirt. Try to look less like a cop." She deftly undid the buttons on his maroon shirt. Thank God it wasn't starched white.

"I won't forget this, Kate." Kevin put his arm around her, and they approached the door.

*

The heavy beat of electronic music slammed Kate as soon as they entered the purple-and-black interior of Midnight.

Every table was filled. The massive ebony bar with its electric-grape neon trim had a large crowd, and every imaginable combination of half-naked men and women were grinding together on the dance floor. Their bodies adorned with glow-in-the-dark body paint gleamed in the eerie black-and-purple lights.

Kate didn't need to go upstairs to smell the sex. The odor wafted down the halls from the bathrooms, from the balcony, from the dance floor itself. The strobe lights alternated with the black lights, and the purple walls lit with glitter. But it was vast and disorienting and throbbing with sexual energy. The stars stamped on their hands gave them access to the more extreme rooms upstairs, but Kate knew it was the lower levels they needed to reach.

Glow sticks, leather, and strange electronic music were big here. They passed a couple—an overmuscled guy in leather chaps and a skeletal blonde in a leather dress shorter than her own—with their tongues jammed so far down each other's throats that Kate thought they'd choke. She realized they were fucking against the wall and turned away.

Kate glanced around the room, trying see through the crowd. She pushed Kevin into a corner and went to the bar to order two drinks, scanning the room. Then she saw the circular booth tucked into an alcove across the room. It sat on a small platform, sheltered by semidarkness. A group sat there, and three large men stood in front of it. Guards. They'd never let Kevin get close.

Kate took a hard look at Bruce Delhomme and his women, who draped over him like human scarves. He sat drinking, a nervous smirk on his face. A thin, blond man sat to Delhomme's right, his arms spread across the back of the seat—Mason. He lay back, a look of contentment spread across his face. So pleased with himself. Lord of the manor, even more so than Delhomme. It took Kate a second to realize that the woman—or maybe it was a boy—hunched over him was in the process of giving him a blow job. She swallowed both drinks and went back to Kevin, stepping into the shadows so Kevin didn't see the fury she knew contorted her face. Her skin itched and stung.

Hinky dinky corny cup, how many fingers do I have up?

Goddamn Novell. He had to know Mason was still alive and in the city. He had to know. Kate pressed her hands against her stomach. She hoped they shot Novell at the back door. Oh Christ, she had to stay calm.

Da said that last walk was the loneliest one of all. You met the Lord alone. She'd do that, or maybe it wasn't the Lord she'd meet at all but the devil, because no matter what she told herself, this one last thing she had to do was surely a sin. And she would surely pay. She wondered if Danny understood her deep-sworn vow. If he cared. Maybe she'd just be another story. But that was all right. She'd be one hell of a story. His very best.

"Kate? Are you all right?" Kevin's voice was filled with concern.

"I'm grand," she said and gave him a tight smile.

If Mason was here, Danny must be in the dungeon. Why else would Mason be sitting in the open? Kate could almost feel Thomas whisper in her ear, telling her not to be afraid.

She opened her purse and palmed the two-shot Derringer she always carried.

"That's Delhomme's table." Kate pushed Kevin back into the shadows, slid off her jacket, and wiggled against him. "Put your hands on my ass." She laughed when he hesitated. "Jesus Christ, you won't get cooties. Do what I tell you. It's a goddamn sex club." His hands touched her, and she moved closer. "Listen to me, Kevin. I know Danny's here. Don't ask how, but I do. If you walk over there, maybe they panic. I can get close. Maybe I can get Delhomme to leave the table."

Kevin's hands tightened on her ass. "No. It's too risky."

"We don't have options. I'm not threatening. You are. Give me a few minutes, then call for backup or whatever you cops do." She saw him wince and knew he hated the thought of sending in a woman to do his work for him. "I can do this, Kevin. Trust me." She gave him a smile that had a lot more bravado than she felt. "Now give me a kiss like you mean it, and then it's time to dance with the devil."

69

The lights had gone. Only the agony remained. It engulfed him until he wanted to use the knife on himself, but he clenched his teeth together. Someone would come.

Danny heard the key turn in the lock, and he gripped the knife.

Lyle entered and stood at the foot of the cot. "You awake?"

Danny didn't answer.

Lyle walked to the side and stood with his hands on his hips. Danny watched him through slitted eyes. "Time to rise and shine." Lyle smiled and bared those crooked teeth. "Well, you put up a fight, I'll give you that. I hate pussies. And kids. I did a kid once. Snapped his neck like a chicken bone. Collateral damage, y'know?"

Heat shot through Danny. An explosion of fury so violent that his blood scarred his veins.

Conor in his car seat. His eyes wide open. Trapped. This bastard the last thing he saw.

Danny heard the locks on the closet door snap one by one. He pressed the knife against his side, clutched the handle in his fist, but he waited for his moment.

The old man's laughter roared in his head. His hands shook. Not from fear. He knew where to stick a blade. Sweet-faced Danny Ryan. *Come a little closer, you son of a bitch.*

Lyle grabbed Danny and yanked off the blanket. When Lyle pulled him to his feet, Danny shoved the curving blade into Lyle's gut and jerked it up. Blood spilled in a hot stream over his hands and chest; its thick odor mingled with the putrid stench of Lyle's rupturing intestines.

Lyle's eyes widened. His mouth opened to scream, but only a gurgle came out. Froth and blood welled up, bubbling from his lips. He held out his hand as if looking for pity, but Danny had none to give. He felt nothing but the fury that burned like blue flame.

Though he knew he was wasting his strength, Danny twisted the knife deeper and deeper until Lyle sagged to the floor, pulling Danny with him. Danny wanted to shout in triumph. But he dragged himself to his feet and staggered to the door.

70

At the service entrance, Novell crouched behind the dumpster and waited. Steam billowed from a grate and hung in the frigid air. Weird techno music pulsed and raged; it was like standing outside hell. Novell stared at the purple neon sign. *Midnight.* Its letters were pointed like daggers. Why had he come here? Ryan was a dead man.

Yet here he stood. Without backup. Out of his jurisdiction with a Philly cop acting on his own. And Kate. How did you begin to classify Kate? Maybe you didn't classify her. Maybe the time had come to let her go.

Novell wished he'd brought a flask and then figured it was better to have a clear head. Just for fun, he let the air out of Bruce Delhomme's tires.

He had just finished with the back tire when he noticed the cellar doors. They were built into the ground and padlocked. Novell looked around. Since the music was booming, he decided he could take a risk. He pulled out his SIG, placed the muzzle against the lock, and fired.

When nobody came to investigate the gunshot, Novell pulled the lock free and jerked on the doors. He expected it to be pitch black beneath the doors, but the narrow steps were dimly lit. He climbed down. It was cold and damp with that musty smell of mold and mildew that made him feel like spores were coating the insides of his lungs every time he took a breath.

Novell found himself in a passage lit by safety lights. He could still hear the music playing. The bass throbbed overhead, but it sounded eerie now, maybe because this place seemed a little too much like a dungeon.

Novell edged his way down the corridor. To his right was a row of doors. Novell opened the first door. The room was a cell, empty save for a chain that hung from the ceiling, a sink, a metal table, and a cot. Video cameras were set in the walls. Each room was the same.

Jesus fucking Christ.

A door stood open, and Novell's heart jumped against the walls of his chest. Inside he saw a body curled on the floor in a fetal ball by the side. Not Danny. A huge guy. He looked like a bear had mauled him. The pink of his intestines leaked out through the massive hole in his gut, and he stared up at the ceiling, his eyes wide and horrified.

Novell turned away.

He recognized the bloody, balled-up shirt that lay on the cot and stuffed it in his pocket. The table in the corner was covered with metal instruments. Scalpels. Knives. Little hooks. Fuck. This was worse than he'd imagined.

A blood trail led down the hall, and Novell followed the splotches of red around the twisting corridors. He paused at an intersection of tunnels to catch his breath, his fingers aching from gripping the SIG. It was a goddamn labyrinth.

He jerked around when he heard something clatter against the stone floor up ahead. Before he could move, a hulk in a black leather jacket appeared in the tunnel on his right and said, "What the fuck?"

71

Trapped.

If Danny moved from his niche, he'd be exposed, and he was too goddamn tired to run. He scooped up the knife he'd dropped when the furry something ran over his foot and tried to shrink into the cold stone wall.

The act of forcing air into his lungs almost drove him to his knees. It sounded like a death rattle in his chest. He didn't know how long he'd been shuffling through the maze of corridors, but he'd almost reached the end of his endurance. His own blood trailed down the hall behind him.

He could hear slow, heavy footsteps. More than one pair of feet. They walked with the care of men picking their way through a minefield. Then a muffled voice.

He flinched when he heard three booms in quick succession. They echoed off the walls and were followed by two thuds. Danny froze. Now what? If he went back, there was only that cell. He gripped the knife against his side and pushed away from the niche.

When he rounded the turn, he saw a big man lying on the floor with half his head blown away. Brain matter, blood, and skull fragments were sprayed against the floor, and an ever-widening puddle of deep red spread around the shattered remains. A second man sprawled against him with a hole in his throat the size of his fist and a second in his chest. He stared at Danny with lifeless eyes. A stream of red dripped from his open mouth.

Danny took a step back, and Novell appeared like some kind of avenging angel from the shadows. His eyes shone a little too bright, and his cheeks flushed deep red. His breath came shallow and fast, and though he wasn't smiling, Danny could sense the big, chest-thumping victory whoop that lay beneath the surface. Novell looked like a junkie on the best high of his life.

He understood it.

Novell assessed Danny for a minute, and his mouth grew pinched. He yanked off his overcoat and draped it over Danny's shoulders. "Put this on. There's a back way. Past those cells. Can you walk that far?"

Danny slid his arms into the coat and tried to ignore the way the fabric pulled at his torn flesh. "No. Mason's upstairs. Novell—"

"What are you talking about?"

Christ, it was a nightmare. He had to explain and was running out of time and air. "I can't—Mason—is here—Kate—Mason was—I promised."

"She told you about Mason?" He saw the understanding dawn in Novell's eyes. "She's here with your brother."

"Upstairs?" Danny slumped against the wall. They'd come for him.

"You'll never make it," Novell said. "And I don't need the liability."

"Go. I'll . . . follow." Danny didn't want to argue the point, especially when he could see the stairwell through the tunnel up ahead. "Get him."

"Goddamn you." Novell's voice shook a little, but he put his arm around Danny's waist. "Lean on me and move. Don't argue."

Danny shuffled with Novell until they reached the stairwell. He looked up. It seemed endless.

"I'm going first. I'm gonna look for a way out," Novell said. "You follow. If something happens to me, find Kevin and get yourself out." Novell squeezed his shoulder. "You do the big guy?"

Danny held out the knife. Novell shook his head, but he sounded almost pleased when he said, "You're a goddamn idiot, Ryan."

"He killed . . . Conor." Danny could feel his last reserves crumbling, and he turned his head away.

Novell leaned close. "Listen to me because I'm only gonna say it once. Keep going. No matter what happens. And keep down. You understand? If you want to get out of here alive."

72

By the time he reached the top of the stairs, Novell had disappeared through the metal door at the top. Danny was coughing blood, and he had to grip the railing with both hands to keep from falling backward. His hands were slippery with sweat. He didn't care what was on the other side of the door, but when he stumbled through it, he found himself in yet another corridor. Purple neon lights edged the matching walls and ceiling. The deep-violet carpet felt smooth and soft beneath his bare feet.

The music was so loud now he thought his head would explode from the shattering bass line. The wall vibrated when he leaned against it. No sign of Novell.

No place to go but forward.

The wall to his left split open, and a woman clad in a leather cat suit stepped out. She wore a mask over the upper part of her face, and her lips were painted black. When she saw him, she paused with her hands on her hips. She tapped her fingers, their tips long and silver, and then she smiled, and he almost did a double take. Her teeth were filed to sharp points.

"You like it rough, don't you?" she said and stepped toward him. "Come upstairs, baby. I'll take care of you."

He stared at her, fascinated and repelled, and he wondered if he was hallucinating. He almost expected to hear the opening bass riff of Jefferson Airplane's "White Rabbit."

"Have to get out," he said.

"You're bleeding on the floor. I think you aren't supposed to be here at all."

"Please."

She hesitated and then looked behind her, like she expected trouble to pop out of the wall. "Give me a straight answer. Did they have you downstairs?"

He nodded.

"Fuck." She pointed straight ahead to what seemed like a dead end. "Pull your collar up around your face. Here." She began to arrange the coat for him, and he tried to ignore the look of pity in her eyes. "You never saw me." She slipped her arm through his and led him down the hall, letting go when the wall at the other end cracked open. Novell appeared.

"Danny. Move it." Novell didn't bother to hide his gun, and the woman stepped back. Her mouth opened like she might scream, but she seemed to think the better of it.

"She helped me," Danny said. The words scraped his dry throat.

Novell looked at the woman. "If I were you, I'd get my ass out of here before the shit hits the fan. Understand?" She nodded. Danny saw a flicker in her eyes, and then her face went blank. He shuffled down the hall to Novell.

*

"Stay behind me and keep down," Novell said. "We're coming behind the kitchen into the club. If I could avoid this, I would, but I can't."

Danny could hear the clink of dishes and smell beef searing on a grill. It smelled like his own burnt flesh. The scent of garlic and basil clung to the air. He pushed his fist against his mouth and willed himself not to vomit.

They passed through a final door into a different kind of horror show. The music and the lights hit him like punches, and he couldn't get his bearings in the vast club. Glow sticks waved as light patterns on the floor changed every few seconds. It was a huge sex emporium. He didn't think he'd ever seen so many people wearing leather gathered together in one room.

"It's over there," Novell said, pointing to a table in the semi-darkness of an alcove.

A beam of purple light illuminated it for a second. Delhomme and Mason sat among a crowd of leather-clad women, and Kate walked toward them. At least he thought it was Kate, though she looked oddly like Beth. With each step, she grew more and more surreal.

He reached for Novell. "There."

Kate wore a short, skintight, black leather dress that laced in front, and she sauntered toward the table with an attitude that had the men turning to stare at her. She should have left a trail of smoke in her wake. The three goons standing in front of the alcove just grinned at her.

Techno music filled Danny's head and the lights flashed. He pushed after Novell through the crowd, but Danny felt a sick certainty they were too late. It was like watching a chain reaction car crash from an overpass: you could see it coming, but you couldn't stop it.

In desperation, he stripped off Novell's coat and watched people back away from him in horror. Mason looked up, and then he was on his feet.

Kate raised her hand. There were two flashes, and Mason clutched his neck. Blood poured between his pale fingers. Delhomme's mouth was open, but his cries were lost in the music. One of the big goons started to swing around, but Novell was already aiming his SIG. Danny heard the gun boom. There were several booms that followed, and Kate dropped to the ground.

People were screaming and running now, and ahead, Novell ducked when one of the guards took a shot at him. Danny struggled through the torrent of people pouring toward the exits, her name echoing through his heart.

Music still blasted and lights pulsed. Someone knocked him down, and he smashed into a table. Legs and feet went hurtling past him. A heavy boot connected with his skull, but he shook off the pain and crawled the last few feet to Delhomme's table to pull Kate into his arms. Her back was slippery, and in the light, the blood looked deep purple. She gripped a tiny derringer in her right hand.

Mason slumped down on the floor, his eyes wide, his dark blood staining the front of his silk shirt. He clutched at his neck with one hand and reached the other out to Danny. "Help me." He choked out the words, the blood leaking through his fingers and out of his mouth.

"Fuck you, Mason."

"Please . . ." Mason's hands reached for him, those long, white fingers stretching. "Please . . ." A single tear glistened on Mason's cheek, and his voice trembled. Mason edged closer until his hands locked around Danny's leg.

Danny could hear him choking in his own blood. "Do you hear the fucking voice of God, Mason?" Mason's face crumpled. "Keep listening."

Kate moved against him, and Danny could feel her shallow breaths feather his cheek when he bent closer. "Kate. Kate, please." He could smell lavender mixed with the caustic odor of cordite and blood. Where was the fucking bullet hole?

She sighed, and her eyes rolled open. Her lips moved, but her voice was so faint he had to press his ear against her mouth to hear. "Not lost anymore."

"Not lost." He pulled her closer. "Kate. We're not lost. We're together."

"I did it."

"Kate, don't leave me. Please. I love you. I—"

She took a labored breath, and he watched her eyes drift shut.

The surge came then with relentless force. Black water spilled over him until he could no longer breathe, and Danny sank into the welcoming darkness.

73

Under a cloudless sky, Danny lay on the beach and let the sun warm his exhausted body. Conor dumped bucket after bucket of white sand on him as waves washed up against the shore.

"If we lived on this island, we could come to the beach every day," Conor said. "We could always be like this." He poured sand and patted it down. A warm blanket on Danny's legs.

"Could we stay here, Conor?"

Conor dumped another bucket of sand on Danny's stomach. More and more sand. "We could always be together, Daddy. I miss you."

"I miss you too. I miss you so much."

Conor smiled. He patted the sand until it felt firm around Danny's body. Then he leaned close. "Mommy's dead. She's in the ground."

Danny struggled to sit up, but he couldn't move. The sand had hardened like concrete. Conor sat back on his heels and folded his arms. His eyes grew distant. Cold.

"You can't stay."

Danny tried to answer, but he couldn't speak.

Conor shook his head. "You can't stay. You let the bad man hurt me."

Conor stood and walked away, and Danny heard the tide rush in. When he called out, black water filled his mouth and poured down his throat.

*

Danny jerked up in the hospital bed and waited for his heart to slow. It would. Eventually. He'd stop shaking, and his breath would come. He closed his eyes, lay back against the pillows, and willed himself to relax.

He knew he was in a private room in the hospital. He'd been here a week, as close as he could determine, while they reinflated his lung, pumped him full of antibiotics, x-rayed his broken ribs, and ran a full spectrum of tests. He no longer cared what they were for.

They told him he would heal with a minimum of scarring and kept him doped up for the first few days. It dulled the horror a little.

Kate waited for him on the edge of consciousness, and he could almost touch her and smell the lingering scent of her perfume before she melted into darkness. The old man was right. Kate should have stayed away from him. She offered him salvation, and he had gotten her killed. Was that what she meant when she made her deep-sworn vow? She knew somehow they would be parted? She sacrificed herself for him, and a miserable sacrifice it was.

To what end? So he could lie in this bed and remember what an idiot he was and then be snowed under only to dream of Conor. Always of Conor. Because he couldn't bear to think of Conor when he was awake. To do so was to slide along the edge of the razor blade into the dark pool of despair. Then he'd lie there and listen to his heart race and watch the numbers on the monitor jump higher and higher until the nurse came with a needle filled with something that sent him back to oblivion.

He promised himself that he'd start to write, and he'd tried to put some words together on the laptop Kevin brought him from home. He wanted to do it, but nothing was there.

He had opened the door, become the monster.

"Don't let me down," Andy had told him that last day outside Linda's room in this same hospital. Andy would be pretty goddamn disappointed if he were here right now. Danny stared at the dark-brown stain on the ceiling tiles. It looked like a rabbit with a drooping ear or maybe like someone giving the finger.

He picked up the shopping bag full of mail Kevin brought and set it on the bed. Kevin was solicitous. Kind. He fetched clothes, the laptop, everything Danny asked him to bring, and he hovered like a St. Bernard whenever he was here. Danny almost preferred the old head-smacking Kevin to this new and improved model. He felt like a bastard for thinking it.

He hadn't seen Novell, and Kevin wouldn't talk about him. Kevin was the censor to all information. He wouldn't allow the television to be turned on. Danny had no newspapers. No telephone. A cop lived outside his door twenty-four hours a day. Danny wasn't sure whether Kevin was protecting him or keeping him under some new form of house arrest.

He was surprised Kevin brought him the mail. Danny rooted through the red shopping bag he'd ignored until now.

He pulled out a flyer for a singles night at the Church of Good News. Across the bottom was written, "I'd love to see you. Please call if you don't want to go alone. Carrie Norton. P.S. Enjoy the cookies."

She left her phone number, and Danny tried to remember who Carrie Norton was and then decided it didn't matter. When he was hanging out with Mason, she was sipping Christmas punch with the Christian singles. Maybe he'd call her just for the hell of it and explain why he'd been unable to attend. Somehow, he didn't think she'd find it amusing.

He dumped contents of the bag on the blanket. Christmas cards and junk mail tumbled out along with one package wrapped in brown paper. It fell onto the bed with a soft thud, and Danny recoiled as if it were a snake. He reached for it with shaking fingers. He didn't have to read Michael's handwriting to know what it was.

The writing was smudged as if with tears, the paper splotched with dark-brown stains. Michael's blood. All the time they were looking for this goddamn package, Carrie Norton had it in a red Christmas gift bag.

Danny pulled the paper off to find five discs in thin plastic cases and a small cardboard box of photographs with matching negatives. All bore the logo from the cards, though they were black, divided with a thin gold line and had that gold tear-shaped flame. One DVD was labeled "Tophet." The last DVD was labeled "For Danny Ryan in the Event of My Death."

74

A foursome in black leather sipped neon-green drinks and watched one naked girl whip a second. Chained to a slab of granite, the second girl's body bowed back and her face contorted in a silent scream. Bloody stripes crisscrossed her buttocks. The girls couldn't have been more than fifteen or sixteen.

An older man Danny recognized as a district justice lay on a similar slab while two young boys pissed on him and a third whipped him.

The pictures got worse.

The Inferno. Its membership list read like a Who's Who of Philadelphia society. Who would guess so many high-ranking civic leaders and philanthropists nursed such peculiar tendencies? Maybe it shouldn't have surprised him. According to Andy's disc, Robert Harlan was the leader of the pack. Unfortunately, while there was hard evidence on most of the other members, there was nothing definitive on the senator. He invested in Bruce Delhomme's enterprises. So did half of Philadelphia's elite. It didn't mean they were all into underage sex or sex clubs.

But Andy wouldn't have accused Robert Harlan if he hadn't been sure. Senator Family Values. It would almost have been funny if it weren't so horrific.

For enough money, the Inferno performed useful services for its members. Sex. Blackmail. Murder.

The senator had presidential ambitions. Danny imagined that was why he wanted to get rid of his prying son-in-law. Maybe that was part of the reason Beth had become so shrill in her warnings to leave her father alone. Who would know better what a dangerous man he was?

Danny didn't understand why they hadn't finished the job.

He closed the file and then glanced at the "Tophet" DVD that lay on the bed. It contained, among other highlights, the torture and murder of at least three kids performed by Mason Scott himself.

Did Bartlett Scott know about his son's horrific employment? Did he care? Maybe it didn't register. Perhaps he considered it the lot of children born to endless nights.

He watched Andy's disc, a confession of his involvement with the Inferno, articulated in Andy's typical style. No bullshit, no apology. He pushed his computer away. Soon the aide would bring him a tray with a bowl of consommé and containers of green Jell-O and orange sherbet. He was stuck in this bed, and those bastards still walked around like they owned the goddamn universe.

It wasn't a conspiracy. It was a club, and one had to be in a certain tax bracket to join. Danny realized with some irony that he now qualified to be a member. It made him more than a little nauseated. Beth always said everyone had nasty little secrets. Maybe she was warning him.

Kate had warned him, but he was Danny Ryan, righter of wrongs, too full of his own shit to listen; now almost everyone he cared about was dead.

Danny watched the IV fluid drip down from its bag and run through the tube into his arm. This time he wasn't sinking into the black hole, and he wasn't going to let Kevin hide him away for his own protection. He dragged himself out of bed and began to go through the nightstand drawers. No wallet. No cash, credit cards, or driver's license. He clutched the bed, a little dizzy, but it didn't matter. He was getting out.

He ripped the IV out of his left arm. It burned like hell, and blood dribbled down his arm. He ignored it, switched off the heart monitor, peeled off the little wires and adhesive pads, and hoped no one would come to check him. It was a hectic time. Shift change. He might be able to slip out unnoticed if he planned it right.

At least Kevin brought him clothes. Thank Christ he remembered to bring shoes and a coat.

Danny stuffed the pictures and discs in his coat pocket and crept to the door. He could see the Philly cop assigned to guard his room chatting with the cute blonde nurse at the central station. The cop leaned against the desk, gave a quick look up and down the hall, and then settled in for some serious flirting. The nurse didn't seem in any hurry to get rid of him, not by the come-a-little-closer smile on her face.

An aide helped an elderly woman in a walker, and the woman from housekeeping pushed her cart toward the nurses' station. When she rolled past his room, Danny took a breath and slipped around the door. The stairs were at the end of the hall, and he wanted to run to them. The trick he knew to becoming invisible, however, was to pretend he belonged. He took his time and made no eye contact, but he didn't try to avoid anyone either.

It was like he was in one of those dreams where he was walking but not making progress. When his fingers finally touched the metal handle of the fire door, he yanked it open.

He took the stairs two at a time.

*

Danny ducked in and out of the lunch crowd at Reading Terminal Market and hustled spare change. He needed to put some space between him and the hospital, and it was easy to get lost here in the crowded market. Women were the easiest mark. He looked cleaner than the average street person, and most of the women were charitable enough to believe his story about being mugged. It wasn't much of a stretch. He was still wearing a hospital bracelet. When he caught a glimpse of himself in a store window, he barely recognized his face. No wonder they hadn't given him a mirror.

He looked not quite human. Or maybe all too human. Most people winced and took a step back from him before they shoved a dollar or two in his hand, but one gray-haired woman bought him a cup of coffee and a sandwich before she gave him a twenty.

"I 'member you, Mista Ryan," she said. "You wrote them stories 'bout the city closin' the library in my neighborhood. You said children needs books, and you got Mrs. Bartlett Scott to come in and get her husband to donate one million dollars. They calls it the Bartlett and Emily Scott Reading Room, but I said it should be called the Daniel Ryan Reading Room 'cause them rich folks never would have gotten involved if it weren't for you."

He kissed her hand. He'd forgotten the library. He'd forgotten so much. He used to care. What the hell had happened to him?

He had almost forty dollars in his pocket when he reached the Broad Street Subway. Once, he'd been a relentless hustler, desperate for the cash he knew brought independence from the old man. The fact that he looked young for his age always gave him an edge.

Vic Ceriano called him his gold mine, and Danny knew if it weren't for the weird quirks of fate, he might have ended up pushing drugs for Vic. He might have ended up in jail for real. He might have ended up like those poor kids in the video. A thousand ifs: if the old man hadn't caught him selling dope, if his English teacher Mrs. Taylor hadn't sent in that essay, if Andy Cohen hadn't taken him under his wing.

Danny peered down the tunnel. He could see the subway headlight glow in the semidarkness and feel the vibration of the train. He leaned back against a pole to breathe in the dank odor of mold and piss.

He'd spent countless hours waiting for the Broad Street Subway. The day he'd left for college, he'd packed a duffle bag, walked out the door, and took it away from his old life.

The old man had laughed at him, called him a goddamn jackass for wanting to study something as idiotic as journalism. The

Ryans became cops. Or junkies like Theresa. He'd been furious when Danny got the letter informing him that he was the recipient of a full scholarship to Temple.

"I give you a week," the old man had said, and his eyes had lit up with a malevolent gleam. "Two at best. You might have some fancy scholarship, but you gotta live down there too. Don't expect any handouts from me. See how long you last, Einstein. You'll be back."

He hadn't returned until the old man's funeral. Didn't know or care what happened to the things he left behind. Those stupid copybooks filled with crap. It was all trash. He thought he knew so much, but what did he know about life then? About anything?

When the subway rolled into the station, Danny slumped into a molded plastic seat. The door smacked shut, and the train lurched away.

That first day, he'd found a care package waiting for him in his dorm filled with the kinds of things parents normally packed for their kids to take off to school. Sheets, towels—the basics he had no clue he needed. At the bottom he'd found a lunch invitation from Andy Cohen, and he'd realized that this too-good-to-be-true scholarship had been a setup.

When he'd met Andy at the Four Seasons Hotel, Danny expected he'd at least pretend ignorance, but Andy just laughed. "What did you think, kid? That Temple just has money to burn on South Philly juvies? What do you care where it came from?"

"I don't want to owe anyone."

"Don't be an idiot. Isn't pride one of the seven deadly sins? I thought you Irish were big on sin." Andy had downed his scotch.

"So why are you so interested in my welfare?"

"Why do you think, kid?"

"Are you gay?" Danny had been sure that Andy would throw him out or smack him. Generosity without a catch was unknown in his world. If Andy was offering money, Danny had figured he wanted some kind of favor.

"Hell, no!" Andy had laughed until tears ran down his face. "Are you?"

Danny had frowned, half annoyed, half embarrassed that Andy had found him so ludicrous. "Why do you give a shit about me? What's in it for you?"

Andy's face had turned pensive. "You're a little young to be such a cynic, aren't you? Must be your old man's cop vibes rubbing off on you."

The waiter had set down Danny's grilled chicken, and Danny had been so hungry, his stomach was doing flip-flops. But he hadn't picked up his fork.

"You know my old man?" The old man had always been his hair shirt. The man who'd single handedly faced down gang-bangers in North Philly with nothing more than a Smith & Wesson and a sneer.

"Thomas Patrick Ryan. The most kills of any active cop in the Philly PD, and the most decorated cop in the history of the department. He's a fucking legend, kid."

"That's him. Dirty Harry without the conscience." Danny had tried to sound flippant, but his voice had grated against his throat. "My brothers are cops. Runs in the family. I've always been the oddball."

"Well, I still have that essay you wrote. You're a hell of a talent, my friend. Suitably tormented." Andy had signaled the waiter for another scotch. "Let me ask you this. What are you more afraid of? That you're like your father or you're not?" Andy had held up a hand before Danny could reply. "I don't really give a shit what your answer is. You want to know why I'm so interested in you? You're my mitzvah, kid. My good deed. I'm a Jew, and we've all got to do our mitzvahs. But I'm also a smart Jew, so when I look at you, I know that my good deed will pay me big dividends."

Danny rested his head against the window. He still didn't know the answer to Andy's question. All he knew was he ached in chunks and wished he could shut it off the way he used to. But it was too late. No matter how hard and fast he ran, he couldn't escape the surge that dragged him under. His body swayed with the rhythm and rumble of the train, the only real thing in a world of shattered dreams and dark water and desolate ghosts.

75

Sam Westfield had been the city editor for as long as Danny could remember. A profane, fire hydrant of a man, Westy always had a red pen jammed behind his ear and a thick stogie that smelled like it had been dipped in horseshit clamped between his yellow teeth.

Danny called him the Cliché, but Westy was also a Haverford School boy who'd gone on to Harvard before he ever set foot in a newspaper office. Interesting street creds, to say the least.

"Christ on a one-legged crutch." Westy scrunched up his face in disgust when Danny emerged from the subway. "You look fuckin' grotesque, Ryan. I almost didn't recognize you." He coughed and spat a glistening blob of green phlegm on the pavement. "This better be good."

"Sex, drugs, and serial killing." Danny watched Westy's eyes begin to sparkle with glee.

He lit his stogie. "What are we waiting for then? You'd better work out of Andy's office. We'll talk there."

*

"Legal has to look over those," Westy said when Danny handed him the discs. "Why do I think they'll have a shit hemorrhage?"

"I'll give you copies, but I get to hold on to the originals. Anyway, it all ties in with what went down at Club Midnight."

"You mean the drug bust?"

Unease tightened Danny's shoulders. "What are you talking about?"

"Major drug bust at Club Midnight. The DEA had the place under surveillance for months." Westy rolled the stogie around his mouth, then yanked it out and pointed it at Danny like an accusing finger. "Some fuckin' reporter you are. Don't even read the goddamn paper."

"No, it wasn't like that." Danny pressed his hands against his forehead. He didn't imagine what happened at Club Midnight. What happened to Kate. "I was there. There was a shooting."

"Yeah, shots were exchanged. Some people got shot up. That Bruce Delhomme, you know him? He's down at Jefferson in a coma. He may or may not ever wake up. In any case, you were in South Philly getting the shit kicked out of you. According to the cops, you were jumped near your sister's house. Cops found you at Morris under the I-95 ramp beat nearly to death."

"No. Ask my brother—"

"Where d'you think we got the story? Detective Kevin Ryan of the Philly PD." Westy regarded him with something approaching pity. "Look, you were beat half to death. How clear d'you remember anything?"

Danny turned away. He couldn't stand to have Westy look at him like he was a used-up has-been who had to be humored for old time's sake.

"Tell me what you know about the Inferno, Westy."

"Jesus Christ, is that what this is about?"

"You were looking into it? You didn't tell me."

Westy gave him a grim smile. "The sex club? Why would I? You gave up on investigative reporting. You were our award-winning columnist. Didn't you ever read your own propaganda? But I had a guy on it."

Danny shifted in Andy's chair. Andy couldn't afford to ignore a story without raising suspicions, but Danny was sure whomever Westy assigned to it got nowhere. He didn't think it was a coincidence that Andy offered him the column right after the Sandman case closed. Christ, had it all been an ego fuck? A distraction? Whatever it was, he'd gone for it.

"It's not just a sex club, Westy. It's an organization. The cream of society. For a fee, they can get access to . . . you name it."

"And you've got proof?"

Danny pointed to the discs. "Michael Cohen was bringing those to me the night he was killed."

"And you've got confirmation of everything on these discs, Ryan?"

"Jesus Christ. You haven't even looked at them."

"I know if you start hurling accusations at people in power, you'd better have some pretty airtight proof and you'd better have collaborating sources. You aren't a rookie. You know how it works."

Danny knew Westy was doing his job, but he'd lived the story. "Have legal look at these after we make copies. I think it's pretty airtight. I spoke to Andy, and he included a confession of sorts. I have financial records of the organization. Initiation fees. Lists of services. It's all documented along with a full membership list."

"And?"

"For most people, being members of the Inferno gave them access to kinkier-than-normal sex clubs. Not your standard ménage à trois stuff, but some hardcore S and M, kids—most of them were street kids who looked very young, maybe fifteen— other grotesque shit. But high rankers got more."

"What do you mean more? More sex? What the hell were they doing? Fucking babies?"

"Possibly, but they ordered off the select à la carte menu, depending on who they were and how far how up the food chain they were. It was all an additional fee, of course."

"You mean like sex and drugs?"

Danny wondered if Novell felt as old and tired as he felt right now. Where was Novell? He had to track him down. Novell needed to see these discs. He needed to be part of this.

"Danny?"

"First, as far as I can determine, at the top, it was a very select group of very high rollers, and they could get anything, and I mean anything. Not everyone got to be a top member; they had to be approved, but once someone was approved . . . well . . . Say I need investors for my club. Better yet, say I want to kill you. I go to my friends, and they can make it happen. It's not just about sex. It's about power. They have it, and they aren't afraid to use it. Christ, if you want to understand, look at the pictures, watch the DVDs. It's all there. Andy included a signed and notarized statement of authenticity."

Westy chomped on the stogy for a moment, his face sober. At last he said, "I'm not going to like what I see, am I?"

The surge punched through his chest. "Not unless you like snuff films."

76

D anny faced Novell across Andy's desk. "The Inferno. I figured you deserved to see these before they hit the Sunday paper." He handed Novell the pile of photos. "According to Andy's confession, there were three of them in the beginning: Bartlett Scott, Robert Harlan, and Andy. Three rich guys looking for a way to have fun on Saturday night. It might have stayed that way except Bartlett Scott had a son with peculiar inclinations."

"He liked to kill girls."

"Not just kill them. He liked to skin them." Danny's voice faltered, and he thought of Kate. The lost girls. They surrounded him. He could feel their cold breath on the back of his neck.

"Go on." Novell pulled out a slim flask, but he didn't open it. He just turned it over and over in his hands, and Danny knew it was only the soothing repetition of the task that kept Novell from leaping from his seat and smashing something.

"When Bartlett Scott discovered what Mason was up to, he was appalled, to be sure, but not so appalled that he was willing to let his son go to jail. It was Bob Harlan who realized there was profit to be made by transporting young girls into the country, using them up sexually and then throwing them to Mason. A virgin is only a virgin once after all, and Big Bob realized there was money to be made in offering special services to very, very rich, influential people. For a fee. So he brought in Bruce Del-homme to run the day-to-day operation and invested in his res-taurants. Nice cover, right? Problem was they misjudged Andy. They figured he was a cokehead without a conscience." Danny looked up at Novell and saw the scorn in his eyes. "They were wrong, Novell."

"Were they?" Novell stopped turning the flask.

"They were." Danny broke off, and it struck him that pictures of Andy and dignitaries he'd met over the years lined the walls. Presidents stretching back to Kennedy, local politicos, movie stars, the famous and nearly famous.

Crowded in among the pictures was one Danny had never paid much mind, though he knew it hung there: a photograph of him at age fifteen with Andy taken the day his essay was pub-lished. He'd been stunned because he couldn't understand why he'd been singled out for anything other than a beating. Andy saved his life.

"He didn't have to make these discs, Novell. He didn't have to confess to anything."

"I guess you don't know the feds very well," Novell said. "First to talk. First to walk."

Danny shook his head. He might have ended up like those poor kids, passed around until they were deemed unusable. Did Andy know Mason never stopped his ritual? Andy swore in his confession that he didn't know what was happening in those basement rooms until he saw the Tophet DVD. He was told it was a fake at first, but Bruce Delhomme enlightened him because Bruce wasn't taking the fall alone if something went wrong.

"But there's no way to prove whether the DVD is real or fake," Novell said.

"No. I guess you could take it to a pro, but it would be an opinion."

"And that would be their defense. It's all fake. You might get them on using underage actors or not. Hard to say." Novell shrugged. "Basically, the DVD doesn't count as hard evidence, though the feds will take a hard look at those kids. They'll try to get a clear picture of their faces, then put them out to local law enforcement. If anyone's been looking for them and they get a hit, it'll be a first step, but that nightmare ought to be seen."

Danny knew he was right. Maybe someone somewhere cared about those kids, but they had dropped through the gaping holes in the juvenile system. The DVD needed to be seen, but it would never make it to court. "Is Kevin dirty, Novell?"

"Kevin thinks he can keep you alive if he looks the other way."

"Has he been looking the other way for a while?"

"I don't think he's been involved with the Inferno, but he definitely called in some major favors with what went down at Midnight."

"Westy said the cops found me in South Philly."

Novell shrugged. "I know. If it means anything, he was trying to protect you."

Danny tried to understand Kevin's logic, but it eluded him. "By keeping me in that goddamn hospital room like a prisoner?"

"Stan Witkowski's dead. There was an explosion at his house. They said he was smoking and it set off his oxygen tank. Him, his wife."

"Jesus."

"Our friends were covering up loose ends. Kevin didn't want you to become a loose end. And he didn't want you to know the cops reached an agreement with Mason's family to keep his name out of what went down at the club."

"They did what?" Danny almost jumped out of his seat.

Novell smiled. "Don't worry. The feds got to go through Mason's private room and gather evidence. But it won't change the outcome of the Sandman killings."

Danny could see Novell was having fun. "And you won't tell me anything."

"Nothing to tell. The feds took over the investigation, and they aren't talking. Apparently, Delhomme's operation has been under surveillance by the DEA for some time. The clubs have been shut down."

"Didn't you know about it?"

"I'm not in the bureau any more, and it was a deep-undercover operation. Nobody is talking to anyone." Novell gave him an asthmatic chuckle. "Bureaucracy is a wonderful thing."

"You're all insane, Novell. And Kate?"

"She's gone."

"She's dead?" Danny pushed his fingers against his temples. He'd killed her. She'd come after him, and now she was dead.

Novell sighed. "Does it matter? She's gone. It's not your fault. It's what she wanted. She wanted to put a stop to Mason."

"We had him. I was too slow. It is my fault."

For the first time, Novell gave him a look of pity. "No. It's not. Kate made a choice. Now you need to decide what you're going to do. Having investments in a sex club may look a bit shady for Senator Harlan. He'll take a hit in the press. I doubt it will do him lasting harm in the long run." Novell's face hardened. "So what are you going to do?"

"My father-in-law's throwing a party tonight at the Pyramid Club. Westy's already sending a photographer. I thought it would be fun to crash it."

77

"Welcome to the Pyramid Club, gentlemen." The blonde in the black velvet cocktail dress almost blinded him with her smile. "The reception is upstairs. If I can see your IDs?"

Danny let out a breath. Kevin had been among the cops standing guard downstairs, but Danny managed elude him and slip in among the crowd of press. Now he and Novell took refuge behind the bulky photographer, Freddie Santos. Engulfed in Westy's coat, the faint horseshit aroma of Westy's stogies gave Danny a strange comfort. He held out his press pass.

The blonde smiled. "Alex Burton?"

"Right," Danny said. "That's me."

It had taken some doing, but he had managed to filch Alex's ID and persuaded the photo boys to whip him up a passable facsimile. Thank God this bimbo had no idea that Alex was a woman.

"The senator is making an important announcement tonight," Novell said to Danny. "You have any idea what that would be?"

Danny nodded. "He wants to run for president."

"Which is why he wanted the financial records."

"Look. They're showing a movie. Why do they always show movies?" Santos pointed to a poster of the senator that sat on a metal tripod in front of the curving staircase that led up to the main reception area. *"Robert Harlan: A Life in Retrospect.* What does that mean?"

"That he's an asshole." Danny glanced at Novell. "Home movies can be pretty boring, don't you think?" He held out a disc.

Novell's mouth twitched. He gave an almost imperceptible nod, took the disc, and slipped up the stairs to blend into the crowd.

*

Danny shrank into a corner of the room behind a potted fern and tried to pretend he was enjoying the view out of the twenty-foot window. He could see the reflection of the hors d'oeuvres arranged in silver bowls. Shrimp the size of his thumb, little crab claws, glistening oysters, and so much more—clearly this was the seafood room. In the middle of the table stood an ice sculpture shaped like a battleship. Light sparkled off its surface in an ever-changing prism of color.

It was an all-star crowd. Judges. Philanthropists. Lawyers. Doctors. Eminent do-gooders. Politicians. Danny felt trapped. The real circles of hell surrounded him tonight.

"There's the man of the hour!"

A jolt ran through him. He didn't have to look around to know that Robert Harlan had entered the room. The senator's presence was electric. Danny was surprised that the ice sculpture hadn't vaporized.

"Senator," the blonde from downstairs came into the room. "We're almost ready to begin."

"In a moment, Janine. Get everyone assembled, please."

She immediately began to herd people toward the dining room, and Danny winced. Kate's replacement. She looked as if she were made of plastic, and he thought of the scar under Kate's right breast. It matched the empty space in his heart. Danny clenched his fists. It was time to stop playing hide and seek. He slid around the fern and blended into the crowd milling out the door.

A reverent silence fell over the room when Robert Harlan sailed in, as majestic as any battleship. He shook hands, smiled, and waved to the crowd as the klieg lights snapped on and Danny took refuge behind Freddie Santos's bulk.

"Ladies and gentlemen, thank you for joining me tonight."

Danny could see Patsy Harlan, who sat at the head table, her helmet hair so sharp and perfect it was probably bulletproof. There was never much of Patsy in Beth. She was always Daddy's girl. But Patsy looked good tonight in an artificially tightened way. Miss Georgia Peach was doing her best to glow. Her wide, fake smile looked painful.

"These are trying moral times, indeed, my friends."

As the senator's golden baritone bathed the room in its warmth, people clapped and cheered. They bought into the Gospel of Robert Harlan. They soaked it up because he made their fears and prejudices reasonable. In his voice of poisoned syrup, he offered them simpleminded solutions, and they sounded reasonable too.

Wasn't that what the devil always did?

"We need a stronger America with real family values. And that is why I am forming an exploratory committee to seek the office of president of the United States."

People stood to applaud, and Robert Harlan beamed, a benevolent sun shining down on his subjects.

Janine said, "Ladies and gentlemen, if you will please direct your attention to the movie screen, we'd like to show you a short film, then the senator will be happy to take questions from the press."

The lights clicked off, and the room went dark. Danny held his breath.

78

The room seemed to recoil as one at the sound of the boy's screams, clearly audible over the relentless guitars. Mason's voice joined in on the vocals.

"Is this some kind of sick joke?" a woman said.

Danny watched Janine fumble in the darkness for the switch on the DVD player. The image of a blond boy hanging naked and bleeding with Mason lurking before him like a malevolent green pixie froze and then disappeared. The lights snapped on.

Danny watched the faces staring at the screen. He saw anger, disbelief, disgust. He wondered if it occurred to any of them that some of the kids who had serviced them at their clubs ended up in that dungeon with Mason. Maybe they didn't care. Maybe they already knew and were pissed off that thanks to this interruption, dinner would be late.

He took a step forward, and the movement was enough to draw Robert Harlan's eyes.

"Senator Harlan," Danny said, loud enough to cut through the indignant voices filling the room. "Do you recognize the man on the DVD?"

The senator's face turned from brick red to purple. "I'm not going to dignify that question with a response. Janine, see to it this man is taken away."

"It's Mason Scott, Senator. Do you have any comment on that?" He looked around, but Bartlett Scott wasn't in the audience. "Does anyone have a comment?"

"Daniel, I think you left the hospital too soon. Clearly, it's affected your mind."

Danny stepped closer to the head table. He wondered how many seconds he had before he was dragged from the room.

"Mason's father was one of your associates in the Inferno. There were three of you in the beginning, but you've grown since then. Andy Cohen left me a package with an updated membership and investor list. That would be the one you were looking so hard for. I'm sure the FBI will find it as fascinating as I did."

Gasps from the crowd at the words "membership list."

"I want this man removed!" The senator's arms windmilled like he was going to take off. He could have lit up the city with the amount of energy he was expending.

Danny could hear cameras clicking behind him, could feel the glare of the lights in his back. This wasn't exactly what he'd planned, but he thought Andy would approve of the melodrama. He went to the DVD player and removed the disc from Janine's slack fingers.

"Somehow, I don't think this is going to look good on the campaign trail. That poor kid was just about sixteen. Where are the bodies, Senator?"

The senator had regained control, though his face was rigid with fury. "Your sad attempt at a comeback is in remarkably bad taste."

"And you will never be president of the United States. I will devote the rest of my life to that. I'll be so close, you'll hear me breathing with you."

Danny heard urgent voices in the hall. His time was up.

"This film proves nothing," the senator said through clenched teeth. But his eyes darted around the room to take in the shocked faces. The urgent murmurs rose to a higher, more intense pitch.

"Maybe not." Danny held up the remaining discs. "But these do. I've got financial records and membership lists, and did I mention the pictures? You'll be reading all about it, Senator." Danny slid the discs into his pockets. "Starting tomorrow."

Patsy Harlan's face was working as though something were alive in the muscles. Danny couldn't help it; he gave her a smart-ass grin. "Hey, Patsy, you were so close, honey." He leaned in. "Stand by your man even when he has a taste for children."

The reporters began to close in a second before Patsy Harlan gave a high-pitched shriek. Then she drove her thick, serrated steak knife into Danny's shoulder just above his collarbone.

"You! You, son of a bitch!" Patsy Harlan had finally exploded in living color.

"Jesus!" Screaming bolts of agony ran straight to his brain, and he sank to his knees. "Jesus!"

"Patricia!" Robert Harlan called.

"Goddamn bastard! I can slit a hog's throat! I'll gut you!"

Danny grasped the table with his right hand.

"Patricia!" Robert Harlan had her now and tried to subdue her. Cops and security guards merged from all directions, and Danny could hear the crackle of the police radios. The clicking and chirping filled his ears.

When the senator dragged her back, Danny struggled to stand, but his legs had turned wobbly. He could see the outline of Robert and Patsy Harlan merged together in one shadow, almost as if they were dancing. The senator shook her. "Patricia, for God's sake, you're making a scene!"

She spat at him. "I'll show you a scene, you bastard." She grabbed a bottle of wine and slugged him with it so hard that he lost his balance and fell, slamming his head against the podium as he went down.

"Mrs. Harlan, don't move," someone shouted.

"Stand still." A chorus of voices. Police at last.

Patsy Harlan backed up against the wall, tears rolling down her cheeks. "You wanted a story? You've got a story," she said to Danny. "I hope you bleed to death."

She laughed as they led her away.

79

Painkillers are wonderful things.

From his bed, Danny watched the activity at the nurses' station come into focus. A tree decorated with red-and-gold satin balls sat on the desk. Multicolored Christmas lights wound around it and blinked on and off in a hypnotic rhythm, and Danny stared at them until they blended into a smear of pulsating color. Fuzzy numbness overwhelmed him, and his eyes drifted shut.

"At the end of the world, there'll be fourteen cockroaches and you."

Danny forced his eyes open at the sound of the familiar voice and tried to focus. Novell's face floated into view.

"What're you doing here?"

"Waiting for you to wake up. You were in surgery for that hole Patricia Harlan put in you. You're very lucky she didn't nick any arteries." Novell laid a newspaper on the foot of the bed and peeled off the front section. "Your friend Westy sent it." He held up the front page. "I guess you're a big deal again."

Danny barely glanced at his own column. Next to it was a picture of Robert and Patsy Harlan performing their tragic dance. Patsy clutched the wine bottle. Goddamn Freddie Santos really knew how to capture the action shots.

"Senator clings to life?"

"You didn't know? No, of course you didn't. When he fell, he hit his head funny and broke his neck. He's paralyzed, but not dead." Novell gave Danny a bleak smile. "Maybe I was wrong. At the end of the world, there'll be those fourteen cockroaches, you, and Robert Harlan."

*

The hospital kept him for two more days, which was as close to walking away from a knifing as Danny figured he would get. The doctors said he was lucky. He'd suffered nerve damage, but after physical therapy, he would probably be at least 95 percent whole. Danny figured that was as good as he could hope for.

"Why did you lie about the club?" he said to Kevin. "You could have lost your badge."

"That night, the mayor's chief of staff was there with two transvestites, and the federal prosecutor was upstairs getting his ass whipped. There was no way I could shut down Delhomme's operation myself, which was a good thing for you. Christ, Danny. You stuck a guy with an eight-inch blade. I damn near shat myself when Novell told me that."

"It was self-defense."

"Did you want to go to trial on that one? Jesus God, when we got to Mason's house, there were pictures of you all over the place."

"You thought I had a connection with Mason Scott?"

When Kevin flushed, Danny knew he had assumed the worst. "I, uh, found out the DEA has been running an investigation for months. They were hoping Delhomme would roll on the operation. He figured first in to cut a deal would get immunity."

"The whole operation?"

"I guess. Nobody wants to do jail as a child killer."

"Will he get a deal?"

"If he ever wakes up."

"And Mason?"

Kevin's eyes shifted away. "Mason's not your concern."

"What the hell does that mean? Do you know what he did to Kate? To those girls?" Cold fury filled him.

"The feds will look into the Inferno. There are plenty of loose ends. It just takes time. And Mason's done. He's just done. Let it go."

Kevin face turned dark and tense, his lips compressed, and Danny saw the monster in Kevin's eyes. The old man's legacy. And he knew that some doors were best left unopened. He would have to accept the fragile trust between them or lose his brother. He gave Kevin the barest of nods.

"Please tell me the truth about Kate."

"I'm sorry, Danny. I truly think she loved you. If it's any comfort, we wouldn't have gotten into the club if it wasn't for her." Kevin looked down.

"I got her killed. The old man was right about that."

Kevin pressed his lips together for a long minute. "She made a choice." He squeezed Danny's arm. "There's a difference between dying and choosing."

Danny plucked at the covers. "So either way, she chose to leave."

"Let her go." Kevin stepped a little closer, his face filled with conflicting emotion. He did the Ryan thing and gave Danny a bat on the head. "I can't believe you just walked the hell out of here."

"You shouldn't have kept me like a prisoner."

"Because I knew what you'd do. What were you thinking, going to that dinner? What the hell did you say to Patsy Harlan?"

Danny smiled. "I said, 'Stand by your man.' Swear to God."

Kevin paced the room for a moment and then came back to stand by the bed. "Why couldn't you just write your story and let it go at that?"

"I had to. For Conor and Beth and Beowulf. For Kate." Danny swallowed. He didn't feel like arguing with Kevin. "If you'd gone through the mail instead of stealing my cookies, you'd have found the discs first."

When Kevin spoke, his voice was almost inaudible. "It scared the shit out of me when she stuck you. I thought for sure you were dead."

"Novell said at the end of the world, there'd be fourteen cockroaches and me."

Kevin made a noise somewhere between a grunt and a growl and then caught Danny in a clumsy embrace that sent shudders of agony across his damaged shoulder, down his left arm, and into his hand. Kevin's body shook with sobs, and it terrified him because to the best of his knowledge, Kevin hadn't cried since their mother's funeral.

"Jesus Christ. What's the matter with you?"

"Dumb son of a bitch."

Danny could feel Kevin's halting breath against his neck, and he laid a tentative hand on Kevin's shoulder. Love left an imprint, not visible, yet indelible.

"I love you too." He wasn't sure Kevin heard him, but it didn't matter. He gave himself over to his brother's embrace.

80

The old stone building rose out of fields covered by a fragile layer of fresh snow. It gave the countryside the look of a postcard. Inside, the persistent smell of antiseptic, the pale-green tile floors and florescent lights, and the hospital beds and special handicapped equipment were vivid reminders that this was no country retreat.

Danny paused outside the suite, knocked on the doorframe, and then approached the figure who sat in the motorized wheelchair by the window. In three months, Robert Harlan had lost a considerable amount of weight, but his black eyes glittered with life. His hair, now closely cropped, was completely white. Danny could see red drill marks on his skull where the iron frame had been screwed to keep his spine from compressing.

"Senator Harlan, you're looking well, all things considered." Danny watched the senator's eyes go a little colder, though he smiled and lifted his right hand with some difficulty. His fingers latched onto Danny's, and the touch of the senator's icy flesh filled him with revulsion. He placed his left hand against the bandage that wound around his neck.

"I'm so pleased you came to see me, Daniel." The senator's voice was weaker these days, but it didn't diminish his presence. "As you can see, I'm on the mend."

SARAH CAIN

"I read you were a quadriplegic."

"You shouldn't believe everything you read. I don't."

The senator took a breath. Air rasped through the gauze-covered hole in his neck left by the tracheotomy, though he no longer used a breathing apparatus. Conor would have said he sounded like Darth Vader.

"I have regained much of my body function. They say my will is very strong. I could be walking in six to eight months."

"I'm surprised that you wanted to see me, Senator."

"Are you?" The senator's lip curled up in what Danny supposed was a smile. "Are you worried that I might be plotting my revenge?"

Danny knew the senator would never be brought to trial. The feds swooped in and took the discs, the pictures, and the negatives while he was in the hospital. They didn't plan to return them. Kevin had already warned him to stay out of it. "It won't just be you who'll be a target," he'd said. "Think of what's left of your family."

Drugs were what the feds were after. All those dead children were collateral damage from the million-dollar cocaine operation that had run through Bruce Delhomme's restaurants and clubs. Of course, it wouldn't wrap up without an investigation, but Bruce Delhomme, the man who could tie everything together, was lying in a coma at Jefferson Hospital. If anyone was talking, they weren't privy to much information. The feds were plodding on, but as Kevin had said, it would take time. In the meantime, Senator Harlan and Everett Scott had donated all the profits they had made from Bruce Delhomme's various restaurants to create an outreach center for runaway teens.

"Why did you want to see me?" Danny wanted to pull away, but the senator tightened his grip. His fingers were already starting to go numb. A gift from Patsy Harlan: his left hand would always be damaged. He supposed he deserved it.

"I wished to congratulate you, Daniel. I'm afraid I underestimated you, but you were much more resilient than I thought."

"I could say the same for you, Senator."

"Did you know they drilled holes into my skull and hung me on a frame? Just like a piece of meat?"

"That's a damn shame." Danny drawled out the words with what he hoped was the right amount of insincerity. "Do you expect me to pity you? If it weren't for you, Beth and Conor would still be alive."

A muscle in the senator's face twitched.

The senator jerked his head at Danny to lean close. "My daughter was everything to me. Everything." The senator's black eyes burned with an intensity that Danny had never seen. Christ, the old bastard had cared for something. Or was Beth the ultimate trophy? Beth once told him her father loved her because she was the perfect daughter. He never quite understood what she meant until now.

"You took her from me, Daniel. You weren't worth the ground she walked on. But you were what she wanted. All she wanted, so I acquiesced. I had no choice but to wait until she recognized her lapse in judgment. I knew she would, so I didn't interfere. She was planning to divorce you. She told me."

"I know."

The senator fingered the bandage on his neck, then took a breath. "And then she changed her mind. I couldn't believe it." Robert Harlan took a choked breath. "She changed her mind."

Danny tried to comprehend his words. "She changed her mind?"

"Oh yes. She wanted to reconcile right as I was considering a presidential run."

Danny stared at him. "So you stepped in to deal with the problem."

The senator blinked. "I told you. I never interfered in her life. What were you to me? An insignificant local reporter. My God. If I wanted you dead, you'd be gone."

Daddy, there's a monster . . .

Conor had always been afraid to go to sleep at night. Maybe he knew monsters wore human faces.

"In any case, you were as good as dead." The senator's right cheek twitched, like he was trying not to laugh. "You should have seen yourself. It was much better than killing you. The arrogant prick of a journalist, so clever with words, the scourge of politicians brought to his knees . . ." He shuddered and wheezed. "You were useless. If Michael Cohen hadn't come along, you'd probably have killed yourself. But he had to leave you that damn package."

"You killed your own daughter."

"No. I wouldn't kill my own child, but someone did."

"And you know whom."

The senator shrugged. "That would be a strange thing to admit."

The revulsion crawled down Danny's back. "And Conor was . . ."

"Collateral damage." The senator leaned closer. "It was unfortunate, but think of it this way: you lived to write the story. You won. Or did you? When you tally up the wins and losses, did you really win, Daniel? Or would you trade it all to have your boy back?" The senator gulped air through his ashen lips, but he smiled. "Don't bother to answer."

Danny couldn't answer. He'd have destroyed the evidence in a minute to have Conor back. He'd have sold his soul. He wouldn't have had a choice. Christ, he was wrong. Love didn't leave imprints. It left the deepest scars of all.

Danny looked into the senator's eyes. They were as black as pitch, yet he recognized something in those depths, something akin to his own pain. He jerked his hand away.

"How is Patsy these days?"

The senator looked away. "Patricia is not doing as well as we hoped, I'm afraid. Her long-term prognosis is not good."

Danny's skin began to crawl. Patsy may have tried to kill him, but he provoked her. He couldn't imagine what it was like living with Robert Harlan. He doubted she'd be doing that much longer. She'd go quietly in her sleep. A heart attack, perhaps. Or a stroke. No questions asked.

"Bruce Delhomme might wake up, you know."

The senator smiled. "Perhaps. But he's been in a coma for three months. How lucid will he be? Anything is possible, of course."

"I hope he wakes up tomorrow and remembers everything. I hope they decide to prosecute you to the fullest extent of the law. I hope you never see the outside again."

"The authorities will do nothing." The senator chuckled, a dry wheeze. "In eight months I'll be back at work, much to the joy of my constituents, who will have forgotten any of my possible business dealings and will cheer my triumph over adversity. With any luck, by this time next year, I'll be walking. The twenty-four-hour news cycle is indeed an amazing thing."

"You were the one giving the orders. I know you were."

"What you know and what you can prove are two different things. In any case, I have always been a man who served the interests of my constituents, nothing more and nothing less. I have never availed myself of the services of the Inferno."

"But you saw no harm in profiting by those services."

"It was a business arrangement, pure and simple. I made an investment in Bruce's restaurant. An unfortunate one as it turned out. All that business with cards and memberships. That nonsense was Bruce's idea. Marketing, really. Exclusivity. Little people like their cards. It shows they're better than others. What insignificant man doesn't enjoy his upgrade to first class? He can sit in his leather seat and pretend to be something he isn't." He jerked his hand in an impatient gesture. "I assure you, I never needed a card. I burned mine immediately."

"You get off on control. Like with Kate. You wanted to control her."

The senator took another rasping breath. For a moment, his eyes glittered with that same emotion as when he talked about Beth. Something human. Something horrible.

The senator's face grew dark and hard. His breathing became more labored. "You will spend the rest of your life wondering whether or not you could have saved her. Or maybe, more to the point, whether she could have saved you."

Danny absorbed the impact of the senator's words. He had failed Kate. She would haunt him forever. "And you will sit in a wheelchair and wonder how the Irish bum brought you down."

The senator coughed and waved his hand. "You pick over people's lives for a living. That's your business. You're no less ruthless about it than I. You, of all people, should know that there are no absolutes, no ironclad truths, Daniel. In this world, everything can be right or wrong. I daresay a skilled journalist can make an argument for anything. Don't pretend we're so different."

Danny recoiled at the man in front of him. He wasn't like Robert Harlan, yet he could feel his father's accusing voice in his ear. *God is watching you, boy.* A vulture. Is that what he was?

The senator's eyes lightened with pleasure, as if he could read Danny's thoughts. "What's the point of arguing? I won't be able to run for president. My affairs can't sustain that level of scrutiny, so I shall remain in the Senate. It too is a club. You, of course, can start over. You are still a young man, but if I were you, I'd sleep with one eye open, especially if you plan to pursue this story any further."

"Is that a threat, Senator?"

"Let's just call it a friendly warning." The senator fixed him with a dead-eyed stare. "Remember, Daniel, it's good to have friends."

81

D anny had to lean against the wall, catch his breath, feel the ground solid beneath his feet. He waited for the surge to hit, but it didn't come this time. There was only a dull ache that came with the recognition that none of them were winners. They had all paid.

In the end, the only innocent was Conor.

Danny approached the information desk, and he managed a smile when he saw the aide. She wore scrubs with shamrocks on them and a light-up pin that glowed "Happy St. Patrick's Day" in Kelly green.

"I know, I know. I'm a day early. But the patients love it," she said and gave him a wide smile. "You okay?"

No. He wasn't okay. He'd just sat face to face with the devil and saw more of himself in Robert Harlan than he would ever admit to anyone. He nodded. "I'm trying to find some information about a former patient. A Linda Cohen. She was here at the beginning of January."

The aide punched the name into her computer and then frowned. "Is that Cohen with a C?"

"Yes. Linda Cohen. She was transferred from Franklin."

"We didn't have any Linda Cohen as a patient here in January."

"But the hospital told me they transferred her here."

"I'm sorry, but I don't have any record of a Linda Cohen."

"Her maiden name was Goldman. Would you try that?"

She punched into the computer again and shook her head. "Sorry. Nothing. Maybe you need to recheck the hospital, honey."

*

Danny rode the elevator to the twelfth floor of the paper. Andy's faithful secretary was not at her desk, and Danny slipped into the office. He took a moment to look around at the pictures and awards.

This was Andy's private sanctum, though Danny could never remember Andy spending more than ten minutes at a time here, unless he brought a bimbo with him and he wanted to get laid. Even then, twenty minutes was his limit. Andy was always afraid he'd miss something.

The new chief had been operating out of here for the last six weeks, but Andy's ghost would always prowl the room, his hair unkempt, his eyes full of mischief, and his heart? Christ only knew what was in Andy's heart.

Danny slipped the picture of Andy and him off the wall then picked up the framed essay that hung below it: "My Night in Prison," by Daniel Francis Ryan.

That essay . . . You'll want it back, Daniel, but I won't give it to you. You'll have to wait 'til I've shuffled off this mortal coil.

When he turned the essay over, he saw a manila envelope addressed to him taped to the back. It had a gold label with a Florida return address in the corner. Inside was one disc labeled "Justin." Andy's just-in-case-everything-else-fails insurance. Danny took the envelope and tucked the photograph and essay under his arm. He headed for the elevator.

It really was time to leave.

82

Novell eyed the "For Sale" sign on Ryan's farmhouse and the new black BMW Z4 that sat in the driveway. A tiny blue lightsaber and a dog's tag dangled from the rearview mirror. He wondered if Ryan had gotten himself a pierced ear and a fancy Italian suit to match the car, but when he approached the back door, Ryan stood there in jeans and a faded black sweatshirt.

Though in the past few months, he'd gained some weight and the skin no longer stretched too tight over the bones of his face, Ryan would never look like a kid again. Lines etched around his eyes and furrows cut between his brows. A pink burn scar skimmed his cheekbone. But it was something in the depths of those eyes that had changed, as though Ryan had gained a secret knowledge, one forged in suffering and burned into his soul.

"Nice wheels, Ryan," Novell said. "You going yuppie now?"

"John Novell. Good to see you too." Ryan's mouth curved into that enigmatic half smile. "I haven't had much luck with Jeeps." He paused and looked down. "My son always wanted me to buy one of these, but he was too small to ride in the front seat. Maybe now he will."

Ryan looked up and met Novell's eyes. Did that agony ever really go away? Novell hoped it faded to a tolerable ache in time.

"Have you come to make an offer on my house?"

"Three and a half million's a little beyond my budget," Novell said.

Ryan waved at a stack of glossy brochures that sat on the kitchen table. "Beth had a talent for decorating. I was the only project that didn't work out as planned." He cleared his throat. "Scotch?"

Novell shook his head. He didn't want to elaborate on his six weeks in detox. That was his business. After today, he'd fade off into the sunset, and maybe he'd finally be able to start that new life he craved. Or pick up the shreds of his old life and weave them into something new. God, now he sounded like one of the goofy new-age preachers at the nut hut where he'd been spending his days.

"I've given up scotch for the moment," Novell said. "I'm tying up my loose ends here before I leave."

Hell, who besides Sean McFarland gave a shit what happened to him anyway? And that was only because they had been partners. Sean had given Novell the speech about how he had so much left to teach. When he turned in his badge and gun, Novell shook his head and handed McFarland a case of Dos Equis.

"Geez, how did you know?" Sean had said.

Novell had just smiled.

"You know, Beth and Conor Ryan's accident was no accident."

"I know. Put it away and forget it,"

"But—"

"You're a good cop, Sean. Don't ever doubt it, but let this one go." Novell had walked away without looking back.

Now he set the cardboard box he'd retrieved from Kate's apartment down on the edge of the granite counter and slipped a small package in among the contents. "I'm retiring. It's time."

Ryan didn't answer, and his eyes remained like the clear surface of a lake under a cloudless sky. Maybe that was what now struck Novell about him. The eerie silence in those dark-blue eyes. Something between resignation and sorrow, but not quite despair.

"Where are you headed, Novell?"

"California. I have a daughter there."

"You're full of surprises. You never mentioned a daughter."

"We had a fight."

"A fight? About what?"

Always the questions. Ryan's old man was right. This kid had ink in his veins. Novell shrugged. "Does it matter? She's there now. She isn't leaving."

Ryan nodded like maybe he understood, though Novell wasn't sure how. Then again, Ryan had an odd sort of understanding of people.

Ryan's eyes strayed to the box. "What's in the box?"

"Kate's things . . . and a gift for you. I think she'd want you to have them." The son of a bitch might have made her happy, but Kate didn't believe in happy endings.

Ryan tilted his head and curved his lips in a half smile. Novell still hated that smile. "Where's she buried?"

"She isn't. She's cremated. You were in the hospital."

"Her ashes?"

Novell shrugged. "Gone."

"You might have waited."

"When you're dead, you should stay that way."

Ryan lifted up one last disc. "It features a kid named Justin. You don't want to watch it."

"It's all out of my hands now. I suggest you put it someplace very safe."

Ryan ran his hand over the box. He hesitated and then went into his office and reappeared with a small bundle of cash. "If I'd known you were leaving, I'd have gotten more. There's twenty thousand. Send me an address."

"I don't want your money." Novell looked at the bundle.

"Think of it as security. I expect you'll need security. You and your daughter."

"Not as much as you." Against his better judgment, Novell felt a kind of pity. "She's not coming back, Danny."

Ryan looked away. "I'll wait."

83

Florida's new Seven Mile Bridge, in fact, only stretched 6.7 miles, but when Danny headed over the turquoise water toward Little Duck Key, it looked like it ran clear to Cuba.

The old bridge stood alongside the new one, and it was missing chunks here and there. When it was completed in 1912, it was hailed as the Eighth Wonder of the World; now it looked like a crumbling fishing pier spotted with pelican shit. Still, it had a strange dignity. It had stood up to the hurricane of '35 and was, in its own way, a survivor.

Danny appreciated survivors.

He thought of the cardboard box he'd left in a storage facility in Atlanta. Kate's things. Funny that so many of Kate's things turned out to be from his family: his old copybooks, the old man's notebooks, a cassette tape of the old man's conversation with Bartlett Scott, the picture of Kate and the old man, and one last thing: the package from Novell. Danny didn't know how he managed to retrieve it. It contained copies of the discs, pictures, and photos plus classified information from the DEA investigation. Novell's cryptic note only read, "Keep it safe. It may keep you alive." He left Andy's letter with the rest of the items.

If he wanted, Danny could finally write the last word on the Sandman killings, but somehow he didn't think he would. Not

316

yet. The dead needed to rest, even if they did so uneasily, and as Kevin noted, he had family. How odd to find himself in the old man's shoes.

He headed onto the Overseas Highway, looked for his turn-off on Big Pine Key, and then followed the wandering road off onto a narrow lane edged with brush, slash pine, and cactus. The late afternoon breeze, heavy with the scent of citrus, rustled the palms and red-barked gumbo limbo trees. It was much wilder than Key West or the eminently more luxurious Shark Key, but perhaps that was the point.

At last he came to the dead end of a hard-packed dirt road where a huge, white house stood behind iron gates. Just beyond, he could see the turquoise water of the Atlantic Ocean sparkling in the sun. He rang the bell and gave his name.

When the gates swung open, he pulled down the sweeping driveway where a woman waited on the steps for him. Her great rolls of fat strained against the fabric of her bright-aqua dress, and her perfect face was dimpled and creased with laugh lines. Two hundred pounds ago, she probably looked like Tyra Banks. Even now her face had a perfect symmetry. Her large, brown eyes, flecked with gold, held his gaze, and he realized she wasn't much older than Kate.

"Mr. Ryan? Welcome to Bella Vista." She smiled, flashing perfect white teeth.

"Thank you."

"I am Asha," she said in a voice, low and musical, not quite British, not of the islands.

"South African?"

"Cape Town. You have a good ear."

"Asha means life."

"That it does. And Daniel went into the lion's den, did he not?" She patted his shoulder, and he noted the thick pink scars that ran up her arms. She nodded as if he'd asked and she'd answered a question. "It is safe here. Please come in. The madame will be happy to see you."

*

Danny stood on the veranda and watched the water lap up against the sand. The faint aroma of orchids drifted in the air and mingled with the salt breeze and scent of lime while a white heron soared overhead and then settled on a rock near the water's edge. He heard footsteps behind him.

"Danny." Her voice was soft.

He steeled himself to face her, but she didn't look all that different. She seemed to float toward him in her dove-gray dress, and he could see the faint red scar from the knife that had slashed her throat before she wrapped a gauzy white scarf around her neck. Her eyes brimmed with tears.

Linda ran her hands over his face, let her fingers linger over the burn scar under his right eye. He put his arms around her.

"I'm sorry," she said at last.

He shook his head. "I didn't come here for that."

"Andy liked the sex. The drugs. He was like a teenager with an unlimited supply of Playboy bunnies and cocaine and booze. The good times never stopped."

Linda cleared her throat, and Danny could feel the weight of her sorrow. He knew she loved Andy in a way he never did comprehend. He would watch the way her eyes followed him when they were at parties together and Andy would abandon her to chase some young thing with mile-long legs and an IQ that was smaller than her bra size. He'd see Linda wince and try to put up a what-the-hell front and recognize that inside, she was hurting like she'd been smashed by a freight train.

"I got old. I wasn't fresh and young and full of adoration. I saw through him. It happens." Linda wiped her eyes and looked up at Danny, her lips curved in a wry smile. "No regrets."

And he knew she either believed that or would talk herself into it. Maybe that was how she got up every morning and lived with herself.

"Linda, I thought you were . . ."

"Yes. Andy thought it better to pretend I was in worse shape than I was."

She placed her hands back around his face. "We're survivors, you and I. That's hard, isn't it?"

"Kate tried to save me." Danny's voice cracked. Linda slid her palms down his arms until she grasped his hands in hers.

"Kate was damaged. Don't you understand that? You can't save someone who doesn't want to be saved. Know this: she did love you."

"I should have run away with her when I had the chance."

Linda shrugged. "Perhaps, but I'm not sure you'd have been happy in the end. Kate never believed she could be happy."

Danny could still feel Kate in his arms, smell the perfume she wore, see her haunted eyes. His Kate. She had crept into a deep recess of his heart and would never leave.

Linda touched his face again. "Remember, thanks to you, Robert Harlan will never become president. That's something."

"Is it?" Danny could see the senator sitting spiderlike in his wheelchair. Robert Harlan was still capable of malice. Of that he was sure. "The story barely made a dent."

Robert Harlan was like black mold that grew behind pristine walls. Patient. Insidious. He fed on people's greed and lust, seeping into them until they were rotten and corrupt.

"It made a dent." Linda squeezed his hands. "You shared credit with Andy and Michael for the story. That was generous."

"There wouldn't have been a story if it weren't for Andy and Michael."

"Yes, and Andy will be remembered as a hero, not the old goat he was. You made him pure again, and for that I will always be grateful."

"I wrote a story." The facts were there, but the characters would always be larger than life. The heroes braver, the villains darker. Because even a true story needed its clichés and color, and nobody knew that better than a journalist.

"And now, here we are, you and I, and life continues."

He supposed she was right. God knew he'd fought to stay alive, killed to stay alive. He still wasn't sure how he felt about that. Maybe he never would be sure.

"I know what you've lost, but you're young, Danny. If I weren't old enough to be your mother . . ." She smiled and patted his arm.

"How did you manage it?"

"You found me."

"It's my job."

She shrugged, and he had to laugh at her coy smile. He wondered how Andy could've ever looked at another woman. Perhaps if he had kept his eyes on Linda, Andy would still be alive.

"You didn't answer my question," he said.

"I don't think I need to."

"You gave Michael the story."

She turned away as if she were trying to come up with a decent lie and then sighed. "No. Andy gave him the story. Not on purpose, of course, but Andy could never keep things like passwords in his head. He wrote everything down. Michael loved machines more than people."

"But you must have known Andy was involved."

"Know? I financed him." She turned back on him, her white scarf fluttering out behind her. Linda, who always looked so insubstantial, had the relentless eyes of a predator. She knew about the Inferno all along. She had to have known. She always was the financial heavyweight in the house. Andy never made any money decision without discussing it with her. "I loved him. Stupid, I know. I never understood it myself, but there you are. The heart doesn't ask the head for permission to love, wisely or unwisely. I loved him. I stood by him all those years, through all those women, because in the end, I knew they meant nothing to him. I paid for his membership, but I didn't look into the Inferno. I didn't know what was going on. I didn't want to know. I suppose I always suspected it was unsavory, so I atoned, like Bartlett Scott. Why do you think he gives so much away? Do you really think he's such a philanthropist? He's trying to save his soul. Andy would not have had sex with a child. I know that."

Danny nodded. "But he knew about the kids."

"I don't know." Linda turned away. "Andy always came home. Then one day he didn't. One day he fell in love. He wanted a divorce. A divorce!" Linda quivered with fury. "And you know who that someone was?"

Danny shook his head numbly, though he could feel the answer in his stomach.

"Your wife. Your Beth. I knew why she latched onto him. She was using him. She thought you were heading for a divorce, and she wasn't going to lose that boy of yours."

"But she wasn't going to leave. She told her father."

Linda shook her head. "Andy didn't want to hear that. He came to me and told me he'd finally found the woman who could make him completely happy. He wanted another child, you know. He wanted another son. Like Conor. The stupid old bastard thought he could get himself another boy just like yours. I told Andy if they went through with it, I'd cut off his funding, but he wouldn't listen. And then, well, you know the rest."

Danny could see desperate Andy in the ICU, grasping his hand, talking about Michael and Conor, and he finally understood Andy's terrible darkness. Had Beth ever cared for Andy or had she been using him? Was she her father's daughter or was that light he had always seen in her real?

"Nothing was supposed to happen to Conor," Linda said.

"I don't believe you. How could they know she'd be driving my car?" The earth seemed to tremble beneath his feet, and he caught the ends of her scarf. "My car, Linda. Did you want to get us both, just to be sure?"

"It was Bruce. I told him I wanted Beth dead, and I paid double. I told him to make it look like an accident. I didn't ask how. I didn't think she'd be in your car. I didn't think she'd have Conor. I thought—I don't know what I thought. I just wanted her dead." She jerked the ends of her scarf from his hands. "I loved Conor too." Tears glittered in her eyes. "I thought of him as my grandson."

"That doesn't make it better."

"No, but I called Bob Harlan after the accident. I'm the one who told him Beth was dead. The bastard screamed then." Linda looked at Danny with a smile of bitter satisfaction on her face. "After the crash, Andy came to his senses. I knew he would. He always came around in the end."

"Jesus Christ, Linda. Do you think that made it okay? You killed my son. My wife." He wanted to grab her, but he didn't trust himself.

She blinked at him as if she didn't quite understand. "No. Conor was an accident."

"Conor was murdered by an ape named Lyle who snapped his neck."

"No."

Danny had to walk away from her and catch his breath. He stood at the edge of the veranda and breathed in the salt air. He listened to the tide wash up against the beach. It should have been peaceful, but he couldn't reach that peaceful spot. Conor. Beth. His family. All those children who died. They had names. They had faces. They stood between him and peace. He waited until his heart slowed before he turned back to Linda. "What about your neck?"

"They sent that creature Mason after me because they thought I'd betrayed them, that I was helping you, but I wore my collar that night. He couldn't make a good cut, and by God I fought the little bastard like hell. As it was, he nicked my jugular but not the carotid artery. I'm a doctor. I was able to slow the bleeding."

"You gave me the disc at the party. You must have known what was on it."

"I did. I also knew I wouldn't be implicated anywhere. I'm on no list. I was never a real member of the club. I just paid for Andy."

"But you were implicating him."

"No. This was going to be the crowning achievement of Andy's career. His paper was going to win the goddamn Robert Kennedy Prize for Public Service. Don't you understand? He even had a spot for it." She stared at him unblinking, and he knew that something inside Linda had snapped. His Linda was gone. Only the husk remained.

Some are born to endless night. He didn't know how to answer. Maybe she really believed what she was saying.

Linda sighed. "You know the worst part? I miss him."

Danny knew he should call the police, but it wouldn't change anything. "So in the end, you won," he said at last.

"In the end, nobody won. I lost my husband and son. You lost Conor and Beth. You lost Kate. Robert Harlan may still be able to cause mischief, but he's done as a presidential prospect. Oh, he'll remain in the Senate, but he won't go further. You might not think that's hell, but for a man like him, the presidency was his life's ambition. The paper won't get any prizes for this story. Too much controversy. You and I get to survive, but to what end? I don't know. It all feels very hollow. There's no morality tale. It just is."

"That's very Buddhist of you," Danny said. He tried to summon up anger but couldn't. She was right. In the end everyone had lost.

"You should stay. Maybe we'll heal each other, and then I'll send you back to the world."

"You know I can't stay."

"Because you still have a column to write."

He shook his head. "I quit."

"Yes. I know. Steinman called in a panic when you just disappeared." She laughed at his confusion. "Danny, my family always owned the controlling interest in the paper. Andy worked for me, though no one knew it. Don't worry. I'll work things out with Steinman. He's an ass, but he's got talent. I'm trusting you and Westy and the rest to break him in."

"Not this time, Linda. I quit."

"I know, darling, but you didn't really. You have a contract, and I won't let you out of it."

"I think you will," Danny said. "I think you'll tell Steinman I'm leaving."

"And why would I do that?" She blinked those predatory eyes at him again, preparing for a fight.

"Because I'm done. I need time to think, to begin something new. I have a mission. I don't like adults who think it's acceptable to use children for sex."

"Do you think I'll let you just walk away and hand something like that to the *New York Times*?" She looked at him not with anger but a tinge of sorrow.

"Yes, I think you will. If not for yourself, for Andy. Because I have more evidence. Much worse evidence that no one wants brought to light."

She put her hands to her face, and he realized she wore no jewelry. He'd never seen her hands without adornment.

"Andy always believed you were his mitzvah. I always looked at you as something else. A lost son, I suppose. Andy wasn't alone in wanting another son. You were everything I wanted Michael to be." She dropped her hands. "I have to live with that too. Atone. So be it."

Danny wanted to tell her to stop talking, but he couldn't. It was too late. He already knew what she was going to say.

"I shot Michael." Her voice was barely a whisper, and he had to lean close. "We fought. He made me watch that video. The children. It was hideous. I knew Andy would be charged with conspiracy at the least. I begged Michael, but he laughed and told me how much he hated me. Something . . . snapped. I didn't mean to shoot him. I tried to get him to come with me to the hospital, but he ran. He ran." She sighed. "I don't suppose I blame him. But it was an accident, Danny. Kate was there. It happened at her apartment."

"At Kate's apartment?" Kate had told him Michael was there that night. She had just left out a few convenient details.

"I knew he'd show up there eventually, and I told her to call when he did. He was raving. He threatened us with a .22. Here's a lesson for you, Daniel. Never pull a gun unless you're willing to fire. He came at Kate, and I shot him. I only meant to wound him." Linda paused and took a breath. When she looked at him, her face was flushed with anger. "Damn it! Why did you have to fall apart? He would have gone to you first, and you would have handled him. Do you really believe I wanted to kill my child?"

"No." Did it matter what he believed? In the end, he wasn't sure anyone cared. "I believe you wanted to save your husband."

"We cleaned up the blood, and I bought her that rug just in case."

"You thought of everything."

"I knew Michael was up to something. I thought Kate and I could reason with him. Since you'd been gone, he grew so despondent. He started visiting clubs, and by God, he stumbled into the wrong one. I'm sure that's how he discovered those discs. He needed money for membership, and he went into Andy's safe. The best part was that he left everything there until he was ready to come to you."

It made sense. Michael could screw his father by finally producing a huge story. "He wanted Kate to tell him it was okay."

Linda nodded. "She was kind to him."

Danny took Linda by the shoulders. "Listen to me carefully. There's still more evidence, and if anything happens to me or my family. Anything. I will bring down a world of hurt."

Linda nodded. "Nobody wants trouble. I think that's a safe bet." She reached up and touched his face, letting her fingers rest on his cheeks. She kissed him briefly on the lips. "You must remember the good times. Andy would want that. Now, it's getting late, and I have a few things to finish. You're free to stay, of course, but I know that's not your plan. You'll forgive me if I don't see you out."

She smiled, but her face was as pale as her scarf, as if purging herself had drained the life from her. When she walked back into the house, she seemed ethereal, and he supposed Linda had become yet another ghost.

He walked down to the beach to stare out at the ocean and wonder if a door had opened or closed.

Danny smelled citrus, stronger now, and for a moment he swore he heard a child's laugh borne on the wind. It seemed so peaceful, only the waves that caressed the shore, the rustle of palms. Still, he could feel the rapid cadence of his heart because he knew that peace was an illusion. A dream. And monsters would always prowl the dark corners of his dreams.

Sunlight caught the edge of a cresting wave. It flared like a beacon—crimson, bright yellow, and then deep violet—before the wave crashed and rushed toward the beach.

Acknowledgments

So many people have been there to support me on this long and very twisted road to publication. First, thank you to my husband, Howard, and children, Alexandra, Michael, and Mary, who have always understood Mom's need to retreat into her writing corner.

Thank you to Gary Zenker and the kind and supportive folks at the Main Line Writers' Group. Special thanks to my very special critique group: Tony Conaway, Matthew Fisher, Brian Mahon, Matt McGeehan, Elizabeth Stolar, and especially Paul Popiel for all his generous help editing and formatting, and Lorinda Lende, my intrepid partner in crime; a talented, funny lady; and an extraordinary friend. You guys rock and write.

Thank you to Julie Duffy, creator of the StoryADay May flash fiction challenge, for giving me a creative kick start when I needed it.

Thank you to Dragon Queen Rebekah Postupak of Flash! Friday for your enthusiastic and generous support.

Thank you, *Philadelphia Daily News* political columnist John Baer for taking the time to read the doorstop and to offer so much encouragement.

ACKNOWLEDGMENTS

Thank you, Susan Settaduccato, for reading many drafts of this novel and remaining supportive, kind, and just amazing. You're a word artist, my friend.

Thank you to my wonderful agent, Rene Fountain, for believing.

Thank you to the delightful people at Crooked Lane Books, especially Matthew Martz and Nike Power, for taking on this book, editing, and wringing out the story.

Last, but never least, thank you to my dear, dear friend and fellow traveler Maria Hazen Lewis, an amazing writer who has spent hours reading, commiserating, hand holding, and just being there. You are quite simply the best.